WHERE SEA MEETS SKY

WHERE SEA MEETS SKY

a novel

KARINA HALLE

ATRIA PAPERBACK

New York London Toronto Sydney New Delhi

ATRIA PAPERBACK
A Division of Simon & Schuster, Inc.
1230 Avenue of the Americas
New York, NY 10020

First Atria Paperback edition March 2015

ATRIA PAPERBACK and colophon are trademarks of Simon & Schuster, Inc.

For information about special discounts for bulk purchases, please contact Simon & Schuster Special Sales at 1-866-506-1949 or business@simonandschuster.com.

The Simon & Schuster Speakers Bureau can bring authors to your live event. For more information or to book an event, contact the Simon & Schuster Speakers Bureau at 1-866-248-3049 or visit our website at www.simonspeakers.com.

Interior design by Kyoko Watanabe

Manufactured in the United States of America

10 9 8 7 6 5 4 3 2 1

Library of Congress Cataloging-in-Publication Data is available.

ISBN 978-1-4767-9640-6
ISBN 978-1-4767-9643-7 (ebook)

To Kelly, my "almost" famous Kiwi

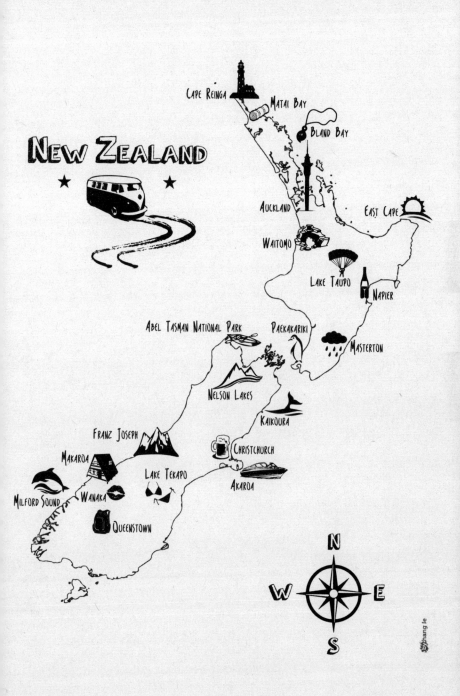

New Zealand

Cape Reinga
Matai Bay
Bland Bay
Auckland
East Cape
Waitomo
Lake Taupo
Napier
Abel Tasman National Park
Paekakariki
Masterton
Nelson Lakes
Kaikoura
Franz Joseph
Makaroa
Christchurch
Milford Sound
Wanaka
Lake Tekapo
Akaroa
Queenstown

N
W   E
S

Glossary of Māori Terms

hāngi: refers to an open-air pit in which food is cooked, as well as the food prepared in the pit and the social gathering or meal during which the food is eaten.

hongi: a traditional greeting in which noses are pressed together.

iwi: a tribe.

Kia ora: an informal greeting that means "hello" or "be well."

marae: a gathering place for meetings and celebrations.

pākehā: a person who is not of Māori ancestry, especially one of European descent.

pāua: a large abalone and the shell used to make jewelry.

tā moko: permanent face markings, distinct from tattoos.

tapu: sacred or forbidden.

whānau: family, especially extended family.

Chapter One

VANCOUVER, CANADA

JOSH

I get an erection the moment I first lay eyes on her. She looks like no one I've ever seen before. Tall, curvy, with thick superhero thighs and a round ass, showcased in black Lycra that hugs every slope. Her big, high breasts and small waist are accentuated by her white tank top. Her body has just enough meat for me to grab a good hold of, and I imagine running my hands over her hills and valleys. I want to imagine more than that, but I'm horny as hell as it is and my erection is already inappropriate, considering I'm in public and all.

She finally looks my way, aware that I've been staring like an idiot. She catches my gaze, her eyes twinkling a vibrant yellow, her pupils large and wet. She smirks at me, causing a shower of glitter to rain from her cheeks, and brushes her purple hair over her shoulder before she bends over to slide a gun out from the harness strapped to her boot.

I try not to stare into the blinding sun of her tanned cleavage. I try to think of something clever to say to her.

Something along the lines of, *I think I know who you are, but shouldn't you have one eyeball instead of two?*

But it's she who comes over to me, gun comfortably in her hand, and stops only a foot away. When she smiles at me, I see fangs.

Now I'm really confused. At least I know what to say now. "Who are you?" I ask her, happy that my voice is hard and deep. I hope it makes her think of sex.

She raises a perfect brow, and up close I'm struck by how bronzed her skin tone is. I don't think it's makeup. Not many people in Vancouver manage to keep their tan into the fall.

"You don't know?" she asks. She has an accent. I immediately want to say she's from England but that's not it. It's not Australia either.

"I thought I did," I say. "But your eyes and fangs are throwing me all off."

"I'm vampire Leela, from *Futurama*."

I grin at her, happy that I was half-right. "Shouldn't you just have *one* eyeball then?"

She reaches into her other boot and effortlessly pulls out an eye mask. It's painted white, with a black pupil in the middle. She waves it at me. "I put it on for photos but I can barely see out of it. I walked into a wall, twice." She raises two fingers for emphasis. "I figured I'll just be a vampire the rest of the time."

I can seriously listen to her talk all day. "I don't remember any episode where Leela turned into a vampire." Maybe it hinted at my secret nerd-boy status, but I watched the cartoon *Futurama* religiously.

She wets her lips for a moment and I try my hardest not to adjust my boxer briefs underneath my costume. "I like to think she'll become a vampire in future episodes. Or maybe she was one once and Matt Groening scrapped the idea. I believe characters have more to their lives than the lives we are shown."

"Kind of like people," I say, hoping I come across as somewhat profound.

She gives me a slight nod—indicating I'm not as profound as I thought—and looks me up and down. "I just had to come over here to tell you you're the best-dressed guy here. I mean, that must have taken some effort."

I grin at her. "*Game of Thrones* fan?" I ask.

Another sly nod. "Of course. But who doesn't love Khal Drogo?"

"Last year I dressed up as George R.R. Martin," I tell her. "People kept mistaking me for Ernest Hemingway, even though I was carrying a bucket of fried chicken around with me and had a pillow stuffed down my shirt."

"So you went for something sexier . . ." she says as she lets her eyes trail over my body, which automatically makes me stand up straighter. I haven't left much to the imagination. Jesus sandals, weird billowy pants that I think some granola dude dropped off at the thrift store, plus a leather corset over my abs and leather cuffs on my forearms. My upper body is bare and covered with bronzer and streaks of blue paint, and I found a black wig with a long braid down the back. It kind of works. I guess if you don't know the show, I look like some sparkling warrior who wears too much eye makeup.

"Hey, girls can't be the only ones to slut it up at Halloween." She raises her brow.

And once again, my foot goes in my mouth. "I mean, not that you're dressed slutty or anything, I just mean—"

She laughs. "Don't worry about it," she says with a wave of her hand. "*Everyone* here is dressed slutty. That's what the holiday is about, isn't it? Pretending to be someone else? This is actually my first Halloween, so I'm feeling a little overdressed. Or super nerdy." She looks around her at the drunk girls—referees and fairies and nurses in wonderfully indecent outfits—and shrugs.

"I wholeheartedly disagree," I say, trying not to ogle her all over again. I pause. "Wait, your first Halloween?"

"First *proper* Halloween. The North American kind. We don't really celebrate it the way you guys do."

I cross my arms, insanely curious now. "And who is we?"

"New Zealand," she says. "I'm from Auckland."

"Nice," I say. "I was going to ask if you were from New Zealand."

Her lips twitch and she gives me a shake of her head. "No you weren't."

"Well, I definitely wasn't going to ask if you were from Australia. I know how you'd feel about that."

For a moment her features look strained, then it passes. "Kind of like if I asked if you were American."

"Exactly."

"So," she muses and steps closer. She lays her hand on my bicep and I suck in my breath. "Are the tattoos real?" She removes her hand and peers at her palm, which is streaked with bronze shimmer shit. "Because your tan sure isn't."

Damn, I hope I'm not blushing. I clear my throat. "The tattoos are real, I assure you. I needed a bit of, um, help to get that Dothraki tan going on."

"And this?" She reaches for my face and I am frozen in place while she gently fingers my goatee and beard. She grabs the end of it, which I had attempted to braid, and gives it a little tug.

"Ouch," I say, though it doesn't really hurt. It turns me on instead. Big surprise.

"So it is real," she says. She sounds impressed.

I shrug. "I had a month to grow it in. I say, it's all or nothing. But tomorrow everything is getting shaved off."

She frowns and lets go. "Pity. I love a scruffy guy."

I can't help but smile. "Lucky for you, I'm scruffy for at least twelve more hours."

Her mouth twists into a wry smile. I realize I'm being kind of forward with her, but at the same time she just felt my biceps and fondled my man hair. Then again, I've never been very good at reading women. Half of them seem to love my tats and black hair and piercings; the other half seem to think I'm a delinquent from skid row.

I'm wondering what she thinks about me when I realize I don't know her name.

"I'm Josh, by the way," I say to her, holding out my hand.

She gives me a surprisingly firm shake in return. "Gemma."

"That's a beautiful name," I tell her. Even though I'm sincere, I'm aware that it's very much a pickup line.

Gemma snorts and it's absolutely adorable. "Right. Well, in New Zealand, Gemmas are everywhere."

"But I bet they don't look like you." Okay, so now I'm totally swerving into pickup line territory. I push it further. "Can I buy you a drink?"

And there the question sits, floating between us along with the haze of pot smoke that hangs in the air. The rejection might come fast, or if I'm lucky, not at all. But it's Halloween, I have a three-beer buzz going on, and I'm feeling pretty good.

Still, when she nods and says "Sure," I feel my whole body lift with relief.

We make our way through the crowd to the makeshift bar set up in the corner. It's a house party we're at, one I try and go to every year. My friend Tobias rents the whole house with three other dudes who go to the University of British Columbia nearby, and every Halloween they go all out with mind-fuck decorations, elaborate costumes, and a haunted house in the basement. This year they even applied for a liquor license since last year ended with a police raid and all of us running for our lives down the street.

While we get in line behind a guy dressed as a one-night stand (complete with a lampshade head) and a girl dressed as some Disney princess, I ask her, "So, Gemma from New Zealand, how did you hear about the party?"

She fixes her yellow eyes on me and I wish she could take out her contacts so I could see their real color. I'm assuming they're brown, based on her skin tone, and I feel like I could get lost in them if she'd let me.

"At the backpacker's hostel I'm staying at. I made friends with the guy who works the front desk," she says, and I can't help but feel my entire back bristle. A guy? Of course she'd be here with a guy. "He invited me and another backpacker but I haven't seen them all night." Her eyes sweep the room then come back to me, sparkling knowingly. "Not that I'm surprised; she's from Holland and has legs up to here." She makes a slicing motion with her hand across her neck. "He obviously wanted to shag her."

"Maybe he wanted to shag the both of you," I say and then try not to wince.

She gives me an exasperated look but still smiles. She has the cutest dimples. "Maybe. But I don't like to share. My parents never taught me to play very well with my toys."

"Sup, Drogo," the bartender says. I swivel my head and eye him, slightly annoyed at being interrupted. He's dressed as a hot dog.

"Sup, dog," I say. "Is that costume supposed to be a hint or something?"

He nods, completely deadpan, which only makes it funnier considering there's just a small cutout for his face in the wall of wiener. "It's a complete metaphorical representation of my penis, if that's what you mean."

Gemma laughs. "You Canadians talk about your dicks a lot."

I casually lean one arm against the bar top. "Well, have you seen our dicks? It's a point of pride for our country."

"No, actually, I haven't," she says and a million clever follow-ups flow through my head. Unfortunately, half of them are serious propositions so I don't dare say them.

"Oh really," the hot dog says, beating me to it. "You know, that can be arranged."

"I'm sure it can," she says sweetly but her eyes are telling him not to bother. "Could I get a beer please? None of that Molson Canadian stuff, though. Do you have any craft brew?"

The hot dog plucks a bottle of Granville Island Winter Ale from the ice chest and plunks it on the counter. "Seven dollars."

I sigh and order one for myself, fishing out my money from a small leather satchel around my waist that I thought maybe Khal Drogo would use when he wasn't slicing people's arms off. "I thought the point of a house party was to have cheap booze."

He shrugs, apparently hearing that complaint all night. "Blame government regulation. Still better than being stuck at some bullshit club downtown."

He has that right.

"Mojo" by Peeping Tom suddenly comes on over the speakers and the rolling beat of one of my favorite songs gives me another boost of confidence. I'm about to suggest to Gemma that we find somewhere to sit, maybe in another room, when she asks if I want to go to the roof deck.

I can't help but oblige.

"It might be still raining," I tell her as we squeeze through the crowd of people and up the carpeted stairs to the second floor. "It's almost winter here, remember."

"Nah, I love the rain," she answers.

"Then you should seriously consider moving here." Suddenly there's a bit of traffic near the door to the roof and she stops in front of me. I'm pressed up against her ass and it's like I've gone to heaven. It's so firm and round that I'm starting to think that she's magic. Of course, I'm also growing harder by the second and I know, *I know*, she can feel the magician's wand.

I cringe inwardly. I really don't want to be one of *those* guys. In fact, I start thinking that perhaps I need to apologize for my public displays of erection but she actually presses her ass back into me. It was subtle but it was there.

Before I drown in over-analysis of the moment, the foot traffic moves forward again and suddenly there is space and we find ourselves up on the flat roof of the building. The air is sharp, cold, and damp, but I have enough alcohol in me that I don't mind the chill. It's stopped raining. There are a few dripping lawn chairs scattered about and scantily clad girls shivering in their costumes, trying to puff down their cigarettes or joints.

In the distance, you can see the dark mass of English Bay peppered with tankers and the night-skiing lights of Grouse Mountain. The glass high-rises of downtown Vancouver twinkle and set the low clouds an electric shade of orange.

Gemma grabs my hand and leads me to the edge of the roof, away from everyone else. Her grip is strong but her hand warm and soft, and before I can give it a squeeze, she lets go. She leans against the railing, not caring if her arms get cold and wet, and stares out at the view.

"I do have to say, I always thought Auckland one of the most beautiful cities in the world, but Vancouver has totally blown it away," she muses wistfully, her eyes roaming the cityscape.

"How long are you here for?"

She sighs. "Not long enough. Ten days."

"Did you go to Whistler?"

She smiles. "So I could be surrounded by Aussies and other Kiwis? I was there for a day. Nice place. But we have mountains like that back home."

I ask her if she was in other parts of Canada and she tells me she originally got a work permit because she wanted to live and work on Prince Edward Island out east.

I laugh. "Really? Why? You a fan of *Anne of Green Gables*?"

In the dark, it's hard to tell if she's blushing. "Actually, yes."

"That's cute."

"Shut up." But she's smiling and brushing her hair off her shoulder. "Anyway, work was hard to find there. I guess all the summer jobs were filled, so after a while I had to move on. Went to Nova Scotia, Quebec, Toronto." I scrunch my nose at the last city and she rolls her eyes. "Yeah, yeah, you guys with your rivalry. Then I went down into the States for a few months. Boston, New York. Flew to New Orleans, drove through the Southwest, then onto California. Disneyland." Her eyes light up at that one. "San Francisco. Took a backpacker bus up the Oregon coast, spent some time in Seattle, and now I'm here, flying out tomorrow."

"And you did all of this by yourself?" I ask incredulously.

She purses her lips and nods. "Yeah. Why not?"

"You sound a lot like my sister," I say.

She frowns. "That's not exactly what you want to hear from someone you find attractive."

I stare at her for a few beats, making sure I heard that right. I try not to grin, but I can't help it.

"Attractive?" I repeat.

"Oh, I've gone and given you a big ego, haven't I?"

"Sweetheart, I already had a big ego," I admit, still smiling. "And I don't mean I think you're *just* like my sister, Vera. It's just that she went overseas to Europe last year—Spain, actually—by herself and now she's living there. It's just . . ." I try and think of the word, "*brave*, that's all. Everyone else I know goes and travels in groups and pairs."

She shrugs. "People can be a pain in the ass."

I nod. "True. But I think it takes some sort of courage to go overseas alone. Don't you get lonely?"

For a moment, I swear she looks lonely. Then it's gone and her expression is blasé. "Not really. I like my own company and I meet heaps of people this way, people I probably wouldn't have met if I were traveling with someone. Sometimes you . . . wish certain people were around, and sometimes you wish you could share a moment or two with someone else, but fuck, that's what Instagram is for."

I raise my beer at her. "Well, let me just tell you that I think you're a pretty awesome woman, Gemma."

She raises her brow and her bottle at the same time. "Woman? Not chick, not girl?"

"You're all woman to me, as far as I can see," I say.

She clinks her bottle against mine. "It's the tits, isn't it?"

My eyes drift over her. "It's a lot of things." The truth is, I'm torn between wanting to tear her clothes off and fuck her senseless or wanting to sit somewhere quiet and talk to her the whole night. It's a curious war I'm fighting, but I'd be happy with either victory.

"So, you," she says, turning around so she's leaning back on her elbows, one boot kicked up onto the other, "tell me about Josh. All I know is you have a sister called Vera who lives in Spain, you watch *Futurama* and *Game of Thrones*, and you have a big ego and a nice dick."

I choke on my beer and quickly wipe my mouth. "Whoa, whoa, whoa. Who told you about the dick?"

She takes a polite sip of her drink, her eyes playful. "You did earlier. You said it was a Canadian thing."

"Right," I say, quickly recovering. "Well, that's where the ego comes from."

"Uh-huh," she says. "And what do you do? You know, work-wise?"

My smile falters. This part is where I kind of suck at life. A big dick can only get you so far. "Oh, I just kinda work. Jobs."

"Oh, *jobs*," she says. "I've heard of those."

I sigh inwardly. "I'm a line cook at a restaurant."

She cocks her head. "Oh, so you want to be a chef?"

"Not really," I say, but what I mean to say is *not at all*. "It's just something that pays the bills." The minute I say that, it's like I'm lying, because while I do pay rent, I pay it to my mother and it's nowhere near as much as what most people pay. The dirty truth is, I live at home and there's no woman alive who finds that sexy.

"So then what do you like to do, if that's not it?"

Here's the thing. On the surface, Joshua Miles is a charmer. I'm tall, have a good body, nice tats, and a dick that I know how to use. I can be shameless but funny enough, which usually works to my advantage with the ladies. But aside from the fact that I work as a line cook and I live at home, I'm also an aspiring artist. A graphic artist. I mean, my dream job is to either work for a place like Marvel or DC illustrating their comic books and graphic novels, or to just create my own one day. But the moment you tell a girl that you like to draw comic books, they look at you like you just took a shit in front of them.

But I don't know Gemma, and since she's leaving tomorrow I don't have a lot to lose. Besides, something tells me she's different from the others, and it's not just her accent.

"I'm an artist," I tell her, deciding to cut out the aspiring crap. "Graphic design, graphic art. I sketch, I paint, lots of digital work. I'm in the middle of illustrating my own comic book, though I just have half the rough drawings complete and none of the dialogue. I've even applied for art school but I'm still waiting to hear back."

She's silent for a moment and I peer at her cautiously, expecting to see her eyes glazed over. Instead, she looks extraordinarily happy. Her smile is breathtakingly wide and it's such a sharp contrast to her ever-present smirk.

"Really?" she exclaims. "That's so awesome!"

"It is?" I thought she'd tolerate it, not actually think it was cool. Goddamn it, who just dropped this dream woman into my lap?

"I used to paint," she says and her smile winds down. A wash of sadness comes across her brow and I have this sudden urge to kiss her and hope it brings that smile back.

I wait for her to elaborate, but she doesn't. "Hey," she says, brightening up. "Come on, I'll buy you another drink." She quickly downs her beer and I can tell she's forcing some cheer into her face. I can't say no to another bottle, though.

She grabs my hand again, but this time she's in no hurry to let go. Neither am I. Just like that, a beer is the last thing on my mind. This woman seems to be everything I'm looking for and I only have her for one night, if I even have her at all. I want to bring her into a dark corner and let my tongue caress hers before sliding it down her neck. I want to feel her smooth, tight body beneath my hands and make her smart mouth open with a moan. Then I want to glide my fingers down her pants and make her moan louder. I want her eyes to stare at me with lazy lust and beg me to do my worst.

But there are no dark corners on this roof deck, so we make our way through the sweaty mess of people again. I immediately miss the relative privacy and the invigorating chill of the outdoors and make up for it by having a cold beer, and then another.

We find a small living room at the end of the hall where we sit down on a couch and watch a few people play Rock Band in the near dark. I'm buzzed and the room is hypnotizing with the sounds and lights and her warmth beside me. I put my hand on her thigh and try to talk to her, but it's too loud and the dark is too inviting, too freeing. I go to whisper in her ear, to ask her if she's having a good time, to ask her what time her flight leaves, to ask her anything at all, and I find my lips grazing her earlobe. I'm losing the war and losing it fast.

She tastes far too good for me to stop. I tease the rim of her ear with my tongue to taste her even better.

She doesn't shove me away. She doesn't flinch. She just turns her head so my lips are next to hers, and for one moment I hesitate, my lips brushing lightly against hers, feeling the heady desire build to a breaking point. Her breath hitches in anticipation.

Then I kiss her. It's sweet and soft and so gentle that all the blood in my body doesn't know where to go.

Then it hurts.

"Ow," I say, pulling back slightly and rubbing my fingers over my mouth. What the hell?

"Sorry!" she whispers harshly, flushed from either embarrassment or arousal, and she quickly removes her fangs from her mouth, tossing them over her shoulder. "I forgot they were in there."

"Good thing we didn't start off with a blow job," I joke.

"No," she says deviously, and her hand goes on top of my erection. My eyes go wide. "That was going to come second."

"Was?" I repeat, feeling myself get harder under her touch. I can't even stand it.

She bites her lip coquettishly and once again I am wondering how the fuck I got so lucky. Must have been the eyeliner and dick comments.

I grab her face in my hands and kiss her, not gentle this time, not slow. It is fast and feverish and her mouth is even sweeter than the rest of her. She's a good kisser, but then again so am I, and I sink into this dizzy well of lust that I'm not sure how to get out of. So I don't even try.

We make out like that forever, my tongue exploring her mouth, fucking it hard and soft all at once, followed by my lips on her neck and her hand stroking my shaft. I think the last time I had a hand job over my clothes was in high school, but now there's something so fucking erotic about it that I have a hard time not coming. Maybe it's the fact that there are five other people in the room, although they're all concentrating on playing "Helter Skelter." Still, voyeurism is a total turn-on.

I quickly remember that I had put a condom in my satchel because I figured that pretending to be a ripped, violent warrior might just be walking lady porn. I pull back, both of us breathing hard. "Want to find a room?" I say to her, my eyes glued to her wet, open mouth. Oh god, did I need those lips to finish me off.

She nods and gets up. I do the same, tucking myself up into the waistband of my briefs and making sure I'm not about to poke anyone's eye out. I take her hand and we leave the room and start exploring the hallway, though I have to press her up against the wall at least once and drive my tongue into her mouth and myself into her hip. I put my hand up her shirt and feel her soft skin through her thin, lacy bra, her nipples intoxicatingly hard. I want nothing more than to pinch them between my teeth and roll my tongue ring over them.

When I'm able to pry myself off of her again, we find a door that's locked. I'm not one to try and bust doors open, not even for the sake of hot monkey sex, so I take out my credit card and slide it up between the door and the frame. I breathe out a sigh of relief as it clicks open and we stumble into a small billiards room that has been stuffed to the walls with furniture and breakables, all put away for the party.

I close the door behind us and lock it.

Chapter Two

GEMMA

I love his accent.

It sounds softer than the stereotypical Canadian one, but it's still foreign to my ears. Though Josh could speak with a Klingon accent and he'd still be every woman's fantasy because he's dressed as a big, beefy warrior. Who knew guys with eyeliner could be such a turn-on?

While he locks the door behind us, I lean back against the pool table and stealthily admire him. This billiards room turned storage facility is the most light I've seen him in all night and I take advantage. He's tall, probably six foot two, which is perfect because I'm fairly tall for a girl. He's nowhere near as thick and muscly as the meatheads I work with at the gym, but his body is toned and sculpted. It looks good—real good. If he's anything like most people in this city, he's earned it swimming, stand-up paddle boarding, mountain biking, whatever. But he's definitely earned it.

And under all the bronzer and the eyeliner and the tribal

facial hair, I can tell he's absolutely gorgeous. Full lips that bear the mark of a lip piercing he's taken out, soulful blue eyes the color of pale winter skies, and strong cheekbones that have a Nordic or Eastern European quality to them. He manages to look both manly and pretty in his getup—not an easy feat. His tattoos help. They're mainly black and white but wonderfully artistic and intricate, covering his arms and shoulders. I wonder where else they are.

I wonder if I'm brave enough to ask.

I'm not normally this forward with men I've just met, but Josh is pretty forward himself. He has this ease and sexual confidence that I rarely see in guys my age, like he knows more than he leads on, and I'm falling for it hook, line, and sinker. He's a bit sexually aggressive, too, but in the way that I feel comfortable with. There's an air of respect coming off him, and I know that if I were to decide I don't want to do this, he'd totally understand.

But of course, I do want to do this. I wanted to the moment I set eyes on him. His lopsided smile, touched with a bit of arrogance, his eyes that were cheeky and playful—it all drew me in like a lion to the kill. I wanted to play with him. I wanted to have fun.

I *need* to have fun. What a way to say goodbye to North America.

"Do you play pool?" he asks, gesturing to the table.

I shake my head and as he walks over to me it's impossible to ignore the butterflies that are swirling in my stomach. It feels like they're escaping, fluttering along my arms, making my nerves dance. I can't help but smirk to myself. After all this time traveling, it's my last day that finally makes me feel the most alive.

"What's so funny?" he asks, his voice lower now. It's deep

and rich and has this way of washing over you. I'm reminded of how incredibly turned-on I am and I momentarily squeeze my thighs together to quell the throbbing there.

"Nothing," I say. I don't dare admit anything. He's still a stranger.

He places his hand on my cheek, cupping my face. I want to close my eyes and lean into his touch but at the same time I'm too afraid to look away. His lips are so perfect, his mouth so inviting. Those beautiful blues are hooded with desire, all for me.

"I don't believe you," he whispers, inches away. Underneath the somewhat flowery scent of the bronzer he's got all over him, he smells fresh and masculine, like he uses some kind of woodsy cologne or shower gel. It's not Lynx like my ex used to spray all over himself, thank god.

I don't have time to come up with a witty remark. He kisses me and the world around us slips away. His tongue is smooth but urgent, the tongue ring stimulating, and our kiss builds with desire until my whole body feels like it's being licked by the sweetest flames. I'm sucked under, in a riptide, into the undertow, and it's dark and I'm tumbling and I don't know which way is up but oh god, how I don't want it to stop. I could drown in his mouth. I could sink into him forever.

I barely know this guy. I'm leaving tomorrow and I'll never see him again.

But I want to drown in every moment we have.

I want him to fuck me with all he's got, until I'm left breathless, washed up on shore and deliriously spent.

It's at least a promising start.

He gently slides my purple wig off of my head and tosses it behind me onto the pool table. He smiles—no, grins, like he won the lottery—and tousles my long dark hair loose and over my shoulders.

"Fuck, you're hot," he says softly, running his fingers through the strands. It feels amazing.

"So I should rethink the purple hair?"

He only smiles and pulls my singlet over my head. I'm glad I'm wearing matching underwear today: intricate peach lace. It's a bit too flimsy for my breasts—the girls need a lot of support—but that doesn't matter the minute I can feel the heat of his fingers through them. I lean my head back and close my eyes as he peels down the lace, revealing my nipples, which sharpen, exposed to the air, to his touch.

Josh brushes them lightly with his thumbs, causing me to shiver. I let out a loud moan that sounds deafening in this haphazardly arranged room. But before I even have a chance to be embarrassed, he places his mouth on my nipples, teasing them with his teeth, running the cool steel of his tongue ring over them. I moan again and I can feel his smile against my skin.

"I'm going to make you come so hard," he murmurs, cocky as all out.

"Just so you know, I don't come on command," I tell him. My voice is husky with desire, it doesn't even sound like me. "I don't care what books you read."

"I won't be saying a word," he says before he starts flicking me with his tongue. Jolts of sweet agony shoot through me. Oh, sweet Jesus, this boy is good.

Just when I think I'm going to have an orgasm from him biting and sucking on my breasts alone, he slides a hand down my pants. I know I'm soaked when he finds me and he groans at the discovery. He quickly pulls my pants down toward my boots, the underwear next.

I have a fit body but I work hard for it. I have to. I'm a personal trainer and a bit of a fitness buff. But even so, there's always been a part of me that blushes and feels insecure when a guy sees me naked. All my insecurities run through my head—my thighs are too muscular, my shoulders too wide, my butt needs its own hemisphere. I could go on.

But tonight, I don't hear anything in my head. No doubt, no cringing, no bashfulness. I feel like I don't need to apologize to Josh for being me. He's too busy making me feel like I am all he's ever wanted. His desire not only fuels my own but gives me confidence. Halloween is all about pretending to be someone else, yet for once I feel completely comfortable, naked and exposed; there's nothing to hide.

Not really.

Josh brings me back around by trailing his fingers up the insides of my thighs. My skin shivers in anticipation and I lean back on the pool table, my cheek resting against the soft green surface. I'd had a couple of one-night stands before; one drunken night on the beach in Napier, the other after a night out at a sweaty club in Auckland's Viaduct. Neither guy went down on me. Hell, neither guy even really knew I was there. They came, I didn't—end of story. Sometimes it had been that way with my ex, too.

But Josh is different. He lowers his head and kisses down along the ridge of my hip bones. I can't help but arch them up toward him. There's a moment of anxiety as I feel his breath over my landing strip, tickling what hair is left there. I wonder if he's going to like the way I taste, the way I feel.

The moment his steel-laced tongue grazes over my clit though, the worry is gone. He's good, very good, and soon I'm coming, moaning louder than before. The room fills with the sound but I'm adrift on a bobbing raft, face to the sun, cool water beneath me. The orgasm takes me away somewhere beautiful until his chuckle slowly reels me back in.

I open my eyes and raise my head to look at him. He's grinning and undoing his pants but keeping the leather corset around his waist. I kind of like that. He's staying in character, the opposite of me.

"I told you I'd make you come," he says. He slides his pants off and I'm caught between wanting to look him in the eye and at his large erection. It's hard to focus on one thing. I think I manage to do both without going cross-eyed but in the end the dick wins. He was right about that, too.

"I never doubted it," I say. I go to sit up, more than ready to lay my lips on him and give him that blow job I promised, but he's bringing a condom out of his bag and tearing it open. He throws the wrapper and the bag to the ground and then slowly rolls the condom onto himself. For some reason, there's nothing sexier than watching a guy put on a condom; the sight of a man's hands on his dick is a pure lust-inducer.

And despite just coming, the lust is pouring back into me again, like a dam unleashed.

The side of his mouth quirks up into that crooked smile. "I don't mean to be presumptuous, but I'm dying to be inside you."

I have a feeling that "presumptuous" is his middle name.

He puts his hands around my waist and pulls me to him. My legs wrap around him while he starts to guide himself inside. It's intimate, perhaps more so than I'd like. The lights are on and he stares right into my eyes, and for a moment I want to look away, to break the tension, the intrusion. I'm already exposed and he peers into me like he's uncovering every last rock. The things I keep hidden deep down. It's mildly terrifying.

But I don't look away. Instead, I tighten my hold around him, my calves flexing.

He grips the small of my back while he thrusts in, finding purchase. I haven't had sex for months, and despite how turned on I am, it hurts for that first moment. I close my eyes and he slows.

"Are you all right?" he asks breathlessly. He reaches up and pushes a strand of hair off my face. His tenderness is jarring.

I quickly nod and smile. I am all right. I'm more than that; I'm flying. He kisses me and I relax into him, allowing him in further until I'm so beautifully full. The pain is gone and the pleasure builds with each controlled movement he makes. There is symmetry in our actions, as if we move as one, as if I'm not precariously perched on the edge of a pool table at some party. We don't move like strangers.

I hold him tight, he holds me tighter, I pull him in deeper, he pushes in further. He thrusts, I rush to meet him. We give and take until I should be close to coming. I move my hand between us, running my finger over the tip of his shaft before helping myself out.

He grins down at my hand and slowly raises his hooded eyes to meet mine. "I'm not sure if I want to watch or if I want to help." But after a few sweaty moments of near bliss, he moves my hand out of the way and places his thumb on my clit. His lips go to my neck where he bites and sucks his way to the smooth spot behind my ears. He picks up the pace, thrusting harder, faster, and I can barely hang on.

He whispers, grunts, moans things in my ear. He tells me how good I feel, how bad he wants to come inside me, how much he wants me. He wants more. I want more.

Just when I feel like he's about to come, his breath hitches, he frowns in deep concentration and control, and I let go. His thumb is magic and we come at the same time. His nails dig into my back, the heels of my feet dig into his. My body rides the wave again, rides him over and over until I'm drowning. I'm sweaty and sated and he steals my breath for a few moments before I come back down.

When I do, I realize we're embracing each other, our

foreheads pressed together as we breathe in unison. A drop of sweat rolls off his face and onto mine and he opens his eyes to look at me. They look soft. Delicate. There's a wound there, something deep and dark and lost inside of him.

Does he even know it's there?

Then he wipes at his face and laughs. He's a mess of running eyeliner and smudged bronzer. Somehow it makes him look even more handsome. It makes me forget that I ever saw him vulnerable.

I wish I had more time with him. I wish I could get to know the real Josh.

But New Zealand is waiting for me. Home.

Eventually we pull apart—hot and sticky. I am absolutely covered in his bronzer, and my hair and makeup are a mess. Halloween is officially over now.

"Where are you staying?" he asks me as he carefully pulls the condom off.

"The Hostelling International on Thurlow," I say as I jump off the pool table. I quickly get dressed, turning my back to him. Now that the haze of sex has worn off, I'm feeling like a wild animal without cover. Exposed.

When I turn around, he's watching me, smiling. His pants are on and his wig is crooked, and with half his body bronzer wiped off he looks like a tawny zebra.

"What?" I ask, trying not to feel self-conscious.

"I don't think we're done with each other."

I raise my brow. "Okay . . ."

"What time is your flight?"

"Three in the afternoon."

"How about I get you a cab home?"

I frown. "I can get my own cab."

He rubs at the braided goatee on his chin. "How about I take you home. I shave this thing off. We do that," he gestures to the pool table, "again, in a bed. You stay the night. In the morning, we'll take it from there."

I admit, it's tempting. But slightly irresponsible. "It sounds a bit too risky when I have a thirteen hour flight tomorrow." I'm thinking it over though and he's studying me, waiting for me to say yes.

And I do, because I want to. It feels right. He's right. We aren't done with each other.

"How about I stay for a while," I tell him, "then cab home before the sun rises. I'll feel better. I have a knack for missing planes, trains, and automobiles."

He bites his lip and nods. "Excellent film, by the way." He comes over to me and kisses me softly on the lips. "Let's go."

We leave the billiards room and step out into the party. There are people milling about in the hallway—a woman dressed as Luigi from Super Mario, a guy dressed as Ferris Bueller—and though we totally look like two people who just shagged themselves silly, everyone's too drunk to even make a remark about it.

Hand in hand, we weave through the party and into the night.

———————•———————

It takes us a long time to catch a cab—no surprise since they're in such high demand tonight. It seems that the province has just as strict drunk-driving rules as we do back home.

We walk for blocks through boisterous suburban streets with houses decorated with all things spooky, listening to firecrackers going off and the subdued beat of music pouring from random house parties. In the distance, police sirens wail. In a way, it's almost romantic. It has to be at least one a.m. and though the world around us swirls with life, it feels like we're the only two people left alive.

I was smart enough to bring a jacket with me—Halloween in the southern hemisphere happens in the spring, not autumn—but even though the air is damp and chilly, I'm still high from the orgasm and subdued by the beer; it keeps my nerves alive, my blood warm.

Walking beside Josh helps, too. Though he doesn't have a coat or anything, he still radiates a kind of heat that draws me to him. I want to know more about him, soak him all up. I want to talk to him about his art but I'm afraid doing so will bring me down, and I can't afford to be that way. Not now. Art used to be everything to me. Now it reminds me of too much loss.

So we talk about travel instead.

"Have you ever wanted to see your sister overseas?" I ask, remembering what he said about her being in Spain.

He nods. "Yeah, for sure."

"Would you go traveling anywhere else?"

He seems to think about that for a moment. "Probably somewhere else in Europe. It depends what she has in mind."

"But would you go *alone* somewhere?" I press. When he doesn't answer I say, "I think you should. It will open your eyes."

He looks at me curiously. "Has it opened your eyes?"

The truth is, I'm not sure that it has. Not in the way I wanted it to. So I smile at him and say, "You should come to New Zealand."

He laughs. He doesn't realize I'm not saying it to be polite. I'm half-serious. He should go there. Everyone should.

"I'd love to," he says. "But you know . . ."

I can hear him finishing his sentence in his head. Work, possibly school. Lack of money. Life. There's always something. There had always been something for me, some excuse not to go, until suddenly it was really my only choice.

"Well, I'd show you a good time."

He squints at me. "Am I showing you a good time?"

I shrug. "Sure."

He reads my bluff. He stops in the middle of the sidewalk and puts his hand behind my head, pulling me to him. "Bull-shit," he whispers before kissing me hard. I almost go dizzy, swirled in desire all over again, like melting soft-serve.

We only pull apart when we hear the sound of an approaching car and the air around us dances in the sharp glare of headlights. It's a cab and he immediately raises his hand to flag it down. He grabs my arm and gives me a look. "I'm showing you a great time."

Of course, he's right.

We get in the cab and make out in the back like horny teenagers, all groping and hungry kisses. It's not long before he tosses money at the annoyed driver and we stumble out of the cab and into the front yard of his house. It's tall and narrow and even in the dim streetlights I can tell it's immaculately kept.

"Wow, you live here?"

He looks away and hesitates. "I live with my mom," he says.

"Are we going to wake her up?" I ask quietly as he ushers me in first through the front gate.

He shakes his head, getting out his keys. "Don't worry, my room is far away from hers and she sleeps like a rock."

I can tell he's embarrassed. I know he probably feels bad that he lives with his mom but if Vancouver is anything like Auckland, the rent prices are hard to afford. I don't live with my mom, but I do have a flatmate.

As if he hears my thoughts, he turns to look at me just as he sticks his keys in the front door. "It's an expensive city," he explains. His face is shadowed and he probably likes it that way. "I pay my mom what I can but if I want a tiny, shitty studio apartment close to work, I have to shell out at least a thousand bucks a month."

I briefly put my hand on his shoulder. "Hey, I'd do the same." Little does he know, if it weren't for my job and the fact that it pays well, and my flatmate, I wouldn't be able to afford Auckland either. He also doesn't know that I'm not one hundred percent sure I have a job to return to when I go home.

We go in the house. Josh moves his tall frame through the dark with ease, as if he's used to coming home in the odd hours. I wonder if he goes out a lot, what places he goes, what girls he sleeps with. The guy has skills and he didn't get them from practicing on himself.

We go into his bedroom and the door softly clicks shut behind us. He locks it and flicks on a small lamp that barely illuminates the darkness. He's got a few framed Melvins and Tomahawk posters on the walls, a messy stack of vinyl beside an aging record player. There's an empty beer and coffee mug on the windowsill and a small bookcase overstuffed with what look like secondhand paperbacks. I see some titles—Asimov, Goodkind, Gaiman, alongside Chandler and Hammett. Sci-fi and detective novels. Interesting.

In one corner are an empty easel and a paint-splattered toolbox. Against the wall, a tower of graphic novels and comic books flank battered sketchbooks and canvas still in their plastic wrapping. He has a small work desk and a large Mac monitor that looks like it's about to topple over at any minute. A few photos and magazine tear-outs are pinned to the wall behind it.

Aside from the fact that his queen-size bed is unmade, it's not too messy. It's comfortable and has a bit of controlled chaos going on.

"It's not much," he says in a low voice. "But it's home."

Home. Tomorrow I'll be heading home. After so long, the

concept seems strange. It makes me both wistful and anxious. I want to go but I also want to stay. If only I could be in two places at once. If only I could be two people at once.

"You okay?" he asks. He takes a step toward me and puts his hand at the back of my neck. It's a possessive move but his hand only massages me as he stares at me intently. "Sorry it's such a mess," he says, misreading me.

I give him a quick smile. "It's all good. Sorry. Just . . ." I don't want to get into it. I'm here to have some more fun with him, to prolong the last night, not to get into the sordid details of my life. "I was just tired for a second. Too much beer, I guess."

He looks a bit disappointed but says, "Well, let's get you to bed then. No harm in sleeping for a few hours. I'll set an alarm."

I grab his arm before he can turn around. "Sleep is for pussies," I tell him. He's taken aback but he likes it. Before he can say anything else, I drop to my knees and tell him to take off his pants.

He wastes no time, and neither do I.

There is no sleep to be had this night. After a blow job and a couple of sweaty rounds of sex on the bed and off, when we finally crawl under the covers for good, we stay up talking until the sun comes up.

I tell him about where I work in Auckland, where I live, what my favorite activities are. We have a similar taste in music—nineties grunge, experimental rock—so I tell him about some up-and-coming Kiwi bands. I tell him a bit about my mother and aunt, who run a winery outside of Napier together, and when it comes up that my dad died when I was a teenager, he doesn't press or ask questions. I'm glad for that. My bad hand starts to tremor at the memory and I have to quell it before he notices.

Josh doesn't talk as much, which surprises me at first. He's so easy-going that I figured he'd be just as open. Instead he listens. I mean, really listens. It's both good and bad. Sometimes I don't want people to listen that closely. But when you'll never see the person again, I suppose it shouldn't matter.

He tells me about the art school he wants to get into, hoping that he can get a loan from either the government or his father to pay it off (his parents are divorced). He figures he has to keep working as a line cook but I encourage him to try getting another job, in a field he likes, if he's going to cut down his hours anyway. It's easy for me to say—it's not my rent, not my bills—but he doesn't discount it either.

Just before dawn cracks open the sky, he goes into the bathroom. When he emerges, his face is clean-shaven, his makeup thoroughly washed off. In his tight gray T-shirt and loose, black pajama pants, he's both hot and adorable and extraordinarily pretty. It's sexy as all out, and I find myself wishing he lived in Auckland. Oh, the fun we could have.

But it's time to go.

"I wish you could stay another day," he says as I slip on my gross clothes, all smelling like pot and beer. "I'd take you out for dinner tonight."

I shoot him a sly smile. "Like, a date?"

He returns the smile easily. "Definitely a date. Bit of food, bit of sex."

"I do like both those things."

"At the very least, I could take you out for breakfast," he suggests and he's hopeful.

I want to say yes, I really do. But this is what it is: a one-night stand. We had our fun—it was essentially the best sex of my life, multiple times—and that's all it was going to be. That's all it could be.

"Thanks," I say, quickly braiding my hair back, "but I've

got packing to do. I may even have a nap since we didn't sleep much."

"We didn't sleep at all."

"No, we sure didn't."

We stare at each other for a few moments and the space between us seems to fill with the unknown. We're both waiting to say something but I don't know what it is.

"Let me call you a cab," he says eventually, plucking his cell from the desk. I thank him and in minutes the cab calls back to tell us it's on its way.

He walks me out of his room and down the hall. I can hear someone in the house stirring but he doesn't try and hurry me out or hide me.

Outside, the air is sharp, bitingly cold, and a layer of mist hangs over the half-bare trees, their branches dark from the damp and reaching into the gray like skeleton hands.

I'm shivering and Josh has his arms around me to keep me warm. I lean back into his chest and close my eyes for a moment, just enjoying his embrace, the feel of his hard body behind me. It makes me feel safe and protected. I could stay like this forever.

But the cab crawls down the road and stops beside us, and Josh is letting go. I shove my hands in my jacket pockets as he leans down and kisses me, soft and sweet.

"Thank you for the best Halloween ever," he says.

"Thank you for the sex," I tell him and he laughs.

"You're welcome. Anytime."

I reluctantly walk to the cab but he's suddenly ahead of me and opening the door. He's got good manners, too.

I slide on in and he hesitates at the door. "Have a safe flight."

I nearly laugh. Why do people always say that? It's not like I have any control over the plane. "I will try my best."

He grins and nods then shuts the door. I wave my fingers at him and he lifts his hand in goodbye. I try and commit his beautiful face to memory but I know I won't forget him anyway.

I tell the driver where I'm going. To the hostel.

Then I'm going home.

Home.

Home.

———————•———————

Home comes faster than I think. I go through the rest of the day in a daze, too afraid to nap in case I miss my flight, which turns out to be uneventful. I even manage to doze off for a few hours despite being cramped between the window and a fidgeting child. The copious glasses of cab sauv that Air New Zealand serves like candy certainly helped.

When I arrive in Auckland, it's like I've gone back in time instead of going forward. I can't explain it except that everything feels old. I feel like I don't belong here in my own country.

But the feeling doesn't last long. After I get my ratty backpack and duffel bag and go through customs, my old life comes crashing toward me. In the arrivals area I see *him* among a sea of people, the man I had wished I'd shared every sunset with. He's holding a single red rose, his dark blond hair even shorter than before, his skin deeper than ever. He's waiting for me.

All of a sudden I realize that the last four months did nothing to change me. I am still the same as I was before I left.

I had gone overseas in hopes of finding myself. In this moment, I know I hadn't been looking for anything.

I had been running away.

Chapter Three

JOSH

On the scale of sex, there are four different ways to measure your fuck. There is sex. Good sex. Amazing sex. And mind-blowing sex. There is no bad sex because, I mean, it's still sex. At least to me. I'm not picky. But what I did with Gemma, that fucktastically hot foreign minx, is in another category of its own.

That was pure, primal, crazy, sweaty, erotic, sensual, rabid animal, life-changing sex. That was the sex that happens once in your life, if you're lucky. I cannot get it out of my head. I cannot get *her* out of my head. For the next few days after Halloween, Gemma and her come-hither eyes and thick hair and infectious laugh are all I can think about.

But I never even got her last name.

When Monday rolls around, however, I'm given something else to think about. I have a morning shift and I smell like Hollandaise sauce and drip coffee when I get home. There's a stack of mail on the kitchen table. My mother, the workaholic Realtor, is out somewhere, probably showing some sad sap a house and trying to convince them that they can afford Vancouver's outrageous housing prices.

I pop open the fridge and grab a can of Coke and start riffling through the pile of envelopes and catalogues. I start getting nervous for some reason and then I see it.

A large envelope from Emily Carr, the art school I had applied for. It was only for a few courses—3-D Computer Animation, Illustration, Comic Book Storyline, Design for Motion, Art Direction—but they would be enough to get my life heading in the right direction. I wanted to ease into it and then see if I could actually get my degree down the line.

I take in a deep breath and rip it open. On the first page it says I've been accepted. I had submitted my work late so it was always up in the air, but there it is. I start my courses on January fifteenth.

I close my eyes and smile. I am beyond relieved. The school doesn't take just anyone and some of the courses are for second-year students, but somehow I made it in. I squeezed through the cracks.

Holy fuck, I'm actually going to be a student. Things are finally going to change, going to turn around. And yet, as I lean back against the fridge, staring at the paperwork, I'm left wondering: Will this be enough?

Before I can continue my thoughts, my cell rings. I pick it up. It's Vera.

"Hey!" I say brightly into the phone. For once I have something to say to my sister. It seems her life is so interesting and exotic while mine never changes at all. But not today.

"Hey, bro," she says. "You sound happy."

"Fucking right," I tell her. "Guess what?"

There's a hesitant pause and then a squeal. "You got into Emily Carr?"

"Yup." I can't help but grin at her reaction: more squealing.

"Dude," she says and I hear her take a sip of something, then swallow. "I am so proud of you. What did Mom say?"

"She doesn't know yet. I just got the acceptance letter."

"Good," she says. "I like that you got to share with me first. Unless, of course, you've managed to snag a girlfriend in the last week."

I'm so tempted to say something about Gemma but I'm fully aware that I'm talking to my sister. I don't discuss my sex life with her, though she doesn't seem to have that problem with me. Sometimes I have to remind her I'm her brother first, friend second, and the freaky stuff she does with her older boyfriend, Mateo, is absolutely none of my business.

"Joshua?" she asks, using my full name to bring me back to attention.

"Yuh huh?"

"So, what are you going to do now? I mean, about your job." I hear her swallow again.

"Are you drunk?" I ask.

"*Drinking*," she says. "Don't change the subject."

"Where's Mateo?"

"He's reading in the living room."

"How exciting."

"It is. I'm drinking on the balcony."

"And you're not freezing your ass off?"

"We have an outdoor heater thing." Interesting. A few months ago, Vera would have said, "*He* has an outdoor heater thing." She's starting to really put down her roots, even after all the shit she and Mateo have gone through. Sounds like she's there to stay now. I don't know why that burns a bit. "Anyway, back to the school stuff. Are you going to look for a new job?"

I shrug, though she can't see it. I don't understand why everyone is so against me as a line cook. I mean, I'm not terrible at it. Sure, there was that one time I used cayenne pepper in-stead of smoked paprika, but anyone could make that mistake.

"I don't know, I *just* got the letter. Give me some time to think."

"Sor-ry," she says, exaggerating the word. There's a pause. "Oh, by the way," she says way too casually, "I'm not coming home for Christmas after all."

I'm stunned for a moment before I yell, "*What?!*"

"Yeah," she says cautiously. "I just . . . I'd rather stay here with Mateo, and we don't want to leave Chloe around this time of year, so . . . yeah."

I feel my head get hot and my stomach sinks like a stone. "Vera, you can't leave me alone with Mom and Mercy. You know that Christmas is at Mercy's house this year, with all those stuck-up fucks. I can't handle them alone. I can barely handle Mom."

"I know, I'm sorry." And she does sound sorry. But that's not enough. "I'll miss you, but I don't know. I have my own life here. I was just at home in September. I just don't see any reason to go to Vancouver and be surrounded by people who don't really care if I'm there or not."

"*I* care."

"Only because you need me to take the pressure off of you," she says quickly. "When I'm there, I'm the black sheep, not you."

She's right. With her overseas, she's no longer the screwup of the family—it's me. And yet I feel that even with her around, I'll still be the one picked on. Vera has grown up a lot in the last year, and it shows. She doesn't give a fuck about our sister, Mercy, or our mom, or any of the things she used to. It's a good thing, believe me. But it doesn't stop me from feeling jealous from time to time. Vera has something, someone. She has a life.

I'm starting to fear that I don't.

"You'll be so busy preparing for school, though," she says. "You won't even notice I'm not there."

It's a lie but there's no point in resenting her. She's got her new life. And come New Year, I'll start to have mine.

But when I hang up the phone and spend the rest of the day working on sketches in my ongoing comic—*Detective Demento*—my mind keeps wandering. I find myself sketching a femme fatale who looks just like Gemma. She's wearing a black sequined gown, her wavy, glossy hair over one eye. She comes from a land of fire and water, and as I draw, I remember the taste of her on my lips, the way she arched her neck when she moaned. She was incredibly, *incredibly* sensual but still had her sass, that smirk, those eyes. She had the whole package.

I sketch her all day in various stages of undress. It doesn't bother me to draw her this way, though maybe it should. Whatever. The female body is meant to be appreciated, replicated. I do have to stop several times and jerk off—the memories are too much for my hormones to handle. I find myself having a fantasy about sketching her live, nude, while she fucks me. Screw Jack and Rose, that's how it *really* should have gone down on the *Titanic*.

But when night falls and I hear my mom's car pull up in the driveway, I realize that Gemma has been a pleasant diversion. My memories of our night together lead me somewhere, to some edge, and all I have to do is grab my dick and jump. Instead, I'm in my room and she's some phantom I never knew, living some life far away.

I feel trapped and frustrated and I find myself crumpling up the last drawing and chucking it hard at the window. It rattles an empty beer bottle but it doesn't fall. I want it to. I want it to fucking smash.

I should go into the kitchen and tell my mom about the school. She'll probably be happy, but it won't be a business degree like every other good son has, or a real estate course that she thinks would serve me better. It's school but it's *art* school, and even though I have the chops—my illustration won a contest that helped pay for my car—it's still a fruitless career. To her, anyway. I know that the arts are hard and the odds stacked against you, but I also believe that the harder it is, the greater the reward. Besides, why not? Millions of artists have their art as their career. Why can't that be me?

It's so easy to think that, but I wonder if I still believe it deep down. I'm great at lying to myself.

But I don't go into the kitchen. I stay in my room, attempting to draw *her*, but after a while it all looks like shit so I toss the sketchbook across the room. I go to my computer instead, put on Tomahawk's "God Hates a Coward" and start looking up everything there is about New Zealand.

It's more than just hobbits and Kiwi birds, I know that. But I had no idea how beautiful it really was, how adventurous, how fun. It looks a lot like British Columbia but with a hint of the tropics thrown in.

Suddenly I find myself wanting to go there. To see something. To see her.

"Jesus, Josh," I mutter, pushing myself back in the chair. I pinch the bridge of my nose, trying to shake some sense into myself. I'm contemplating some crazy fucking stuff that might just make me a pathetic stalker.

Yet I realize it's not about Gemma at all. I don't know her. Yes, we had amazing sex and I can't stop thinking about her, but the fact remains: I. Don't. Know. Her.

Of course, I want to know her. I want to get to know everything about her. I want to touch her. Kiss her. Fuck her. Be with her. Just to see if it was everything I remembered. Just to see if it's the same girl in my drawings, or if I conjured her up from thin air.

But what intrigues me more than her is what she represents. She's the freedom. She's the unknown. She left her home for whatever reason and went traveling by herself, to a whole new land. She had boobs *and* balls. I saw this life and vitality and courage in her that I didn't realize I lacked in myself.

I want to feel her, I want to feel *like* her. I want to do the running man and throw caution to the wind and do something a little bit crazy. It worked for my sister, after all. Why should she get all the adventure that life has to offer?

I'm not as impulsive as Vera, though. I take a look at my bank and credit accounts, take a look at my work schedule, take another look at the acceptance letter. There has to be some strategy when you're dealing with such a big trip and such little money.

I've almost got it all figured out when my mother knocks on the door. I tell her to come in and she does so cautiously. She looks tired and wired, her hair starting to come out of her tight bun, her glasses perched on the end of her nose. I remember how scared Vera was when she told her she was moving to Spain to be with a man. I remember how mad Mom was. But I feel no fear. I feel clarity jiggling through my bones.

I haven't decided anything and even that is enough to get me revved up. Gotta get your motor running, your engine humming.

"Haven't seen you all evening," she says to me, stopping just a few feet away. She always acts like she has to wear a hazmat suit whenever she's in my room.

I nod and try to contain my smile. Smiling too much around her is dangerous. "I have some news."

She tilts her head and appraises me. "Oh?"

"Two things, actually," I say. I lean over and pick up the

acceptance letter, handing it to her. "One is I got accepted to Emily Carr. I start January fifteenth."

She looks skeptical at first. Then she takes the paper from me and she nods as she looks it over, as if she's impressed. "Very good, Joshua. I guess that means you'll have to cut your hours at work." A line of worry threads her brow. "Have you talked to them about this? Will they let you?"

I lean back in the chair. "It doesn't really matter. I'm going to quit. Tomorrow."

And then I'm smiling because I said it and it's real.

"Well, you need to have a job, Joshua," she says, tossing the paper back on the desk. She tips up her chin and folds her arms. She looks like a disgruntled schoolteacher from an Archie comic.

"I'll get something," I say. "Don't worry about me."

"Someone has to," she says. Her voice is still stern but she seems to be relaxing a bit.

So I ruin it. I'm good at that. "So the second thing is that I'm going to New Zealand for a few months. I won't be home for Christmas. I will be back for school."

She's stunned. She's trying to process what I said and realizes it doesn't make a lick of sense.

"New Zealand?" she mouths.

"I just bought a plane ticket," I tell her but I'm lying. I haven't done that yet, I'm just curious about her reaction. If I say it, it will happen. "I leave November twenty-third and come back on January tenth." She's still speechless, so I go on to add, "I'll find a new job when I get back. Something I want to do. Something that works with my school schedule. I'll pull it off, I always do."

"But you don't," she says, and I'd be lying if I said that didn't sting like a wasp. But as with a wasp, I swat it away.

"I will, Mom," I tell her. I'm starting to feel defensive, and when I get defensive I get angry. There's no use being angry with my mom; she always uses it against you. It's her weapon, along with her overly pointy fingernails. "It's just a short trip, what's the big deal?"

She narrows her eyes. "The big deal is you have no money."

"How do you know? You have no idea what I save." And that's the truth. I have been saving for emergencies, for rainy days, for the moment I'm sure she's going to kick me out of the house. It's probably the most responsible thing I've done, and I'm about to do the most irresponsible thing with it.

"A credit card—" she says and I raise my hand, cutting her off.

"My credit card limit is low, my payments are manageable, and I don't think I really need to explain myself anymore."

She raises her eyebrows, eyes wide. She's not used to me talking back.

"And anyway," I continue, "I'll still pay my rent when I'm gone, so don't worry."

She sucks at her teeth and looks around the darkened room, as if it will give her answers. *Where did I go wrong?* I can imagine her saying.

Finally she looks back at me and she seems tired, like the lines around her eyes suddenly deepened. "This is just so . . . impulsive, Joshua. You're just like your sister."

That was meant to cut like a knife, but it doesn't hurt. "And just like my sister, are you going to let me back into the house when I return? Or will the doors lock on me, too?"

Her eyes narrow into slits. "That is not fair. Vera went to live with a married man. That behavior is unacceptable."

After all this time, my mother still doesn't get it. It doesn't matter that Vera is happy, that Mateo got a divorce pretty much right away, that things are great for them and they've beaten a lot of those heavy odds stacked against them. None of that matters. Your fuckups will never let you shine in the Miles household.

"Well, she did it anyway, despite what you think, and I'll be doing the same."

A weird softness comes into her eyes for one moment, like she's peeled off a mask.

"Why do you hate me so much?" she asks so quietly I can barely hear her.

Now I'm the one who's stunned. "What? I don't hate you." *I just don't really like you most of the time*, I think, and it surprises me. It's strange, actually, to think about your parents in terms of liking them or not, like they're some person you kind of know and you can form an opinion of them based on how they act, how they treat you, whether you click or whether they annoy the shit out of you. We're all thrust into our parents' lives without a choice, and you grow up together as they raise you. You love them and they love you.

But liking them, as people, to be around—that's a whole other bag of balls. I love my mom because, well, I do. I'm her son. She's my mom. But for the first time, I realize I actually don't like her at all. It's fucking weird.

"I've gone wrong somewhere," she says, going into her dramatics. Whatever vulnerability I saw, that little thing that made me like her a bit more, is gone.

I contemplate saying, *Look, Mom, I love you but I don't like you*. But instead I indulge her and say, "Well, Mercy turned out great. Married to a rich husband with a stick up his ass. Nice house, though."

"Joshua," she says. "Watch your language." But she doesn't argue my statement either.

After that, she leaves, looking defeated, as if she just lost a sale to another Realtor. The funny thing is, I wasn't one hundred percent sure I was actually going to quit my job and buy a plane ticket to the land of Gandalf and flightless birds and backward draining toilet water. But now, after her reaction, now I'm sure. I'm going.

And I don't even know why. It comes back to Gemma, of course, but I don't think she's the reason for me taking flight so impulsively. I don't even plan on looking her up—how could I find her anyway? I don't even know her last name, and the last thing I want to be is a stalker.

But she was at least the catalyst, the push I needed to go into the great unknown. You can only ignore the call so many times before you know it's time to go.

Life is spreading her legs for me.

I'm going in.

———— • ————

Everything happens so fast. The next day I quit my job. They aren't too sad to see me go, which makes me realize that even if New Zealand goes tits up, at least I made the right decision. I'll get a new job; a better one.

I collect my vacation pay and put it aside in the bank. I did save money, that was no lie, but it's really not a lot. I can put the flights on my credit card but everything else has to come from the savings account. I start looking into hostels, into backpacker buses, into camping. Everything seems so expensive but I see some cheaper options out there to make every dollar stretch. I can work on farms in exchange for room and board. I can do the same in some backpackers. I could probably even find some under-the-table work if I really got stuck. I could eat ramen noodles and drink cheap beer. I could make anything work, if I had to.

The fear doesn't set in until it's a few days before November twenty-third, the day of my flight. I talk to Vera on the phone and she's still in disbelief over the whole thing.

"I can't believe you're actually going," she says.

"I guess it's a bit out of character," I muse, rolling up a joint in my room.

"Well, no that's not it," she says. "You've always been a bit impulsive. I just never thought you'd be this way for a girl."

It was probably a mistake to tell her about Gemma. I didn't tell her much, but it's enough for Vera to get the wrong idea.

I sigh. "I'm not going *for* her. She just . . . made me think if she can do it, I can do it."

"What am I, chopped liver?" I know she's a bit hurt that I'm going there and not to Spain, especially over Christmas-time.

"But you're really tasty chopped liver, Vera," I tell her as I light the joint, taking the first puff. I used to smoke a lot more but I've seriously cut down over the last year.

"Thanks, dickhead."

"Seriously," I say, "I don't know why I picked New Zealand but it just seems like a good place for my first time overseas. It's small, they speak English, it looks a bit like Canada . . ."

"There's a hot chick there that you want to bang," she adds.

I grimace at those words. "That helps, but that's not why I'm going."

"You keep saying that."

"I don't actually know her."

"You keep saying that, too." She pauses. "It's okay to be infatuated, I understand. Believe me."

"You and Mateo," I start, searching for the right words. "You had a connection but you also knew each other. It wasn't . . ."

"Insta-lust?"

"No. Well, maybe. Hell, I don't know what I'm talking about."

"There's nothing wrong with insta-lust, Josh. I mean, isn't

most lust instant? You see the person and right away you're like, damn, I want to get in their pants. If insta-lust didn't exist, there wouldn't be one-night stands, would there? You saw this Gemma chick and you wanted to fuck her right away. The fuck was good enough to make you want more. It's simple."

"I don't think we should talk about this anymore."

She sighs. "You're so weird about this stuff."

"I'm not, you're the weird one."

"Fine. Well, anyway, I say go have fun. You'll have the best time of your life, I'm telling you that right now. And Josh . . . I'm proud of you."

I roll my eyes. "Thanks."

"No, seriously. It takes guts to do something like this. I hope you get the girl. Just remember to keep me updated."

"I'm not getting the girl," I tell her again sternly.

"Just like I didn't get the guy." Then she tells me she loves me and hangs up.

The funny thing is, my closest friends, they obviously know about the trip and are super excited for me. My friend Brad has even been to New Zealand and gave me his Lonely Planet guidebook stuffed with all his highlighted recommendations and shit to do. But I never discussed Gemma with them. I guess because I don't want them to assume the same thing that Vera does: that I'm going there for her. They'd never let the pussy jokes stop. And, if I'm being honest, a part of me is afraid that if by chance I do come across her, it won't be anything like I remembered. I'm afraid that I'll lose her before I have a chance to have her.

I really should go back to lying to myself.

Chapter Four

AUCKLAND, NEW ZEALAND

JOSH

I have no idea where I'm going. I'm unbelievably tired, sore, strung-out. People are speaking with funny accents. The light in the airport is too bright. I don't know what time it is. The customs officials are asking me too many questions about soil and seeds and fruit. I'm in another hemisphere, another day. I'm in the future. I'm a traveler through both time and space, yadda yadda. Led Zeppelin must have been talking about jet lag.

Somehow I find my way into the arrivals area of the Auckland airport. I'm here. I made it. I'm really here.

Holy fuckfarts.

This was a huge mistake.

The weight of all my impulsive decisions come crashing down on me like rolling rocks, picking up speed. I drag my overpacked backpack to a chair and plunk myself down on it, head in my hands. I could have thought this over yesterday. I could have had second thoughts on the long-ass plane ride, when I watched thirty million episodes of *New Girl* and *How I Met Your Mother*.

Instead, all my doubt smashes into me the minute I'm on New Zealand soil.

I'm alone in a foreign country with a finite amount of money to my name. I only have a backpack with some random shit I didn't need to bring. Outside the large windows it's summer. My head is in winter. I quit my job to do this. I may be doing this for a girl I don't really know.

I'm an idiot.

I don't know how long I sit like this. Maybe minutes, maybe an hour. I only raise my head when I feel someone sit down on the chair next to mine.

It's an older, heavyset man with a bushy beard, a baseball cap on his head. He's got a stuffed Kiwi bird in his worn hands and twirls it around.

He catches me staring and gives me a knowing look. Just add a twinkle in his eye and a pipe in his mouth and he could be fucking Santa Claus.

"Jet lag is a bitch, aye?" he says in a gruff Kiwi accent.

I nod. "I guess you could say that."

He narrows his eyes, sussing me out. "Where ya from, mate?"

"Canada," I say, turning my backpack over so he can see the freshly affixed Canadian flag patch I placed on it.

"Where in Canada?" he asks.

"Vancouver, British Columbia. West Coast."

"Where in Vancouver?"

I raise my brow. "Uh, in the city, near downtown."

"Where in the city?"

"Commercial Drive?" I say, as if the truth isn't the right answer.

Finally he smiles. "Love that area. My cousin lives on

Broadway, near the Drive. Last time I went was just before the Olympics."

My mind is blown. First person I talk to in a foreign country and they pretty much know exactly where I live. I'm not sure if this is good or bad.

He's watching me. Then he says, "Small world, aye?" Suddenly his attention is caught by a load of passengers coming through the arrivals area. "Excuse me, my granddaughter is here."

He gets up and I watch as he greets a young couple and their little girl in a pink dress. There's a lot of hugging and tears and he gives the girl, his granddaughter, the stuffed Kiwi bird. She hugs it, delighted, albeit still shy around her grandfather. The reunited family leaves together, looking happy as pigs in shit.

I've never felt more alone. And I know the feeling will only get worse if I don't get up. I need to get to the backpackers in the city, I need to unpack and sleep and take comfort in the idea that the world is small. It's something I can handle.

I go outside and wait for the next airport bus. I have a moment of panic when I realize I never got any New Zealand currency out from the bank machine, but it turns out the buses here accept credit cards. I hold my breath, praying there's enough room on the card for the twenty dollar ticket after all the plane tickets I bought. There is.

Throwing my backpack in the bins at the front, I find an empty seat and take a moment to get a grip. I feel discombobulated, like a gumball bouncing around in a gumball machine. I feel like I'm in a dream, like I'm here but not here at the same time.

By the time the bus engine roars to life, my leg is jumping up and down to a restless beat. I'm anxious, nervous, worried about things I'm not even aware of. But when we pull away from the curb and chug down the road on the wrong side, I'm hit with a thrill. I'd forgotten that everyone drives on the left here.

Suddenly, a mere bus ride turns into a novelty. It trips me out, going against everything I'm used to. It's foreign. It's exciting. I'm not at home. I'm elsewhere.

I'm free.

Bright fields of French lime and forest green fly past the window, dotted with cows and sheep. Cars zip down the highway with names I've never heard of before, like Holden and Peugeot and Daihatsu. Everything is so much the same and yet so different. It hits me, smacks me, time and time again, that I'm not in motherfucking Kansas anymore.

I feel high. It's the jet lag. It's the lack of sleep. But the unknown is all around me, and kilometer by kilometer, I am falling in love with it.

By the time the bus winds along narrow suburban streets, well-kept houses, and yards filled with lush, subtropical foliage and bright flowers, and then through downtown Auckland with its concrete and glass buildings, my body is fighting a war between the need to explore and the need to close my eyes.

The bus drops me off near my hostel, the Sky Tower Backpackers, located across the street from the famed tower, a building so tall that it puts the CN Tower to shame. It makes me nauseous to crane my neck back and stare at the top, and even more sick when I see a tiny person jumping off the top and descending it while attached to wires, like they're rappelling some cliff, not a thousand-foot-tall structure among city streets.

The girl at the front desk of the backpackers is cute and friendly and giving me the eye, but I'm suddenly in no mood for chit-chat. Part of me wants to talk about a million things, do a million things, but most of me just wants to crash for a few hours.

She gives me the key to the hostel and the bunk room and tells me a few rules that I don't really pay attention to. Then she shows me the way.

The room wasn't the cheapest—it has only two bunk beds instead of four or six, but I figured the first few nights I was in Auckland I'd need all the extra privacy and sleep I could get. To my relief the room is empty and clean enough and the only available bunk is on the top, which means no one will be disturbing me.

It seems like there are only men in the room, judging by the state of their backpacks and the mess around their beds. There are lockers and I use one to store all my valuables, like my passport and credit cards, then I change into a new pair of clothes and climb onto the top bunk, cradling my backpack in my arms like it's a girl who refuses to spoon. I had heard horror stories about people's shit being stolen from their bags, and even though my roommates don't seem to care about their stuff, I figure it doesn't hurt to be cautious on the first day.

In seconds, I am out.

I wake up to shaking. It takes me a few moments to figure out where I am, then why the bunk is swaying back and forth. I try to open my eyes and it feels like I need a crowbar to finish the job. Dim golden light is coming in through the window. I don't know what time it is or what day it is. I barely remember I'm not in Canada.

"Aw, sorry man, did I wake you?" A strange accent jabs into my skull.

I slowly turn my head to see what jackass has dared to wake the sleeping giant.

A short dude with a mess of brown hair is standing by the bunk and staring up at me expectantly with a big smile on his face. Though I feel like I've been hit by a truck and my body is begging for more sleep, I can't really be mad at this guy. He's got one of those faces.

"I was sleeping, so yes," I tell him groggily. One of my arms is numb under my backpack.

His grin broadens. "American? Canadian?"

"Canadian," I tell him.

"Right on, I've been to Toronto." Before I can tell him I'm *not* from Toronto, he gestures to the other guys in the room. "We're from Germany. I'm Tibald and this is Schnell and Michael."

I lift my head and see two other guys sitting on the bottom bunk. They raise their hands in hello. They all seem to have this wholesome, enthusiastic vibe that I can't seem to wrap my head around.

"What's your name?" Tibald asks, stepping up onto the bunk below so he can get a better look at me. I move back slightly, not used to having my personal space invaded by strange men (which is probably a good thing not to be used to).

"Josh," I say, clearing my throat. I eye the golden cityscape outside of the window. "What time is it?"

"Seven," he says. "At night. You must be jet-lagged. You should have seen us for the first few days. There's an eleven-hour difference between here and Koln, where we're from. We were batshit crazy."

His English is very good. I nod. "Jet lag, I guess. I didn't sleep on the plane either."

"Well, you got enough sleep now," he says, smacking the railing. "If you keep sleeping, you'll wake up in the middle of the night. Come out with us. Have you seen any of Auckland yet? Did you come straight here?"

There are too many questions for my brain to handle. "No, and yes."

He breaks into a smile again. "Well, then, you have no choice but to come with us. We're just about to get something to eat at a pub."

I slowly sit up. "I should shower . . ."

"Shower? What for? Are you planning on meeting any women and bringing them back here? I hope not. The bunk seems barely able to support you alone."

I stare at the boisterous little man blankly. "Suit yourself," I finally say. "You're the ones who will have to put up with my stink." I hop off the bunk—does teeter dangerously under my weight—and quickly brush my teeth at the sink they have in the room. I finish off with a spritz of cologne, just in case.

Twenty minutes later, Tibald, Schnell, Michael, and I are all at some Irish pub around the corner. I'm still tired but the beer is perking me up. I snack on potato wedges dipped in sour cream and sweet chili sauce before moving onto meat pie.

The Germans are an affable bunch. Tibald is the loudest and most talkative, while Schnell is silent and stone-faced and looks eerily like Paul Bettany in *The Da Vinci Code*. Michael, with his baby face, is happy and eager to please. I learn that they're all triathletes back at home and Michael was thinking of doing his degree in sports medicine at one of the city universities, so they all came down to check it out together. They've been here one week already and in a few days are joining some multi-week bike tour, heading toward the South Island.

"So what are your plans?" Tibald asks me after he goes over their route in detail.

I shrug and take a sip of my beer. "I'm staying at the backpackers here for a few more days and then . . . I dunno."

Tibald laughs. "You're serious? No plans, nowhere you want to go?"

"Nope."

"Milford Sound, Mount Cook, Lake Taupo, Bay of Islands, Abel Tasman? None of those places tickle your fancy?"

"There will be no tickling," I tell him.

"So why are you here?" he asks.

I pause before I gulp down the rest of my beer. Why am I here? Wasn't I still in the process of figuring it out?

Aware that the Germans are all staring at me, waiting for my answer, I say, "I just figured it was something I should do."

"I see," Tibald says, leaning back in his chair. "Just get here and figure out the rest later."

"Something like that."

"And you don't know anyone here? You randomly picked New Zealand?"

I tilt my head, considering the question. My eyes quickly dart over to him and he slowly nods, smiling.

"You do know someone. Who is she?"

Now Schnell has perked up, seemingly more interested in my nonexistent story.

"Who said anything about a she?" I ask, but I realize I don't want to pretend anymore. These guys are strangers but that makes it easier. I sigh and then launch into everything about Gemma.

When I've finished, the three of them look impressed, like, *Hey this guy is actually a dedicated stalker*. I must make them feel better about themselves.

"Are you going to go see her?" Michael asks.

I shake my head. "No. Like I said, I don't even know her last name and she was right, there are a million Gemmas here, at least on Facebook."

"But you know where she works."

"Not really. I forgot the name. She just said an Australia

rugby player, or ex-rugby player, owns it, has a chain of them or something."

Suddenly Michael is on his phone, Googling something. "Murphy's Gym?" he asks, looking up at me. "There's an Australian rugby player, Nick Murphy, who used to play for the Wallabies. He owns a gym here called Murphy's Gym. Could that be it?"

He slides the phone over to me and I stare at the smug face of Nick Murphy on the website's home page. His neck is thick, his blond hair buzz-cut and he has the body of a meathead. I quickly scroll through, trying to find out if Gemma works there, but her name isn't listed as one of the personal trainers.

"I don't know," I say warily. "It doesn't seem like the place. I mean, she's not listed as working there."

"Well, maybe stuff happened between then and now," Tibald says. "We should all go there tomorrow and see. It's in Mission Bay, not too far from here."

I feel sick. Must be the jet lag. "I'm not sure that's a good idea," I say.

"Sure it is," Tibald says, slamming his beer down. "You'll have moral support. If she's there, then, well at least you'll get to see her again. If she's not there, we'll just head to the beach anyway. It's sweet-as there." He slurps the foam off the sides of the beer and gives me a look. "You know what 'sweet-as' means, right?"

"A weird way of saying awesome?" I ask. He nods and I sigh. My heart has been racing for the last minute. "I don't really need moral support, you know. I mean . . . I don't even know you guys."

"Sure you do," Tibald says. "That's the beauty of traveling. Haven't you caught on yet? There are no strangers here, just friends you haven't met yet."

I roll my eyes. "How cliché."

"We only learn the clichés in Germany." He grins then raises his beer. "Here is to tomorrow and Josh's first night in New Zealand. *Prost!*"

Well, I have to *prost* to that.

———•———

When I wake up the next morning I literally have no idea where I am. I'm facedown on the scratchy carpeted floor. I can hear two people snoring on and off, like dueling piano players from hell. My mouth is so dry I can barely swallow and my nostrils are filled with the odor of stale beer.

Cautiously, knowing my brain is about to explode from dehydration, I raise my head. I'm in the backpackers. I'm in Auckland, New Zealand. I have the worst hangover of my life.

Tibald is passed out in his clothes on top of his sleeping bag. Schnell is snoring in his bed, but he's all turned around and his feet are on the pillow. Michael is snoring on my bed, having fallen asleep on top of the wrong bunk. Why am I on the floor? I have no idea but it doesn't bode well for my first morning in this country.

I lie there for a few minutes, trying to piece together the last night. We were drinking at an Irish bar, I remember that. Then we were walking down the city streets and eating sushi-to-go from vendors on the sidewalk. I remember being by the water, seeing the lights of the city reflecting on it, the span of the harbor bridge and the land across the dark bay. The memory is peaceful, and then I'm bombarded by spliced images of drunk girls and laughing faces, shots spilling over on crowded bars, and shitty, shitty dance music.

Ugh. First night in a foreign country and I can barely remember it. Perhaps that's for the best.

I gingerly get to my feet and stagger over to the communal showers. I find one stall unoccupied and stand under scalding hot water until I feel remotely clean. I hear people talking as they stand around waiting for the showers, a blend of accents, but I'm in no rush, no hurry. Part of me prays that the Germans are too hungover to want to make the trip out to Mission Bay.

No such luck. When I get dressed and back to the room, I'm shocked to see all of them are awake and already showered. Smiling, even, though I guess that's not surprising for Tibald.

"Hey, you're alive!" he says, slapping me on the back.

I narrow my eyes at him suspiciously. "Why are you guys so chipper? Did you drug me last night?"

"We're just more manly than you, Josh," he says, spritzing himself with deodorant spray. "Germans can outdrink everyone. Ready to go meet your woman?"

"She's not my woman," I tell him, my eyes even more narrow now, trying to burn holes into his smiling façade.

He seems to thrive on it. "Sure, sure, she may not be yours but she was for one night and that's enough."

Actually it wasn't enough, that's why I'm here. But I don't say that.

He continues, slipping on his sneakers. "And, if she made that kind of impression on you then I'm guessing you did the same to her. Women are very into . . ." he wriggles his fingers at me up and down, "this."

"He means to say tattoos," Michael speaks up. "At least back home the women go crazy for them."

I open my mouth to say something about it being more than the tattoos that made the night memorable for her, but I decide to keep quiet. Sometimes I forget that my humor doesn't always translate.

I barely have time to pour myself a cup of coffee from the

machine in the hostel's communal kitchen before we're out on the streets of Auckland. It seems like a different world in the daytime. It's sparkling clean, the strong sun bouncing off the glass buildings, and in minutes I am regretting wearing jeans. The change from Vancouver's fall to Auckland's spring is fucking me up, and I'm soon taking note of the stores we pass by, wondering where I could pick up some board shorts and summer gear. Once again, I am ill-prepared. Story of my life.

When we reach the end of Queen Street and come up against cruise ships and ferries leaving for exotic-sounding islands, we hop on a bus and head out along the water. Tibald tells me about the volcanic island of Rangitoto that is peeking out on the bay like a green cone, and how the three of them had run straight to the top of it. You know, just for fun. I do my fair share of running and hiking back at home to keep in shape, but these guys seem to have a death-by-exercise wish.

The scenery whizzing past the bus is beautiful. The sky here seems brighter, clearer, giving everything a sharp intensity. I want to paint the glare of the sun on the water, silver skimming green. I want to sketch the mound of islands in the distance—all, according to Lonely Planet, remnants of old volcanoes. I want to duplicate, create, expand upon.

Yet even if I had brought my sketchbook on the bus with me, I wouldn't be able to work. I'm in a stranglehold, caught by the beauty of my new surroundings and the fear of what I'm about to do. What if Gemma isn't there? What if there's no way of finding her? I'll pretend I won't feel disappointed, I'll go on and travel and see the country the way I said I would, but it will still hurt. Maybe for only for a second, but it will be a sharp, swift kick.

And then there is the even greater fear: What if Gemma *is* there?

Then what?

I still have no plan. Going to this Mission Bay place to see her, that was the German's plan. It wasn't my own. I still have no next step. What do I say to her? What will she say to me?

Why am I doing this?

"Guys," I say slowly, my fingers drumming along the edge of the window. "How about if she's there, you don't mention anything about me being a stalker. I know it's funny ha ha to you and all, but girls freak out about this kind of shit. It's cute in a book or a movie but the moment it happens in real life, women are bringing out the pepper spray."

"No worries, mate," Tibald says in a horrible Kiwi-ish accent. And yet, I am worried. Never trust the Germans.

Eventually we get off the bus by a long stretch of golden white beach. It and the surrounding park are packed with families and douchebags in Ed Hardy and hot chicks in skimpy bikinis. The air smells like salt and sizzling hot dogs and suntan lotion.

I gaze at the azure water with its gently lapping waves and feel the pull to it. Maybe I should jump in and swim and swim until I reach the green shores of Rangitoto on the other side of the bay. It seems safer.

But Tibald is tugging on the end of my shirt like a little kid. "This way," he says, nodding his head to the busy shops across the street. Michael has his iPhone out and is navigating us past leafy trees with spiky red flowers until we're on the other side of the road and heading down a side street.

My heart starts to hammer the moment I see the sign for Murphy's Gym. I'm starting to hate myself, I'm acting like such a pussy-whipped tool. It was a one-night stand. It was just for that one night. That's what they are there for. I've had at least eight one-night stands before and every single one of them remained exactly that. Wham, bam, thank you ma'am, and oh, you're welcome, too.

Why was this one different? What did she do to me? What the hell was it about her that made her stand out from all the rest?

When did I lose my motherfucking mind?

It's a strange time to be having this argument with myself. I should have figured it all out before I hopped on a plane, not while entering the gym where the woman in question works. But I'm doing it, sucked into a spiral of fear and self-loathing.

What if I had built her up to be more than she was? What if she doesn't look or act the same as I remembered? What if this turns out to be nothing more than a colossal waste of our time?

But when the receptionist peels her eyes away from her phone for just long enough to tell Tibald that Gemma doesn't work here but we're welcome to check out the gym anyway, I know the whole thing has been for nothing.

"I'm curious," Tibald says, unfazed, "let's go see how the Kiwis work out."

I mumble something but follow the guys into the gym room. I was right about the disappointment. I feel it deep down but I can already tell it's not going to last. I never let it linger for long.

While I stand on the side of the room, absently looking at the few people on the ellipticals or free weights, I take in a deep breath and make a note of starting over. I'm in New Zealand, I've made some friends already, I have seven weeks to explore the country, and though my budget may be limited, it's not enough to stop me. I came here for one reason but I'm staying for another.

This is going to be the best goddamn time of my life.

I feel a smile lift the corners of my mouth and silently thank Gemma, wherever she is, for bringing me here. Now, the adventure begins.

When the Germans come back to me, having inspected the place and wearing mild approval on their annoying bright faces, I say, "Shall we go to the beach then?"

"Bouncing back already?" Tibald asks. "Let's go then. At least you tried."

I shrug, marveling at how at peace I already feel about everything. I guess we could come back another time and try again, we could pester the receptionist for her information, but I'm taking it as a sign. "I tried."

We open the door and step out into the corridor, heading toward reception, heading toward the heady sunshine.

And that's when I see her.

That's when I see Gemma.

And the peace inside me shatters.

Chapter Five

GEMMA

I wake up with pain in my heart and the tremor in my hand. I lie in bed for a few moments, my eyes closed and my fingers spreading apart and coming together. I do this until the shakes in my muscles subside.

The ache is still there, though. I breathe in deep and stare at the ceiling. Despite everything I've done, this feeling haunts my chest, digging deep, and I have no idea what it is. It's just longing and sadness that coats my pores. It's a subtle suffocation, but it's there.

My alarm sounds but I take my time before turning it off. I sigh, letting out the air slowly. I know in a few seconds there will be scratching at my door. Chairman Meow, my roommate Nyla's cat, always acts like a snooze button. It's usually a good thing but today I can't be assed getting out of bed.

I pull the duvet up over my head, blocking out all the morning light, and I stay that way until it gets too hot under the covers. Chairman Meow starts scratching at the door.

Eventually I get up and pad over to it, my muscles sore

from yesterday's bike ride. I let the cat in and he immediately snakes between my bare legs. I've always been more of a dog person but Mr. Meow is an exception. On the days that Nyla isn't home—which is often—he's the only thing I can talk to. Lord knows I can't talk to my guy friends, or even Nick. My mother has never really been an option.

I think about Amber, my cousin. She's only been in Auckland for a few days but she's staying at a small hotel in Parnell. I had invited her again and again to come stay with me for free while she was in the city, and though at the time I was relieved she said no—I cherish my personal space—now I'm wishing she was here. She's a nice girl, just turned twenty-four, so two years older than me, and we're about to spend a month together cruising the country. Getting to know her better would be a good thing.

I put the kettle on and fish out the last packet of instant coffee, dumping it into a coffee cup that has a picture on it of a zombified Sleeping Beauty. Even if I do end up bonding with Amber, I doubt I'll be able to explain to her what I've been feeling. How do you explain the sadness and anxiety gnawing away at you every day when there is no cause for it? I know most people, my mother especially, would say that it's leftover from the accident, from when my father died.

But that's not it. I've done my grieving, I've gone to the counselors, I've worked through those feelings. This is something else. This is that feeling like you should be doing something else with your life and every day that you're not is another waste of your existence. The only time the feeling had stopped was when I was traveling, but now that I've been home for a month, it's all back in full swing, worse than ever.

It doesn't help that I still don't really have a job. No job, no purpose.

"All right, pity party over," I tell myself as the water boils and I pour it into the mug. I sit down at the wood-hewn island in the middle of the kitchen, stir my coffee rapidly and stare out the window to the pōhutukawa tree outside. The red flowers are just starting to pop, signifying that Christmas is on its way. Amber and I will be spending the holiday at my mum and aunt's, at the vineyard I grew up on. Christmas has always been hard without Dad but I feel that this year it might be nice to have Amber around. Maybe my grandfather will have us over for a New Year's *hāngi* again up north.

I start to perk up a little, though I'm not sure if it's the coffee or the idea of having something to do, about showing Amber the ins and outs of Kiwi culture. There is still the whole job problem. Nick can't fit me in as a full-time trainer until February, so I've just been taking shifts when one of the trainers is sick or if they're all booked up.

Of course, Nick has no problem fitting me into his bed. Then again, I have no problem fitting him into mine. Yesterday was amazing—taking our bikes on the ferry to Waiheke and racing around the island, stopping at the occasional beach for a swim and at as many vineyards as we could fit in. We arrived back in the city good and drunk, weaving on the ride back home, to my flat in Mount Eden, and followed up our day with a night of turbulent sex.

As usual, though, Nick didn't stay the whole night. He was up and out at two a.m., once again claiming that his early morning workout routine would be too much of a hindrance to me. When I arrived back from being overseas and saw him at the airport waiting for me, I really thought things were going to change. I thought he was going to change. That was the whole reason I left, to get away and figure out what I wanted. To find myself, yes, but find a way to get over him.

I thought it had worked. And for one day it did. When I met that Josh guy in Vancouver, it was like everything finally made sense. I realized there were people out there that you could click with, that could ignite you with their kiss, that could wake you up like a splash of cold water. Then the next day he was gone, I was gone, and Nick came back into my life.

When Nick broke up with me six months ago, I knew it had been for the best. He was always splitting his time between Auckland and Sydney, so he was rarely around, and when he was he could hardly focus on me. He liked me in bed a lot, he liked to show me off to his athlete friends, and we had fun being active together. We never opened up to each other or got closer than just our skin on skin. For some reason I liked that. It was safe, and even though he never once in our year of dating told me he loved me, that was okay, too.

But even as noncommittal as we had been with each other, he'd done a number on me. I'd invested way more in the relationship than I should have and when he ended it because the long distance was getting too hard, it dug deep. I'd been protecting my heart but it hadn't been enough. Even without the I love yous, I fell for him and all the shit and false promises that he came with.

I know that seeing him again is wrong, that it's bad for me. There's a feeling of distinct disapproval that rolls off of Nyla every time I mention his name. She's lucky she's a nurse and barely has to see him.

But I am seeing him and things are exactly the same as they were before. We connect in the bedroom but not outside of it. We get down and dirty but never open and real. This time I'm going to have to be okay with it. At least he's going to get me a job. At least he looks good on paper. At least I know I won't get close this time. I won't get hurt. Things will continue to just be . . . *fine*.

I finish the coffee and put the empty mug in the sink. Chairman Meow hops up on the counter and slides himself along my arm, wanting attention or perhaps wanting to comfort me. That ache behind my ribs is still there, that longing for something that probably doesn't exist.

I take a shower and get dressed in my gym clothes—black capri tights, sports bra, white singlet—thinking that I'll go to Nick's and see if I'm needed. I know I'm not. They'd call me if that were the case. But I'm feeling especially anxious today and staying around the house wouldn't do me much good. There's some gardening to be done in the back of the house, my favorite lazy day activity, and a few books I wanted to dive into, but I feel like I have to get out and interact with people, put myself out there. I'm an introvert through and through but sometimes it seems detrimental. Besides, maybe by showing my face at the gym I'll manage to attract the interest of some of the men. I know they never really *need* my training but a job is a job and I'm not above working what I have.

Since it's Sunday the drive to Mission Bay takes a bit longer than normal. The traffic downtown is all right but once you hit Tamaki Drive, everything starts backing up with people bound for fun in the sun. Though it's technically still spring, the weather is hot and perfect, paving the way for what seems like a good December. I hope it holds up for our road trip.

It's too bad Nick said he might go back to Sydney early for Christmas, otherwise he'd be joining me and Amber. I kind of want him there as a buffer, in case Amber and I don't get along, and having him along for the experience would be nice. He often says he wishes he had the time to really explore New Zealand, and I want to be the person to show it to him. I want to make an impression, having something of mine be his first.

But when I asked him about it, his answer was guarded and cagey, saying stuff about going home earlier than he thought. I didn't press it. The invitation still stood and besides, now that I'd already gone out for a beer with Amber, I had no worries about us hitting it off. She's quiet, but I can be, too, and I don't think any silence between us would be awkward. She also seems to just be happy breathing the air. To say she's easy to please is an understatement.

By the time I reach Murphy's Gym, I'm irritated and sweating up a storm. The AC in my car, a piece-of-shit Suzuki, is broken and even with the sea breeze and the windows down, it's not enough to cool the sweat on my brow. All the parking on the side streets is taken by beachgoers or people jonesing for Mövenpick ice cream. They often parade past the gym with their dripping cones of Swiss gelato, like visitors taunting animals at the zoo.

When I finally walk into the gym, I know I look buggered, my hair coming loose from my ponytail and going haywire with the humidity. It shouldn't bother me since most people there are sweaty and red-faced, but Nick has always drilled it in my head how important my looks are in this industry. The prettier I am, the less body fat, the sleeker my limbs, the more work and money I'll get. It's pretty fucking ridiculous, because really, none of that has any measure on my physical fitness—I can kickbox most men, let alone women, into the next hemisphere. But I'm not naïve. I know how the world works.

I take in a deep breath and wiggle my left hand around. Funny how I can lift weights, grip bike handles, and block a punch, but the things that really matter to me, I can't do. In life we adjust. After the accident, I adjusted.

Once inside, I'm met with the blessed burst of air-conditioning. I smile into it, closing my eyes, finding my peace and make my way over to the front desk.

Nina, the receptionist, is glued to her phone and barely

looks up at me. She doesn't mean to be rude, but when she's reading it's hard to get her full attention and I know that she's using a Kindle app on her phone.

"Busy today?" I ask her.

She still doesn't look up but she shakes her head, her brown bangs skimming her eyes. "No. I think everyone is running outside."

"It's hot-as though," I say, wiping my brow.

She nods absently. "Nick isn't in yet."

Well, that doesn't surprise me.

"That's cool, I'm just going to do a set and see if anyone needs me."

"All right. Ta." And she's back to reading. She'll barely remember talking to me. "Oh right, Gemma?" she suddenly asks and I turn around in surprise. She is staring at me with vague interest. "There are people here looking for you."

I frown. "Who?"

"Dunno," she says with a shrug. "Some American and a bunch of Germans."

My frown deepens. *What the—?*

Before I press further, I hear the door to the gym open behind me. My heart starts beating fast for no reason at all and I wonder if I'm dehydrated.

I slowly turn around and am absolutely floored by what I see. If my good hand didn't have such a death grip on my water bottle, I would have dropped it in some overdramatic fashion.

It can't be.

But the guy walking out of the gym and into the reception area is tall, toned, covered in tattoos and has a mess of black hair slightly spiked at the ends. He's wearing dark blue jeans and a plain black T-shirt and checkered Vans. He has a swagger that he knows about, killer lips accented with a lip ring, and stunning eyes. He doesn't belong here. Not in this gym, not in this country.

And yet I'm smiling wide just the same.

It's Josh.

How the hell is this possible?

How. The. Hell?

I am stunned. I can't move.

Then he sees me and he stops, too. We lock eyes. There is fear and happiness in his. I have no idea what he sees in mine.

I barely notice that he's with three other guys, but if it weren't for them I'm certain the two of us would have remained statues, frozen to the ground, tongues tied but blood pumping. At least, he's having that effect on me.

"Is that her?" one of the guys says in a mild German accent. He's short but good-looking and very fit. Actually, they all look athletic, but Josh is the one who doesn't give off the health and "good for you" vibes. He gives off the hot and bad for you vibes.

Except I know that's not true. He may look like the quintessential bad boy, and he may have a bad boy's skills in the sack, but when I was with him for that brief time, he treated me with utmost respect. It was a combo that had my mind and body in a tizzy for days after.

"Josh?" I find myself saying, surprised I can talk. "What the . . . what are you doing here?"

He smiles at me sheepishly, and for a moment he looks away, biting his lip. When he looks back, he is all charm.

"I guess 'surprise' won't really suffice, will it?" His accent, combined with the deepness of his voice, is turning me into a puddle of goo. He and his friends walk over to me. He gestures to the short one. "Gemma, this is Tibald. That's Michael and Schnell. Schnell is actually a lot more fun than he looks."

I barely look at the other guys. I'm staring at Josh, still

trying to make sense of what's happening in front of my eyes. The memories of that night come flooding back like it was just yesterday. The feel of his hands, the stroke of his tongue, the brush of his lips. My mouth opens but I'm not sure what to say except "what the fuck?" Luckily, the guy he called Tibald comes forward and extends his hand.

"Nice to meet you, Gemma!" he says enthusiastically, pumping my hand before taking his back and looking at it. "Nice shake you got there. Listen, Josh has said . . . well, not too much about you but what he has said has been very nice." He shoots him a look over his shoulder. "I've been assuring him that he's not too big of a stalker, but I suppose that's up to you to decide. He almost didn't come here today."

Josh presses the back of his hand into his eyes and groans. I can't help but smile, even though the word *stalker* is ringing in my ears a bit. He's not actually here for me, is he? I mean, I know I invited him to New Zealand but he hadn't taken it seriously at the time.

"So," I manage to say and fumble for the rest of the sentence. "What—what are you doing here? I mean, it's nice to see you." Because it *is* nice to see him. Despite how weird the whole situation is, it is almost a relief to be staring at him again.

Josh glances at the Germans, who are staring back and forth between us like they're watching a tennis match. "Hey guys, why don't I go and meet you at the beach?"

Even the Schnell guy smiles.

"No worries," Tibald says with a wink. I'm surprised they don't all go "ooooooh" like a bunch of primary schoolers. They all give us a wave and disappear out the door. Now there is only Nina, who has abandoned her book and is staring at us with keen interest as she sips her bottle of L&P soft drink. She's probably wondering what I'm doing with this guy who so doesn't fit in here. I know she doesn't care enough to say something to Nick, but I'm suddenly feeling on display.

"Want to go for a walk?" I ask him, gesturing to the door.

"Oh, I don't want to interrupt your day, I just wanted to say hello."

"You're not interrupting," I say reassuringly. "And like I'd let you say hello and just leave."

"Well," he says, scratching at his head, his expression bordering on a wince, "after the term stalker was just used, I wouldn't blame you for running far away."

I give him a wry look. "Hey, I can take care of myself."

His eyes trail over my body and I can feel the heat in them. "I definitely believe you can. You're looking good."

"Sweaty and gross is preferable to purple-haired and drunk?"

"You know I'll have any version of you."

My stomach swirls, feeling peppery and light. His gaze is back to mine, holding me in place, and I'm captivated by the icy depths of his blue eyes. His presence is doing a million things to me—bad, unacceptable things.

Nick. I'm seeing Nick. I am with someone else. I shake some sense into me and shoot him a smile but Josh is already looking away, putting a subtle amount of distance between us. It's probably for the best.

"Come on," I tell him, touching him lightly on his arm. His skin is both soft and warm and rough, and I want to touch him again but I shouldn't. I don't. I walk to the door and open it. He follows and we step outside into the blinding heat.

"There's a park around the corner," I tell him, "has a lot of shade." I glance at his jeans. "You must be hot."

He laughs, low and rich. "Yeah, I didn't really pack for the whole summer thing. I was at least expecting a Vancouver-like spring. You know, rain and more rain."

"Normally we do get nothing but rain in Auckland, but summer has come early this year." I pause and notice I'm staring at him a bit too much. I turn my gaze to the street. "So, erm, what brought you to New Zealand? I mean, how did you find me?"

He clears his throat, sounding a bit uncomfortable. "Uh, well, I guess a few things we talked about, you know, *that* night, kind of resonated with me. It took time but I couldn't stop thinking about just packing up and leaving. Going off on my own, someplace new. The things you said . . . I wanted to feel that, discover it for myself. You gave me a push in the right direction."

I smile. I actually affected someone. It feels good. "And your job? You were working as a cook, right?" I phrase that as if I don't remember every single thing I learned about him.

"I quit," he says proudly. "I got into art school for the spring semester, so I figured it was as good a time as ever to quit and do something else, something more . . . rewarding? Something less shitty and life-draining, anyway. Still don't know what, but at least being here buys me some time to think and figure it out."

I feel a pang of jealousy over his art school. I shouldn't—I should feel happy for him, and I am, but it's a bit buried under the sharp stab of yearning. That should have been my future, not the one I was currently staggering through.

"Anyway," he goes on, shoving his hands in his pockets. "I didn't really have any plans except just coming here and hoping to figure the rest out as I went along. I didn't think I'd see you again because, I mean, I don't even know your last name. But then I met Tibald and his friends last night and they kind of made it their mission for me to meet you. We figured out where you worked and . . . well, here I am, ironically in *Mission* Bay."

He's smiling but it's stiff. He's unsure of how I'm going to act. I don't know whether to let him sweat it out a bit or tell him the truth—that I'm flattered.

I go another route. "Wait, so it was their mission for you to find me? You wouldn't have done it without them egging you on?"

He shoots me a look of surprise, his dark brows snaking together in confusion. "Oh. Uh. Well, you see I was more concerned about coming across as desperate and stalkerish."

"And *are* you desperate and stalkerish?"

He suddenly stops. "No," he says adamantly. He hurriedly runs his hand through his hair and looks away. "I knew it was a mistake to come here."

"Hey, I'm just taking the piss out of you," I tell him. I reach over and grab his forearm, giving it a squeeze. His muscles are firm beneath my touch, his skin sun-warmed. "Seriously. You can stalk me all you want."

He glances down at my hand on his arm but he's still stressing. "I just wanted to say hello. I didn't expect . . . I don't expect . . ."

I apply more pressure. "And I'm glad you did say hello. Really. It's just kind of crazy, don't you think? When did you get here?"

He smiles and I realize I have to let go of him now. It's not easy, but I manage to do it.

I should tell you I have a boyfriend, though, I think to myself as I take my hand back. *I should tell you I have a boyfriend, I should tell you I have a boyfriend.* Hell, Nick's not really my boyfriend, he's just kind of my . . . whatever he is. But Josh still should know, he should know.

But I don't say anything. This is going to bite me in the ass very soon.

"I just got here yesterday," he says. "Everything has been

kind of a blur. We went out last night but I don't really remember where. It was loud, though, and there were a lot of drunk douchebags in dress shirts."

We reach the memorial park at the end of the road and walk over to an empty bench under the wide shade of a banyan tree.

"You were probably at the Viaduct," I tell him, taking a seat. I wait for a moment, wondering if he's going to sit next to me, how close he's going to sit. I feel like I'm a hormone-frenzied teenager all over again.

He sits close enough that his thigh brushes against mine. I suck in my breath instinctively as he turns his head to face me. I'm needing nerves of steel here and I'm not finding any. Why does the urge to lean forward so that my lips touch his feel so palpable and impossible to ignore?

"Yeah," he says throatily, his eyes resting on my lips. "That's where it was. Terrible place."

I nod, swallowing hard. "So what are your plans?" I'm almost whispering, like the strength has been squeezed out of my lungs.

The corner of his mouth lifts into a dry smile. He raises his brow. "I told you. I don't really have any plans. My vacation is an open book from now until January thirteenth. It feels kind of nice."

You know what else would feel kind of nice? Kissing him again. That would cure what ails me. I especially want to know what that feels like now that he has his lip ring in.

Tell him, I think. *Say, I'm seeing someone.* The words are so close to coming out of my lips. I'm afraid if I don't say it, I'm going to do something stupid, though probably not regrettable.

"You should come traveling with me," I suddenly blurt out. "Me and my cousin. We're taking Mr. Orange to the South Island."

All right, that's it. I'm not allowed to talk anymore.

His head jerks back. "Mr. Orange?"

I sigh, trying to compose myself. I said it and I can't take it back. "My cousin, Amber, she's from the States. She's here visiting. On Wednesday we're heading down to the South Island, going to spend the month tooling around there and then come up to Napier for Christmas, maybe the North for New Years. My uncle Robbie has lent me his old VW bus called Mr. Orange. It sleeps six. Got one of those pop-up bunks up top. Would be nice to have someone split the petrol money with us." I pause, catching my breath. "You know, if that interested you."

He studies me carefully. "Didn't you just go on vacation?"

I tilt my head back and forth. "Yeah, but I never get the chance to see my own country. With Amber here, it just seemed like a good opportunity to get away."

"And don't you have a job?"

I shake my head, feeling the tiniest bit ashamed. "No. I mean, I will in February but until then I'm kind of on-call, freelancing, that sort of thing. I'm supposed to be a personal trainer for the gym and their kickboxing instructor but it's just not happening right now."

An appreciative look passes over his eyes. "So we're both kind of in limbo for the next while, aren't we?"

I can feel my face light up. "I guess so."

He grins at me. My god, it's as panty-melting as I remembered. "Well, all right then. I would love to come with you. But first, you have to tell me your last name."

"It's Henare," I tell him, smiling. "Sort of the Maori version of Henry."

"You're Maori?" he asks, sounding intrigued, which is good. I'm never really sure which people are going to have problems with race, though I never would have pegged that on Josh.

"Yeah," I tell him. "I mean, my grandfather is practically full-blooded, but for all intents and purposes, yes."

"I thought you looked a bit exotic," he says, appraising my face. "Your sexy eyes and those cheekbones."

I gulp loudly at his mention of *sexy eyes*. "You know, some people say that the word exotic isn't quite PC anymore."

"Well, I'm not a very PC kind of guy," he says, leaning in closer to me. "But I can use the term *erotic*, if that helps." His voice lowers over the word and it takes all my willpower to keep from biting my lip like a coquettish virgin.

I've already invited him on a trip with me and my cousin, to be squashed together for weeks in a '70s campervan. I have to get out of here before things go too far.

So I stand up abruptly. "Okay, good. I'm so excited you're coming." I stare down at him, smiling like a crazy person. I *am* a crazy person. What the hell am I doing? I can't just invite some guy I barely know, a one-night stand, on a trip like this when I'm actually seeing someone else, someone who *isn't* coming.

He looks up at me, perhaps puzzled by my burst of energy. He slowly gets up, his tall frame towering over me. "Well, I'm glad you invited me. This should be fun."

We gaze at each other for a moment and I'm wondering just what kind of fun he has in mind. I have a guess. It's probably the kind of fun we already had together, something that, unfortunately, can't happen again. Talk about bad fucking timing.

With that settled, we walk back to the gym and I tell him a bit about our proposed route on the road trip. Just like Amber, he seems happy to just come along. It's funny how at ease I feel with him, like we've known each other for a long time.

I keep my distance as we walk, though, just in case he's

getting the wrong idea. Although, who am I kidding, I'm the one misleading him. I'm giddy and nervous and scared about all of this, and with each step I take I know I'm painting the wrong picture.

We get to the front door and I'm about to tell him about Nick, or at least figure out the best way to say it without ruining everything, when the devil himself shows up, his rental convertible roaring into his reserved parking space.

Ah shit. It's all going down.

"Hey babe," Nick says as he gets out of the car, sliding his sunnies up on his forehead. "Didn't think I'd see you here today."

He eyes Josh briefly, failing to hide the mild disdain on his face, and then comes over to me, putting his arm around my waist and pulling me in so he can kiss the top of my head. Nick's not normally physical in front of people, and I try not to cringe for Josh's sake.

But Josh seems to take it all in stride. There's a flash of revelation in his eyes and then his face is curiously blank.

"Who is this then?" Nick asks, nodding at Josh. He's smiling, trying to be open, but I can pick up the thread of derision in his voice. I know what he's thinking. Josh doesn't belong here.

"I'm Josh," he says, not missing a beat. He holds out his hand and Nick gradually returns the shake.

"Nick." He looks him up and down. "You Yank thinking about joining the gym?"

Josh smiles but his eyes look menacing. "I'm a Canadian, actually."

Nick just shrugs. "Same difference. So are you a back-packer looking to get into shape or have you moved here?"

That pisses me off. Josh is in shape, he's just taller than Nick and his muscles aren't so bulky. In fact, compared to

Nick, I'm much more attracted to Josh's body type—strong, toned, and lean. It feels wrong to think, but it's true.

"I'm just a backpacker," Josh says, his eyes briefly flitting to me. "I met Gemma in Vancouver and she told me to look her up when I came to the country. So I did."

Nick nods slowly. "Good on ya, mate, New Zealand is a nice country," he says rather begrudgingly. He looks at me. "You never mentioned meeting anyone over there."

I blink. "I met heaps of people."

He holds my gaze before turning back to Josh. "Well, Gemma must have made quite the impression on you if you remembered her." Josh frowns but Nick goes on, "So, I guess you're not interested in the gym at all."

"Not really my scene," Josh says. The look in his eyes is darkening, and I hate the way things are turning out. "I should be going."

"No wait, Josh," I call out. "I need your phone number." Josh pauses, unsure.

"Phone number?" Nick repeats dumbly.

"He's coming with me and Amber on the road trip," I tell him. His eyes narrow, and it makes my heart race but I stand my ground. "It will help with petrol cost."

"What?" Nick is flabbergasted. Still, I take out my phone from the hidden pocket in my pants, ready to get Josh's number. "You barely know this guy."

"I barely know my cousin, too," I tell him. "Besides, I know him enough. I can take care of myself." I look at Josh and manage a smile. He looks awkward as all hell. "Okay, so what's your number?"

"Um," he says, thinking for a moment before telling me a long-distance one with too many digits. "But I don't really have a plan here so I guess only text, and maybe do it all in one go."

So I can't text you during all hours of the night? I think to myself. If Nick wasn't here, I would be flirting my ass off. I'm a little disgusted with myself. But only a little.

"Wait, wait," Nick says, raising his palms, "*when* is this road trip?"

I glare at him. "I *told* you. We leave on Wednesday." Doesn't he ever listen?

"And where are you going?"

I try to contain my annoyance, taking in a deep breath. "To the South Island. Then we're coming back to my mom's in time for Christmas, maybe even go up to the bach for New Year."

"What's a bach?" Josh asks.

I forgot that when I was in North America, half the people couldn't understand what I was saying. "It's what we call a beach house or a cottage," I explain, trying not to let my aggravation show to him.

"Sounds choice," Nick says. "Count me in."

I raise my brows, feeling a surge of panic. "You said you couldn't come. I invited you and you said you had to go home early for Christmas." I'm practically complaining.

He folds his arms across his chest. "Yeah, now I'm changing my mind. I can at least go for a couple of weeks. I've never seen the South Island aside from Christchurch, and that was before the earthquakes anyway."

An hour ago this would have been music to my ears. Now it just felt like this bag of crap was ready to fall on my head. It's not that I had been planning anything . . . *illicit* with Josh. Lord, I hadn't even gotten that far. And it's not that I suddenly didn't want to be with Nick at all. But being in an old VW bus for weeks with the hot-as-fuck guy I had a one-night stand with and the antagonistic, ex-rugby-playing entrepreneur I'm seeing is bound to be the most awkward thing I've ever done.

Mr. Orange is already uncomfortable to be in; I can't imagine how it's going to be now.

Nick looks at Josh. "That alright with you, mate? Having another dick in the bus to break up the pussy?" Judging from his unfriendly tone, it's more of a dare than anything else, and I'm so certain that Josh is going to back out.

But Josh only shrugs, a carefree look about him. "Not a problem with me," he says and it sounds genuine. "The more the merrier."

They both look at me expectantly and I paste a smile on my face. "Well, Amber is going to be happy. I think she was worried there would be too much estrogen."

"Hey," Nick says, coming over to me and putting his arm over my shoulders. He gives me a squeeze and then jerks his thumb over at Josh. "Maybe this bloke and your cousin can get their bonk on. She's American, she'll like the whole rock star, drug addict look, won't she?" He smiles at Josh, all teeth. "But we'll establish some rules—'When this van is a rockin', don't come a knockin',' and all that."

Though it shouldn't, the idea of pretty little Amber and Josh together makes me feel a bit sick.

"That won't be a problem," Josh says with ease and rocks back on his heels. "Well, I better go back to my *mates* at the beach." He throws in the Kiwi speak and I give him the thumbs-up. "So, I guess, text me before Wednesday where to meet you and I'll be ready."

"Sweet-as," I say, and Nick squeezes my shoulders just a bit harder.

Josh waves at us and then saunters down the street, disappearing around the corner.

As soon as he's gone, Nick takes his arm off me. "Really, Gemma," he says with disapproval all over him.

"What?"

"Where did you find that guy, in a druggie's den?"

Anger flares inside me. "No, of course not. Just because he's got tattoos and piercings doesn't mean he's a fucking drug addict."

Nick waves me away with his hand. "You don't know this guy. I'm surprised you even talked to him to begin with."

"Why?" I ask, totally annoyed now. "Why wouldn't I?"

He grins. "Because you're one hot chick and he looks like he should be on skid row, that's why. Look, I know it's none of my business what you did when you were traveling, but the Gemma I know wouldn't have befriended someone like him."

I'm surprised he thinks we only *befriended* each other, but I leave it at that.

"Well, maybe you don't bloody know Gemma at all."

He rolls his eyes and grabs my hand, pulling me back to him. "You're so dramatic. You know what I mean."

And maybe I do know what he means, but just because I surround myself with certain types of people doesn't mean everyone else is off limits.

"Anyway," he says, "you'll need me with you. Who else will make sure he stays in line? Last thing you need is for him to rob you of everything you have and leave you stranded in Milford Sound while he goes off looking for his next fix."

I can't believe his narrow-minded view of people and the world. Then again, I shouldn't be surprised. I'm so tempted to tell him the only drug users I know are him and his friends, since I know they're all hopped up on steroids half the time. But that will open a can of worms that I don't want to deal with. Though Nick is nearly thirty and has a successful business, he deals with personal problems like a five-year-old child.

"Nick, seriously," I tell him, taking my hand away. "If you're going to come, you can't be a dickhead the entire time.

Josh is a nice guy, he's not a drug addict, and he's not going to rob anyone. This trip is for Amber anyway, so you have to learn to be nice and get along for her sake, if not for mine."

"I am nice," he protests. "But if anything goes wrong, it's all on you."

"Fine," I tell him. And though things aren't going to go wrong in the way that he thinks, I know there's no way that things are going to go right either.

Chapter Six

JOSH

"Josh, do you know what the Kiwi term *munter* means?" Tibald asks me casually in his near-perfect English.

I don't lift my head up from the pub table. "What?" I mumble into the wood.

"It means *you*, Josh. You, right now, are a *munter*."

Tibald, Schnell, and Michael all laugh. They are "taking the piss," another Kiwi term I've learned since seeing Gemma.

Whatever a *munter* is, I'm sure there will be a picture of my face next to it in the New Zealand slang dictionary.

I lift up my head and rest it in my hands. "To be fair," I say between my fingers, "when she invited me on the trip, she had just said only she and her cousin were going. This boyfriend, Nick the Dick, or whoever he is, he pretty much invited himself along once he learned *I* was going."

"And that's probably when you should have said, you know what, on second thought, *no*," Tibald says before he signals to the waitress for another round of beers.

"It will be like that American sitcom, *Three's Company*," Schnell says without a trace of a smile. I think it's like the second thing he's ever said to me.

"Except her cousin will be there," I say. "So, Four's Company."

"Never heard of it," Schnell says.

I ignore him and look at Tibald. "So, what, you think I should have bowed out?"

Tibald shrugs. "Sure."

"Would you have?"

"No way," he says adamantly. "I don't back down."

At that, Michael drums on the table and starts singing the Tom Petty song, *I Won't Back Down*, in German.

"Yeah, well, neither do I." Everything until that moment when Nick showed up was absolutely perfect. Naturally, I had been nervous as fuck. Seeing her in the flesh made everything much more real. She was as gorgeous as I remembered—that body, that smirk—and within seconds I felt like talking to her was the easiest thing in the world. Okay, maybe it wasn't the easiest, I was trying my hardest to not come across as a stalker or some obsessive guy, and I was trying even harder to hide the growing bulge in my jeans.

But, all that aside, being around her felt . . . right. It felt natural. I felt like I had worried for nothing, and from the signals she was giving—the way she locked eyes with me, the toss of her hair, the nervous shake to her hands—I assumed she felt the same.

Obviously I am a total *munter* when it comes to reading women, because she does not feel the same. She has a boyfriend. His name is Nick. He's a total roid-monkey douchebag. His smile reminds me of a donkey that's used teeth whitener. He looked at me as if I were beneath him. In fact, he said something about me looking like a drug addict, and it took all I had at the time not to punch him in the face, let alone pretend that it didn't bother me.

Never in a million years did I think that Gemma was with someone. Obviously I never would have come to New Zealand if I had known that. Hell, I probably wouldn't have slept with her either, since I know what it's like to be cheated on (though there's still a chance I would have—I'm still a human with a penis).

And now, well, now I'm going on a road trip with her, her cousin I don't know, and her fuck-face boyfriend. And why? Because I'm stubborn? Because I didn't want to lose face in front of the turdburger?

Or because in some deep, terribly hopeful part of me, I feel like I still have a chance. Like I can win her over. Like it's not over. I mean, I'm here aren't I? That's still something.

As if reading my mind, Tibald suddenly says, "Maybe she'll change her mind." The waitress comes over with our drinks and he stops her before she can leave. "Excuse me, miss?"

She gives us a tense smile. She has a million tables to wait on, the bar is full of backpackers and other riffraff, and she looks all kinds of exhausted. She can barely humor us.

"Yes?"

Tibald nods at me and I groan inwardly. "See this man here. He's a good-looking guy, right?"

The waitress looks at me and smiles. It's genuine. At least *she* thinks I'm mildly fuckable. "Mmmhmm."

"Well," Tibald goes on, "he's come all the way to New Zealand for a girl. He meets with her and then she invites him on a road trip to the South Island. He agrees, naturally, and then she adds that her boyfriend, whom he did not know about, will be coming with them. Now, in your wonderful opinion, does he still have a chance with her?"

She frowns in thought and taps her tray against her thigh. "I don't know," she muses. She looks at me. "Were you always good friends?"

I clear my throat. "We had a one-night stand, just before she came back here."

Her eyes widen and she looks a little less tired. "Oh. You came all the way here after a one-night stand? She must have been a good shag."

I'm not amused but Tibald takes the reins. "So," he quickly says, "do you think he has a shot with her? I mean, you wouldn't invite a guy you shagged along on vacation with you and your boyfriend unless there was a chance that you'd hook up again."

She sighs and notices a table waving her over. "I don't know," she says. "Maybe she just wants to have her cake and eat it, too." Then she leaves, scurrying off into the crowd.

"Great help," I tell Tibald.

"Why would you have cake and not eat it?" Schnell asks, seeming seriously puzzled.

As I drain my new beer, the rest of the conversation goes to their bike trip, which starts tomorrow, a day before I go off with Gemma and her crew. I don't know our route at all, but I already made tentative plans to meet up with the Germans, if possible. We'll at least stay in touch by text and e-mail.

I'm going to miss these weirdos, that's for sure. Ever since I saw Gemma, I'd been spending the days with them, taking in all of Auckland's sights. We went hiking on Rangitoto, went up the Sky Tower, took a ferry to Devonport, got thrown out of a strip club, and visited the Auckland War Museum. They kept me busy and my mind off of her. I think they thought at some point I'd give up on the whole trip and just join their bike tour.

But not only would I be unable to bike more than thirty

kilometers a day without dying, the truth was I just didn't want to back down. So what if Gemma had a boyfriend—we *had* only been a one-night stand. She didn't owe me anything and I didn't owe her anything. I liked her company, plain and simple, and I could push past this. Perhaps Nick the Dick was right and I'd hit it off with her cousin. For whatever reason, I just didn't want to miss any more opportunities in life.

———•———

When Wednesday morning at eight thirty a.m. rolls around, I'm standing outside of the backpackers and waiting for Gemma to arrive. My backpack is even heavier now, thanks to the extra summer clothes I'd bought, and I'm zonked from lack of sleep. I was tossing and turning all night, worried my alarm wouldn't go off, and my new roommates, a bunch of Israeli guys, were bigger party animals than the Germans were.

It's a workday, so the streets are busy with people heading to their jobs. The sun is just slicing over the tops of the buildings and the air is sea-fresh. I like Auckland—it feels like home. But just like home, I'm ready to leave. I want to leave the concrete jungle behind and step into the unknown again.

Suddenly my ears ring with the deep rumble of an old engine, and the unknown pulls to a stop in front of me. It's a bright orange, vintage VW bus, and the driver is smiling at me.

It's the most beautiful sight.

Gemma jumps out of the driver's seat and for a moment I think she's going to come over to hug me but she slides open the side door and gestures to it. "You ready?"

I nod and come over to her, taking my bag off my shoulders. She's wearing white shorts that show off her toned legs, flip-flops, and a black tank top. Her hair is pulled back into a ponytail. She looks excruciatingly wholesome. This is going to be harder than I thought.

"Definitely ready," I tell her as I swing the backpack onto the floor of the van and step inside. Gemma slides the door shut behind me and I see Nick in the passenger seat, giving me the head nod but nothing else. I nod back and then, hunched over, walk down to the bench at the back. A petite, curvy girl with a mess of blond curls and a pretty, angelic face is strapped into the bright blue seat and I ease my frame down beside her.

"Hey, I'm Josh," I tell her, holding out my hand.

She gives me a shy smile, her eyes making contact with mine for only a second as she shakes. "Amber." Her voice is soft and her American accent sounds strange after being around Kiwis and Germans for days.

I'm about to tell Amber something like "nice name" but Gemma struggles with the clutch as she pulls away from the curb and the van jerks forward. I quickly slip on my seat belt while Nick turns to her. "God, Gemma, ease up."

"Sorry," she snaps at him. "I'm not used to driving this old thing." She gets used to it fast though, and we're zipping through the city as quick as the van can go, which isn't saying much.

It's an old thing, but it's pretty fucking cool. Her uncle must have taken really good care of it. There's a sink, a fridge, a counter than runs the length of the back, seats behind the drivers, passenger seats that flip up, a table that pulls out in the middle, loads of cupboards, and colorful curtains at the windows. The bright blue seat Amber and I are on folds down into a bed, and above us you can see where the top pops out into a bunk. It's surprisingly spacious considering there are four of us in here, and there's a lot of distance between where I'm sitting and where Gemma is.

When we finally make our way out of the inner city, I lean forward on my knees. "Got any tunes?" I ask loudly, trying to see if they have an MP3 outlet for my iPhone.

Nick laughs. "The radio in this shit-heap is broken and we only have a cassette player. Total dodge."

"But," Gemma says, flashing me a quick smile in the rear-view mirror, "my uncle left us all his cassette tapes. I hope you like Pink Floyd because he only has *The Wall, Dark Side of the Moon, Wish You Were Here,* and *Meddle.*"

I do like Pink Floyd, though I can tell the music will color the trip a little differently. But driving round New Zealand in an old VW van seems like the perfect time to listen to them.

After we pull over for "petrol" and get a few coffees to go with strange names like "flat white" and "long black," we're on the motorway heading south. Gemma slips in one of the cassettes and the sound of whistling wind comes over the scratchy speakers before the overly dramatic bass line of "One of These Days" kicks in. It certainly sets the mood, making the start of our trip even more epic.

"Nice," I yell at her and she gives me the thumbs-up in the mirror.

I lean back in my seat and see Amber is staring out the window, lost in thought. She's not one for small talk, which I don't mind at this stage of the morning. I sip my coffee and am lost in the passing scenery and the psychedelic sounds. Despite the potential awkwardness of the four of us in this van, I'm curiously content. A bit anxious, a bit nervous, but I'm also happy. I try not to question it. I just relax and let the morning sun wash over us, coloring the passing fields a million shades of green.

Though Gemma and Nick occasionally chat up front, we're all silent for the most part. By the time we pull into the city of Hamilton to grab a few egg "sammies" and quiche from a bakery, plus more coffee, Amber perks up and becomes more talkative. She tells me a bit about herself, how she's been living at home with her parents in San Jose, California, since graduating from one of the state universities with a degree in English.

"Pointless degree," she says quietly, shaking her head. "I really thought there would be jobs for me. I thought my work experience and my education would be good enough, I mean, I'm smart, I have a lot to offer, but it took me all summer to find a stupid office job. It barely paid and they let me go two months ago so they could hire fucking interns for free instead."

She sounds bitter. I don't blame her.

"Well, you're definitely not alone in this," I tell her, trying to make her feel better.

She sighs and sips her coffee. "I know. That almost makes it worse. I'm out there competing with a million other hungry grads. You know, they could have warned us in high school. Instead they told us we were all fucking special snowflakes and the world was at our feet. Such bullshit."

She swears an awful lot for being such a quiet little thing. She looks at me with big green eyes and seems abashed for a moment, as if she's aware that she doesn't know me very well. I smile back and she relaxes. "Anyway," she goes on, brushing her curly hair behind her ear, "I decided to take all my savings and say, 'Fuck you America, fuck you economy. I'm taking my money and I'm spending that shit somewhere else.' So here I am."

"Is New Zealand your first stop?" I ask her.

She nods. "Yup. After this I'm on to Australia, then Thailand, then Europe. My dream is to find a small village somewhere on the Mediterranean and teach English." A wistful look passes over her eyes. "It could happen."

"I'm a big believer in anything is possible if you want it bad enough," I tell her, and my eyes briefly fly to the front where Gemma is concentrating on driving shift and eating at the same time. Nick is listening to his own music with headphones so he doesn't have to put up with Pink Floyd—or us, I suppose.

"So what brought you here?" she asks me, and I have to watch my words. I can't exactly say Gemma with Nick sitting up there with her.

"Curiosity," I tell her. "That, and *Flight of the Conchords*."

"Good choice," she says appreciatively. She really is quite pretty. Maybe a little too innocent looking for my appetite, but she balances it out with a style that reminds me of Stevie Nicks.

She's not Gemma though. She doesn't have the mischievous eyes I keep trying to get a glimpse of in the rearview mirror.

"So, Gemma tells me this trip is pretty much all for you," I say. "Which would definitely put her in the running for cousin of the year, wouldn't you say?"

"She's pretty awesome," Amber admits.

"My ears are burning!" Gemma shouts from the front and flashes us a cheeky grin over her shoulder.

"I'm only saying good things," Amber protests. She looks at me. "I said I would be happy going wherever Gemma wanted me to go, but she's thrust all the responsibility on me. Now you're here though, so you can choose."

I shrug and lean back in the seat. "Honestly, I have no idea. Everything I've read about sounds amazing. I'm happy with pretty much everything, too."

"Great," Gemma says, "the plans are in the hands of the most indecisive people in the world. I thought you North Americans were all about enforcing your choices on people."

"Well, I'm just being polite," I say. "All the blame goes to Amber for being the American."

Amber playfully punches me on the shoulder and giggles. "Hey, I resent that."

I grin at her and sense Gemma watching us. I glance up and see her eyeing me briefly before looking away. For that one moment, she looks kind of bothered.

Gemma clears her throat. "All right, kids, since you both can't make your own decisions, I'll let you know what we're doing. We're heading down to the Waitomo Caves for two nights. I haven't booked any of the tours yet, but the one I want to do is tomorrow morning so just give me the okay and I'll call them. The cheapest one is ninety-nine dollars so I don't know if that's out of your budget."

I raise my hand. "Excuse me, teacher, but what are the Waitomo Caves and why would I pay a hundred bucks to see them?"

Amber looks at me aghast. "You haven't heard of the caves? Glowworms! Like, for real."

I frown at her. "Okay . . ."

"The whole area is a spelunker's paradise," Gemma explains. "Hundreds of caves, big and small, though there are only a few that have tours available. The tour that I think would be choice has blackwater rafting, abseiling, and the whole glowworm thing."

"Blackwater rafting?" I repeat, confused by everything she's just said.

"They outfit us in wet suits and we sit in these inner tubes that take us down an underground river, through caves. You can see the glowworms hanging overhead. I've never done it but I've always wanted to." She looks at Nick to see if he's going to jump in, but he's still got his headphones on and he's looking out the window, totally oblivious. A flash of annoyance comes across her face but she shrugs it off and then smiles at me. "In order to get to the cave we have to abseil into this fern grotto type thing. I think it would be fun."

"Wow," I say. "Kind of a crazy introduction to the country."

She shrugs. "Oh, you haven't seen anything yet. Go big or go home, we say. Or, I say. Wait till we hit Rotorua on the way back and you get shoved down a hill in a giant hamster ball."

I have my budget written down in my sketchbook but I don't feel like pulling it out and analyzing it like some cheap bastard. Traveling around in Mr. Orange and having most of the accommodation and transport covered is saving me money in the long run. I have enough money now to make the occasional splurge in the adrenaline capital of the world.

"Count me in."

"Me too," Amber says quickly, and I have to wonder how much money she's saved up for her around-the-world trip. Something tells me that her parents are helping out a lot.

"Awesome," Gemma says. She turns to look at me and me alone, it seems. "You'll be starting your trip out right. Good thing you're fearless." Then she nearly swerves into oncoming traffic and quickly corrects, swearing under her breath.

I'm not fearless, but I let her believe that.

It doesn't take more than two hours before we're pulling into the village of Waitomo and everything is *cave* this and *glowworm* that. We stop in a local grocery store and get beer for me and Gemma, wine for Amber, and nothing for Nick because he says he only drinks twice a week before noting that sugar is the enemy of metabolism. I briefly wonder how on earth Gemma deals with him, but seeing as she's eager to drink beer, I think she's dealing with him just fine.

We pile our cart with sausages, buns (gluten-free for Amber), eggs, bacon, water, and other foods that will tide us over for the next few days, then putter to the local camping spot, or "holiday park," which happens to be close by.

Even though it's a busy time of the year, it's still mid-week and doesn't take us long to secure a spot. Gemma has stored a tent and extra camping chairs under our seats. The flip-up table inside of the bus is removable, and soon we've set up camp outside by a fire pit.

It's hard not to feel immediately at ease. Even though the holiday park is commercial and filled with neatly mowed grass, noisy families, and fences, there's this total sense of wilderness just beyond the trees. The birds here are different—even the pigeons are pretty—and the plants have this tropical feel that you don't see at home. The late afternoon sun shines down on me with a kind of clarity and strength I haven't seen before. It burns beautifully and the sky reaches above us in never-ending blue.

I itch to sketch, to paint, but I know I won't produce anything good here. There are too many people, too many distractions. I'm drinking too much beer called Tui, with a bird on the can. I need focus and privacy to do this world justice.

When the sausages hit the grill, we're all eager and relaxed, even Nick. He eventually starts drinking Gemma's share of beer. I guess it was too much being the odd one out. I know it's petty to feel triumphant about that, but I can't help it. The guy rubs me the wrong way, and it's not just because he's with Gemma.

It's because he's a fuckmuppet.

We run Mr. Orange's battery for a bit to play side two of *The Wall*. Gemma starts singing along to "Comfortably Numb," and though I want to join in, there's something about her performance that seems very private. Her voice is clear and strong and it seems she's just singing for herself, lost in her little world with the band. I can tell the song means something to her, and because of that it means something to me.

So I just watch her and appreciate it, even while Nick goes for another beer and Amber downs her gluten-free hot dog. They don't get it. But I do.

When the tape is over, we turn off the engine and are enveloped by the sounds coming from various campsites. Someone has an acoustic guitar and is playing Eric Clapton—badly.

Another site is listening to children's songs, like the classic "Banana Phone" by Raffi. The couple closest to us is bickering. Our fire provides enough crackles and pops to blend them all into one strange melody.

"So, Josh," Amber says as she pours white wine into a red cup. "Gemma mentioned something about you being an artist."

It's not exactly a secret but I still find myself shooting Gemma a furtive glance. She looks a bit melancholy for some reason but manages to smile at me. "Cat's out of the bag," she says.

"An artist?" Nick almost scoffs. "What kind? Graffiti?"

"Actually," I say, giving him a steady look, "I *have* done street art before, and I'm pretty good with a spray can. But I got charged for vandalism after high school, just for painting a woman on the side of an abandoned building. Charges were dropped but it scared the shit out of me."

I'm surprised I'm even admitting it to them—I haven't told anyone about it, not even Vera. Of course, Nick tilts his head back in an *I knew it* manner. Yes, yes, I am a dastardly criminal. Naked ladies, ooooh.

"Josh is writing and drawing his own graphic novel," Gemma says, and I'm begging for her to shut up. Who knew she'd remember all that shit I told her? It's not that I'm ashamed of what I want to do, but it's funny how easily someone can twist *graphic novels* into *draws silly cartoons for fun*. At least that's how my family seems to view it.

Nick is no different. I can see amusement in his donkey smile, but he doesn't say anything. I'm not an especially violent person, but I'm wondering how many days it will take before I hit him. He thinks he's stronger and that's why he can be a douche, but I can take him. Probably.

"Have you told him about your dad, Gemma?" Amber asks, and Gemma seems to freeze.

"No," she says, taking a sip of her beer. She looks uncomfortable.

"Why not?" Amber asks, shaking her head at her. She looks to me and smiles. "Gemma's dad married my mom's sister, so he's my uncle in a way."

"Was," Gemma says bitterly.

Amber frowns. "Just because someone dies doesn't mean they stop being related to you." I'm not sure if she's oblivious to how sensitive Gemma seems to be about the subject or what, but she goes on. "Anyway, he was an artist, too. A really good landscape painter. I grew up with his paintings all over our house. I felt like I knew New Zealand before I even got here."

"His stuff was big even in Australia," Nick says, rubbing Gemma's back appreciatively. Hmmm. I think I like the guy better when he's being an ass.

I want to ask Gemma more about her father but I can tell it's something she doesn't want to get into. I could tell that the first time she brought him up, when she was lying in my arms, in my bed, naked. Dear god, sometimes it seems like a crazy dream that I had ever been inside of her.

At that, I gulp back the rest of my beer and take another out of the cooler.

Then I have another.

And another.

Darkness descends upon the campsite and the air is filled with dying embers and a choir of crickets. There's a chill with the sun gone. Before too long, I'm growing tired, and so is everyone else.

It's time to decide where everyone is sleeping.

Gemma flicks on a light from inside the van that illuminates us, making the shadows darker, and pulls out the tent. "I guess we should have set this up earlier," she says, throwing it to the ground like she's already given up. Setting up a tent in the dark, when you're drunk, is the worst.

She looks at me. "Do you guys mind sleeping up top? Nick and I can take the foldout at the back of the bus."

I exchange a look with Amber and shrug. I had assumed that's where we would be sleeping anyway.

With some effort, we manage to pop the top up so it expands like a giant blue tent over the bus. It miraculously turns into two sleeper bunks, with space to put our bags and shit at either end. There are even plastic windows down the side and at the front that you can uncover by peeling off a Velcro flap.

The beds are narrow but long enough for my height. I sit slouched over on the edge of my bunk, my head pressing against the roof, while Amber sits on hers across from me, our legs dangling into the middle of the bus. "I hope you don't have a habit of tossing and turning," I tell her. If she does, she'll roll right off onto Gemma and Nick below.

She smiles impishly. "I guess it depends how much I have to drink."

"No one is falling on us," Gemma warns from below as she folds out their bed. It occurs to me there's zero privacy in the bus, which might get extremely uncomfortable for me and Amber if Gemma and Nick start fucking. Make that extremely uncomfortable *and* nausea-inducing.

I grab my gear and head to the block of washrooms and showers in the middle of the site. When I return in my loose pajama pants and white T-shirt, the bus looks downright cozy from a distance, a single light emitting a warm glow from the inside.

Once I look through the open the door, though, I see just how cozy it is. Nick and Gemma are under the blankets, giggling and moving around.

I wince and look up at the bunks. I can see the edge of Amber lying in her bed and the soft sound of her snoring comes over me. Just fucking great. Now I have to be the only one awake to listen to this shit.

I step into the bus and close the door behind me—hard. They jump under the covers and stop whatever the hell they're doing but they don't poke their heads out either.

Deep breaths, Josh, I tell myself.

I pull myself up into the top and wriggle into the sleeping bag I bought a few days ago. I close my eyes and the light below switches off. I can hear Gemma giggling again but then she's whispering for Nick to stop whatever he's doing.

The envy I'm feeling at this moment is incomparable. It sickens me, straight into my bones, and I hold my breath, trying to ignore and listen at the same time. I've touched her before, felt her skin beneath mine; I've seen her eyes roll back in her head because of something I gave her. I felt that sexual, feverish frenzy that enslaved us both.

And now she's with someone else who can have that same thing anytime he wants.

But it wouldn't be the same. It can't be. I know I'm acting like a bit of a chump thinking this, but that one night, it was far more special than any of that shit they're doing. It has to be. Gemma's face when she looks at Nick, it's not the same as it was with me. And for the life of me, I can't figure out why someone like her is with someone like him. They look good together on the surface—all fit and wholesome as shit—but what about underneath?

Thankfully Nick doesn't try to harass Gemma anymore, and the two of them quickly lapse into silence.

I lapse into a fitful, dreamless sleep.

Chapter Seven

WAITOMO

JOSH

BANG.

"Son of a fuck!"

One moment I'm in the abyss, the next I'm on my back on the floor of the bus, staring up at the blue tent above me, my vision spinning until it corrects itself. Pain radiates from everywhere.

What the fuck just happened? Did I just fall out of the bunk? I haven't fallen out of bed since I was a wee shit at swim camp.

Amber pokes her head over the edge, absolute fear sharpening her angelic features while her golden hair spills over her. "Oh my fucking hell!" she swears. "Are you okay?"

I groan. "No." Nothing's broken. I lift my head and hear the peal of laughter from outside the bus. I sit up and see Nick just outside the door, hunched over from laughing too hard, tears in his eyes.

I want to be annoyed but I have to admit it's kind of funny.

Or it will be, once the pain of my bruised ass begins to wear off. I guess I should be thankful that Gemma and Nick got up early and had already put their bed away, or else I would have landed on them.

That said, I do mourn the chance of crushing his spine.

It isn't long before we're packed up and heading toward the caves, this time with Nick behind the wheel and Gemma beside him. It feels weird to leave a campsite we'll only be returning to later, and I make a joke about defending our fort from pirates.

Gemma doesn't smile. She doesn't even seem to hear me. She stares out the window as we make our way down the winding road, the thick canopy of trees on both sides slowly lit by the morning sun. Everyone else seems to be in good spirits; Amber hums to some song and Nick is less douchey as we approach the meeting point for our adventure.

We're a little bit late and the tour group has already gathered in the gravel parking lot beside a van splashed with pictures of people smiling and having all the fun you can have while being in a cave. We pile out of it and are met by an instructor who reminds me of Tibald—all gums and good vibes.

There are only four other people in our group—two couples just a bit older than us, which makes me and Amber seem like we're paired together. A couples trip. The idea doesn't make me uncomfortable, but it doesn't seem right either.

The guide, who introduces himself as Blair, gets us to fork over our cash and sign some waiver sheets before outfitting us with helmets, wet suits, and what look like wrestling shoes, all white and flexible. There's a damp chill in the air, even though it's about ten a.m. and some of the sun is spilling over the verdant forest and onto us.

He explains to us that we'll be in water only about ten to

fifteen degrees Celsius, which isn't very warm, even by Canadian standards, and though we'll be guided, the expedition will test anyone with a fear of heights or dark, enclosed spaces.

I'm not a fan of either of those things. When I went into the Sky Tower with Tibald and the Germans, I didn't go near the windows, let alone the section of the floor that was made of glass. And the idea of being trapped in a dark, small place makes me feel breathless.

But I don't dare say anything. Fears are meant to be faced, meant to be overcome. At least that's what I tell myself when my only other option is shitting my pants.

Within ten minutes, we're armed with our equipment and marching through the dense, green bush, heading toward the unknown. I'm walking right behind Gemma and I find myself wondering if she has any fears at all. She seems so . . . in control. Fearless.

I'm also having trouble tearing my eyes away from her body. Her ass sashays a bit when she walks, just enough to draw your eyes. Her waist is narrow and begs me to put my hands around it, and her long legs are both strong and feminine. I remember the way they wrapped around my waist as I pushed into her, how sweet and tight she was inside and out.

I have to stop thinking like this—it isn't helping. I keep walking, training my gaze on the back of her head instead, but even then my fingers long to brush through her hair and feel the silky strands between my fingers. She's so close but I can't touch her.

Ten minutes later we've stopped in the middle of the forest beside what looks to be two outhouses. We take turns getting changed into our swim gear we were told to bring, then head back out to put on the wet suits. Nothing like fumbling into a damp, skin-tight sausage casing in public.

Gemma is wearing a rather modest bikini with boy shorts,

and I should know better than to stare at her, but I can't help it. I can feel Nick's eyes boring a hole into mine, and I quickly look away at Amber, who is dressed in a one-piece. She's not as crazy fit as Gemma but she still looks pretty good, with curves in all the right places.

Now Amber is looking up at me, catching me staring at her body, and she gives me a little smile. It's more coy than shy, and right then I know she's getting the wrong idea. I give her a quick smile back.

"Listen up," Blair says, clapping his hands together. "When you're all suited up, make sure to slip on your helmets. I'll come by and make sure everyone is done up correctly. Then I'll quickly go over the abseiling technique and we'll make our descent."

I raise my hand. "Uh, descent into where?"

He smiles and makes a sweeping gesture to the forest behind him. "Just over there."

There's nothing but ferns at first glance, but when I stare a bit longer I can see the shades and heights of the greenery change.

Once we put on our helmets, complete with a light on top, and look like a bunch of scuba-diving astronauts, Blair does a quick demonstration on abseiling technique. And when I say quick, I mean, like, lawsuit-ready quick. Something about keeping a steady grip on the rope and your knees relaxed and trying not to plummet to your death. That's all I get out of it.

I look at everyone else in the group but they seem more excited than worried as Blair leads us over to the place he was gesturing toward earlier.

The ground in front of us opens up into a wide hole in the ground, a very mini version of the Grand Canyon filled with ferns and other prehistoric-looking plants. There are no hobbits here but I wouldn't be surprised if a velociraptor came darting out of the bushes.

There's the distinct smell of fresh water wafting up toward us and the sound of it babbling from somewhere down below. When I gather the courage to step closer to the edge and look over, I can see the ropes are already in place. Down where the canyon seems to disappear under the lip of a rock, there's a stack of inner tubes. I have to remind myself that these tours run several times a day, every day.

I'm not going to die.

But it's not long before I'm tempting death and Blair is hooking me up to the ropes. I don't know why he's chosen me to go first; maybe because I'm the tallest and most expendable.

Or because I'm Canadian.

I can't back out now. I'm hanging off the side of the cliff, my feet against the rock face, trying to keep my knees from locking. I'm gripping the rope for dear life and I've forgotten everything that Blair has said. The only thing I can see is Gemma, peering over the edge at me. All the other faces, all the other voices, meld together until they're nothing.

But she's there. Watching me with concern, with wonder. A few strands of dark hair hang loose against her cheekbones, and I remember brushing my fingers along her skin, pushing her hair away. I don't think I'll ever stop comparing that night—what we were—with what we are now.

In some ways, I wish I had never slept with her. Then I could appreciate being with her more, revel in her company, in getting to know her. But I can't even do that, because I already feel like I know her. I've come inside her mouth. She's come into mine. I've felt her heartbeat beneath me. So much intimacy in such a short amount of time.

And now I'm forced to start at square one, and it's killing me that there's this distance, that I'm hanging from this rope and going into the abyss alone while she watches with her boyfriend by her side. I'm falling, slowly and controlled for now, but I'm still going down.

I wonder if she'll follow.

She at least follows into the canyon.

As soon as my feet reach the ground and I let go of the rope, unhooking myself, Blair is readying it for her. I step back and stare up at her as she descends with ease. She has obviously been abseiling before.

When she lands, light on her feet, and it's just us two, I have a very Neanderthal moment, imagining we're Adam and Eve. I could just scoop her up in my arms and run into the cave with her and we could start a new life in this secret little world.

But Nick is next, blasting down the ropes like a stripper on a pole, and he gives Gemma a hard high five, accompanied by a few Tom Cruise-ish hoots and an "Aw yeah, awesome!" If I let my real caveman come out, I would have to club him over the head with a rock and steal her from right under his nose.

Soon we're all gathered on the overgrown canyon floor and Blair is leading us toward the stack of inner tubes. Once we've each picked one up and swung it on our shoulders, we're told to flick on our headlamps and follow him into the cave.

It smells like, well, like a cave—dank and earthy—and while at first there's a lot of height to the ceiling, it gradually slopes lower and lower until we're all hunched over. The sound of water increases to a roar, and through the glow of our headlights I catch glimpses of a river. The light from the outside world is far away, a dim glow of blue at the end of the cave.

I shiver. "Has anyone seen the movie *The Descent*?"

Amber glares at me, her face washed out against my lamp. "Shut the fuck up, don't talk about that movie while we're in here."

Blair laughs. "Every day, someone brings that film up. Well, rest assured, we aren't going to be squeezing into any tight spots, and there are no creepy half-man, half-animal blind cannibals hiding in the dark. Besides," he says, reaching forward and grabbing Gemma's biceps, "it looks like Gemma here can take care of them herself."

Gemma gives him a small smile at the slight intrusion, but Nick immediately smacks Blair's hand off of her, stepping in between them with his chest out and his neck muscles all strained and ropey.

"Hey, ease off," he snarls, getting in Blair's face.

And I thought *I* was the caveman here.

Blair's eyes go wide and he raises his palms in surrender. "No harm, mate. I was just saying she's pretty strong. No monsters will mess with her."

Nick jabs his finger into Blair's chest and I hear someone in the back of the cave suck in their breath. "She's not yours to touch."

I exchange a look with Amber, both of us uncomfortable as hell. Everyone is, especially Gemma, who is going beet red and looks like she wants the ceiling to collapse on her.

"Nick, it's fine," she says, her voice low but harsh, like she doesn't want to bring further attention to herself. "Just forget it."

Nick doesn't seem to hear her. He stares at Blair for a beat before jerking his head at him like a posturing dog. Then he turns around, putting his arm around Gemma and leading her away to the back of the pack.

Now, I'll admit that I'm naturally a jealous person. I've gotten in fights over ex-girlfriends before, I don't like it when guys hit on my woman, and I can be fairly possessive—if she's mine, she's mine. That said, I could see that Blair meant no harm, and I wonder if Nick is always blowing his top like this around her, or if it's a new thing. Gemma doesn't seem like the type of person to put up with it.

Then again, maybe the Gemma I met in Vancouver wasn't really her at all. What did she say about Halloween again? Everyone wants to pretend to be someone else? I put that revelation away for now.

Blair attempts to shake it off, though as he addresses us for the rafting procedures, he avoids looking in their direction. I'm barely listening to him myself. I look over my shoulder at Nick and Gemma. He's still staring at Blair with murder in his eyes, but Gemma briefly looks at me. I give her a sympathetic smile that she doesn't return. Her eyes shine dully in my light.

"All right, let's do this," Blair says, clapping his hands together. "Let's do four to a group, which seems to work out perfectly here. I'll take the lead."

Blair walks to the edge of the black river with his tube. I look to Amber, feeling like I missed something. "Wait, what's going on?"

She rolls her eyes. "Way to pay attention." She peers at Nick and Gemma. "Were you guys at least listening?"

They stare at her blankly. She sighs and looks even smaller under the weight of her helmet. "When we get in the river, we have to attach to each other by hooking our legs on each other's shoulders."

I glance at the gently rolling water and observe the other four in our group, trying to sit in their tubes and splashing awkwardly in the water.

"Come on," Blair yells at us, now sitting comfortably in the black tube and holding on to the riverbank with one hand, his white boots glowing against the black. "You don't want to be left behind."

Seeing that we're in near-pitch dark except for our headlamps, which paints the rugged and slick cave walls in an eerie glow, while an underground river rushes past us and disappears into the fathomless depths of the cave, no, it's not a place we want to be left behind in.

Amber goes in first and shrieks a bit as she steps into the water. I follow behind, and even with the wet suit it's still a sharp, biting cold that seeps under my skin. It's a bit unnerving to be going into water where you can't see the bottom at all. Everything is unnerving right now.

Getting into the tube itself is also a bit of a challenge, but once I'm in I do as the others did and hook my legs over Amber's shoulder. She grabs hold of my calves, holding me to her, which in turn keeps the rim of my inner tube pressed against hers.

To my relief, it's Gemma who comes floating from behind, bumping into me. I turn my head and try to glance at her. Without my light shining directly on her she's cast in shadow, but I can see the whites of her eyes reflecting in the dark.

"Wanna hook up?" I ask playfully.

I can tell she's smiling. That's something.

"You can have my legs," she says as she carefully places the backs of her knees on my shoulders. I wrap my hands around her calves, holding her firmly to me. It shouldn't be strangely intimate, and yet it is. I half expect Nick to tell me off for touching her, but there's not much he can do about it here.

"This is like a PG version of the human centipede," I joke, to which Amber laughs.

"Seriously Josh, you have the worst taste in movies," she shouts back at me, her tone flirty.

"Hey, I'm not saying they're good films," I protest.

"Stop your yapping and hurry up," Blair yells from somewhere up front, his voice echoing off the walls. "We're ready."

"I'm going to punch that fucker," Nick growls from the back, still sore over what happened earlier.

Gemma's legs tense under my grip. "Nick, stop."

"All right guys," Blair says, projecting his voice so it reaches us. "Lean back and let the current take you. I'll be in the front, leading the way. Keep your arms inside the tubes at all times and hold on to your partner. If you bump into the wall or get stuck, just gently push off. If anyone starts panicking, just call out and we'll all stop. It's going to get very dark, very narrow, and very low in places, but the cave opens up often, so there's always relief. So keep your heads back and look for the glow-worms. Enjoy the black-water rafting."

There's a twinge in my stomach as the adrenaline builds. I tighten my grip on Gemma's calves and she gently presses them into my chest.

We float, slowly at first, moving together as one, like a giant fish. It doesn't seem possible but it really is getting darker, so dark that even the light from our headlamps seems to be swallowed up. No one is talking but I can hear their breaths echoing off the low walls. Even though the water is cold, Gemma's contact keeps me warm. All I can think about is how close she is, and I lament the layer of wet suit between my hands and her skin. I want to feel her again. This is my only chance. I slowly run my hands up and down her shins, gently squeezing her calves as I go.

I know I shouldn't be doing it. I know it's risky, wrong. It's not a friendly gesture, and I think she knows that. But I'm still doing it, still massaging her as she's draped over me, with her own boyfriend draped over her. With each press, I'm trying to tell her something in case she doesn't know it.

I want her even though I know I can't have her.

But it doesn't change anything. So I keep feeling her as much as I can while the river below us twists and turns until a collective "oooh" rings out from in front of us. The walls above us suddenly widen and it feels like I'm staring at a giant night sky.

Everywhere I look there are bright blue-white dots of glowworms shining down on us. They reflect faintly off the water, and it's as if we're astronauts, soaring through the Milky Way. I briefly think about Vera and her love for astronomy. She would love to float among the stars like this.

"It's beautiful," Gemma whispers in awe, so faintly that I can barely hear her.

"Don't you have this all over your country?" I ask, still massaging her legs.

"I've never seen it like this before." Her voice is full of childlike wonder that does funny things to my gut. She almost sounds vulnerable. My fingers tighten.

As the cavern widens, the ceiling lifting, the walls stretching out, the current slows down and we're no longer moving in a perfect line. I can see the dim lights of the group in front of us, but they seem farther away than they should be, their voices growing fainter.

"What's the hold up?" Nick grumbles, and I hear a splash from behind me.

Gemma says, "Nick, what the hell?" and I turn my head to see him loose and floating past us, his hands paddling him along.

"You guys are too slow," he says, as if this is supposed to be a race, and he floats down, disappearing in front of Amber just as the cavern starts to narrow again and the current quickens.

We whip back into the dark, the glow of the worms fading behind us as the cave's ceiling begins to press down on us oppressively.

I can hear Nick let out a "woo-hoo" from down the river

as the current picks up speed and feels more like the rapids I had imagined.

Suddenly someone cries out in annoyance and I hear a scraping sound that travels back down the tunnel. We twist with the river and Amber bumps into part of the wall that juts out. She lets go of my legs and pushes off but the current spins her away and she's loose up ahead, her headlight shining around the walls in a circle.

Amber lets out a cry that's half scared, half having fun and she stays in my sight until Gemma hits the same spot on the wall as she passes. For a moment she seems stuck and is jerked out of my grasp.

"Agh!" she cries out, and I hear her splashing as she tries to push off back into the current. I spin around so I'm facing her and reach out with my hands, just managing to grip the edge of her foot. I pull her toward me, wrapping my arm around her tube, squeezing in between it and her thigh.

The light from my helmet catches her eyes and she looks afraid, her brows raised high, the whites of her eyes shining. I don't know if she's scared because the others are no longer in our sight, if she thought she was going to lose me, or because I'm even closer to her now.

She swallows, her throat bobbing, and I have the urge to lick her there and feel her pulse under my lips. We might be wearing the unsexiest things on earth, but she's still radiating that same sexual energy as she did when we first met. Here in the dark caverns with me, she is more luminous than the glowworms we just passed under.

"I've got you," I tell her, my voice automatically going lower as the swift river sweeps us forward.

She smiles, close-lipped. It's not quite a smirk but it will do. "I think we lost everyone else," she says. Her voice is hushed, delicate.

Even though it's not easy to maintain eye contact without blinding each other, we do it. Her eyes are even darker in here, blacker than the water we're floating on. "I'm sure we'll eventually run into them," I tell her reassuringly, even though catching up with everyone else is the last thing I want. "Unless the river branches out and we go down the wrong arm and over some underground waterfall."

"You're just full of the wrong things to say," she says, smacking my arm.

I can only grin at her, which means I'm not looking at where we're going as my foot catches the side of the narrow wall, sending me spinning off. I remain attached to her though, my arm still wrapped tight around her tube. We drift side by side until the passage narrows like a tie and I'm still holding on. I don't want to have her legs wrapped around my shoulders; I want her as close as possible. The voices of the rest of the group occasionally drift toward us from the never-ending darkness and I know we're in no real danger.

We're alone. Very alone. I want to take advantage of this.

"So," I say, keeping my voice low so it doesn't bounce off the walls and down the tunnel. Even so, it echoes, mixing in with the sound of the gurgling water. I rub my lips together, my words waiting. I could make things a lot more awkward for us. "Why didn't you . . ." I begin and then start over. "How long have you been seeing Nick?"

I'm not looking at her, so I don't know if the question surprises her or not. When she answers, she's cautious, almost ashamed. "We broke up before I went away. We weren't together when you and I . . . well . . ."

"And you came back here and picked up where you left off." I try not to sound bitter. It's none of my business, really, and I have no right to be annoyed.

"Pretty much," she says with a heavy sigh. "I'm sorry . . . I . . ."

"You have nothing to apologize for," I tell her quickly, not wanting her to think I'm suffering, that I think I have claim to her. "We had a one-night stand. It happens. When I came here, I really didn't think I'd see you. And I didn't think you'd be sitting around waiting for me either." I grow quiet while I think something over. "If we hadn't run into Nick, would you have told me about him?"

Now I turn my head to see her answer. The water whisks me to one side so I can only glance at her for a second, but she looks pained. "You know what," I say quickly. "Don't worry about it. It doesn't really matter, does it?"

A loaded silence hangs over us, lower and more oppressive than the cave ceiling.

Finally she says, "I wish things were different."

I can't help but let out a laugh. "Me too. But you know what? I'm glad I came. I'm glad I'm here."

"Really?" she asks.

"Really," I say with a nod. "Though I do have to ask . . . why the hell are you going out with such a dicknugget?"

She snorts but she seems more shocked than amused. "Excuse me," she says indignantly.

"Sorry," I say. "I know he's your boyfriend and all, but you can do a hell of a lot better, Gemma."

"And I suppose you're volunteering for the job."

"If there was a *position* available, yes," I tell her and let the word *position* sink in.

She's quiet again before she says, "He's not my boyfriend, you know."

"Fine. Your fuck buddy is a—"

"Josh," she warns. "It's just the way things are."

"And I don't understand it."

"Because you don't *know* me," she says, rather bitingly.

It doesn't hurt, because I suppose it's the truth. But it sure makes me feel like a fucking idiot.

I guess not, I think. *I guess the girl I met in Vancouver was someone else. I guess you were just a ghost, just a figment of my imagination, another drawing from my sketchbook.*

But I don't want to play that role, go that route, be *that* guy, not here in the dark where everything seems deeper than it is.

"Well," I measure my words out carefully, "I would like to know you."

I wait for her to shut me down, but instead she says, "Okay."

"Oy, guys!" Nick's voice carries toward us, and as we round a bend we can see another cavern up ahead with a smattering of bobbing headlights gathered near the entrance. We shut up and let the current run us into the group.

Nick narrows his eyes at us suspiciously while Amber looks relieved.

"I'm so sorry, Josh, I was trying to hold on," she says, although she looks all right. They all do—happy to see us but having fun of their own.

Blair gives us an enthusiastic smile and the thumbs-up sign while he holds on to the edge of the wall. "Right on, you made it." He looks to everyone else. "Okay, we're about to go into another cavern. It's not as wide as the previous one but it's just as pretty. I'm going to get you to stay together as we go into it, so try hooking your legs under the next person's arms instead of over the shoulder, for more traction. You won't separate as easily. But after the cavern, we'll need to break apart—the cave gets so low that you'll need to place your hands along the roof to push yourself along. It will feel like a coffin for a few minutes and you could hit your head. But that's why we have helmets, aye?"

Oh great. Who doesn't love being in a coffin?

This time when we hook back together, I don't massage her legs or squeeze them. I just hold on, and after the brilliant blue glow of the cavern subsides and fades away, like stars disappearing at dawn, I let go of her for good.

The rest of the trip did in fact include a portion where it felt like I was in a coffin. If I really started to think about where I was and what I was doing, I nearly flipped the fuck out. I mean, I had to lay flat back and there were still only a few inches between my body and the roof of the cave.

But eventually the cave opened up again and there came a few times when we had to leave one cave system and climb into another by way of a ladder and drop in over a small waterfall in our inner tube. My hips are so narrow I nearly sank right through my tube once I crashed into the water but I managed to stay afloat. Thank god for my broad shoulders.

I don't know how many hours we were underground but we eventually emerged into a fern grotto, climbing out of the dark and into the light, which even though it had grown overcast, was extra blinding. We all blinked at it like newborns in a strange new world.

Once we were done, we were allowed to use their showers before getting back into our regular clothes. Being dry never felt so good. Then we were treated to a bowl of homemade tomato soup and a bagel, but to be honest, all I wanted to do was drink a gallon of beer.

Naturally, once the four of us got back to the campsite, that's exactly what we did. It was still the afternoon, but we loaded up on more supplies and parked our asses down in the camping chairs, refusing to move. We filled up on hot dogs again, copious amounts of alcohol, and at some point during the night Nick stopped being a douche long enough to play several drinking games with us.

It was actually a lot of fun. The caves had somehow made us all bond together in one way or another, but by the time the sky grew dark and the stars peeked through the clouds, we could barely move our tired muscles.

We called it a night.

And I, well, for my own safety I slept in the tent.

Chapter Eight

GEMMA

"Please tell me you have Advil," Josh moans, his hands together in mock prayer. "I will do anything you want if you just give me one. Just one."

"Anything?" I ask, cocking my brow.

We had to get up bright and early again to make it to just outside of Wellington tonight, but that was easier said than done. We all ache from our necks to our toes—even me and Nick, and we're used to physical exertion. Being in that cave absolutely slaughtered us and made us strain muscles we never knew we had, and though I wish I had packed some ibuprofen with us to ease the pain, we're all going to have to suffer.

"Anything," Josh says, and I can see he wants to make it sexual but manages to rein himself in. Or maybe it's me who wants him to make everything sexual. I push that thought away as I shove a piece of hair behind my ear and spy Nick coming back from the washroom block. I'm already feeling extremely guilty for what happened yesterday.

Armed with the chilly bin packed with leftover food and

drink, I press past Josh, who is sitting in the doorway of the van, begging for mercy, and start placing stuff in Mr. Orange's fridge. Bacon, eggs, hot dogs, potato salad, cans of beer. At least it will be on during the drive and our stuff will stay cool.

"I wish I could make you do anything," I say, shutting the fridge door and placing the chilly bin in the storage space behind the backseats. "Because I have a wicked imagination. You should be glad we didn't play truth or dare last night. But I don't have any drugs, and it's called Nurofen over here, by the way."

"Right," he says. "And what did you call that cooler earlier? A chilly bin?"

"Well, it's a bin that keeps things chilled," I point out defensively.

He starts ticking off his long fingers. "Right. And a truck is called a ute, and the hood is called a bonnet, and the trunk is called the boot, and you fill up with petrol before you drive your tyres, spelled with a y, on the bitumen."

"Everything you said makes perfect sense." I try to keep a straight face but his exasperated expression is just so cute. His upper lip snarls just so, like it's taunting me, daring me to bite it and show it who's boss.

"Almost ready to go?" Nick asks, suddenly appearing at the door and giving me a fright. I look at him and nod. That wash of guilt comes over me again, like someone has doused me with petrol. I haven't even done anything but I still feel it soaking me to the core.

I'm in danger of igniting.

My problem is, no matter what I do, I can't stop being attracted to Josh. I've tried, but the moment he first threw his backpack into the bus and climbed aboard, I began a wrestling match with my hormones. And, though I've kept myself totally appropriate, I can't help my body from the physical reaction it gets just by being near him, I can't help my mind for wanting to focus on him all the time, and I can't help the butterflies that seemed to have escaped my gut and moved into my heart.

I can't help any of it, but that doesn't stop me from trying to fight it.

So far, being squeezed in an underground cave for hours has been the easiest part of the trip.

Once Amber comes back from the showers, her hair piled high in a wet, messy bun, Nick gets into the driver's seat and taps the passenger seat for me to sit down. I do so somewhat reluctantly. I want Amber or Josh to have the front row of the journey down to the south tip of the North Island, but if Amber sits with Nick then I'll be in the back with Josh and things might get weird. And forget about Josh sitting at the front. Nick would probably say something asshole-ish, and I now know that Josh is not a fan of him. What had he called him again? A dicknugget?

We pull away from the holiday park and hit the open road. Pink Floyd's "Flutter" seemed to work yesterday as good morning music, so I put it on again, sliding it into the cassette deck with a satisfying snap. I don't know why Uncle Robbie only had these tapes in Mr. Orange, but they bring back old memories of my childhood and will hopefully make some new ones here.

Because everyone is worn out and aching, we all keep quiet, stopping only once outside Waitomo to get coffee. It's a beautiful morning, though—warm, golden sunlight hits the damp cool of night, causing clouds of mist to gather in the fields and flank the base of rolling green hills. When I can tear my mind away long enough from the problem at hand, I'm caught up in a sense of adventure and freedom that I've never had in my own country before.

And yet it's all an illusion—the adventure will be short-lived and there never was any freedom. Not here, not when I'm caught like a fish on a line, not strong enough to fight.

I glance at Nick. He's concentrating on the road, his brows together. I know he wants the old bus to go faster, but it just can't. It's not built that way. It's built to take its time, to do more than get people from point A to point B. It wants you to savor the journey.

Nick is all about speed. Even his features—sharp and short nose, small eyes, straight brows—move quickly and dramatically. You get a glance at him and you have an idea of what he's all about. You don't need to keep staring. But still, he's handsome, in that overly athletic way—deeply tanned skin, thick neck, white teeth. It was his smile that won me over the day we first met in his gym, that and the fact that he was successful, had a career behind him, and a new one in front of him. But he's not smiling much these days.

He's not happy to be here. He's always been a rather hot-headed person—especially when he was playing rugby—but for the most part he's aloof. He keeps that all buried, and all you see is the professional. Here, though, everything seems to put him on edge. What he did with Blair was embarrassing, yelling at him like that and smacking his hand away just for touching me. I want to say it's out of character, but something tells me it's not. I may not know Josh but I'm not sure I know the guy I'm seeing all that well either.

It's like being here is the last thing he wants to do. He's sullen, moody, immature. At first I assumed that Nick was coming because he wanted to do this trip with me and Josh had just spurred him on. But now I'm starting to think the only reason he's beside me right now is because he doesn't want to lose face. He doesn't want to *lose*, period. He's competitive to the very core, and I'm just a prize.

As the easy acoustic notes of "Fearless" play out over the speakers, I glance at Josh in the rearview mirror. He's sitting back beside Amber and staring out the window, his legs splayed, wearing flip-flops, jeans, and a tight black T-shirt. His tattoo snakes masterfully down his arms, like an organic extension of his shirt, and his thick, rich black hair is free of product and occasionally falls across his forehead. He's lost in thought, his pretty blue eyes taking the passing scenery in.

Josh's face invites you to stay awhile, to spend some time taking him all in. You want to dwell on his features—the soft, Elvis-like curl to his upper lip, his arched dark brows, the slant of his cheekbones. Most of all, you just want to stare into his eyes. Sometimes they're so easy to read that you think you can see right into his soul. Other times they're clouded, like a storm rolling down a blue glacier, and you have no idea what he's thinking, what he's wanting.

I want him to want me.

I want him to not want me.

I don't know what I want.

But when he was massaging my legs yesterday in the caves, I couldn't deny there was something between us. There always had been, there had just been too few opportunities for it to spark.

It scared me, the feelings he brought out.

But so far my fear is greater than my want.

And so I'm with Nick, not with Josh, because Nick is my future. And Josh, he's a ghost from the past, staying for a spell before he's pulled back to where he came from. He's not permanent. He's like the wind. He'll be with me long enough to ruffle my feathers and then he'll be gone.

Just outside of Tongariro National Park, we pull over for greasy fish and chips wrapped in newspaper. The imposing volcanic peak of Mount Ngauruhoe, still fringed with snow, pokes its head in the distance. We sit down at a picnic table nearby, a scenic spot for lunch, and I can't help but watch Josh as he takes it all in, the contrast of white against all the green. I wonder if it reminds him of home.

"Do you miss Canada yet?" I ask him, pouring an illegal amount of vinegar all over my chips.

"Not even for a second," he says, eyeing the carcasses of vinegar packets as they pile up in front of me. "When did you start missing New Zealand while you were gone?"

I thought he'd already asked me that question, back when we were talking in his bed till dawn. I don't look at Nick as I answer, "I didn't miss it at all."

I'm not sure why I say that since it isn't exactly true. I had missed some things—our chocolate for one, Watties tomato sauce (not ketchup), and a few friends and family. And I guess, on occasion, I had missed Nick. But things are different now, and I'm not about to admit anything.

"Well, I'm homesick," Amber admits, and I look at her in surprise.

"You are?"

She nods and exchanges a look with Josh. "I was just telling Josh last night that I don't really . . . feel like I'm here yet. It's like my memories of home are more tangible and this is just some dream."

"Could it be jet lag?" Nick suggests.

She shakes her head, a few curls coming loose and framing her fairylike face. "No, physically I feel fine. Mentally I feel like I'm in a cloud."

"I told you, it's because you're placing too much pressure on yourself," he says, and I feel like an animal when someone pets them the wrong way, my hair all raised. It actually bothers me that the two of them are having private moments together.

I blink and try to shake it off, and Josh eyes me closely. I put on my mask and tell him to elaborate.

"I don't know," he says, running his hand along the dark stubble on his jaw. I'm glad he didn't shave this morning. I like it. He looks more rugged. "I'm just now figuring this out for myself, but it seems like when you travel, at least for the first time, 'cause, fuck, I don't know any better, there's so much pressure to take it all in. You're short on time and money and you panic, thinking, 'I better be present in the here and now or I'll never remember anything, I'll never feel like I'm here. It will be a waste of time otherwise.' But the more you concentrate on being here, the more it clouds over. Amber said she was feeling the same way, so maybe I'm onto something." He shrugs, as if suddenly aware that neither Nick nor I might understand.

But I do understand. I went through it myself.

"So then what do you do?" I ask.

His mouth quirks up into a smile. "Just relax and have fun. Do what we're doing right now. Embrace the fog, I guess. Eventually it has to clear up."

"I have no idea what the hell you *munters* are talking about," Nick says as he rolls up his chips into the newspaper and tosses them into the rubbish bin. He never eats chips and usually picks all the batter off of the fish.

"You wouldn't," Josh says under his breath, and I shoot him a sharp look. He doesn't look the slightest bit apologetic and meets my eye with determination. I can almost hear what he's thinking—*I told you he was a dicknugget.* Thankfully Nick is already halfway to Mr. Orange and doesn't hear him.

"Maybe the fog is a good thing," I tell him as I get up. "Maybe clarity shows you the ugliness underneath."

"You say ugly like it's a bad thing," he challenges.

"Okay, now I'm confused," Amber says with a whine. She

turns to me, stuffing the last of her chips in her face. "Speaking of confusion, where did you say we were staying tonight?"

"Paekakariki," I tell her.

She snorts. "Kakawhat?"

New Zealand place names never get old for these two. The minute I told them about a place called Whakapapa ("Wh" in Maori is pronounced as an "F," by the way), they couldn't stop laughing for minutes. "It's a little beach town outside of Wellington. I've booked us a hostel there so we can get a short break from the bus." Before they can ask, I say, "Don't worry, you're in a dorm room. It's cheap. Much cheaper than Wellington. Anyway, that's why we're staying there. Plus, it's about time you guys see a real west-coast Kiwi beach."

As we walk back to the bus, I turn and give Josh an impish look. "Did you want to try driving?"

"Uh, what?" he asks, stopping in his tracks. "Isn't that illegal?"

I roll my eyes. "You have a driver's license. It's valid here, too. You just drive on the other side of the road; everything else is the same."

"Except I'll be sitting on the wrong side of the van, driving on the *wrong* side of the road, and changing gears with the wrong hand," he points out.

"Don't be a chook."

"That's *racist*," he says with a face of exaggerated disgust.

I slap him lightly on the back, though I really want to slap him on his ass. "Chook means chicken."

"Oh." He looks at Amber, who shrugs.

"I don't care who drives," she says, "just don't kill me."

I cock my head and look back to Josh expectantly. "I rented a car in the States, drove through a part of the southwest. If I can do, I think you can do it." I raise my brow at him and look him up and down. "Or maybe not."

He bites the bait. "All right, I'll drive."

I grin at him. I'm not sure why I think this is a good idea. I guess I just want to share *something* with him, even as simple as driving.

Naturally Nick is pissed off, even though I can tell he's tired of being behind the wheel.

"It's going to take twice as long now to get there," he says as he begrudgingly sits in the back beside Amber.

"He's not going to drive the whole time, let him have some fun," I admonish him.

Josh climbs into the driver's side and tilts his chin down, looking up at me through his dark lashes. "Fun?"

I smile and shut the passenger door, snapping on my seat belt. "You can at least drive stick, right?"

"Of course," he says, staring at the wheel and instrument panel with thinly veiled trepidation. "Herman is manual."

"Herman?"

He gives me a grin. "Yeah, I named my VW, too. He's a Golf though, so half of Mr. Orange's size. Bought him last year with the money I won from an art contest."

I'm impressed. "Nice." I'd seen Josh's work in his room, so I knew he was talented, but it says something when other people recognize it, too. For a moment I feel like throwing a smug look over my shoulder at Nick—he who believes the arts are a waste of time—but I keep my attention on Josh instead.

He turns the key and Mr. Orange starts with a throaty grumble. He moves his feet around and gives off a small sigh. "At least all the foot pedals are in the right spot."

That said, we still lurch around for a moment. I'm glad we're on a side road and not the highway. "The clutch is sticky," I say, trying to make him feel better as Amber and Nick get tossed around in the back.

"The whole bus is sticky," he grumbles, but his eyes are

dancing and he's looking more alive than he has all day. I settle back in my seat, my feet propped up on the glove compartment as Josh gives me a sidelong glance, not so subtly ogling the length of my legs that my shorts show off.

He catches my eye and doesn't look ashamed to have been caught checking me out. In fact, his expression lights up. He likes that I know.

I like that I know, too.

By the time we reach the highway, he seems to have gotten the hang of shifting with his left hand and doesn't even flinch when traffic passes on the "wrong" side.

Josh ends up taking us all the way down to Paekakariki. We spend the next three hours talking and laughing, and it's like our own little world up here, where it's just the two of us and the passing green scenery. There's just something so easy about him, about the way I can relate to him and the way he relates to me. All those wicked little feelings I had about him during our night together come back with more punch.

My brain wants to do battle again and I reluctantly let it win. Whatever I'm feeling, it can't stay.

By the time we roll into Paekakariki, the sun is low on the horizon, coating the wild Tasman Sea in waves of gold. Most people would pass by this tiny settlement on the way to Wellington, our nation's capital, and I only know about it because I'd gone to Wellington once with an ex-boyfriend and all the affordable places were booked. We took the train out to this town because we had heard good things about the sole backpacker's hostel they had. Though the ex moved on, the memories remained.

"This is cute," Amber says in a hushed voice from the back, her wide green eyes taking in the "town," which consists, basically, of one street. There's a dairy, or corner store, with all the basics, a pizza shop, a real estate office, a white clapboard church, a post office, a pub, and an empty storefront with a for lease sign.

On one side, right beside the highway, are giant, imposing green hills dotted with sheep. They loom over the town, begging you to touch them, climb them. On the other side of the town is a long strand of wild beach, roaring waves, and the long, crocodilelike body of Kapiti Island, a nature sanctuary.

"Where's the hostel?" Josh asks and I tell him to take his next right. There are basically only two blocks between the highway and the beach, but we tempt fate by bringing Mr. Orange up a long, twisting driveway to the top of a small rise. He puts the bus into park, slamming on the hand brake, and peers at the house.

It looks like a quaint residence, not a hostel, but that's part of the appeal. In fact, you would never know it was a hostel if it weren't for the discreet sign at the base of the driveway that says PARAKEET BEACH BACKPACKERS.

We carefully climb out of the bus, our sore muscles extra tight from all the sitting, and see a black-and-white cat hanging around the front door, our welcoming committee. Leaving our gear in the bus for now, we walk into the house. It already smells amazing as bursts of basil and sizzling garlic hit my nose. The kitchen to the left is being used by two tall guys who are taking advantage of the stove. They give us a friendly wave then go back to cooking.

"You must be Gemma," a woman says, coming out of a small den to our right. She's got a wild mess of hair—even more unruly than Amber's—and her aging face is pointedly makeup free. She wears a long flowing cape and seems extremely secure in herself, a vision of poise. I wish I could be her someday.

I quickly shake the woman's hand, her many bracelets jingling as she introduces herself as Kate. When we're all paid up, we go back to get our bags and lug them through the ramshackle living room, complete with cozy couches and board games, and through the French doors out onto the patio. As I had remembered, the view is still spectacular, overlooking the beach, Kapiti Island, and in the far distance, the tip of the South Island.

"Shit," Josh says from beside me, sucking in his breath as he takes in the view. "Good choice, Gemma."

I shrug like it's no big deal, but secretly I'm over the moon that this is making an impression on him.

"So where are we staying?" Nick asks, and I realize we're just standing in the middle of the backyard, between a crop of gardens and a soothing koi pond. I nod at what looks like a little shed poking out around the corner, half hidden by lush banana and yellow-blossom kōwhai trees.

"That's our room," I tell him. Then I point to a pair of French doors to the side of us that open to the yard. "And that's where Amber and Josh are sleeping."

"Sweet," Amber says enthusiastically as she makes her way to the doors and goes inside.

"You wanted some privacy, aye babe?" Nick asks, wrapping his arm around my waist. I nod and let him kiss my neck and press up against me. I make sure not to look at Josh, who I can tell is now following Amber over to their room. The truth is, I originally wanted us all to stay in the dorm, but there were only two beds available in the four-bed room, so Nick and I snapped up the private one.

I can't complain, though. When we step into the tiny one-room cottage and see that it has its own queen-size bed with mosquito net, Nick wastes no time in shutting the door and throwing me to the mattress.

I open my mouth to protest, to say that Amber and Josh will be wondering what happened to us, when I realize they won't be wondering at all. They'll know. And even though I don't really feel like it, perhaps a romp in the hay will fix what's ailing me. And Nick. It has been a few days without real privacy, and usually sex is the only thing that holds us together.

That's probably why you've been falling apart, I think to myself as he kisses me and starts taking off my shorts.

Nick is a good-looking guy. He's a hot jock, like most rugby players are. He strips down to nothing and his erection stands stiff and swollen. He has a nice cock, too, considering his weakness for steroids. Any woman worth her salt would want to sleep with Nick—I mean, if they were into the clean-cut, overly muscle-y, athlete look. I know it's what attracted me to him in the first place.

But even though my shorts and underwear are at my ankles and his fingers are pressing down into my folds, I'm very conscious of how *un*-wet I am. I need this but my body isn't so sure.

Nick is persistent as ever and there's no real time for foreplay with him. Soon he's flipped me over and taking me from behind as he stands at the foot of the bed. It hurts at first but the position allows me to pretend Nick isn't there at all.

I'm thinking of Josh. I pretend it's him filling me up, his balls slapping against my ass, his grunts filling the room. It's not hard to imagine—I've had him this way before. He's more than a fantasy, and if I let out a scream, he could hear me. He's real and tangible, and for these few moments, he's mine again.

It's not long before I'm coming, and I owe it all to him. My hands grip the clean duvet and my face is pressed against it, my mouth obscured, and I'm glad that I can't accidently call out Josh's name because that is so close to happening. I can taste it. I want to yell it, scream it. *Josh*. I want him to know.

When Nick comes, a little too loudly considering where we are, he pulls out and smacks me on the ass.

"Fuck, I needed that one."

I roll over on my back and nod at him through the quickly fading haze. Usually after sex I find myself feeling closer to him, both mentally and physically. Now I just feel this cold distance between us.

"Hey babe," he says as he slips his shorts and T-shirt back on.

"Mmm?" I should get dressed, too, but I feel too spent. I'm trying to relive the few minutes before.

"I'm not sure what you have planned tonight with those two," he says, gesturing toward the house, "but whatever it is, count me out. I saw the pub down the street. I think I'm just going to head there."

I sit up. "Are you sure? Do you want company?"

He gives me a pointed look. "No, I do not want company. That's why I'm going."

"I meant me."

He blinks at me for a moment, as if to say, *I know what you meant.*

I swallow. "Okay, well whatever you want to do. We'll just be here. I was thinking of going down to that pizza place and getting some takeout, then just having some food and drink on the terrace."

"Pizza?" he repeats, and his eyes settle on the tiny pooch of my stomach that I can never seem to get rid of, no matter how hard I train. "You better not let yourself go soft or you're not going to have a job come February."

I glare at him. "It's a road trip, Nick. Crap food is going to be involved."

"Well, just remember that good nutrition doesn't have to be difficult." He's taking on his trainer voice, and it annoys the shit out of me. "Kale chips here, a protein shake there. It's easy. Plus I haven't seen you keep up with your exercises. It will be hard for you to catch up when this is all over."

Now I'm getting out of bed and angrily slipping on my shorts, hyper-aware of my large boobs and poochy stomach. "How can I keep up with my exercises?" I ask defensively. "I spent hours in a cave yesterday using muscles I never knew I had."

He shrugs and stares at his face in the mirror on the wall. "I get up every morning before you do to fit in my routine. It's about time you start making this part of your life a priority. It's not enough to just want something, Gemma, you have to fight for it, too. If you don't have the passion for this career then maybe you should be doing something else."

I stare at him, balking at his words that seem to hit me like hammer blows. I don't even know what to say, because for once he's being smart. Worse than that, he's being true. Do I really have the passion anymore? Did I ever?

He glances at me and frowns when he sees my face. "I'm just looking out for you," he says with complete sincerity. "No need to freak out. You're gorgeous in *any* shape or form, you know that." His voice softens now, trying to appease me. "If you want to eat your pizza and drink your beer and get soft like the rest of them, that's your choice. But it's a choice you better know you're making if you really want to cut it as a trainer. This is your job we're talking about, and I just don't want you to forget that." He heads for the door. "I'll see you later."

He closes it behind him and I am left half-naked.

Alone.

And scared.

Chapter Nine

JOSH

I can hear them fucking. It's got to be the worst sound in the world.

Amber doesn't seem to be bothered. She's busy unpacking her backpack and hanging up an array of floaty skirts from the railings of the top bunk, as if she's making a privacy curtain for the bottom bunk, all while humming to herself.

The French doors to the courtyard area are open and I can hear Nick's groans waft in with the breeze. She may be able to ignore it but I can't take this.

"I'm going to go take a look around," I tell Amber. I turn around and leave, even though I feel like she's opened her mouth to say something.

The hostel is tiny and it really is no more than a house. It's something special though, and I wish I could sit on the patio table and just stare at the horizon. But I can't. I would need earplugs and alcohol to do that.

Instead I go into the living room area, shutting the door to the moans, and start flipping through a book about New

Zealand. Then I peruse the guest book and I'm shocked to see the name of a girl I went to high school with, dated a few months back. Small fucking world again.

Gemma had told us we were going to spend several days in Abel Tasman National Park tomorrow, kayaking and tramping—which I assume means hiking and not whoring ourselves out. I go to the giant map on the wall and find where we are, just this tiny dot on the southwest tip of the North Island. Directly across from us is the tip of the South Island.

I turn around and look at the silhouetted peaks of the mountains across the water. That's what our view is of: tomorrow. It's amazing to think I'll be there, on another island, in another place I've never been.

I start to relax a bit at that thought and wander into the kitchen, where I meet Craig and Braydon, two post-college kids from Dublin. They invite me to have a beer and the pasta they just made, but I politely decline. The food, that is—I never turn down a beer.

Sitting there and talking to these guys makes me remember why I'm there—to travel, to meet people, to open my eyes and get a fucking life. All this shit with Gemma and Nick has started to mess me up and forget the big picture. I have to remind myself she was only my reason for being here. She isn't my everything.

Curiously, I'm not listening to their travel adventures for long before I see Nick walk past the kitchen and out the front door. He gives me a nod of acknowledgment, which is big for him. I expect Gemma to follow behind any minute.

She doesn't. Strange.

A little while later, when the sun starts to set behind the mountains of the South Island and the two Irish lads move their beers to the patio, Amber and Gemma come by and ask what kind of beer and pizza I want. Half an hour after that, we're all on the patio, enjoying good Kiwi beer and shitty Kiwi pizza.

"No offense," I say, shoving the last bit of pizza into my mouth, "but your pizza sucks. It's like eating cardboard with tomato sauce."

Gemma sticks her tongue out at me. "Then why did you eat it all?"

"Because it's food."

"I thought it was fine," Amber says, always diplomatic. She eyes me mischievously. "It's hard to cook cardboard just right."

"Well, yours is for sure," Gemma points out, ignoring our jabs. "You're eating gluten-free."

The air around us has settled to a soft, silvery blue. Dusk is here and the sun is long gone, though the light seems to stay, burning the area where the sea meets the sky and the mountains fade into the night. There's a fresh breeze coming off the water and you can hear the steady rhythm of the waves as they pound into the shore.

Gemma had told me that Nick went to the local pub, needing some alone time, and I guess that's why the Irish guys have moved in on our little group. I don't mind; it's nice to have them break up our unit, which has started to feel a bit claustrophobic at times, plus they've introduced us to a crazy drinking game.

For once, I'm not the most drunk. I'm taking it easy, not entirely trusting myself these days. Not around her, anyway.

Instead it's Gemma who's tying one on. She has one beer, then another, trying valiantly to keep up with the Irish boys. I want to tell her that's one battle she doesn't want to win, but I'm not sure if it's my place.

Finally, the hippie-lady owner of the hostel has to come out and tell us all to be quiet—there's too much laughing, too much shrieking, too much spilling. At this, the Irish decide to join Nick at the pub and invite us to come along. Gemma, suddenly growing stone-faced and silent, vigorously shakes her head no. There's no way I'm going without her.

Amber decides to go with them, though—she's been flirty with the Braydon guy all night—and soon it's just me and Gemma, alone in the chairs. It's dark, save for a faint light from inside the hostel, and the sound of crickets competes with the crashing waves.

It's romantic. So uncomfortably romantic.

And quiet. Gemma isn't saying a word and I have to stare at her closely, her features muddy in the dark, before I realize she's staring right at me.

"Are you okay?" I ask quietly, taken aback by her hidden perusal.

She swallows, licks her lips, then looks to the sea. "I don't know."

"Drunk?"

She nods. "I guess that's it."

It doesn't take a brain surgeon to be able to tell when something is bothering a girl. They wear it plainly on their face, in their tone, in their posture. It does take a brain surgeon to actually *extract* that information from the girl. The most you'll get is a hard "I'm fine," and the rest remains buried.

Still, I care about her and I can't let things go. "What's wrong?"

"Nothing."

I sigh and lean back in the chair. I finish another beer, the silence thickening between us, before I say, "You know you can talk to me about everything. I know we aren't close or anything, but if you need someone . . . I'm here."

I can see the white of her teeth as she smiles but her voice is dry. "You are the last person I can talk to."

I frown. "Why?"

She doesn't say anything. I can almost hear those wheels in her head turning. Without thinking, I reach over and I grab her left hand, hoping to get her to spill.

It's trembling in my grasp.

"You're shaking," I tell her, and she quickly snatches it back, far away.

"It's nothing," she says, her voice raised and almost panicky.

"Are you cold? I can get you my sweater." I begin to rise from my chair.

"No," she snaps. She sighs and rubs her other hand down her face. "I'm sorry. I don't mean to be rude. I just mean, it's fine. I'm not cold. My hand just shakes sometimes."

I sit back down. "Just the left one?"

"Yeah," she says softly.

"I don't mean to get personal," I say, even though that's exactly what I want, "but why?"

I can barely see through the dark but I can feel it. She's giving me a look that says, *None of your damn business*. But it doesn't scare me off. I stare right back at her.

"What happened?" I press on.

She exhales slowly. The waves continue to crash. There's a sound in the bushes, rustling, but then it stops.

"It's not a big deal," she says in a warning tone. "I hurt it a long time ago. In an accident. It was crushed and I had a bunch of operations on it but it's fine now. It just shakes once in a while. I was left-handed, but now I have to write with my right. It's steadier, though it's not the same."

I have so many questions but I'm not sure how far I'll get. "But your hand is okay for the most part. Obviously you can lift weights, throw a punch, drive a stick."

"And give a hand job," she says. "Yes, it's fine."

"So you can handle big things," I tell her, grinning to myself.

"Yes, if you want to think about it that way. But when it comes to the smaller things, stuff that takes precision, I can't." Her voice falters at the end.

"What was the accident?"

I sense her freezing up. I should apologize, tell her I don't need to know. But I don't. I want to know.

"You know, you're very nosy," she says.

"I'm just interested," I tell her. "Remember what you said in the caves. I could get to know you. This is me getting to know you. But I want the real you, the one you hide deep down. Not the you that everyone else sees. Not the you that Nick sees."

"Don't bring him into this," she says.

"But he *is* in this. You know it."

"You don't know what you're talking about."

"Then tell me. Tell me something. Tell me about your accident."

"Persistent bastard," she mumbles to herself as she shakes her head.

"That's true," I admit. "I'm here, aren't I?"

A few beats roll by, thick as the night, then she says, "Fine. If you must know, when my dad died, I was with him. I was fifteen and coming back from an art exhibit in Hastings. Our family winery is about half an hour away and my dad had a small showing that night. My mom had gone earlier but left because of a headache, and I stayed behind with my dad for company and other stuff."

I can already tell this is going to be bad, and I'm sorry for being such a nosy son-of-a-bitch.

"My dad only had two glasses of wine that night and he had a pretty high tolerance since he operated a vineyard when he wasn't painting. So he was fine to drive. They later said it wasn't his fault. We were about fifteen minutes outside of town when a truck came around the corner too fast and in our lane. It hit us head-on. Most of the impact was on my father's side of the car, but then we spun out and went crashing into a tree. My arm was pinned beneath the steel. My dad was alive for a few moments. He called my name and I told him I was scared and I loved him, and then he stopped breathing. When the ambulance came, it was too late. We both had to be removed with the jaws of life."

I am shocked. Horrified. I can't even breathe. I can't even tell her how sorry I am. My heart feels like it's drowning at the bottom of the sea.

She goes on, her voice harder now. "So, they pulled me out and my hand and arm were broken in a bunch of places, and so was my ankle. My ankle and arm healed up the easiest though, but my hand was a real problem. I had a lot of operations on it."

Suddenly she picks up my hand with her right one and guides my fingers over her open palm. It's warm and soft and there are a few raised lines inside that I hadn't paid attention to before. I feel like I'm reading her past, the real her.

"I was in physiotherapy for a long time. I'll never be as good as I used to be. But I'm okay."

"Gemma," I whisper softly. Before I know what I'm doing, I'm raising her palm to my lips and kissing along her scar. She smells so good, feels even better.

She lets me do it for a moment then she awkwardly clears her throat.

Don't make me let go, I think. *Please don't make me let go.*

The rustle in the bushes is back again. Gemma jerks her hand away, as if we're about to be caught by Nick the Peeping Tom, as if we're doing something wrong.

Are we doing something wrong?

Suddenly the air around us fills with squeals, and the rustling increases. The nearest bush to us at the base of the yard, near the fence, starts to move back and forth.

I stand up out of my chair to get a better look and see what looks to be little creatures waddling out of the bushes and heading for the side of the house. Once they hit a patch of light coming from the house, I can see what they are.

Little blue penguins.

"What the fuck?" I say softly, feeling like my mind has just imploded. "What the hell are those?"

"Little blue penguins," she says proudly.

I turn to her in disbelief. "Are you serious?" I thought I was making that up. In my head.

She nods. "Yup. Little blue penguins."

And she's right. They're about a foot high, miniature versions of the ones I've seen on TV, and they're entirely blue in color. I thought it was just the darkness playing tricks on me but no, once they hit the light, you can see the color on their oily feathers.

"I don't get it," I say, watching as the last of their group quickly scampers out of sight. That might have been the cutest and weirdest thing I have ever seen.

"You never head of them?" she asks. "They probably have a burrow under the house. It's actually quite common for beach houses."

"Look, I wasn't lying when I said I didn't do a whole lot of research about the country."

"I can see that," she says. "Well, how about that, then."

"How about that," I say, sitting back down. The penguins' magical appearance has somehow taken Gemma's heartbreaking story to another place, and she's quick to jump on the transition. She tells me all about the interesting birdlife in New Zealand, from yellow-eyed penguins on the Otago Peninsula down south, to the kea—cheeky green parrots that live in the snow-covered Alps. She's animated as she tells me all she knows, and I absorb it like a sponge. I drink my beer and she goes back to drinking hers, and before Nick, Amber, and the Irish show up all sloshed, she's painted a beautiful picture of what's to come. I can only hope I'll continue to be part of the picture.

———•———

"So how is the art coming along?" Vera asks me, her voice sounding so crazy clear over the cell phone. It's nuts to think that not only is it eight p.m. where she is—yesterday—and eight a.m. here, she's literally halfway across the world. Yet I'm able to talk to her like she's right beside me.

"It's picking up," I tell her. "I didn't start sketching until we were in Abel Tasman Park, but it was like I couldn't stop myself. I wish I brought more than my watercolor pencils though."

I breathe in the fresh mountain air and look around me. If we weren't leaving in ten minutes, I'd be trying to paint this place as well. We're in Makarora on the South Island, a place by an area called Haast Pass, sort of the halfway point between the resort towns of Wanaka and Queensland and the Wild West Coast that we were just on. There's nothing to Makarora except maybe the holiday park we stayed at and farms scattered about, bastions of civilization trying to survive among the encroaching wilderness. But shit, is this place ever beautiful.

I'm sitting on top of a picnic table, the air sweet with morning dew while the sun slowly starts to heat up. I'm still amazed at how strong it is down here and how quickly you can burn. I learned that all too well during a kayak trip, though the burn on my upper body has turned into a deep tan.

Everywhere you look are mountains—big, ridiculously

hefty mountains, like someone has placed sugar-dusted anvils at the sides of the valley. What I like most about them is how bare they are. Though the valley floor is green, green, green, with grassy fields of sharp-bladed flax and palmlike cabbage trees, the foliage peters off halfway up the mountains, leaving their upper halves bare. They're brown and tan and nude, covered in what Gemma calls tussock grass, and because of this you can see every little cranny and crevice. It's like looking at living velvet, and I can literally just stare at them for hours.

Vera clears her throat. "And is that the only thing picking up since we last talked?" she asks, trying to hide her curiosity.

I last talked to her the morning after Paekakariki and the little blue penguins. I bought a calling card at the ferry terminal to the South Island and spent the majority of the rough and wild voyage across Cook Strait filling her in on the trip so far.

That was ten days ago. Everything since then passed by in a dreamy, hazy blur. Sometimes it felt like a good dream. Other times it was a nightmare.

"Well," I say hesitantly before launching into it.

After we left the North Island, Nick and Gemma's relationship became a bit strained. Normally, that would have made me happy—I wanted nothing more than for them to break up. But it only made things awkward and Gemma miserable.

Somewhere during our Abel Tasman trip, though, things went back to normal. At least it seemed that way. That's when the dream got nightmarish again. If anything, they seemed closer, more affectionate.

By day I was sharing a double kayak with Amber and slowly paddling through pale turquoise waters occasionally peppered with dolphins and, yes, little blue penguins. The sun was hot and heavy and we were navigating ourselves through the shallow coves of what looked like a tropical paradise.

By night, we were hauling our kayaks up onto soft, golden sand beaches and camping out between the sea and the forest. Gemma and Nick had picked up an extra tent in the eclectic city of Nelson, a place I wouldn't have minded spending a few days in, which meant I had to share with Amber.

At first this wasn't a problem. But by the third night, Nick and Gemma were back to their horrifically loud fucking, and Amber started to get ideas of her own.

Naturally, being a hot-blooded male, I didn't quite have the energy to fend her off. Not that she was doing anything more than snuggling against me as we fell asleep, but I started to fear that if she *did* start getting horny, I would be powerless to stop her. Powerless, as in, I was getting pretty fucking horny, too, but not for the reasons she'd want.

After our tramping and kayaking trip was over, we gladly piled back into Mr. Orange, filling him with sand and the smell of salt water. We made our way to a place called Nelson Lakes for a few nights, a place of sublime alpine scenery and a lake so still you'd swear it was holding its breath. It reminded me of back home a lot, particularly the area around Lake Okanagan, and for the first time I felt a twinge of homesickness. I sketched and painted my way out of it.

Next we hit the Wild West Coast, which was this prehistoric mashup of ferns and native palm trees and rivers flowing down lush green mountains, and walked along dark beaches strewn with driftwood, beaten by the raging azure sea, a blue so brilliant it hurt my eyes. There's not much to do there but take in the sights, so we looked at strange rock formations called the "pancake rocks," ate something called whitebait (it tastes better than it sounds), and watched as a dumpy weka bird waddled up to Amber and stole her sandwich.

The highlight, though, was yesterday when we went glacier hiking. I had to put up with all the snarky questions, like,

"But you're from Canada, don't you have to glacier-hike to get to work?" to which I said it rarely snows where I live. (Hello, don't you remember the Vancouver Olympics when we had to truck in snow for our mountains?) But aside from that, it was a fucking trip.

We had to get up at the ass-crack of dawn and make our way to the glacial center in the middle of the small but touristy village of Franz Josef. Nick really wanted to do the helicopter tour version but none of us could really spare the expense, so he went off and did that on his own while we did the cheaper version. I could tell Gemma was pretty pissed off about that.

The tour was pretty straightforward. Walk for what seemed like forever across the alluvial plain, crisscrossed with streams of melting glacial water (hey, geography was my best subject in high school after art), the imposing face of Franz Josef glacier slowly getting closer and closer. On either side, waterfalls spilled down in thin ribbons from forested cliffs and the clouds clung to the edges, obscuring the peaks in mist.

Finally we were up close to the giant wall of blue and gray ice towering above us, and the only way through was up. You have to climb up steps your guide carves out of the snow, everyone in single file, with only metal-spiked hiking poles for stability.

I brought up the rear of the group, with Gemma in front of me, and I had this incredible view of everyone walking along the ice like a row of ants. We walked across planks over aqua-tinged crevices that seemed to cut straight into the earth, made our way through caves and holes cut right through the ice, and moved up and down passageways that were so high on either side that the glacier was the only thing we could see. It was pretty unbelievable, and at one point I had to stop and take it all in with my eyes. I knew my photos wouldn't even do it justice.

"What are you doing?" Gemma asked. I guess I did look strange, standing there, pole in hand, staring wildly at everything around me. In the distance the group was getting farther and farther away, heading back down the glacier now.

"I'm trying to remember this," I told her. "I'm afraid my photos will lie and I'll forget."

I could feel her eyes searching mine for a moment and I turned to take her in. She looked so fresh, so beautiful, her eyes and hair so dark against all the white, the tan of her skin glowing. There was something else, too, something in her expression that made me want to stare at her longer. What was it? Longing? Yearning?

For what?

She gave me a quick smile, as if realizing she'd been found out, and then said, "Are you going to try and paint this as soon as we get back?"

I nodded. "I'll try. That's why I'm hoping I can remember this sight just so." But now she would be in the picture, her curious face standing out amid the white ice and green mountains. I was suddenly aware of how small, tiny, and helpless the both of us were on this cold mass of advancing history.

"Do you ever paint?" I asked her. I wasn't sure why, she just always seemed so interested in my art, asking to look at my sketchbook every day. I'd been more than happy to show it to her. Her expression turned to fear. I couldn't figure out what I said wrong.

Then it hit me. "Oh," I quickly said, feeling like an idiot. "Sorry, Gemma. I forgot that your father was an artist. That must be a question you hear all the time."

She looked away, a cold breeze sweeping silky chocolate strands across her face. "No, it's okay." She rubbed her lips together for a few long beats. Somewhere above us, hidden in the clouds, a helicopter whirred. "I did used to paint, actually," she admitted. "I was pretty good. My paintings were being shown alongside my dad's the night he . . . the night of the accident. But I didn't paint after that."

"Why not?"

Her eyes blazed as she glanced at me. I was sure she was going to tell me to fuck off with the constant questions but she didn't. She took in a deep breath and composed herself. "Because of my hand. I loved the landscapes, just like my father, but my thing, what made me special, was being extremely detailed. My canvases were small and my subjects were smaller. I loved just spending hours and hours and days working one dot, one stroke at a time. It took me away some place, all that concentration, you know?"

I nodded. I knew very well. Life would pass you by while you were in that world, but it was the only world I needed.

She sighed. "But I can barely write my name neatly now and so I certainly can't fucking paint the way I used to. If I try and do anything with my left hand that requires too much precision, I get the shakes. And though I guess you could say I'm ambidextrous now, I can't get that same exactness again. The details are all lost and it looks like mush . . ." She trailed off and looked away, her focus on the group that had just disappeared over a mound of ice. She blinked a few times and I was certain she was about to cry. "I just can't paint."

I'd never heard her sound so sad.

Instinctively, I reached out for her arm and pulled her to me. She lifted her feet, the crampons strapped to her boots coming out of the ice and allowing her to fall into my arms. I didn't know what I'd do if I didn't have my art, and it broke my heart to see that Gemma had suffered that loss, along with so much.

I held her there, aware that it was only for now, that I could only try and give her comfort, until someone in the group called out our names. Before they could think we had both fallen into an ice hole, we broke apart and hurried after them.

"Wow," Vera says softly after I tell her about the glacier hike, having stayed silent the whole conversation. "That's heavy shit, Josh. When was this again?"

"Yesterday," I tell her.

"Have you talked to her about it again?"

"No, I haven't been alone with her. After the hike, we met up with Nick the Dick and got some lunch before we came here. Amber and I spent the night in one of the cabins they have here. Reminds me of the ones we used to stay in on Salt Spring Island, you know the A-frame ones? But Gemma was with Nick in the bus, by his side the whole night."

She makes an annoyed growl. "Ugh, that's frustrating."

"Right," I say, exhaling loudly. I look over my shoulder to see Gemma packing the rest of breakfast away in the bus but she's too far away to hear me. "I just don't know why she's with him, you know? And why did she invite me along with them? I mean, she's not making any plays for me. Fuck, I can't even read her half the time."

Vera is silent for a moment before she says, "She's scared."

"Scared? Of what?"

"Losing everything, maybe. If I were in her shoes, I'd be scared to leave the person that I'm with and take a chance on the one that's fleeting. You're just a visitor, Josh. You're leaving next month. I think it's just too big of a risk for her, ya know?"

"Is that what Mateo would say?" Vera's man friend went through pretty much the same thing. He was married when he met Vera and took a chance on her, even though she was as fleeting as it gets. Of course, that all worked out for the best for her. To Mateo, the risk, Vera, was worth it.

To Gemma, I'm not.

"*Sí*," she says, putting on her Spanish accent. "And if Mateo were there I'm sure he could talk some sense into her. But, I'm just saying, try not to take it too personally. She likes you, that's why you're there. But she's freaking out over what to do. If you want her, you have to prove that you're a risk worth taking."

"That's kind of a dickish thing to do when her significant other is right there."

But of course, that's kind of what I've been doing anyway, whether I'm aware of it or not.

"True," she says. "Look, I don't know. Just keep having fun. You're in fucking New Zealand, you should be frolicking with orcs and shit and doing stuff that gets your blood pumping." Pause. "What about that Amber chick? Why not go for her instead?"

"She's hot and sweet and very endearing, in this quietly kooky way," I tell her. "But she's not Gemma."

"Then you're shit out of luck, broseph," she says with a sigh. "I'd say you need to protect yourself and your heart and all that bullshit, but you know what? I've never witnessed you behaving this way over a girl before. You're falling hard. Maybe it's about time you fell."

"You're sadistic."

"I'm just trying to look on the bright side," she says breezily.

"Yeah, for you." I don't want to fucking fall. I don't want to hit the ground.

"I guess it comes down to whether the fall is worth it. You want Gemma to think you're a risk worth taking. It has to go both ways. If you want her, you have to be willing to fall for her."

"Stop being rational," I tell her.

"Hey, you were the rational one for me and Mateo. If it

weren't for you egging me on and telling me to take a chance, I wouldn't be living in Madrid with him. I wouldn't be so fucking happy. I want you to be happy, too. Take the leap, Josh, or you're going to regret it."

I swallow hard, feeling uneasy. Man, is my sister striking fear straight into my heart.

After we hang up, I make my way to Mr. Orange, which is purring like a jackhammer. Gemma is driving today, Nick beside her, and I climb into the back, buckling up beside Amber.

"How is your sister?" Gemma asks, eyeing me in the mirror.

I shrug. "Good, as always."

"Do you miss her?"

"Not when she's being a pain in the ass," I say, and then look out the window as we pull onto the highway and start making our way farther south toward Wanaka and Queenstown.

And especially not when she's right.

Chapter Ten

JOSH

The movies were the last place I thought we'd end up, but when we rolled into Lake Wanaka late that morning, a storm was in the process of doing the same.

We parked Mr. Orange at a campervan park beside the lake. With the dark clouds that seemed to rush together above the lake and the churning gray-blue waves, it was a spectacular sight, the surrounding mountains shrouded and only hinting at their hidden size. Unfortunately the rain that started to pour down on us confined us to Mr. Orange and eventually gave us cabin fever. We were lucky that the weather held out for as long as it did on this trip.

After I examined a tucked-away cupboard and brought out a stack of vintage porn magazines from the late seventies—apparently Gemma's uncle had left more than just Pink Floyd behind—Gemma remembered there was a really cool movie theater in the lakeside town. They only took reservations and there wasn't much choice of what to see, but none of us really cared as long as it got us out of what would forever be known as the Shaggin' Wagon. I mean, Pink Floyd and porn? Gemma's uncle must've been a busy guy.

After a quick phone call to reserve seats for whatever movie was playing in the evening, we busied ourselves with a trip to the nearby Puzzling World, which consisted of a bunch of visual exhibits engineered to make you feel high as fuck. When we were appropriately disoriented, we headed to the cinema early to grab dinner there.

I've never seen a cinema quite like this. From the outside it looks like your average mountain chalet, other than the fact that there's this weird sculpture on the roof. Inside there's a brightly colored bar and café filled with movie posters. We order salads and burgers and split two bottles of wine between the four of us.

The wine is almost gone when the doors to the cinema open. The waiter tells us we can order more food or drinks and take them inside if we want. Amber asks if I'll split another bottle with her, and because I'm feeling buzzed I can't say no.

Armed with alcoholic provisions and full bellies, we head into the theater part and I am blown away. Though there are a few old-fashioned theater seats on the rows leading down to the projection screen, the rest consist of a smattering of airplane seats and couches from the seventies and eighties. There are plaid love seats and velvet chaises, and at the very front is a fucking car. Yeah, like a yellow fifties convertible. Some lucky bastards are already climbing into it and claiming their seats.

"Holy schnikes," Amber says from beside me in her best Chris Farley impression. "This is the coolest place ever."

Even Nick gives out an impressed, "Wow."

But while we stand there gawking at the gloriously haphazard room, the couches and seats are all filling up fast. It's a rainy night in the outdoor capital of the world, and it seems all of Wanaka and maybe even nearby Queenstown has come to the movies.

Nick grabs Gemma's hand and leads her down toward the front, snagging a love seat before another couple is about to sit down.

I'm looking around wildly, not wanting to end up in the boring theater seats when everything else is so cool.

"Hey hot stuff, over here," Amber calls out, and I see her down the back row, snagging what looks to be an oversized armchair, the kind that Archie Bunker used to complain in all day. I bring the wine over and try and figure out how we're both going to sit on this thing.

"You can sit on my lap," she says with a coy smile and I laugh.

"Right," I say. "I'm a foot taller than you and twice as heavy. I'll crush you like an itty bitty ant."

"You're right," she says. "I remember in Abel Tasman when you accidently rolled over me in the night. Thought I was going to die more than once. Death by Josh."

"Lies," I tell her, though knowing my predisposition for falling out of bunks, it might be true.

I sit down, placing the bottle of wine and glasses on the small table beside us and make room so she can fit in between me and the cushy arm. She's small but her ass is big (nothing I would *ever* complain about), so she ends up sitting half on me. I've been known to get boners at inappropriate times, like when a hot chick sits on me, so I really hope it doesn't happen now and give her the wrong idea.

The movie starts, some art house flick starring Scarlett Johansson that I wouldn't normally see, but we didn't have a choice, and hey, it's Scarlett. We drink our wine, even though I have to reach over her every few minutes to either pick up my glass or put it down, and each time I do, I brush against her breasts.

My dick stirs in my pants.

This isn't good and I know, I *know*, that Amber can tell.

I try and concentrate on the film. This is also a bad idea. Naked Scarlett isn't helping at all, she's just making things worse.

When the room goes really black during a nighttime scene, I feel Amber turn into me, her breathing hard and loud. Before I have a chance to prepare myself, her fingers are in my hair, her hand on my crotch, and she kisses me.

Her lips are light at first, and there's enough time to pull back and protest, if I want to. What I'd say, I don't know. I've never been very good at rejecting girls. But then she's kissing me harder and my mouth opens, letting her. The feel of her tongue in my mouth elicits a small moan from me, and I can't help but get sucked into it, the feeling of her want and need for me.

I'd be lying if I said it doesn't feel good, that it doesn't turn me on, this feeling of being *wanted*. She's fumbling for my zipper and I'm afraid this can't end well. The problem is, I do find Amber hot and funny, and I do like her as a person. But she's not the one I want to be with, and because of that I can't lead her on. If I didn't like her, well, sad to say but I wouldn't have a problem with it.

I'm gathering up all of my strength to pull away and put some distance between us, preparing what I'm going to say to her after the movie, that I'm not interested in her that way and then be faced with the bone-crushing awkwardness that will surely follow, when suddenly the movie stops playing and the lights in the theater flick on.

The door to the café opens and the smell of fresh-baked cookies wafts in.

What the fucking fuck?

As if expecting this, some people in the theater are getting out of their chairs and heading toward the café. Even Nick, who is halfway up the aisle when he spots us, with Amber's hand down my pants, her lips on my neck. There's no time to make ourselves look appropriate.

He raises his brows at us but keeps walking, disappearing into the café with everyone else.

Amber quickly removes her hand and I zip up my pants before anyone else has a chance to see.

Holy shit. This isn't good.

"Whoops," Amber says, her cheeks turning red. "That was unexpected."

I'm not sure if she means the intermission or the fact that her hand was wrapped firmly around my erection. Unexpected, indeed.

Luckily, I don't see Gemma get up and Amber soon excuses herself to go to the washroom. She comes back a short while later with two still-warm chocolate chip cookies. She gives one to me as she settles back down in her spot. This time, however, my dick ain't playing.

"I guess this is their *thing*," she says with a mouthful of cookie. "Intermission and cookies." She shakes the near-empty bottle of wine at me. "More wine?"

"No thanks," I say, quickly adding, "I'm not really feeling too well."

It's a total lie but suddenly she's feeling bad for me and isn't touchy-feely like she was before. The movie starts again and I'm able to relax and watch the rest of it in peace.

The only thing I keep thinking is that I hope Nick didn't tell Gemma what he saw. But when the movie ends and we meet up with them outside the theater, she isn't acting any differently around us, and Nick even gives me the wink as if he's saying, *Your secret is safe with me, dawg.* Even in my imagination, I still want to punch him.

The next morning is gray and calm. The rain has stopped, so I go for a quick walk along the lake, just to get some breathing room before we head to Queenstown. I'm on my way back when I see Amber heading toward me, looking freshly showered and ready to go.

"Is everyone waiting?" I ask when she reaches me.

She shakes her head. "No I think they're doing push-ups or some shit. Listen," she begins, then looks away. She briefly chews on a strand of hair. "Can we talk about last night?"

"Cool theater, eh?"

"Yeah. But I meant more like the touching of the penis and all that."

"Right, that."

"It wasn't so cool, was it?"

I really don't know what to say to that. My face has awkward written all over it. "Well, I mean, I don't know any guy who would complain about a girl like you touching his dick."

"But you're not interested in me." The funny thing is, she doesn't seem that hurt or rejected by the possibility. Still, I have to be real careful.

I try and give her a reassuring smile. "It's not that I'm not interested . . ."

"But that you're interested in someone else."

I eye her suspiciously. "What do you mean?"

She laughs to herself, throwing an arm to Mr. Orange far in the background. "You're in love with Gemma."

Whoa. Whoa. Whoa.

No.

"I am not in love with Gemma!" I nearly yell it.

She crosses her arms, looking amused. "Fine. Maybe you're

not in love with her, but you're going to be. It's the same thing."

I frown and mouth, "The same thing?"

"I've seen the way you look at her," she says. "You have it bad. It'll only get worse. That's how love starts, you know. Like a fungus."

I want to protest but there's no use. I run my hands over my face and groan. "Is it that obvious?"

She smiles softly. "Well, I've noticed. I'm pretty sure Nick doesn't appreciate the little connection you two have. And Gemma definitely knows, that's why she's been so nuts."

"Nuts?"

"I don't know my cousin *that* well, but she was a lot different before she started this trip. Now she's, like, manic or something. I blame you." She pauses. "I blame you in a nice way, though. I can't say I blame her. You drive me nuts, too."

I scrunch up my face, feeling all awkward again. "Thanks. What did you mean about Nick not appreciating our connection?"

She shrugs. "I don't know. I just think it's obvious you guys are both drawn to each other like crackheads to a pipe. She smiles more when she's with you, way more than she does with Nick, or even me. She likes you, you know."

I ignore the rise of hope in my gut. "But if she likes me, why doesn't she just leave Nick?" I realize I sound like some pitiful shit on the playground, pining after his childhood crush, but fuck it.

She breathes out through her nose and looks at the lake, which is slowly turning from slate to navy as the clouds roll away and the blue sky shows through. The sun pokes its head around a tussock-dusted mountain and shoots a slant of pale light on the lake. It's all so surreal—the scenery and this conversation.

"Maybe she doesn't want to make things awkward for us," she muses. "Though you know what I think? I don't think Nick is the problem. I think he's, like, the result of another problem."

I give her a quizzical glance. "What problem is that?"

She shrugs again, throwing up her hands. "Who knows? Like I said, I don't know her that well. I think I only know her as much as you do. You guys have talked a lot more during this trip than I have. It's just what I feel. My father is a shrink, if you can't tell. I can psychoanalyze the moon."

In the distance, I can hear the sound of Mr. Orange's engine. We both turn to see Gemma by the bus, waving us over. "Guess we better go," I say. "Hey, I'm sorry if last night gave you the wrong idea."

"It's okay," she says quickly. "I wanted to see for myself. You're a good kisser but I can tell the difference between hormones and passion."

"And I've got hormones."

"You're a young dude. I'd be offended if you didn't," she says. "Come on, let's head back. Your not-so-secret secret is safe with me."

———•———

Queenstown is a bit of a clusterfuck. It's remarkably paint-worthy—the mountains that line the depths of Lake Wakatipu are called The Remarkables—but it's packed to the gills with tourists. It seems like every adrenaline junkie in the world has descended on this place the same time we have. The restaurants are full, the bars are full, the hostels are full. It's lucky that we even have a spot for Mr. Orange.

We're only in Queenstown for one night before we tackle the famed Routeburn Track, a hike that Gemma says she's been dreaming about for years. I'm not sure what to expect.

I'm normally in great shape, and the last few weeks have really got my cardio up, but four days of hiking up and down these mountains have me a bit worried.

But Amber doesn't seem nervous—at least she isn't once Gemma assures her there are no predators in New Zealand and we have a zero percent chance of being mauled by a bear—so I man up for the journey.

We wake up early, quickly filling our thermoses with hot water and instant coffee. It's colder here in the mornings than anywhere else we've been, and we're shivering as Mr. Orange heats up. With Gemma behind the wheel, her brows knitting together in keen determination, her lips wriggling with excitement, we make our way along the long lake toward the settlement of Glenorchy, where one end of the track starts.

I'm living in a postcard. Every day I wake up and I'm part of a scene that steals my breath and brings tears to my eyes. If it's not Gemma, it's this goddamned scenery. The sun is just barely rising over the sharp, bare peaks of The Remarkables, bathing the surrounding mountains in shades of gold. The lake is turning from silver to blue. Snow seems to have fallen at night at the upper elevations, making the mountain ranges look like they were dipped in whipped cream.

Even though I easily get car sick, I bring out my sketchbook and try and capture the moment as quickly as I can. When I'm done, my drawing nowhere near as beautiful as the landscape that unfolds before us, I catch Gemma's eyes in the mirror. She couldn't look more melancholy if she tried, and once again it breaks me.

Why don't you just try? I want to say. *Forget about your hand, find another way.* I would do anything to fill that loss in her heart. I just want to bring her peace.

She looks back to the road, which is good considering it's

growing more narrow by the second and we're high above a rugged, green drop to the lake. Soon the lake disappears behind us, the mountains come closer, and the road turns to rough gravel.

Mr. Orange slowly, carefully makes his way along the rocks and dust before we finally come to the end of the road. There are a bunch of cars in the car park and a modern-looking shelter composed of wood and glass where a few people are picnicking and studying displays on the walls.

The signs around the car park warn us that it's unpatrolled and not to leave any valuables in our car, but since we can only carry our backpacks, camping gear, and tents, we have no choice but to leave the majority of our stuff inside Mr. Orange. We'll be back in four days and apparently there's a tour that will pick us up from the other side of the track and take us to see the infamous Milford Sound before dropping us off back here.

Gemma locks the doors and pets the spare wheel on the grill. "You stay strong, Mr. Orange," she says and the sincere look in her eyes as she speaks to the bus is so fucking adorable.

"I thought we were changing his name to Shaggin' Wagon," I say as I sling on my backpack.

She glares at me. "Don't you dare. My uncle is a good man."

"The best men I know like to jerk it to porn," Nick says, and for once I find myself laughing with him, not at him.

The trail starts out easy enough and I find myself relaxing when I see families and old people passing us by, coming from the other way. If they can do it, I can do it.

We cross a swing bridge, then meander beside the Routeburn River for some time, a slice of rushing water that is so unbelievably clear and blue it looks like the waters of Tahiti, a striking contrast against the moss-covered rocks it winds around. The trees are beech and some other weird New Zealand kinds that harbor tiny yellow birds and colorful pigeons. The air is filled with bird-song.

"This is so pretty," Amber whispers from in front of me. "It makes me want to puke."

The beauty does make you a little sick. It's too much and it gets worse the higher we climb. Soon we move through tall beeches flanked with bright green lichen and waist-high ferns, the sunlight dappling through the branches at all the right moments. I take picture after picture, hoping they'll help me to draw the route later on. I was never one to draw or paint landscapes, but now that I'm here it's all I can do.

After we make our way past streaming waterfalls and gorges, the climb evens out and we find ourselves in a high valley. Here the river widens, soaking into the tussock plains and stretching out until it hits the surrounding mountains. The sky has turned gray and the mountaintops disappear into the mist, only to reappear minutes later.

Gemma, who is at the front, stops to get water out of her pack and then points to the distance, where the valley and river seem to converge with the mountains.

"See that lip," she says after a drink of water. "We'll be staying up there tonight. I booked us a room at the hut."

Damn. That lip, that little area high between the mountains, is way the fuck up there. We've already been walking for hours, or at least it feels that way.

But this is an adventure and there's no turning back on an adventure. My muscles are not sore yet, so that's a good sign. We bring out some energy bars and almonds and drink more water before heading forward.

In another couple of hours we're rewarded with the most epic views over the valley. We're up even higher than I thought and we can see the river below us, meandering through the tan grass for kilometers and kilometers. Little colored dots slowly move along the river, hikers going to and fro.

Further up, the Routeburn waterfall spills down the mossy banks of the mountains, spraying us in fine mist every time the breeze picks up, and there's a massive wooden building jutting out of the trees. This is apparently the Routeburn Falls hut, but it's nothing short of a hotel. There's a wide deck with people leaning against the railing, steaming mugs in hand, waving at us and admiring the view that won't stop taking their breath away.

The four of us nearly collapse once we reach it—even Gemma and Nick are sweaty and red-faced. We stagger into the hut and haul our bags through the giant mess hall and over to the bunk beds. It's just row upon row upon row of bunks, but at least they're divided into groups of four and have the illusion of privacy, even though there are no doors.

The first thing I want to do is take a shower, but even though there are toilets and running water, there are no showers. I have to make do with my sweat. Tired and "buggered," as Gemma would say, we decide to cook up our favorite staples—hot dogs—on the stoves in the communal kitchen and break out the bottle of whiskey that I decided to buy before we came. You can't exactly carry a bunch of beer or wine with you.

We do a few shots, play an old board game, and then it's time for bed. Even though I'm starting to get sore and I can barely keep my eyes open, I stay up sketching for a couple of hours, hoping to capture all the passing moments before they fade forever.

The last thing I draw is a picture of Gemma as she sleeps in the bottom bunk across from me. While drawing Gemma from memory back in Vancouver felt slightly intrusive (okay, so it didn't help that she was naked), drawing her asleep with her eyes closed, her face open and vulnerable is . . . necessary. I hope that by the end of the trip I can give her the whole sketchbook, so she knows just what kind of effect she's had on me. I don't know if I'll ever be able to let her know otherwise.

I'm still too afraid to fall.

Chapter Eleven

GEMMA

If you ask most people from New Zealand what's on their bucket list, they'll usually start listing places and activities far, far away from their home country. I mean, driving through the American Southwest in a pale blue convertible was always high on my list, and I finally did it (though the car ended up being more navy than powder blue). But there have been a few other places on my list that are in New Zealand itself.

Tramping the Routeburn Track in the Southern Alps was one of them. Skydiving over Lake Taupo is another, as is swimming in Lake Tekapo. And even though I grew up on the East Coast of New Zealand, I'd always wanted to venture to the remote East Cape and see the first sunrise of the world grace the beaches there.

Now I can cross Routeburn off the list. Even though it's only day two, the trip has been absolutely amazing. Yesterday went perfectly and everyone woke up happy and not too sore. My thighs burn in some places, mainly my hamstrings, but that's always a good thing; it means you're pushing yourself. And I need to be pushed.

This morning we've almost made it to the top of Harris Saddle. It's a side trip off the main track, but since we made good time yesterday I don't want to miss an opportunity. Luckily everyone was game, even Amber, who is the least athletic out of all of us.

Still, she can't help but whine. "Are we there yet?"

I turn around to look at her. She's nearly falling backward into Josh, with Nick at the very back. The last bit of the hike is always the hardest but I know if we keep pressing on, we'll get to the summit.

"Just a bit farther," I tell her, as I have been again and again.

Finally I can see the top of the A-frame shelter poking its head out among the rocky outcrops and endless waves of tussock grass and I nearly yelp with delight.

It's so fucking stunning, I can barely believe my eyes.

The tiny, windowless A-frame shelter looks so small against the valley and mountains that it looks as if it could blow off into the abyss at any moment. All around us the wind crackles around our limbs like lightning; the hum of the land can barely be contained.

We are so, *so*, insignificant here and the mountains go on forever and ever, the distance so vast and great between us and the peaks. I'm almost getting dizzy and I lean back for a second. A small hand goes around my arm and I know Amber is keeping me upright.

None of us says anything, we just suck in the air, suck in the view, suck in the life around us. I feel like the wind rushing up from the far-off lands below is feeding us. It's feeding me, deep inside, giving me strength.

We have a quick lunch of protein bars and water, sitting

among the dry tussock and trying to get our small brains to believe the world around us. Then we head back down the track, passing other exhausted trampers on the way and encouraging them to keep going, that the pain is worth it for the beauty.

Back on the main track heading to the Mackenzie Lake campsite, the out-of-body experience doesn't end. It amplifies as we walk along exposed ridges, the brown and green grass and subalpine plants rolling off on either side of us until they end, dropping off, and then there's nothing but space between us and the Hollyford and Ailsa Mountains.

I'm watching my step on the trodden rock path but I wish I had eyes on the back of my head. Not only to keep taking in the views but to watch Josh. Out of all of us, he seems to be just as affected as I am. He's thirsty for the experience and his passion is revving my heart. I'm already awake and alive and he's adding to it, making me want him more than I ever have.

I don't even have the decency to chide myself. The feeling is freeing and freedom is all I need.

Though it's a breathtaking hike, it's a long one. When we finally reach the campsite, down a steep descent to the rich, blue-green waters of Lake Mackenzie, we've been walking for six hours. It's almost dinnertime and the rumble in my stomach, my body screaming for protein, forces me to set up the tent in record time. I bring out the food from my pack—freeze-dried organic chili and a roll of gluten-free bread—and Amber cooks it over the portable stove that Josh pulls out of his backpack.

It's cold up here, and though summer has swamped the rest of the country, it's still spring in the mountains. We're all wrapped in our sweaters and jackets, ample amounts of mosquito spray covering our faces. The bottle of whiskey gets passed around the fire and soon the sun sinks behind molten clouds and the stars start to pop out in the sky.

Nick heads to our tent early. Soon after, Amber goes to hers.

I'm alone with Josh and I don't want to think. I don't want to be afraid. I don't want to stop being free. I want to get up and strip naked and run into the lake. I want to dance under the stars and the sliver of moon poking its head in the distance, rising from the hidden sea.

I think he can feel it in me, this wildness. I want to pretend the rest of the world doesn't exist and the rest of my life doesn't exist and the only thing that's certain is here and now.

I want him to kiss me. I want to kiss him.

I've wanted and yearned my whole life, but I don't think I've ever wanted quite like this. It pulls from my gut and mingles with those feelings I've ignored, the ones that tell me I'm looking for something and haven't found it yet.

Is it Josh? Would he fill that void?

Or is he just the sleight-of-hand in a card trick?

He's sitting across from me on a mossy rock and his eyes keep catching mine through the flames. If I were to lean over and kiss him, I would catch fire.

But I think I'd enjoy it.

"I think I'm going to turn in," he says, his voice careful, and I look down to hide the disappointment I know is etched on my face.

"Yeah. Me too," I reply, hoping I sound free.

But I'm not free. My stupid fucking heart is nothing more than a cage. I have to learn better. I have to watch myself.

I tip another shot of whiskey into my mouth and feel it burn as it goes down. I wish there were no tomorrow.

Josh seems hesitant to leave me so I get up and go to the washroom instead with the one dying flashlight that we have. I relieve myself and then spend a few moments milling around the campsites, staring at the glow from the tents against the glow of the stars above.

I wish I could paint this. I wish I could capture it as it is, all the details. I wouldn't need to embellish or elaborate. The reality is as beautiful as art.

With that thought in my head, I crawl into bed beside Nick and go to sleep.

———— • ————

The next morning I wake up with a fuzzy head and a frozen nose. It's the only thing poking out of the sleeping bags, and when I open my eyes I see frost on the top of the tent. Lord, it's cold.

I turn against Nick and try and snuggle, try to get warm. But he cries out and pushes me away.

"Fuck, babe, you're pure ice," he says in annoyance and he keeps me at arm's length so I don't bring the chill to him. Now I kind of want to freeze him out in a different way.

"Cuddle me," I demand, half joking, half serious.

But he only covers himself with the rest of his sleeping bag and rolls away, facing the side of the tent. "Fuck no, cuddle yourself, ice queen," he grumbles.

Maybe he doesn't mean for it to sting, but it does. It shouldn't. He meant it as just a joke, a jab at my frozen limbs, not anything more than that. The truth is I don't really need to snuggle up to Nick; he's just a warm body and I'd probably snuggle up to a fat, bearded trucker named Earl if I had a choice, but I don't.

I sigh, my breath catching in a cloud above my head, then decide to get on with the day. I get dressed as fast as I can, my teeth chattering as I go, pulling on singlets and T-shirts and flannel shirts and sweaters.

I noisily zip out of the tent and emerge into the mist. I can barely see Josh and Amber's tent across the fire pit. Everything is hidden by cold, heavy fog.

My teeth are still chattering as I quickly get the fire going for warmth and then the stove going for our breakfast. It's not long before everyone else is emerging, hugging themselves and spewing obscenities over the weather. But that's the thing about the South Island and especially the mountains. You can have four seasons in one day and the weather can change drastically in a short amount of time. The number one killer for tourists is hypothermia.

Thankfully we've all planned ahead, and though it takes a while and we have to wear all the clothes we've packed and wait for the fire to get hot, we eventually warm up and get ready to continue on with the hike.

The track from the campsite is a lot of up and down, and though I know that the cliffs don't suddenly drop off from the path, it's still scary making our way through with limited visibility.

I guess I'm going too slow for Nick because he takes the lead in front of me.

"We're not going to fall off the mountain," he tosses over his shoulder at me. "Pick up the pace."

I exhale noisily but keep one foot going in front of the other. Compared to yesterday, I'm in a bad mood. The low cloud makes me feel boxed in and claustrophobic, plus the slight whiskey hangover and Nick's rejection this morning doesn't help.

We pass through an area known as "The Orchard" where the path turns into a grassy plain dotted with ferns and ribbonwood trees. Josh says they remind him of arbutus trees back in British Columbia, the way their thin trunks bend and reach. In the fog they just look like ghostly, frail hands trying to hold the mist, but they can't hold on any better than I can.

Today's hike feels longer than yesterday's, and though we pass by waterfalls and lush beechwood forest, I feel like that moment I wanted to hang on to has passed forever. I didn't want a tomorrow and yet here it is. Cold and gray and trapped.

We reach Lake Howden Hut around three p.m. and just before the torrential downpour starts. Unlike the first hut we stayed at, this one is much smaller and feels cramped, thanks to all the other trampers taking shelter from the rain, plus the addition of my own foul mood.

Nick cooks dinner this time—parboiled rice and rehydrated vegetables, which actually taste better than it sounds—and I barely finish the bowl when the clouds suddenly clear a path for the sky and the rain stops and the sun shoots us a barrel-wide ray of light.

"I want to go to Key Summit," I announce suddenly, getting to my feet.

"What?" Nick says, reaching for me to sit back down.

I move out of his grasp and eye them all. "The weather has finally cleared up and if I stay in here I'm going to go crazy." Amber and Josh exchange a look. I ignore it. "I wanted to go to Key Summit earlier but what's the point if you can't see anything."

"It's almost sundown, babe," Nick says. "We can go tomorrow."

"Fuck tomorrow," I say. "I want this today. I want the sunset. It's only twenty minutes up and it's totally guided by signs. There's a boardwalk up there. It's safe. I've seen the pictures."

They all avoid my desperate eyes.

"Don't be mad," Amber admits sheepishly, "but I'm not moving an inch."

"Neither am I," says Nick, folding his arms.

Hesitantly, I look at Josh. He just nods and gets up, his empty dish in hand. "I'd love to go. But let's just pack a backpack just in case."

My nerves jump at the idea of being alone with him. Where was the brave girl from last night? Was she still hidden in the fog?

But he's right, we need to be smart, even for a short hike. He comes back from the bunks with the small daypack that detaches from his larger one and I see he's put in a first-aid kit, two rain jackets, sweaters, socks, the flashlight, and a handful of energy bars.

"All set?" I ask him, almost afraid to meet his eyes.

He gives me an easy smile that puts my cagey mind to rest. "Let's go." He looks at Nick and Amber. "I'll send you a postcard."

We leave the hut side by side, the trees around us touched by fading sun at their tops and hidden by darkening shadow below. Once we're back on the track and heading south toward the turnoff for the summit route, we go into single file. This time Josh is leading the way. I like it.

Maybe I just like staring at his ass.

The track ascends through thick beech forest and ferns, everything growing darker and darker the more the sun sets, like the land is preparing for the night. And then the final ten minutes it opens up into bogs and tussock and pastel sky. I feel so much better with the forest beneath us, like my head is clearing.

We reach the summit just in time. The sun is starting to sink in the west over the peaks, and the sky is turning shades of orange and blue, tingeing the edges of the clouds with magenta, like a child has taken a neon marker and outlined them. The boardwalk among the bogs, ponds, and low shrubs ends at a lake that reflects all the colors of the sky back at us.

I want to cry. The tears are there, rushing to my eyes because my soul can't contain them. It's all too much but they still don't fall.

Instead I let out a quiet sob that seems to echo across the mountains and all the way to the unseen sea.

Suddenly Josh wraps his arms around me from the back, holding me in place. He rests his jaw on top of my head and keeps his focus forward, on the beauty changing, melting, evolving in front of us.

My nerves change, too, slipping into something more comfortable. He's just holding me, providing comfort, giving warmth, support. He's a friend and he's here for me. He can feel the ache in my heart.

But I also know he's more than a friend. He's on the brink of becoming something else, if only I have the courage to try.

We stand like that for a long time. Too long. It's getting cold and dark but now the moon is out and the stars are like the glowworms we saw in the cave. I don't want to turn around. I don't want to go back to the hut or to my life as it was. I want to keep standing here with his strong, hard arms around me, staring up into infinite space.

"We should go back," Josh eventually says, and I hear a bit of trepidation in his low voice.

I turn around and face him, my chest pressed against his. I rub my lips together, wishing I could ask for what I want, even though I don't know what it is. I want him to help me.

"Okay," I say quietly. So we're not going to talk about it. So it was just a friendly embrace. So that was it.

He sucks in his breath, hesitating for a moment, then he steps back and away from me, removing his backpack. He digs the flashlight out of the front pocket and flicks it on. The light is weak but it works.

But by the time we get to the end of the boardwalk, it doesn't. Clouds roll in from the sea, hitting the mountains and covering the moon.

Our light is gone.

We are alone in the dark.

We are alone on the mountain.

I try not to panic. I take out my Samsung Galaxy and try to use the flashlight feature. It kind of works, painting the route in front of us in a dim gray. But when I hit rocks and nearly stumble over a low ledge into a mess of trees below, and Josh has to yank me back to safety, I realize we can't use it to navigate.

"Shit," I swear. "Shit, shit, shit, fuck!"

I can't keep the panic out of my voice.

Josh grips my arms, and in the dimness I can barely see his face. "Gemma," he says, calm and steady. "It's okay. Save the battery on your phone. I know there's no reception right now, but you never know what tomorrow will bring. If we try and go down that path in the dark or with those phones, we're asking for trouble. Do you know what they teach you in Boy Scouts?"

I shake my head.

"Neither do I," he says. "I was kicked out after the second day for lighting shit on fire. But I did take an outward bound class in high school. You stay in place. You don't move. You wait for people to come to you. Trust me, this happens all the time at home, people going off to hike in the mountains above Vancouver, and if only they didn't move, they would have been found. They would have survived."

"It was so cold last night," I say, the terror rising in my throat, the image of Nick rolling away from me when I was freezing.

"It was cold," he says. "But that's why we packed a backpack, to prepare for this. There are two of us for heat, plus I know how to make a good bed and shelter from the elements. We're going to be fine, and as soon as dawn breaks, we'll be on our way. We know where we are. They know where we are. We're not lost. We're just delayed in getting back, that's all."

I stare at his face in the dark as a cold breeze whips up my hair. I'm putting all my trust in him. I don't know how he knows this stuff but I believe him. He'll take care of us. He'll take care of me.

As if hearing what I'm thinking, he places his warm hand on my chilled cheek and says, "Trust me, I've got you."

And he does. With the weak light of the phone we head back a few feet from where we were and stop at a grassy area beside a low shrub. On the opposite side of it, against the direction of the wind, Josh starts ripping up grass from the ground and leaves from the surrounding trees.

I do the same, adding the occasional hunk of moss that feels dry. We spread it out on the ground beside the tree, then on top of all the foliage he lays down a silver emergency blanket that he brings out from the first-aid kit.

Next he brings out an extra pair of socks and a sweater and orders me to put it on. I do so quickly and he does the same. Then he gives me my rain jacket. As I'm slipping it on, he walks a few feet away to relieve himself. I should do the same but my adrenaline is running too high.

"All righty," he says as he comes back and gestures to the makeshift bed. "Lie down." He puts on his jacket but he doesn't zip it up.

I carefully lower myself to the ground. The low bush really does block the wind and I immediately feel a lot warmer.

He gets down on his knees beside me and puts his hands on my waist, lifting me up slightly. "Here, flip over. We're spooning tonight."

A faint smile touches my lips. I roll over so my back is to him and he lies down right beside me, his body pressed flush against mine. For once I can luxuriate in the contact and I move my body back against his, craving his heat. He tangles his long legs over mine and wraps the open flap of his rain jacket over me like it's the end of a blanket. One arm goes up over my head, making sure my jacket hood is covering me, while the other holds me in a tight embrace.

"You okay?" he whispers in my ear. Even through the hood, his breath is hot and sends shivers running down my spine.

I nod. It's all I can do.

"We'll be okay tonight," he assures me. "The bush will block the wind and all the stuff between us and the ground will let us keep each other warm. That's why most people die in the wilderness. They think it's more important to have shelter over them, but it's the ground that kills them. It will steal all your warmth."

"What if it rains?" I manage to ask. "Or snows?"

"I don't know if it will snow. But where we were camping last night was at a much higher elevation and it didn't snow there. If it rains, then we'll huddle under the rain jackets, but until that happens it's best if we get some sleep."

But I can't sleep and it's not just that we're lying in the open in the dark in the middle of the Southern Alps. It's that Josh is holding me as tight as he can and I've never felt so safe because of it.

My chest is begging for release but I don't know how to start or what to say.

So I find myself saying something I never thought I would.

"Josh?" I ask softly.

"Yeah?"

"Do you ever find yourself wanting something so badly but you don't know what it is?"

His breath is heavy in my ear for a moment. Finally he says, "Yes. I do."

I swallow, my throat feeling thick. "I have this . . . I don't know what it is exactly. But I wake up and it's there and it's been there for a long time. It's just this absence. It tells me that either something was there before and now it's gone or that something should be there at this point in my life. But I don't have it. I feel this lack. So much that it hurts. And I don't know what it is. It just makes me sad. It makes me long and ache and I need something to fill it. It's a constant pain and I'm so fucking tired of it."

My voice chokes up a bit at the end and the tears that didn't come during the sunset are coming now, slowly, cold on my cheeks. "I think I ache for things I may never have. I long for purpose, for life, and yet sometimes I think I'm too afraid to live." I pause. "Do you ever worry that there's something out there that you're missing?"

"I do," he answers quietly, pulling back the edge of my hood. His warm lips brush against the rim of my ear and I close my eyes to intensify the feeling. "The feeling that you won't be happy until you find it."

"Yes," I say, relief flooding through me at the realization that he understands. "Do you know what yours is?"

He pauses. "I have an idea. It's becoming clearer day by day."

I suck in my breath, waiting, hoping, wishing on what he will say next. If he says it, then I'll take the plunge.

"What is it?"

"Well, coming here has helped," he says. "I feel like I'm actually living my life instead of just getting by. I'm doing something, being somebody. Before this . . . I was just going through the motions. Now I am the motion."

Knowing what happened to me, I ask, "Are you afraid that when you go back home you'll change back to the way you were?"

I can feel him smile against my neck. "No. I'm not afraid

of that. The things that have happened here . . . they're permanent."

Permanent. I can only wish he was permanent in my life.

"You're lucky," I tell him.

"Why?"

"Because no matter what happens, you'll go back a better person. I came back a worse person."

He flinches like he's been struck. "What?"

"It's true," I admit, and even though it's painful to do, that sense of freedom teases me with each word that comes out of my mouth. "When I was traveling I became whatever I wanted, whoever I wanted. When I came back home, it was almost like it was all for nothing. I regressed—and then some. All those months of finding myself were gone in a matter of weeks. And the hollowness has only gotten worse. Sometimes I think I'm just a shell of who I used to be and I don't think I'll ever feel whole."

I can't believe I'm admitting this much. It's not even a life or death situation, at least it doesn't feel that way in Josh's capable arms, but I can't help but open up to him. He wanted to know the real me and now he's getting every ugly bit of her. But he still has no idea of what I could be like and only a small glimpse of what I could have been.

A few seconds roll past and I wondered if I've stunned him. Then he shifts against me, closer, warmer.

"Gemma," he whispers into my hair, kissing the top of my head. "You're beautiful. And that's all I can say—you're beautiful inside and out, and I'm here only because of you. You've given me the life that I needed, just being by your side, just being there for a fucking night, let alone all these ones we've spent together. If you could only see how amazing you really are, you wouldn't be so hard on yourself. Maybe you wouldn't feel that ache."

Another tear rolls down my cheek and I'm speechless at his words. They've built a small, flickering fire inside me and I'm torn between putting it out or adding fuel to the flames.

I don't speak for a long time. I just let him hold me, his breath steady with the occasional cricket or buzzing insect against the white-starred sky.

"Thank you," I tell him. "For being so nice." To lighten the load I add, "And for making sure I don't die."

"Anytime," he says. He presses his face into my neck. "And when we're both alive at dawn, you can thank me again."

I fall asleep when the ache subsides. I barely feel the cold.

Chapter Twelve

GEMMA

We survived the night. Even though I could only doze for a few hours here and there, the ground hard and uncomfortable even through all the foliage, we made it.

The sky above us begins to lighten. I want to roll over onto my back to watch the stars disappear one by one but I know I'm only breathing because Josh is holding me and keeping me warm. My face feels frozen. I know that it's terminally cold out.

"Hey," he says into my ear, voice groggy. "Good morning."

"Morning," I whisper.

"How did you sleep?"

"I slept. That was more than I thought would happen."

"Same here. It's going to be freezing the moment we break apart."

"I know. Let's just stay like this until the sun rises."

But we get up before that happens. Even though the cold is bitter and biting, I'm glad that we're on our feet just as the sun slides up from the Humboldt Mountains to the east. It paints the other peaks, making their fresh snow glow rose gold.

The little lake near us—which, according to Josh is called a *tarn*—is like a mirror, gradually lightening to match the sky, while the valleys on either side of the summit are all covered with a thick layer of mist. Today we're above the clouds.

We turn to make our way down the hill just in time to see a couple coming up; an older man with his camera out, a woman behind him, and just behind her, coming into sight, is Amber.

"Oh my god!" Amber cries out, running for us. She wraps her arms around me and then Josh, her eyes watering. "You guys, what happened? Oh my god, I thought you were dead, you never came back, I thought you were just going for a bit but then this morning you weren't back. I was so worried!"

The couple make their way to us. The man smiles, his bushy mustache moving. "Didn't quite make it last night?" he asks, his accent Swedish or Danish or something.

Josh shakes his head. "No, the flashlight died and it wasn't safe to make it down without it."

The man nods and his pale partner, her head half covered by a knit cap, hands us a thermos full of coffee. "For you," she says. "To wake up, though with this view maybe you don't need it."

I thank her profusely, feeling embarrassed, and take a grateful sip. I pass it over to Josh, meeting his eyes briefly.

Amber squeezes my arm. "We were going to get the ranger to come with us just in case but I guess he went to rescue someone else last night."

"Yah," the man says, lifting up his camera and peering through the lens. "In the fog I think someone fell down a ravine and broke their leg. Had to be helicoptered out."

Shit. That could have been us. I'm suddenly even more

grateful for Josh and that he kept us alive up here on the mountain.

Josh looks at the man. "Not to seem ungrateful or anything, but how come you only came now and not last night?"

Amber looks chagrined, biting her lip. "We didn't tell anyone that you didn't come back."

"What?" I ask.

Her eyes widen in shame. "But I set my alarm for this morning and when I was getting ready, I ran into Janne and Ana here who were going to see the sunrise and I just tagged along. I even suggested getting the ranger, but with him gone, this was our best bet."

"Wait," Josh said slowly. "Why didn't you tell anyone last night?"

She looks away. "I thought maybe you did this on purpose. That you wanted to be alone. You know, like it was part of a plan." When she looks back, she's giving Josh a loaded stare.

He frowns. "I only came because I wasn't about to let Gemma come here on her own."

"I know, I know," she says quickly.

So was Amber trying to play matchmaker between Josh and me? I could have sworn that she was into him. Why would she do this?

I push those thoughts aside. "But," I begin, "if that's what you thought . . . what was Nick's excuse?"

She shrugs with one shoulder. "He said you'd be back at some point." Her voice lowers. "And then he fell asleep. I didn't bother waking him this morning."

Heat floods my cold cheeks. Again, I'm embarrassed and hurt.

The man, Janne, clears his throat. "Well, I hope the rest of your day gets better. Glad to see that you're all in one piece."

I know what he's not saying: *I hope you have fun dealing with that shithead back at the hut.*

And that's when I know it's over with the shithead. Ending it with Nick will throw my future up in the air and will leave me naked and vulnerable, but I have enough self-respect to kick him to the curb. He didn't even *care*. I was in the dark with Josh, way past sunset, in the mountains, in the wilderness, and he didn't care. He just didn't care. He fucking went to sleep instead.

How could he sleep knowing I was out there? Even if he really does believe I can take care of myself, how could his ego let me be out there with Josh?

Had I been sleeping with a monster this whole time?

We say goodbye to the couple, and as we walk down the hill I ask Amber, "Did Nick seem mad?"

"Uh," she says. "He didn't have an outburst or anything but there was a vein popping out on his forehead and it seemed like he was trying to grind his bottom jaw right out."

So he was at least being possessive. That sounded more like him.

After a few beats, Josh, in a low, hard voice, says, "Gemma, I know I've already asked you this before. I know you're going to tell me to fuck off or whatever. But I have to know, because I don't get it." He pauses and I hold my breath. "Why the fuck are you with that asshole?"

I don't say anything.

I hear him stop behind me and he grabs my arm, pulling me toward him. His grip is strong, his eyes on fire as they search mine. "I'm serious. The guy doesn't even give a shit that you're out here. Why the fuck are you with him?" His voice is growing louder. "Tell me!"

I can hear Amber inhale behind me, watching this unfold, probably waiting for an answer, too.

"Because," I croak, trying to find my defiance. "I know exactly what to expect with him."

"And what is that?"

I pause. "Nothing. I expect nothing and that's just what he gives."

Josh frowns, looking a little broken. "How can you want that?"

I don't say anything.

He grabs my other arm and there's a wildness to his eyes, his hair catching on the wind. "Gemma." His voice is rough and heated. "Some people may expect nothing. Most people expect something. But you, *you*, should expect *everything*."

Will you give me everything? I want to ask. I look away before he can see the question in my eyes.

I don't want the answer.

Fifteen minutes later we reach the hut and my nerves are squirming. I'm actually kind of glad that Amber didn't tell anyone other than Janne and Ana, and that all the trampers here are none the wiser.

But once we step inside the communal dining hall and see Nick storming toward us, I know that everyone's about to know all of our business.

He's mad. Amber said he didn't have an outburst but I don't think I'll be spared one. Nick's going to blow like a volcano and it's not going to be pretty. That's when the caveman rugby player comes out, the kind that picks fights and spits in faces.

"Where the fuck did you go?" he yells, and the trampers who are trying to eat their oatmeal and cereal look up at him aghast. He ignores them, coming right over to me and grabbing my forearm tight, yanking me hard.

"Hey," Josh warns, stepping in between us, putting a hand on Nick's chest and trying to push him back.

"Oh fuck off," Nick barks at him, his face going red. "I know exactly what's going on between you two."

"Nick," I cry out softly, my eyes darting to all the people watching us. "Calm down, there's nothing going on."

"Bullfuckingshit," he says. His eyes settle on me, hard, mean little dots. "Like you actually just wanted to look at the sunset. You're not that daft."

"I did!" I say.

He turns his gaze to Josh and his lip curls into a snarl. "So she's a good lay, isn't she? A good little root."

"It's not what you think," Josh says, though now the anger is starting to creep into his voice, too. "We got stuck up there, the flashlight died."

"And you fucked the night away, is that it?" he turns to me, yelling, spittle flying in my face.

"Nothing happened!" I yell right back. I'm getting defensive and can't help myself. I try to lower my voice. "Nothing happened, we got stuck and waited until morning to come back, when we could see where we were going."

"Right, likely story. Like you haven't wanted to fuck this loser for the last couple of weeks."

"Nick, *shut up*," I grind through my teeth. "Let's take this outside and deal with it and not ruin these people's breakfasts."

"Fuck them," he growls. "And fuck you. I should have known better than to take you back." He steps closer to me, his chin raised. "You're beneath me, you ugly slut."

Amber gasps from beside me. My heart stops.

The dining hall fills with a *crack* as Josh's fist slams right into Nick's face.

Blood sprays from his nose and he goes stumbling backward. Josh has caught him off guard, putting all of his height and weight behind the punch.

Nick grabs his nose, crying out, then springs forward, fists swinging at Josh. Josh ducks and spins out of the way and Nick is too crazed to act with precision or grace. He stumbles into a table and orange juice spills and cutlery clatters and people scramble to their feet to get out of the way.

"Stop!" I yell but they don't hear me.

Nick goes for Josh again and clocks him on his chin but Josh moves with the blow and then twists around before throwing a hard punch into Nick's solar plexus. Nick coughs, stunned for a moment, and then Josh is going for another punch.

But someone has grabbed Josh's arm, holding his fist back, and another guy holds back Nick, and I'm able to safely launch myself in between them. "Stop it, please," I say again and my attention is on Josh because, out of the two of them, he's the only one who will listen. I press my splayed fingers on Josh's chest, feeling his breath heave in and out, the heat he's giving off. "Please. Don't be like him."

His eyes are crazed, pupils small against his glacier blues. A thin sheen of sweat covers his brow. But he peers down at me, understands what I'm asking, and gives me the most subtle nod. His body relaxes slightly and he steps back, turning away.

I look back at Nick, who is fighting to get out of the restraint of two men. They're burly, seasoned-looking trampers and they mean business, but that doesn't stop Nick from yelling, "Don't think I won't forget this, Gemma Henare!" He says my last name like it's a joke. "I know what you did. You won't have a job to come back to now, so don't even try. I'll make sure your name gets trashed all over town."

"Mate," the biggest man says to him, his eyes a stiff warning. "Don't make me send you back to Australia, aye? Calm down. It's over." His grip tightens on Nick for emphasis. "You hear me?"

Nick eyes him and the other guy holding him back but eventually concedes. They reluctantly let go of him, though they seem poised to take him down if he tries to go after Josh.

I don't know what to fucking do. Nick was supposed to come back with us; some of his stuff is still in Mr. Orange.

The tough man looks to me. "If I were you, I'd pack up and get out of here. This is a family place. No one wants any more trouble."

"Of course not," I manage to say, shooting him a weak smile. I grab Amber, who seems to have been shell-shocked this whole time, and we hurry over to the bunks.

Josh is leaning his forehead against the top bunk, eyes closed, breathing in and out.

"Josh," I say gently. I carefully lay my hand on his arm. "We need to get going before things get worse. We can pack for you if you want to leave now and take the door that leads to the deck. We'll meet you on the trail below."

He slowly rolls his forehead along the wood and looks straight at me, frowning. "I'm not taking the back door. I'm not afraid of him."

"I know you're not. That's the point."

His brows knit further together. "He called you an ugly slut, Gemma. How can you let him get away with that?"

"It doesn't matter," I tell him, "because *you* didn't let him get away with it. And I appreciate that you stood up for me. But we need to get going before things get worse. We have a bus to catch to Milford Sound anyway."

He sighs but pushes back from the bunk and starts packing. He's fast, and to his credit, he slips out the other door.

When Amber and I are ready, our packs on our backs, I give her a look. "Pretty exciting morning, huh?"

Her eyes are wide. "Tell me about it. I felt like I was in an episode of *Buffy*. But without the vampires."

"Well, it ain't over yet."

As we quickly walk through the dining hall, keeping our heads low, we're left alone. At least until I can see Nick getting to his feet out of the corner of my eye, his chair scraping loudly on the floor like nails on a chalkboard.

"Oye!" he yells. "Where the fuck are you going?"

I don't even look at him.

"Hey! Gemma! What about my stuff?" he cries out, louder now.

I open the door and Amber turns to him. "We'll mail all your crap to your shitty gym," she says. "Don't worry, we won't forget about the steroids."

The door shuts behind us and I can hear his embarrassed protests, but now we're on the trail and we're quickly running down the path, the sneakers I have tied against my pack banging on my ass as we go.

We round a bend and see Josh standing up ahead. He's got his whiskey bottle in hand and is taking a shot.

"It's like eight in the morning," Amber admonishes as we catch up to him but she grabs the bottle and takes a shot herself, wincing all the way.

"Yeah," Josh says, "but I've already been punched in the face so I think I've got a head start on the day."

I take the whiskey and tip a bit down my throat. I cough, wiping my mouth with my sleeve, and give it back to Josh. "It's five o'clock somewhere."

"In China, I think," Amber says, glancing at the time on her phone.

We head down the track, our feet quick.

And then there were three.

———— • ————

"You know," Amber says to me as we lean against the rails of the ship, the towering peaks of Milford Sound rising above us on either side, like mystical overlords, "if you want to make a fuss about Nick, you know, letting you go from your job, you could. I don't know what the rules are in this country but back home you could totally sue his ass."

"Nah," I say, my eyes trained on the rock faces, marveling at the way time and ice have sculpted them. "I'm not going to bother with that."

"But how can you get another job at a gym if he's going to" she says as she makes air quotes "'trash you all over town'?"

"Maybe I won't get a job at a gym."

"What are you going to do?"

I don't know. I can only shrug, wanting her to drop the subject. It's all too much to think about right now. I just want to be numb.

Josh comes back from downstairs holding paper cups of coffee, trying not to spill as the ship rolls back and forth. We're nearing the mouth of the sound, Anita Bay, where the Tasman Sea funnels in, and it's starting to get rougher.

He hands one to me and as I take the cup, his finger brushes against mine. I try and ignore the thrill it shoots into me. He's only adding to my confusion and yet I can't stop bringing my thoughts to him.

When the three of us finally made our way to the Divide Shelter, at the other end of the Routeburn Track, we had to wait around a bit because we were early. The whole time I kept looking over my shoulder, thinking Nick was going to come running out of the forest like a crazy ape, beating his fists into his chest, but luckily the bus showed up before that could happen.

Milford Sound wasn't too far away, and soon we were boarding a small ship with a bunch of other tourists, swatting at the sandflies that gather around the shore.

The Sound is exactly how you see it on all the New Zealand postcards and travel advertisements. Mitre Peak is the focal point, a giant, soaring monolith sticking straight out of the water, but all the surrounding mountains, with their waterfalls and sheer cliff faces, are equally impressive.

I think normally I'd be oohing and aahing a bit more, but after seeing the beauty of the Routeburn Track—and after everything that had happened this morning—it's all a bit anticlimactic.

So my thoughts keep going to Josh. He leans against the railing beside me, sipping the coffee, and I want to stare at him instead of one of the world's wonders. He's the wonder of my new world. His arm is pressed up against mine and I'm caught in a tangle of conflicting feelings.

On one hand, if I want to pursue things with Josh, I'm free to. I'm not with anyone. Nick and I are over. I don't have to feel guilty, I don't have to make the hard choices. There's no one in our way.

Yet *I* am in our way. Because there is the other hand, the one that tells me getting involved with Josh would be a bad idea. I care too much about him now for this to be just a fling, and eventually he is going to leave and that ache in my chest might turn into a full-on wound.

The only way this can possibly work is if I can find a way to detach even further. Have fun, a lot of fun, a lot of good, hot sex, and try my hardest to keep my heart where it belongs.

I just don't know if I'm strong enough to take a chance.

But as I stare up at Josh's strong, beautiful face and he catches my eyes, his lips quirking into a cocky smile, I don't think I'm strong enough to not take one.

The butterflies are taking flight again, their wings tickling my insides, and I swallow hard, looking away and breaking the connection.

"Dolphins at the bow!" someone yells from the front of

the ship, and everyone around us starts to head on over, some slipping on wet patches on the deck. It's pandemonium and Josh's face lights up like a Christmas tree.

"Go see them," I tell him.

He looks at me like I'm crazy. "You don't want to?"

I shrug. "Dolphins, I've seen them all."

He raises a brow. "Well, look at you, Miss Too Cool for Dolphins." Then he runs off up the deck with everyone else.

I look at Amber. "You're not interested?"

"I'm a bit seasick," she says. She nods her head at the wheelhouse. "And this is the one place where the wind isn't killing me. I'm from California, you know, I'm not used to this during the summer."

"Well, it's not summer yet," I tell her. "And I'm fully aware you're from California, you won't shut up about it."

She smiles and takes my coffee from my hand, having a gulp of it. I have to say, I've grown really fond of my cousin in this last while. I'm going to miss her to pieces when she's gone.

As if sensing my hidden affection, she gives me back the coffee, her eyes sparkling. "So," she says, and the way she draws it out makes me hold in my breath. "Now that you're not with Nick . . ."

I don't have time to play games. "Yes?"

"Oh come on, you know what I'm asking."

"I don't."

She rolls her eyes playfully. "Are you going to go for Josh?"

I give her a blank stare. "And why would I do that?"

"Because, the guy is, like . . . obsessed with you."

I raise my brow and try to keep my face as blank as possible. Obsessed with me? My chest fills with a wonderful warmth and a smile fights its way to my lips.

"What do you mean?" I ask super casually, keeping the smile at bay.

She doesn't seem to buy it. "Like you don't know. He wants you. Bad. And I don't know but I've caught the way you look at him. You guys need to combust. With each other, preferably. That's why I thought you guys were going off together last night."

I shake my head, even though the smile has crept onto my face. "No, I seriously just wanted to see the sunset." I pause. I want to grill her for more information but I need to do it in the most delicate way. "I, erm, I thought that *you* wanted to get with him or something."

She waves that notion away with her hand. "No, not really. It just happened that one time and we talked about it afterward."

My smile disappears. Something sinks inside me, heavy and deep. "*What?*"

Amber frowns. "What?"

I swallow uneasily, my pulse starting up in my throat. "What happened that one time?"

She's uncertain now. "Um, the thing in the theater."

"What thing?" my voice is hard, my eyes harder.

She shrinks slightly. "I thought Nick told you. He saw us." I just stare at her. "You know, making out and stuff."

I purse my lips, my eyes widening, as if that helps me to absorb this awful information. "Nick saw you and Josh making out in the theater?"

"It wasn't anything nasty, I swear," she says, starting to panic. "Just kissing and groping, that's it."

Oh my god, I'm going to throw her overboard.

"Oh my god," I say. "Oh my god. Oh my god."

"Shit," Amber swears. "Fuck. I'm sorry Gemma, I thought you knew, I thought Nick told you. Otherwise I wouldn't have said anything."

"You wouldn't?"

"No, well, it's just that it happened once and it didn't mean anything and I could tell Josh wasn't into it."

"Of course he was into it," I snap. "He's a dude and you're a hot fucking chick and not the one with the asshole boyfriend."

"Gemma, seriously," she says. "I didn't think you cared this much. You've had Nick with you this entire time."

"I don't care this much," I say, trying to hide all the emotion from my voice. My stomach swirls with rotten green jealousy. It shouldn't sicken me, I have no right whatsoever to care about what Josh did with Amber, especially seeing as I was with Nick, but it still makes me feel like I'm going to chunder.

I wish I could blame it on being seasick.

With trepidation, Amber places her hand on my shoulder. "I'm sorry."

I sigh angrily, blowing a strand of hair from my face. "It's fine."

"It's not," she says pitifully. "Please don't let this ruin things between you and Josh and please don't tell him I told you. He'd kill me."

I bet he would, I think. Suddenly the risk of going after Josh seems higher. He couldn't really like me all that much if he was willing to feel up Amber and stick his tongue down her throat. If I'm already this bothered by the image of them together, how bothered am I going to be when he leaves New Zealand?

Amber is staring at me with big, pleading eyes and I manage to give her a smile. I'm pissed off as hell but she's actually doing me a favor. She's helped make my choice. My heart will stay buried but intact. I won't have to lose any more pieces of myself.

"I won't say anything," I tell her, and it's a promise. "It's fine." *That's* a lie, but one out of two ain't bad.

When the dolphins seem to have gone on their way, Josh joins us. He has his swagger and his easy smile and I realize nothing I choose is going to be simple.

"How was it?" Amber says a little too brightly.

He shrugs. "Meh, dolphins, you know, whatever," he says, mimicking me and my accent.

I can barely crack a smile and his expression falters, as if he thinks he's offended me. I turn away from him, concentrating on a waterfall that the ship is approaching. I stay turned away for as long as I can.

Chapter Thirteen

JOSH

"Maybe Nick isn't the problem."

Amber had said that to me on the shores of Lake Wanaka, and at the time I had completely brushed it off because, hello, obviously the roid-monkey douchebag boyfriend is the problem here. With him out of the picture, everything would be smooth sailing for me and Gemma.

But that's not the case. Something happened, something I can only seem to pinpoint to the boat ride on Milford Sound, when Gemma switched off. She grew cold and withdrawn. At first I thought it was toward Amber as well, and that made a bit of sense. She'd just had her boyfriend, fuck-buddy, whoever that ass was, accuse her of something she didn't do, call her disgusting names, and then tell her she'd never get a job again. Anyone would be ruined by that.

Gemma seemed resilient though, if not a bit quiet, and by the time we were cruising around the bay on a boat full of Japanese tourists, she seemed to open up. Lighten up. It was like watching the sun come through the clouds.

Then I went and saw some dolphins jumping about and when I came back, it was like she had turned to ice. And as we get on the bus that will take us back to Mr. Orange, the ice only seems to thaw in Amber's direction, not mine.

I can't figure it out. I sit behind them on the bus, beside some young dude who keeps elbowing me and playing his headphones too loud. The drive back from Milford is actually just as stunning as the Sound. The mountains loom high overhead, there's a fuck-ton of waterfalls we keep stopping at, and we pass through Homer Tunnel, which cuts through the ranges. We even see kea parrots hopping around at one of the waterfall car parks and trying to make off with a picnicker's food.

It's here, as most of the bus group goes to look at waterfall number one billion, that I pull Gemma aside. I can't help it.

"Are you okay?" I ask.

She tugs out of my grasp, and from that alone I know she's not. "I've been better, Josh."

I bite my lip, wanting to ask her if it's all because of what happened or if it's something I did. But I let it go. She's been through enough today and I don't want to add to her problems.

"Well, if you need someone to talk to," I say, but I know she won't be turning to me. There's this strange emptiness in her eyes that chills me. I remember everything she said last night. Her fears.

She walks back to the bus, uninterested in the waterfall and all the curious green parrots roaming the area, looking for handouts.

She's uninterested in me.

I refuse to let that deter me, though. I've come this far. I've just got to take my time.

But I'm leaving in three weeks.

I don't really have time.

We all get back on the coach and finish the rest of the route. It takes about four hours for us to finally reach Glenorchy where we left Mr. Orange, and I find it kind of funny that the drive feels just as long as the days of walking we just did. I can't believe I just walked over a mountain range. As active as I am at home, the most strenuous thing I've ever done was the infamous Grouse Grind up Grouse Mountain. It takes about forty minutes to the top. That was nothing compared to what I just accomplished.

The minute the bus pulls into the Routeburn car park, I can feel that something is wrong. It's instinct but it's huge and unwavering.

We hop off the bus and make our way over to Mr. Orange. At first the VW bus looks fine, but on closer inspection it looks like the back window has been busted out.

"Oh shit," I yell and start running but Gemma has already beaten me to it. It looks like someone has bashed it in completely and the gravel around us is peppered with sharp shards of glass.

"Oh my god," she cries out, her hand to her mouth. "My uncle is going to kill me."

"Gemma, it's okay," I say, even though it's not really. She's had one hell of a day.

"How is it okay?!" she cries out, and her eyes start to water. "I don't have a job to come home to, how am I going to afford to replace the window?"

I raise up my hands and come toward her. "Don't worry about it. I'll help, I'll pay for it."

She glares at me as if I said the wrong thing. "Who do you think you are, some Prince fucking Charming swooping in with heroics? I don't need your saving."

Whoa. I blink at her, shocked by her sudden anger.

I'm about to retort with a "What?!" but Amber is peering through the window and screeching.

"Holy fuck!" she yells. "There are things living in it!"

We all gasp and immediately leap backward away from Mr. Orange. Not one of my finer moments.

"Okay, hold on," I say, manning up. I quickly run along the forest edge and pick up a long stick. There are a few other cars in the lot that also have their windows smashed, victims of hooligans, but there's no one else around to see this.

I edge back to the bus and try to look through the part of the window that Amber was at.

She wasn't wrong. I can see small fuzzy bodies moving along the floor of the van and on the front seats.

"I've got this," I tell the girls and grip the stick harder. I motion for Gemma to give me the keys. She throws them to me and I catch them in one hand. I creep my way over to the driver's side. There's a lot of condensation and fog inside the windows so I can't see much except the shadows of something moving inside.

I quickly go over what Gemma had told me, that there were no big predators in New Zealand. Still, I'm being overly cautious as I unlock the door. I take in a deep breath or two, then fling it open.

All I see next are claws coming at my face and a whoosh of wings. I duck and whack the air with my stick but it doesn't hit anything but empty space.

Beside me a kea parrot lands gracefully with a few beats of its red and green wings and stares at me, as if to say, *Why do you have a stick and why are you breaking into my newfound sanctuary?*

I straighten up and look back into the bus. There are at least three other parrots inside, perched on the back of seats and the steering wheel.

Gemma and Amber squeal girlish sounds that I may have made when the parrot flew at me. They come to stand behind me.

"Jesus," Gemma swears, holding on to my arm, and for that moment I don't regret my decision to become the parrot fighter. "Keas."

"Wow," Amber says breathlessly. "Why would parrots break into our car? Unless . . ." she looks at me with quizzical eyes. "Unless instead of *Planet of the Apes* . . ."

"Amber," I say, holding my palm out to her. "Stop."

". . . this has become *Planet of the Parrots*," she finishes.

I throw my head back and sigh and it takes us a good ten minutes of poking them with the stick and waving our arms around like monkeys to make sure every parrot is out of the bus.

Miraculously there doesn't seem to be much stolen. Amber is missing two bottles of Waiheke Island wine she picked up in Auckland and Gemma can't find her iPod, which is another financial blow for her, but everything else, including her uncle's stash of seventies porn, remains in the van.

Naturally, both the thieves and the parrots have left a colossal mess but it's getting dark and we need to camp somewhere. We throw towels over our seats and head out along the road, me in the back and the girls in the front. The wind is cold as it whips in through the back window and the moon is out when we finally pull into our next stop, Arrowtown.

We find a holiday park that has a spot for us and it's not long before we're all getting settled for bed. Naturally, I let Amber and Gemma have the foldout below while I take the bunk. The last few times I've slept up here I haven't fallen to my death, and besides, it's the only place in the bus that the pooping parrots didn't have access to.

I don't tell them that, of course.

The next morning there's dew covering the tarp above my head and everything feels slightly damp, but it's warm compared to the last few nights out in the bush. I wake up before the girls and try to land in the bus below without waking them. I make good long use of the showers at the campsite. It's the first shower for days—and it's a hot one—and I stay in it as long as possible, even though it means pumping more twenty-cent coins into the machine.

By the time I emerge, my skin is pink and red like a newborn but I don't care. I feel like I've washed all the grime and controversy of the last few days off of me.

Thankfully, all the beauty stays with me. The sunset and sunrise over Key Summit. Gemma's honest words. The look on her face while she took in the world, so new to her. The feel of her between my arms.

I want her so badly and it's more than I can bear. Her sudden frost keeps me back and I'm constantly misreading her looks and her words, wanting to believe that she feels something for me but so afraid that it's all in my imagination. It was almost like she flirted more with me when she was with Nick, and now that she's not, I'm nothing more than some guy paying for petrol.

After a quick breakfast, we work our way out of tiny, quaint Arrowtown and onto a narrow winding road that's supposed to lead us from here to Christchurch. Before the Routeburn Track, I'd contacted Tibald to see where he was and it seemed like Christchurch was the only place where our paths would intersect.

In our original plans, we were supposed to stop overnight at a bed-and-breakfast in a town called Twizel and go on a Lord of the Rings Tour, which my inner geek was flipping out over, but now with Nick gone, Gemma seems hellbent on getting us to decent civilization.

She drives Mr. Orange as if her life depends on it, and even when we stop at Lindis Pass to take pictures of the yellow flowers dotted on rolling suede brown hills, she seems like a woman on a mission. None of what we're witnessing seems to be sinking into her brain, and her face remains impassive and dull, as if she's not really here.

The ache she was talking about, well, I'm starting to feel it now. I look at Amber and she doesn't seem to notice that Gemma has gone into autopilot, her own attention focused out the window at the rolling hills of tussock under a saturated blue sky, not on our driver. But mine is, and I just want to beg her to stop driving, to just take a moment and breathe.

Luckily—or unluckily—Mr. Orange decides to do that for us, and it's all thanks to me.

Outside of Twizel there's a turnoff for Mount Cook, the tallest mountain in New Zealand. I get Gemma to turn onto what looks to be a private drive. From where the main road is, it looks like it climbs and snakes its way up a hill, providing spectacular views of the brilliantly blue Lake Pukaki and Mount Cook. I want a view that will knock Gemma's socks off. I want her to feel.

Mr. Orange has gone through a lot and I assume the Shaggin' Wagon can take some more. We're about three minutes up this rough, steep, drive when the bus starts to cough and shake and then comes to a stop.

Then it starts rolling backward.

"Put on the hand brake!" I manage to yell before the back wheels go over the side of the hill and the bus slumps to a stop amid a cloud of dust. Wind whistles in through the open back window.

Gemma slowly turns around and eyes me, her face pinched

and panicked. I hate being the voice of reason. I want to flap my arms and panic, too.

"We're good," I manage to say. "Let's take a look at her."

I get out of the bus and come over to Gemma, opening her door. Once again she's clad in shorts and I have a hard time concentrating on the bus instead of her smooth, fine legs, but I manage. Either Mr. Orange has run out of gas way before his time or he's overheating.

One look at the engine tells me that it's not the problem.

We've run out of gas and in the worst place possible.

Gemma looks absolutely embarrassed, and though she should be, I also can't blame her. Considering everything that's been going on with her, I should have been the one driving, not her. She needed to sit back and pull herself together. Or let herself unravel. I would be fine with either one.

"I'm such an idiot," she moans, her head pressed against the steering wheel.

I place my hand on her back and rub. She flinches at first but I try not to take offense. I keep doing it, persistently, and eventually she relaxes into me. She's saying more than she realizes; I just wish she'd let her body call all the shots.

"It's just petrol," I tell her, remembering to use the proper term. "I'm sure there's someone just up the road who will give us some. People tend to understand this shit out in the country. I bet whoever lives here gets people like us once a week, dumbasses like me who think it's a great idea to come up here and take pictures."

Naturally, it's up to the dumbass to journey up the rest of the steep, winding drive to find out if anyone actually lives up here. Gemma and Amber stay behind, keeping each other company, and I start the climb, hoping I don't run into some backward sheep farmer.

Of course, that's exactly who I run into.

I get to the top of the crest, my body covered in sweat, when I see a small, ramshackle farmhouse amid rolling fenced pastures as far as the eye can see.

There's a man between it and me, holding a shotgun, a border collie at his side, staring up at him as if waiting for directions. *Do I kill the punk or not, master?*

"Uh, hi," I say loudly, raising my arm in a wave. "We had a bit of car trouble down the road."

The man stares at me. He's wearing a leather coat over dirty jeans and a thick wool sweater, a cowboy hat on his head. His face is smudged with oil or something. He couldn't look more stereotypical if he tried.

Somewhere in the distance, among the waving tussock, a sheep baahs.

I feel like I've wandered into an episode of *Flight of the Conchords* and someone is having a laugh at my expense.

I continue, slightly unnerved. "It's nothing major, we just ran out of gas—sorry, petrol. We're wondering if you have a jerry can and any petrol to spare, or maybe you could give us a ride into the nearest town?"

"Nearest town is Glentanner," the man says, totally monotone. "Nearest petrol is Twizel. They're both out of my way."

"Okay," I say, trying not to sound panicky. Guess I'll be going back down to the bottom of the hill and trying to hitch-hike or something. "Thanks anyway."

I turn around and he calls out, "What will you give me?"

I stop and look at him. "Sorry, what?"

He just nods. "I said, what will you give me for the petrol. I have a jerry can in the shed if you'd like but petrol is expensive out here."

"Oh, sure," I say quickly and bring out my wallet from my jeans. "Um, I have some coins," I say, rifling through it.

The last cash I took out was in Wanaka, which reminds me that I owe Gemma a lot of money. "I have eighty cents," I say pathetically. "But the girls probably have a load of cash."

All right, now I'm just saying all the wrong stuff.

He raises his brow. "The girls?"

"My friends, they're back at Mr. Orange, waiting for me."

I can tell he wants to ask what Mr. Orange is but he only nods stiffly before turning and walking away. I wait there for at least five minutes as he disappears behind his house, debating whether to just give up and head back to the bus or stand there like an idiot and hope he comes back out.

My patience and/or stupidity pays off and he eventually emerges carrying a small red can of petrol. I do an inner whoop of joy in my head and then start walking back along the road just before he reaches me so I don't have to do the awkward walk with a burly, silent sheep farmer.

The views are amazing on the way down, though, just as I thought, with the powder blue of Lake Pukaki stretching out to the bare suede hills of the east and up to the jagged white peaks of Mount Cook to the north. I want to stop and take a picture to paint later but I don't dare with this man at my heels.

When we get back to Mr. Orange, Gemma and Amber are waiting, leaning against the side of the bus, facing the views and the sun. Once they see Mr. Friendly coming, they straighten to attention.

"Girls," I say, "this kind gentleman has agreed to help us out with some petrol. Do either of you have some cash we can give him?"

The two of them start frantically digging. Amber pulls out a five-dollar bill and a bunch of lint and candy wrappers from her purse. Gemma frowns, flipping through her wallet.

"I just have my credit cards and my bank card," Gemma says, her voice shaking slightly. "I spent my last bills this morning."

I look at Mr. Friendly hopefully. "Will five bucks do?"

He gives me a level gaze. So does his dog. "It's worth more than that. What else ya got?"

Oh boy. "Well, you see," I say, scratching the back of my neck, "we were broken into the other day and they stole everything valuable."

The farmer walks over to the bus and peers inside the window. "Sure is a nice specimen, though you should know better than to try and take her up roads like this." Then he pauses. "What's that?"

I join him by his side. He smells like strong cigarettes. I follow his gaze to the stack of seventies porn on the backseat. I had been rifling through it earlier, comparing the bushes of 1977 to 1979.

"Uh, really old *Penthouse* and such?"

He grunts. "All right. I'll take it."

"Say what?" I glance at Gemma and Amber huddling by the end of the bus.

"Petrol for the nudie mags. Fair trade. Keep your five dollars."

"Really?" I ask, feeling momentarily torn up about it. "You sure you want those?"

"Oh, just give him my uncle's porn stash, Josh," Gemma hisses.

I do as she says, bringing them out of the bus and placing it in Mr. Friendly's arms. "Do you want some Pink Floyd tapes to go with it?"

He scrunches up his face, the first emotion I've seen from him, and passes me the jerry can, before walking back up the hill, the dog trotting after him.

"Thank you!" I call after him. I look at Gemma who is shaking her head, her brows pinched in worry as she pushes past me to the driver's side.

"Hey," I say, touching her arm for her to stop. "I'll drive. You just relax."

"I'm fine," she says, lying once again.

So I let her be, knowing if I insist, she'll snap. She seems very close to losing it. I go and pour the can of petrol into the bus and Amber gets in the backseat, making sure I'm up in the front beside Gemma.

She starts the car and slides *The Wall* into the cassette player, as if to punish me for trying to sell the tapes to Mr. Friendly.

"Hey You" starts to play and my mind is focusing on the lyrics, applying them to Gemma. Is she feeling so desolate, alone, wanting to give in without a fight? It's a tumultuous, heady song and it takes us down the steep dirt road, to the paved one that runs along Lake Pukaki. To my surprise she takes a right, heading back the way we came from Twizel.

"Aren't we going to Mount Cook?" I ask.

She shakes her head. "Lake Tekapo."

I shrug, but I'm actually relieved that we're heading back toward civilization. The whole running out of petrol and trading porn with a sheep farmer has put me in a weird mood, and tensions in the bus are running high, crisscrossing like threads in danger of snapping.

"What's in Lake Tekapo?" I ask, trying to get her to talk, to open up. She's slipped her sunnies on her eyes so I can't try and read them.

"A very blue, very cold lake," is her simple answer.

I eye Amber in the rearview mirror and she gives me a worried look in exchange. We're just along for the ride.

We motor away from the mountains and toward the

cloud-filtered sunshine and rolling brown hills of the east. Lake Tekapo seems to be a popular stop, and as we get closer I can see why. The lake is even bluer than Pukaki was and the town along the banks is a pleasing slice of civilization.

But we don't stop there like I thought we would. Gemma keeps driving until we come to a turnoff and then she's gunning it toward the lake. On one side of us the road curves along pine trees and holiday homes; on the other there is a stream and a picturesque stone church surrounded by snap-happy tour bus groups.

At a gravel lot at the very end, not far from the shore, she angrily slams Mr. Orange into park and jumps out of the bus. Instinctively I do the same, jumping out after her.

As I stand there watching, I know the memory is being ingrained into my head. The van is still running and "Comfortably Numb" is blaring from the speakers as Gemma strips down to her underwear and runs to the edge of the lake. She's barefoot and she doesn't even slip on the rocks as she goes. She's running from something, she's running to something. The water will be ice cold.

It's just what she wants. She wants to be numb.

I've listened to this album enough damn times now to know that "Run Like Hell" will play soon. So I do. I run like hell toward her. I leave Amber in the back of Mr. Orange, puttering on Lake Tekapo's shore, and I'm sprinting toward the water, unwilling to let her out of my sight.

She's already splashing into the water, like a mermaid returning to a kingdom of blue milk. If the cold is shocking her, she doesn't show it, it doesn't slow her down. The lake splashes around her in Technicolor brilliance, her darkly tanned skin shimmering from the reflection.

In seconds she is diving under and I hold my breath as my legs and blood pump me forward. I'm bizarrely, acutely aware that she might not come up again. I think about what she told me, huddled in my rain jacket. *I think I ache for things I may never get. I long for purpose, for life and yet sometimes I think I'm too afraid to live.*

My fear is in *not* living.

We need to meet in the middle.

So I go into the lake after her. I'm stripped down to my boxers and T-shirt, my dusty jeans and flip-flops discarded somewhere between me and the bus, in a patch of purple and pink foxgloves.

It's so cold I think I'm going to die. My lips open to yell, "Fuck me!" but my mouth is more intent on chattering my teeth together. Each step stabs stones into the soles of my feet and jagged knives of ice water into my legs until the feeling—all feeling—subsides.

I'm breathless, surrounded by ice blue, a color I've created myself when I've touched too much eggshell into too little cerulean. The shores are granite, a soft warm gray, peppered by the unimaginable greens and pinks of foxglove and whatever plants happen to spring up in this country. I'm swimming in a painting, numb, and I'm going for her, the bronze mermaid who wants to swim forever.

But she's not mythical. She's very real. It seems to take forever and eventually she breaks the surface, shrieking out in surprise and agony from the cold. It doesn't numb her after all.

Perhaps in this case, the number you are, the closer you are to death.

Though she swam for a while under, it doesn't take me long to catch up with her. I was an avid swimmer for years.

"What the hell?" I say to her between chattering teeth, spitting out lake water.

She stares at me, wide-eyed, her head above the surface as she treads water. Her wet, dark hair is slicked back from her forehead, an inky wave between her shoulders, her cheek-bones highlighted by sun and water.

"I told you I wanted to come here," she says, as if suddenly abandoning your van and stripping to your underwear in public is the norm.

I can't help but smile at how blasé she tries to be about it. "A little warning would be nice."

"Don't worry about me, Josh," she says.

I pause because something in my heart has swelled. "But I do."

Oh god, how I fucking ever.

She holds my gaze and my fingers itch to reach through the water and touch her. A few days ago I wouldn't have, not in public like this. But I want to see just how numb she is.

My hand glides forward, sluicing through the water in slow motion until it rests on her light and silky waist.

She stares at me, her eyes glowing white against her brown irises, and her brows thread together in contemplation, as if she's trying to unravel me, uncover some truth. I know something is bothering her and I know it's about me more than anything else. It should be a good thing that it bothers her because it means she cares.

I want to tell her that she's all I've ever wanted. I want to show her.

She relaxes into my touch for one sweet moment of victory before she slowly ducks her head under the water. I'm not sure what she's doing so I take in a breath and submerge my head.

The cold shocks my face and when I open my eyes under water they seem to immediately freeze. Gemma is a hazy vision of pale blue, her hair swirling around her. She is so beautiful it makes my chest ache more than the cold does.

Her eyes hold mine and I see that yearning in them again. She reaches forward, grabbing my face, and pulls my head toward her. She kisses me, full on the lips. It's so warm against the cold and I'm afraid I'm about to drown from happiness. I want this and I want more than this.

I don't know how long the kiss lasts—we seem to float through time and space—but our bodies foolishly decide oxygen is equally as important. She breaks away and I am left sucking in ice water before I break through the surface.

I gasp in the dry air, fingers touching my lips as if I can't believe it, but she's back to the way she was before. Impassive. Immovable. Numb.

"We should go back before Amber freaks out," she says in a brisk tone, and in that moment I wish to be as numb as she is.

We swim back to shore and Amber comes running out of the van with towels for us. I know they're the same towels that we put down to cover the parrot poo, but I'm too cold to care.

We run out into them and huddle together briefly, Amber yelling at us for being crazy, then head back into Mr. Orange. We get changed in the back, no one caring about nudity at this point, even though I can feel the girls' eyes on my body as I strip, then we head into town to get a bowl of hot soup and coffee.

Gemma seems to brighten up a bit after that "swim" but I'm watching her closely and I don't think it will last.

She's too comfortable being numb.

Chapter Fourteen

JOSH

"Looks like you have to answer that age-old question, my friend," Tibald says as he raises his beer. "Can I sleep with a woman that I deem to be fucking crazy?"

I give him a steady look. "Gemma isn't *crazy*."

"Maybe not fucking crazy, but she's not normal. Then again, neither are most girls and we sleep with them anyway. Some even marry them." He finishes his thought with a shrug and a long drink of beer.

Pink Floyd's "Breathe" comes on the speakers and I hunch over, groaning into my Speights ale. No matter where I go, I can't escape this fucking band.

He pats me on the back. "But at least this fellow, Nick the Dick, is out of the picture."

"Yeah but it doesn't change anything," I mumble.

Tibald and I are sitting in the Dux Live bar in Christchurch, the one place we've been able to meet up. Schnell and Michael are off at some fancy nightclub and Gemma and Amber are off doing their own girly thing. I needed a break from all the tension and was more than happy when they agreed to split for the night.

"Change is relative," Tibald says. "Use your balls and act on it."

I roll my eyes. "Tell me, Tibald, are you always spewing advice to people or do you ever get a taste of your own medicine?"

When his features go stony and grave, I feel like I've said the wrong thing.

"I did love someone," he said, his voice flinty. "I was engaged to her. But she left me for my brother."

I grimace. "Oh, dude, I'm sorry. I didn't mean anything by it."

He exhales sharply out of his nose, then shakes his head and smiles. "It's all right. It was a few years ago. It got me in the best shape of my life, so I can't regret everything. Everything that happens, I believe, leads us where we need to be." He finishes his beer and starts toying with the Speights coaster. "I know that sounds cheesy but whatever. It's my belief and so it's true." He fixes his eye on me. "What do you believe, Joshua?"

It's weird to hear my name like that. It reminds me of my mom. It reminds me that I haven't talked to her since I left home. I could be a better son, that's what I believe. A better brother, too. I could be better, full stop.

"I believe," I say slowly, "that everyone you meet leaves an imprint on you. By the end of your life, that imprint has shaped who you are and what life you've lived. So, I guess it's kind of the same thing."

"We're getting awfully deep for a couple of blokes, don't you think?" he asks with a smile.

"Blokes? You're really turning into a Kiwi now."

"So are you, bro. It suits you, makes you sound less like a dumb Canadian." He places the empty bottle of beer on the table and spins it around. "Look, I figure I'm only a few years older than you and it's not my place to tell you how to live your life or even prepare for it. But I will say this . . . if you find that person who makes you feel like everything going forward is worth living, hold on to her."

"Is that what you had?" I ask.

"Yes. It was. And I don't regret a moment of it, because in the end it was mine and she could never take what I felt away from me. I could turn to anger, and I did, but I had to admit to myself that I loved her because she was worth loving, no matter what happened."

"And your brother?"

He shrugs. "Brothers are brothers. It's blood. But it doesn't mean anything beyond that. Just because I'm bound to him, forged by our parents, doesn't mean I owe him anything more than a polite smile at family gatherings. My brother is dead to me and I'm sure I'm dead to him, otherwise he never would have slept with her. But that's the difference that people don't get about family. They think it's their right to take them for granted when it's not. I didn't choose him, or my parents, and they didn't choose me. Choice, in the end, is freedom and freedom is everything in life."

I'm a bit shocked at Tibald's revelation. From what I knew about him before, he was the fun-loving jokester. But there's a serious side to him that I didn't know about. He had been good at hiding it, especially around Schnell and Michael, but around me now, it's a different story.

I have to wonder about Gemma. What was she hiding from me, Amber, Nick, everyone around her? What she said to me on Key Summit still rang through my ears. That night she was afraid and open and spilling her confessions to me. I took them in like water for a dying man. She was broken and bruised and aching for something she didn't know.

I had my theories. Selfishly, egotistically, I hoped I could be the one to cure her ache, to make her feel fulfilled. But maybe it would take more than that; maybe she was harboring lost dreams. I saw it a lot, when I used to work at the restaurant. I would take my breaks and eat my hot fudge brownies out on the dining floor and watch the people around me. There were so many of them, young and old, alone and sad, eating to fill the void, being out in the open just to get the comfort of a polite server. It broke my heart, time and time again, to see these lost and lonely people. They seemed to have no one, and if they had someone, they seemed to have nothing to keep their days going. No passion, no dreams. Just a life in the wake of what could have been, discarded attempts at trying to live better.

I was no better. I had no one either, no life, no motives. But I had passion, even if it had to be excavated from me. I had a passion for the arts and the moments that made me love life. The buried passion was what got me going from day to day until my sister fucked off to Spain to live with some man she barely knew.

And that's when I knew I was missing out. I wasn't living at all. I was barely any better than the lost souls I saw at work, hiding their sorrows with beer and greasy burgers. So I applied to school, hoping to at least get that ball rolling, and then I met Gemma that fateful, drunken, horny night, and everything seemed to click, click, click into place, like a key turning a lock.

Now I'm here, transient, unsure of where the door leads and where I'm going next.

"Sorry to bum you out," Tibald says. "I think I like smiling, stupid Josh a lot better."

I glare at him. "You should like all of Josh."

He shrugs, grinning. "I'll leave that to Gemma."

"Right," I say despondently.

"You got to her once before," he points out. "You can do it again."

"By being a forward, cocky, horny-as-hell animal?"

"Whatever works."

I clink my pint of beer against his and say, "Then here's to whatever works."

We drink ours down, fast, and order another.

———•———

The amount of beer I've consumed in New Zealand has been pretty ridiculous. People always say that Canadians are the beer drinkers of the world—as in we drink a lot of it and all the time—but I think the Kiwis have us in a headlock over that one.

The next morning I wake up in a six-bunk dorm that seems to stretch on forever. There's someone snoring in the bunk beneath mine and across the room, Gemma and Amber are just getting out of theirs. Gemma opted for a cheap hostel in Christchurch since we'll be spending a few days at a nice one on the Banks Peninsula.

You get what you pay for. This place has weird stains on the carpet, bathroom doors that don't lock properly and they charge you five dollars to use the Internet for ten minutes. And if I hadn't come home drunk last night after being with Tibald and passed out right away, I would have been up all night listening to the backpacker bus group whoop it up in the shoddy communal lounge.

Needless to say, we're all dressed and packed in record time and piling into Mr. Orange, with Amber worried she's caught some contagious disease from the bed. Our trip to the Banks Peninsula is supposed to be a short one but I volunteer to drive anyway.

Gemma declines, telling me it's not an easy drive, and thanks to the remnants of a hangover, I'm okay with that.

She wasn't kidding. The peninsula used to be a volcano, and now it's this massive, tall lump of land jutting out into the ocean, like a round thumb. The mountains in the middle are high, with rolling brown and green hills dotted with sheep and pockets of forest. The road winds back and forth, switchback after switchback, past deep valleys along the edge of the original crater. Occasionally you can see fingers of rich, jeweled blue as different harbors reach inland.

Mr. Orange growls and purrs like an angry cat as it motors up the hills and around the bends, but somehow we make it all the way to a place called Le Bons Bay and a backpacker's hostel sitting at the crest of a long, wide valley.

After last night, I am more than happy to just spend the night in the bus, but I change my mind as Gemma leads us to the big red farmhouse and we're introduced to the owners. They ask if we'd like to have dinner with them and the rest of the backpackers. I get this feeling that we're at some weird communal hippie resort but then Gemma explains that this is what they're known for. The wife is a cook and they do fabulous homemade meals. There's just enough lamb for us to join them tonight, and tomorrow they're doing fresh pasta.

We can't say no to that—besides, we only have a little bit of food to last us for the next few days and it's a long drive to the French-settled town of Akaroa to get groceries. They also ask if we'd be interested in a wildlife-viewing boat trip tomorrow, weather permitting. They have a small boat they can take about six guests on.

Amber shakes her head no, looking a little green at the thought. "I'm good."

But the cost is reasonable and I don't want to miss out. I look at Gemma. "Dare you to come with me."

She gives me a look. "Oh, really."

"We could see dolphins, your favorite."

That's when the owner, Hamish, speaks up, his eyes volleying between us. "Actually, we probably will see dolphins. Hector's dolphins, the smallest and most rare species in New Zealand."

"Oh, well, Gemma here says she's seen them all. She's a bit of a dolphin hipster."

She rolls her eyes. "Fine, I'll go."

"All right," Hamish says. "So far you guys are the only ones signed up." He smiles, as if he knew that would make us feel uncomfortable.

Little does he know, it doesn't make me uncomfortable at all. I can't wait to be alone with her. It's she who looks a bit out of sorts at the thought, but at this point that doesn't surprise me.

Instead of staying in the red farmhouse with the other backpackers, Gemma has secured us a cabin at the edge of their property. It's rustic, just a wood fireplace, a small table and chairs, a full bed downstairs, and a full mattress in the loft above, accessible only by ladder. But it has a wide porch out front with sweeping views of the valley and the bay in the distance.

I take the bed in the loft because Amber said it looked "creepy" and we crack open a bottle of wine on the porch, sipping out of mugs, staring at the sun-drenched hills and killing time before dinner is served.

I can't help but grin. "This ain't a bad life, is it, girls?"

"Hell no," says Amber, raising her mug to the view. "I could stay here forever. Literally, just keep feeding me wine and I'll keep sitting here."

Gemma doesn't say anything but she briefly catches my eye and offers me a small smile. It's not a lot, but it's something.

Naturally I want more. I'm grateful that Amber bowed out of the boat trip. I need to be alone with Gemma again.

I sigh inwardly and stare out at the endless view. It's so strange to think that we're here, one person from San Jose, one from Vancouver, one from Auckland, and we're together, sitting in a valley at the edge of the world. There's something about being on New Zealand's east coast that I find a bit unnerving. It isn't until after we're done with the fabulous lamb meal in the farmhouse that I identify the cause.

With working flashlights this time, we make our way back to the cabin in the pitch dark and sit back down on the porch to finish off the rest of the wine.

Far off in the distance I see lights scattered near where the horizon line should be. They glow brightly in the black, artificial against the stars above.

"What are those?" I ask no one in particular. The crickets are so loud and intrusive here that I keep my voice to a hush, afraid to interrupt them.

"I think they're prawn- or crab-fishing boats," Gemma answers, her tone matching mine.

I stare at them for a few moments. It's hard not to. They're so far away and yet the brightest spots in all the dark. It's frightening. The desolation feels real.

"What's out there?" I ask.

Gemma pauses, seeming to think. "Antarctica."

I shudder. "That's it? Beyond those boats is Antarctica?"

"Maybe the Chatham Islands or something in between. I don't know. But they're small."

I swallow uneasily, feeling like I'm about to slip off the edge of the world. "God, this is a lonely place."

I can feel their eyes as their heads swivel in the dark toward me.

"What do you mean?" Gemma asks.

"Can't you feel it?" I ask, knowing I can't be the only one. "There's nothing out there, nothing at all. Even at home, if I make it to Vancouver Island and stare across the Pacific, I know Japan and Asia and Russia are out there. Civilization. Here . . . it's just waves of nothing and then a giant, uninhabited continent of ice. It makes you feel . . . alone. Like the earth could swallow you whole right here and no one would notice."

We lapse into silence for a moment.

"It *is* kind of creepy," Amber concedes.

"I like it," Gemma says simply.

But how could she? I wonder about the whole country, these slivers of islands balancing at the edge of nothing, and if everyone thinks they're this close to being lost.

It doesn't help that I'm sleeping on the loft that night.

I have dream upon dream about falling.

I *am* falling.

Chapter Fifteen

GEMMA

I'm still not used to waking up in a different place each day. As soon as I open my eyes, it takes me a moment for my world to realign. Then, as I remember where I am and shrug off the blissful abyss of sleep, I have to wrestle with my crap reality.

Before all the shit went down with Nick, I was battling my growing feelings for Josh. Now, I'm still doing that and trying to figure out what I'm going to do with my life. It's hard to adopt the same attitude as Josh and Amber. They weren't just dealt a crap hand. They're on vacation. I'm trying to put one foot in front of the other and I'm stumbling with each step I take.

I want to reach out to Josh so badly. I want to lean into him, feel his arms around me, hear those words he once whispered, that he understands, that he gets me. But I'm too much in my head, too far down the spiral, and I know that when our time is up together, he will be gone and I'll still be trying to deal.

Time is flying, swooping past me, and I have no idea where I'm going to end up in the end.

Amber turns over under the covers, her butt bumping into my hip. I sigh and stare up at the ceiling, at where Josh should be sleeping on the loft above my head. I think about getting out of bed, quietly, and climbing the ladder to him.

What would he say? Would he kick me out of his bed or welcome me with open arms? Would he be wishing I was Amber, or someone else, someone who smiled more than smirked, who took in the world eagerly, like he did?

Would he take away the pain, the dull ache in my chest? For that night on Key Summit, he at least took the emptiness in his hands and held it. He shouldered it. Sometimes I think he keeps wanting to shoulder it.

But my thoughts can't be trusted. My mind keeps thinking about him and Amber and how he could so easily put her aside. I know that Amber was really starting to like him. However he might've felt about her then, Josh is indifferent now.

How do I know that he won't be that way with me? When I get back to Auckland, I have to find a job and I have no idea where I'm going to start, considering the one steady job I had for the few years is gone and my best reference is gone with it. Josh won't be there to shoulder anything for me—why should I ask him to start now?

I sigh more loudly than I meant to, and I hear the wooden boards of the loft creak. Josh stirs and I see his long, lean legs coming down the ladder. I watch—unwatched myself—as his boxer briefs come into view, a hint of morning wood snug inside. Then his washboard abs and his tattoos. I want to ask him about them and wonder if we'll ever have the time. Next is his firm chest, the black ink snaking over him. Then his arms, wide shoulders, kissable neck.

Then it's his face, and I mean to look away before I see it, but I'm too slow, caught up in morning haze, and I'm staring into his eyes. He smiles with them, cocky but warm. I don't know if I've ever seen him look at me so fondly.

It unnerves me. A ghost of a smile traces my lips and I look away.

"Good morning," I say softly, not wanting to wake Amber. Josh and I are the only ones going somewhere today; she deserves to sleep in.

"Morning," he says. "Want to take a shower with me?"

I raise my brows to the heavens.

He grins. "I mean, come with me to the showers. We don't have to shower together. Unless you'd like to."

I give him the look, the one that says I'm so not impressed, even though I secretly am.

"Suit yourself," he says and grabs a towel and clothes out of his backpack. It reminds me that I should do laundry tonight.

Then he's gone and I realize that I've turned into a mute statue around him. No wonder he's often approaching me like I'm a wild animal about to flee.

It's a gorgeous, sunny morning with the valley lightening from dark green to light green, bit by bit by bit. I stand on the porch, watching it all unfold, and once again I feel that strange pinch of envy about being unable to re-create this in the way I want to, and the fact that Josh can.

I close my eyes to it and wait a few minutes, then head out on the path after the showers. There are two in a little building between the cottages and the main house, and he's waiting outside of them, talking to some girl with long willowy legs and no hips. She's got flawless white skin—no cellulite on this chick—and blond hair braided down her back. She's making him laugh and I'm struck, like a slap in the face, by how ridiculously handsome he is.

That envy strikes again. Not that I can't make him laugh, because I can and I have and nothing sounded better to my ears than hearing his rich laughter and seeing that smart-ass twinkle in his eyes, but that this girl could probably sleep with him and not understand how fucking lucky she is, while I'm too fucked up to even let it happen again.

He doesn't even notice as I walk past him, and I'm hoping there's a shower free inside the farmhouse. There isn't so I turn around, ready to go back. I wait though, paused in the doorway of the house, watching the showers on the ridge. One opens up and it's the one that the blond chick is waiting at.

To my horror and surprise, she gestures to it and to Josh. And not in the, *Hey you take it instead of me*, but in the, *Let's shower together and "conserve water"* kind of way. I hold my breath, watching what he's going to do. She's fucking hot, way hotter than me, and thin in that celebrity kind of way that I could never be. I'm either curvy with muscles or I'm a blimp.

He smiles at her and I'm sure that beautiful grin of his is saying, *Yeah, why not*, and my mind is flooded with the image of them naked in there together, her on her knees, putting his big cock in her mouth. It both turns me on and disgusts me and makes me feel afraid that I was nothing more than that to him.

But he waves at her dismissively, like, *Thanks but no thanks.* She seems taken aback and then starts pouting but he only laughs and wiggles his fingers at her. *Bye-bye.*

She shrugs, like it was no big deal being rejected by the tall, dark, and handsome guy covered in tats, and goes inside. Maybe she hides it well. Maybe she's got enough armor around her that it doesn't hurt at all.

That's what I need, what I want. That kind of armor. The kind that lets me go into battle and walk out with my heart still intact.

I'm impressed, beyond impressed, that he turned her down, but it doesn't stop the fear. In fact, it makes it worse. Because Josh is a good guy, the best guy, but he's still just a visitor in my life. That's all he will be, all he can be.

I suck in my breath, needing to get a grip. I need to see a shrink again, like I did after the accident. I'm running out of time and may be throwing away the next few weeks out of fear of getting hurt. Everything has been horrible and lovely these past few weeks, alternating every other day at times, occurring simultaneously on others. But I know, I know, that if I followed my instincts, my hormones, my body, that the rest of the time could be nothing but orgasms and strong arms and the support of someone who truly understands me.

I hate that I've become so afraid.

I hear the door open behind me and see someone emerge from the indoor showers. I quickly snap it up before anyone else can. When I emerge, less than ten minutes later, utterly conscious of other people waiting for it, I feel better.

An hour later Josh and I are gathered in the parking lot of the backpackers and waiting for the owner, Hamish, to show his face, as well as any other people.

But when Hamish appears, it's apparent that Josh and I are the only ones going. My pulse quickens in my wrist, excited, scared, but also relieved for some reason. There's really no one I'd want to experience this with more than him. There's no one I'd want to experience anything with more than him.

"So I'll meet you at the bottom of the hill," Hamish says.

"Uh, what?" Josh responds for the both of us.

"I have to get the tractor and then get the boat," Hamish says as if he has to say this every day, which I'm sure he does. "Unless you want to wait up here."

I look at Josh. He's trying to put together the words *tractor* and *boat* and they aren't making much sense.

I put my hand on his shoulder and give him an affectionate squeeze. He stares down at me in shock and then at my hand. I suppose I haven't been very touchy-feely lately.

"It's a Kiwi thing," I say. "There's no dock."

He looks like his mind has been blown but he manages to shrug. "All right, so just walk down the hill . . . how far?"

Hamish laughs. "When your feet get wet, you've gone too far."

Josh gives me a look and I can't help but laugh, too. "Come on, you Canadian," I tell him, pushing him forward onto the gravel road that winds down the hill.

"You're awfully violent this morning," Josh says. "Should I be worried?"

"You should always be worried," I say, and I try to ignore the pang of guilt that comes right after. Yesterday I ran into Lake Tekapo wanting to feel numb from head to toe, hoping to quell my raging heart. I ended up kissing him again. I can still taste him on my lips.

"Don't worry about me, Josh," I had said.

"But I do," he answered. And the look in his eyes, it was the same as this morning, full of warmth and concern and all the things that might heal me from the inside out.

I turn my attention to the road and start marching down it, my legs pumping briskly. I haven't done anything physical since the Routeburn Track, and even though that was just a few days ago, I feel like I haven't been pushing my body. The funny thing now is I'm not even sure that I'll be continuing my crazy fitness schedule. I'll never stop being active—I definitely picked up that habit during my physio training after the accident—but I won't have to beat myself up over missing a workout here and there.

"What are you thinking about?" Josh asks, his long legs easily keeping up my fast pace.

"Why are you asking?"

"You have that look on your face."

I narrow my eyes at him. "What look?"

"The one that says you're so far gone inside your head that you can't even come out to play."

I stare at him for a few strides and he stares right back. He can see me at times like this and I hate it.

I kick at a stone and watch it go tumbling down the road. "It's nothing."

"It's always nothing and it's always something," he murmurs but doesn't say anything else.

When we turn a corner, the blue bay of Le Bons comes into view and the sight of that endless ocean, the one that makes Josh feel so alone, spurs something in me.

"Fine," I say carefully. "I was just thinking I haven't worked out in a while."

He scoffs incredulously. "We were just hiking for like four days straight. What the hell? That has to count for something."

"It does," I admit. "I'm just used to keeping goals and records and trying to keep on top of stuff."

"But that's your job talking," he says.

I give him a pointed look. "Old job," I remind him.

"Sure. But old or new, it's a job, right? No way to live your life. Is it your passion? I mean, in the way that painting was?"

My heart sinks for a moment. "No. Not at all. It was just something I enjoyed and was good at."

"Lots of people think that's what passion is."

I rub my lips together. "Most people are wrong."

He stares at me and I can't read his face for the life of me. But I also don't want to spend too much time doing so. Soon we're walking across a large expanse of hard, wet sand, out toward a tractor hauling a small metal boat.

"Now that," I say, grabbing Josh's phone out of his pocket and swiping across the screen in order to take a picture, "is a real Kiwi scene." I snap the shot and hand it back to him. "You're welcome."

He takes the phone. "Hold up," he says, coming around the front of me. "If you're going to use my phone to take a picture of a tractor and a boat, I'm going to use it to take a picture of you. *You're* a real Kiwi scene."

I freeze, totally unused to having my picture taken. I know, it's weird in this day and age of selfies and Facebook and Instagram. But the Instagram pics I take are usually of Auckland scenery or healthy meals I made, not of myself.

"Smile, weirdo," Josh says.

My frown deepens and that's when he takes the picture. He glances at the screen and shrugs. "Well, at least it's accurate," he says before shoving it back into his pocket. "Shall we see a man about a tractor and a boat?"

I make a humorous grunting sound and follow him to the water's edge where Hamish is backing up the tractor.

"Need help?" I yell at him.

He shakes his head and keeps backing up until he slams on the tractor brakes and the whole boat goes sliding backward off the trailer and into the water where it lands with a splashy thud.

Hamish hops off the tractor and gestures to the boat with one arm. "All right, everyone in!"

Though I've known not to expect a dock in places like this, I also wasn't thinking about having to wade through water. I take off my jandals and hold them in one hand, glad I'm wearing shorts as usual.

Josh, on the other hand, is wearing jeans and his skater shoes. He takes the shoes off and rolls up his jeans to the knees.

"You look like Tom Sawyer," I tell him.

"I love Rush," Hamish says, hopping on the boat and flipping through the radio channels, as if he expects to find the band and song playing right this minute. "Canadian band, aye?"

Josh and I walk up to the boat, the water reaching to midcalf on me, before it starts to float away. Josh gets in first and I'm quickly hauled up by him until I'm sitting down on the cold metal seat that stretches across the boat's middle.

Hamish lowers the propeller into the water. He gives us some quick info on the bay and the surrounding environment, though I've heard of most of the birds and sea creatures before. Then he slams on the thrust and we propel forward over ice blue waves that mimic the color of Josh's eyes.

For the most part, the boat ride is a bumpy trip. The Southern Pacific Ocean rushes into the bay and we bounce around, the cold spray coating my bare limbs. At one point the boat really slams down after a sharp swell, as if we're landing on a turtle's back, and Josh's arm goes around my waist, holding me tight and close.

I don't protest. He can hold me all he wants here because I have this feeling that if I even move, I'll be swept overboard. Partly because it's wet and windy and wild out, and partly because it would be ironic. The girl who's trying so hard not to drown would literally drown in the end.

Hamish takes us past the white, ribbed walls of the sea cliffs, and all the cormorants and gannets and other seabirds that lodge there, perched precariously. I wonder how they can even survive living on the absolute edge, in danger with every breath of their lives.

"Here are your dolphins, Gemma," Hamish suddenly says, and the boat guns it further into the open ocean. That thing that Josh feared, that unending emptiness and loneliness, well, I'm finally aware of it, finally fearful. The waves are so big and the boat is so small. We could keep going and going and going until New Zealand was just a dot on the horizon, and we'd be alone forever.

I suck in my breath, trying to calm the panic rising at the bottom of my throat, and Josh instinctively holds me tighter. Maybe he can tell. But he's just letting me know he's there.

Suddenly gray and black bodies are shooting out of the water to the left of us and then to the right of us. The smallest dolphins I've ever seen are propelling themselves out of the water while others are racing us just below the surface, a stunning contrast against the thick, aqua blue of the water. They ride the waves and the current like underwater surfers.

Josh may have been making fun of me for being a dolphin hipster, but I'm sincerely impressed by these tiny, quick guys. I wonder if I should let him know that or keep up my reputation.

"Ah, dolphins," Hamish remarks earnestly. "The llamas of the sea."

Josh and I exchange a look at that.

When we're cold, a bit wet, and utterly enthralled, running on delicious adrenaline, Hamish turns the little boat around and we head back toward the sharp, guano-stained cliffs of Le Bons Bay. After we make our way past the sharp hills and toward the wide beach, he runs the boat into the sand and then ushers us off.

As far as tours go, this one was utterly rudimentary. But that's part of the charm. It was personal—just Josh and I, getting to experience the little Hector's dolphins and that terrible taste of the open sea. It was real to the bone, and I knew because of that it would stick with me for a long time.

With Hamish in the background trying to hook up the boat to the tractor trailer, we make our way across the beach and back toward the road. The sand is extra cold beneath my feet and I'm trying to walk faster because of it.

I look beside me at Josh. He looks pumped, elated, yet when he meets my eyes I see a thread of darkness in him.

"So, what did you think?" I ask.

"You actually care what I think?" he answers. My smile falters for a moment but he's already looking back at the hills in front of us. "I thought that was pretty fucking amazing."

"A bit of a low-budget adventure," I say, feeling as shy and unsure as a girl at her first school dance. What the hell is wrong with my head?

Once we reach the end of the beach, we slip our shoes on. Hamish seems to be taking his time. He's actually abandoned the tractor and boat and is walking to a shed on the opposite side of the beach. It looks like we'll have to walk up the hill without him.

Together.

On our own.

The thought fills me with unwarranted trepidation, and I'm not sure if I'm more scared of myself or of Josh.

We're halfway up the hill, the rugged brown cliffs rising from the road on one side, gently sloping into green fields and trees on the other, when Josh says, "So, the 'us' that happened in Vancouver . . . is that ever going to happen again?"

The question stuns me. It's so blunt. I stop walking, glued to the road, a tiny plume of dust rising up around me. I can only stare at him blankly.

He throws his hands up in the air. "Oh, come on Gemma, it's a valid question."

My heart is starting to hammer against my rib cage and my breathing deepens. But instead of answering honestly, I answer with spite. "I don't know. Is the 'us' that was you and Amber in the movie theater ever going to happen again?"

Josh jerks his head back, blindsided. He blinks, his mouth opening and closing, searching for words, but he has none that can help him right now.

"Amber told me," I quickly fill in, knowing what he's trying to ask. "Said that Nick caught the two of you."

Josh lowers his head until all I can see is his jet-black crown. When he looks back up, he's running his hand down his face, stretching his features, his eyes turned to the sky. "Gemma," he manages to whisper, but he can't go on.

"It's fine," I lie, "but I just find it funny that you have the nerve to bring up the way that we were once when you were with her so recently."

He pinches his eyes shut and shakes his head. "That is *not* fair."

"Life isn't fair," I say plainly and start walking past him.

"No," he growls and grabs my forearm, pulling me to a stop. "You can't walk away after dropping this."

"You're the one who made out with and groped Amber!" I cried out.

"You're the one who was continuously fucking her boyfriend, loud as hell," he retorts and his grip tightens. "And don't tell me he wasn't your boyfriend. Whatever he was, that asshole was in you repeatedly. Do you think that was easy for me to watch? To hear? To be around?"

"Well you certainly had a willing distraction."

"Amber," he seethes, his eyes blazing, "came on to *me*. And I was nice to her about it. And yeah I got hard 'cause I got a fucking dick and she's a nice, pretty girl. But she's not you and I made that very clear to her. No one is you but you, and you don't even seem to know it, let alone believe it matters."

"Because it can't matter."

He grabs my other arm and pulls me to him, my chest

almost pressed against his. "It can matter now. Nick is gone. What's stopping you?"

I try to pull away but his grip is strong, his muscles flexing to keep me in place. "I think I just told you."

"Amber," he says breathlessly. "Is that it? Is that all? Is that the only reason I'm not deep inside you right now?" His gaze is suspicious, roaming all over my face, searching my features for the truth. If he finds it I wish he would tell me, tell me my truth so I can know for myself.

He watches me and I don't think he's found what he's looking for. His frown deepens. "This is ridiculous."

"What?"

"I *like* you, Gemma," he says. His tone is hard and honest. There is something so brave about this moment that I can barely take in what he's saying. "I like you a lot. I've liked you a lot since we first fucked and you got in that cab and I thought I would never see you again. You invaded my dreams. You invaded my art." I raise a brow at that, struck by this revelation. "You invaded my life. I started to think that perhaps you were never real, just something I made up, or a ghost you can't hold on to. Most guys would let it go but I couldn't. I came here hoping I would have the balls to find you, and with some help I did."

He pulls me closer to him so I can feel the heat of his skin between us. His voice lowers and his eyes soften, gazing down at me with a hint of carnality. "I found you. And after everything, I'm still here because of *you*. I could go on a backpackers bus, I could hunker down in a hostel somewhere and be quite content. But I'd never be so happy alone out there as I am by your side, even when we're dealing with the most bogus shit like psycho meathead ex-boyfriends and hooligan parrots and running out of gas on what's probably the set of Rob Zombie's next horror film, I'm still not going anywhere.

I'm here right now because of you, I'm here in this country because of you, and I've been the horniest motherfucker for the last few weeks all because of you. Because of *you*."

I look away from his face, trying to ignore the sincerity in his voice, and stare straight ahead at his chest, absently focusing on the designs of his black T-shirt. He means his words and they're trying to get under my skin, loosen my defenses, melt what little armor I have. I want to believe them so badly but I know if I do I'll have a hard time holding on to the person I need to be. Josh has this uncanny ability to lift my fingers, one by one, from my tight grip on myself, but I'm not letting go yet.

I swallow, feeling shakiness in my limbs. He traces my jaw with his thumb. I don't want to think anymore. I need to distract, deflect.

"Horny?" I repeat. I'm trying to be funny, to make light of everything, but a lustiness comes through my voice, surprising even me. I slowly raise my chin to look up at him, to see if he noticed.

He grins at me for a moment, then his mouth hardens and a dark, fiery cloud comes over his eyes. "You have no fucking idea," he says, his voice low and rough enough to cause the hairs on my arms to spike up and a rush of warmth to flood my core.

Suddenly his hands are on me, one sliding around my waist, tugging me to him, the other going into my hair, making a fist and holding tight. His mouth covers mine, soft and wet and wanting, and all the muscles I worked so hard for in my legs suddenly go limp.

Damn him, I think as his tongue fucks my mouth, sliding in feverishly as my own tries to keep up. I'm vaguely aware that we're standing in the middle of a country road, halfway up the hill to a place where we will have no privacy.

Josh seems to think the same thing. He pulls away, long enough for me to inhale sharply as I try to catch my breath, and tugs me to the side of the road, to a crop of trees. He spins me around and lifts me up until I'm pressed back against the smooth bark of a tall beech tree.

I wrap my legs around him for stability, but he pushes them away and starts undoing the fly of my shorts. In seconds he's pulled them and my thong down to my ankles, then I kick them off into the bushes. Part of me thinks he's moving too fast, part of me thinks he's not moving fast enough. My body aches for him and as soon as he undoes his jeans and takes his cock out, my cunt aches as well.

There is no time to admire him under this soft sunshine. He poises the head at my opening and pushes in just as he bites down on my neck, groaning. I'm lucky I'm wet, because he's as long and wide as I remembered, and he drives himself in deep with one hard thrust.

I suck in my breath, my body trying to accommodate him, to accommodate the fact that Josh is fucking me against a tree in broad daylight. I'm still not sure how we went from arguing to this, but it feels so fucking good, I don't care. The muscles in his back are tight under my fingers and my other hand disappears into his hair, tugging on the thick black strands until he moans against my skin, deep and guttural. I wrap my legs around him tighter, pulling him so he's inside me to the hilt and I can feel the tickle of his balls against my ass. There is something so incredibly sexy about that.

He pulls out, slowly, and I can't help the moan that falls out of my mouth.

"Wait," he says, his voice manipulated by sex and desire. "You're still on the pill, aren't you?"

I know he's seen me taking them every morning. "Yes," I re-assure him. "Though it's a bit late to ask; what if I had said no?"

He grins at me, breathing hard. "I'd pull out right now and come all over your tits."

"And what's in it for me?"

"Oh trust me, sweetheart, you'd like it."

Sweetheart. He's using that term again like he did in Vancouver. This is Josh's sex talk. I love this side of him.

He slams back into me and I let out a gasp.

"You okay?" he murmurs against my mouth before thrusting hard again. It feels like he's trying to nail me to the tree.

I half-mumble, half-groan something and readjust my hold on his neck and back. I just want him to keep going.

He does. Each pump is controlled and hard, slow and teasing, coming out until I feel empty inside and heavy and swift coming back in.

"Do you feel me?" he whispers into my ear, his breath warmth, voice gruff.

I can barely nod. I feel everything.

He thrusts again and again. "How do I feel?"

"Good." I can't tell if I've said it or just thought it loud enough. My eyes close and my head starts to bang against the tree trunk.

His thumb goes to my clit and slides up and down with each thrust. "How about now?"

My body is expanding, greedy, hungry, spurred by the hot, heady pressure on my clit. He rubs his thumb expertly, slickly, and it's making me insatiable.

"How do I feel now?" he repeats, determined for an answer.

"Oh god, Josh," I groan out, "just keep fucking me."

He bites my ear, tugging at it. "Just tell me. I want in deep. Do you want me deeper?"

"Yes," I cry out, my nails digging into him.

"I want you to feel me." His voice is now more hard than breathy, like he's determined to pound me within an inch of my life. "I *need* you to feel me. Feel me fucking you, my cock so fucking deep you'll never get enough."

His dirty fucking words and his heavy hitting are doing a number on me. That, combined with his fingers and the fact that we're having hard sex on the side of the road that anyone could drive down at any moment, means I am seconds from coming. I can feel that wave coming, ready to flatten me to the ground and pull me under. The tide inside me starts receding as it builds.

"Keep going, please," I cry softly as the pressure builds to the breaking point.

"Always," he answers and the wave crashes. My whole body shudders, shatters, and I'm swept under that delicious riptide. As I tumble, my cries and moans and little utterances of orgasmic nonsense fill the air. I'm not sure which way is up and I don't care if I sink or swim.

Josh comes loudly, too, his thrusts harder and faster, and I can feel the heat of him as he pours inside of me. "Fuck," he utters. "Fuck. Oh Jesus, oh Gemma you . . . you . . ." and his words fail him. He doesn't have to continue. I understand. I feel the same.

When the wave loosens and I pop up for breath, I realize I'm a sweaty mess, holding on to him like he's a life raft keeping me afloat. He stares at me with a lazy, heated gaze and a smile tugs at his lips.

I want to kiss him. I want to lie down in the grass and curl up beside him. Then I want to do that again and again and again until I'm raw and worn out and I don't feel anything.

Because right now, I feel something; everything.

I swallow and look away from his softly probing eyes. The haze of sex and orgasm is wearing off and I carefully try to unhook my legs from around him. He gently pulls out and lowers me to the ground.

"Excuse me," I say to him and then disappear behind a bush to relieve myself. No one wants to walk up a hill with cum streaming down their legs.

When I reemerge, he's fastening the belt on his jeans and smiling. He looks like he's just been laid. There's the relaxed peace about him that I haven't seen in a while.

"I guess we should head back," I say, nodding at the road. I walk over to it, avoiding him.

He tries to reach for me anyway but I slip out of his grasp. "Where are you going?" he asks and I can hear the puzzlement in his voice. "What's the rush? Stay and relax awhile."

Just then there's the sound of crunching gravel, and at the bottom of the hill I see Hamish's truck coming toward us. I step out into the road and wave at him.

"Gemma," I hear Josh say but Hamish is pulling the truck to a stop.

"Did you guys have a nap or something?" Hamish asks, his arm hanging out of the window. "Come on in."

I smile my thanks to him and quickly get in the passenger side. I look over my shoulder at Josh but he's standing there, his gaze jagged. He looks to Hamish. "Thanks, but I'll walk. I could use it." He nearly spits out those last words.

I feel a sting but push it aside and close the door. The truck starts up the road and I avoid the side mirrors. I don't want to see Josh walking through the wake of dust from the truck.

I feel like a bitch. I am a bitch. We fucked and I bailed and that is so not what Josh deserves. But I don't know how to keep sex as just sex, and I don't know how to keep a friend as just a friend, and Josh is a friend and sex all rolled into one.

And he's something else, too, something that gets under my skin, and that's the thing I'm afraid of discovering, the thing that wants to loosen my grip. If he gets too far under my skin, he'll stay there.

Chapter Sixteen

JOSH

I've never been so happy to leave a place in all my life. I sit down in the back of Mr. Orange and my leg bounces from nerves and it doesn't stop until Gemma starts the engine and we're pulling onto the road.

Yesterday felt like the best day of my life combined with the worst. It went from fuckawesome to fucking terrible in a matter of minutes, but I guess that shouldn't surprise me when I'm in a country where the weather can change at the drop of a hat and I'm with a woman who's so fucking moody it's like being around two different people.

I still don't know what went wrong. One minute we were having it out, yelling at each other in the middle of the road, and it was good, it was brilliant, because finally Gemma was giving me something—her feelings, her fears. The fact that she actually cared what happened between me and Amber—it should have made me feel guilty but I only felt happiness. Here was the validation I needed, evidence that she cared.

Then it led to hot-as-fuck sex, and I knew she could feel

me, I knew I was in deep and she was letting me in. It was physical but it was the start. Everything I'd been holding inside I let loose into her. I wanted to fuck it out of her, her emptiness, her coldness, the person she hides behind.

I thought I was succeeding.

And then it was like that beautiful, soft, vulnerable light I saw shining in her was snuffed out. I didn't expect her to start spooning me and whispering sweet nothings in my ear, but I also didn't expect to see that blank chill in her eyes, for her to treat me like nothing had happened.

Everything had just happened. Now she just wanted to sweep it under the rug. We fucked and that was that, and now we're back to being extremely awkward around each other.

But that's not what I want. At this point I want more than just a hot fuck, but you know what, I'll take more of that if I can get it. But she doesn't even want to give in to the physical and it blows my mind because I know she came and loved every rough minute of it. She's great at faking life but she can't fake that.

Naturally the rest of the day was all strained bullshit. She kept to herself and to Amber, and the closest I got to her was during dinner when we sat beside each other. She wouldn't even look at me.

Now we're supposed to head up to Kaikoura before taking the ferry back to the North Island, and I'm having second thoughts. I can't stand being in this bus anymore with her, and with the way things are, I've had enough, frankly. It's too bad because, for all the mind games and craziness, she has an inner beauty that comes through when everything is just right; that beauty is the only reason I've been able to hang on for so long.

But I've got my limits.

"Hey Gemma," I say as we roar down past the blue-harbored town of Akaroa. "How much do I owe you so far for the trip? You've paid for a bunch of things already."

She eyes me in the rearview mirror, seeming surprised that I'm talking to her. "I'm not sure. I'll look, I have it written down on my phone."

"Can we stop by the nearest ATM?" I ask.

She frowns slightly. "Of course, but I don't need it right now."

I take in a deep breath. "That's fine. And can you drop me off in Christchurch?"

She blinks as if she doesn't hear me. Amber turns around in her seat. "What are you talking about?" she asks.

"I want to be dropped off in Christchurch. I think I'm going to do my own thing from now on. Maybe head down to Dunedin."

Gemma is watching me more than she's watching the road. I meet her eyes for one second and she nearly flinches when she sees I'm serious. She looks back to the road and I watch as her knuckles grow white against the steering wheel.

"Okay," Gemma says in a small voice. "Shouldn't we talk about this?"

"Do you really want to talk about it?" I ask.

Amber is looking between the two of us, chewing nervously on a strand of hair.

"In private, sure," Gemma says. "I'll just pull over."

"Nah," I say with a wave of my hand. "There's no point. Just drop me off at Christchurch please, beside an ATM. I'll pay you and we'll part ways."

"Josh," Amber says quietly. Her eyes are big and starting to water. "What happened? What did I do?"

It's sweet that she thinks it's something *she* did.

"You didn't do anything," Gemma says, and then she bites

her lip, as if to prevent her from saying something else. I know what it is but she manages to choke back her pettiness. Gemma's issues no longer have anything to do with Amber groping me, and they never even had anything to do with Nick. Gemma's issues are all from her, and I just don't have the fucking patience anymore to deal with it.

I feel my chest harden and I like it. I hope it stays. Is this what it's like to be her, to have this power where nothing can hurt you?

"Amber, you're awesome," I tell her. "I just think it's time for me to go." There is so much more I want to elaborate on but I don't want to air our dirty laundry. "The trip had to end sometime."

"But you'll be alone at Christmas," she protests.

"It's still better than being at home for Christmas, believe me." I give her a placating smile. The poor thing seems to be taking this worse than Gemma, but that shouldn't surprise me. "It's all good, really. This is for the best. Might as well end on a high note." Even though everything since that night at Key Summit has felt low.

Suddenly Gemma brings the bus down a small road that hugs the edge of a stream. It starts to wind up, and I'm about to warn her about Mr. Orange's inability to handle the hill, when she pulls over to the side and shoves the bus into park. She shuts the engine off and then jumps out of the van.

For a moment I think she's going to do something crazy again, like jump into the river, but she slides open the back door and climbs inside, grabbing my arm.

"Come with me," she demands, pulling hard. She's fucking strong when she really wants to be, and I'm actually halfway off the seat before I pull back.

"Why?"

"We need to talk," she says.

"I really doubt it."

She tugs harder but her eyes grow softer and I see a hint of that light again. She's begging, pleading with them. She's desperate. So I relent.

She leads me out of the bus and then slams the door shut. "We'll be right back," she yells at Amber and then leads me a few feet up the road. I pull out of her grasp but continue walking by her side.

"Jesus, kung fu grip much?"

When we're far enough from the bus, she stops. "Why are you doing this?"

"Why do you think?"

She crosses her arms and looks away. "Just . . . don't go. Please. Stay."

I love that she's saying this but I don't believe it.

"Give me a reason to stay," I tell her. "And I'll stay."

She bites her lip. "Because I'm a fun person?" she asks unsurely.

"You can be, when you're not . . ."

"Being a bitch?" she supplies.

I shake my head. "I only use that word when I'm really fucking mad, and I'm not even mad anymore, Gemma. I'm just . . . I'm tired. I can't figure you out for the life of me, and I don't think you want me to try. Things are just so weird now and I think it's best if I just go. You and Amber will be a lot happier without me."

"We won't be," she says, and I hear the sincerity in her voice. I have to ignore it. "Will you be?"

I sigh and run a hand through my hair. "No," I answer honestly. Because I don't want to go, I just feel like I need to go. I need to move on and forget her and the big tangled mess I've gotten stuck in.

She grabs my hand and squeezes it tight. "Then please

don't go. I know I have issues and I'm trying to deal with them and it's not fair that you're caught in the middle."

I step closer to her. "What *are* your issues?" I implore her.

She shrugs helplessly. "I don't know. Everything."

"Am I your issue?"

She shoots me a quick glance but doesn't say anything.

I put my hand on her face, making her look at me again. "Am I your issue?"

"I . . . I don't want to become attached to you," she says, and I can see it took a lot of effort to admit it.

I frown though something inside me is growing warm. "Why not?"

She balks like I asked a stupid question. "*Because.*" She sighs harshly. "Attachments hurt when they're taken away. You're *leaving.*"

"So what?" I tell her. "*I'm* attached to you already and I'm still leaving. I almost left right now. Doesn't mean that the pain negates everything, that none of this was worth it."

She swallows, looking surprised. "You're attached to me?"

I shake my head incredulously and run my thumb over her lips, marveling at how fucking clueless she is. "Gemma, Gemma, Gemma," I murmur. "I told you how I feel about you. I told you why I'm here. Of course I'm attached to you. And I know very well that I'm leaving, but that isn't stopping these feelings from happening. In fact, it only makes it sweeter, stronger, because I know we don't have much time together."

She seems to take that in. I want her to believe it so badly. I have never in my life been so open with a girl. Always in the past it was my girlfriends or random chicks that wanted more from me, wanted a piece of me. I never wanted shit from them. But being with Gemma is like getting blood from a stone, and I may be a fool for trying but I finally understand what it's like to be on the other side.

She relaxes a bit, her eyes softening. I'm think I'm finally getting to her.

"At the very least, we should be screwing each other's brains out until I get on that plane," I say with a smile, pressing my thumb into her wet mouth. I could definitely screw her right here. I spy some sturdy trees over her shoulder. If not, she could easily get on her knees and suck me off. She was good at that.

She bites my thumb then pulls back. "So you're not going."

"Are we going to screw each other's brains out?"

She smiles coquettishly, which makes my dick harder. "If you'd like."

"Sweetheart, it's what *you'd* like," I tell her. "And if I remember correctly, you liked it an awful lot."

She seems to consider that. She looks over at Mr. Orange. "Maybe we should wait until Amber's not with us anymore, or at least until we're at my mom's and we're not all cramped in the bus together."

I cock my head and give her a blank look. "Are you serious?" She's saying yes to sex and now we have to wait?

"It will make things super awkward and weird, don't you think?"

"Gemma," I say with a laugh, "it's been super awkward and weird as fuck for weeks now. This is the most uncomfortable road trip I have ever taken in my whole life, and I've been stuck in a car with my divorcing parents and my sister for a trip across the province before."

"Three more nights," she reiterates. "Two in Kaikoura, one in Masterton, and then we're home in Napier for Christmas."

I squeeze her hand. "No promises," I tell her gruffly. But secretly I'm grinning inside. For her I could wait forever.

Well, I could try, anyway.

Then I'd have a great time relishing the failure.

We stay the two nights in Kaikoura at a holiday park by the ocean. It's a beautiful place—wild blue ocean on one side, towering snowy peaks on the other. It's like the marine mammal and aquatic shit capital of the country, and we're there to go dolphin swimming. It was Amber's idea and Gemma agreed to come along, but when we got up at five a.m. to go out on the boat, we discovered it was cancelled due to high surf.

We end up going for a walk on the Kaikoura Peninsula instead. It's windy as hell and what looked like a quick jaunt is taking us hours of just walking along seal-strewn shores and sheep-covered bluffs. It's pretty though, the contrast between the pebbled beaches and the blue-gray water peppered with whitecaps.

When we stop at a low stone wall on the bluff to eat the sandwiches we bought earlier, I take out my watercolor pencils and sketchbook and start drawing the scene. Eventually Gemma comes over and peers over my shoulder.

"That's gorgeous, Josh," she says softly. I look up at her and see the wistfulness in her eyes.

"Here," I say, handing her the book and the slate gray pencil. "You try."

Fear lines her brow. "You know I can't."

I shrug. "I don't know. Maybe you can. It's just a pencil and it's just paper." I can't help but beg her with my eyes. *Please*, I tell her. "Come on."

To encourage her, I flip the page so it's nice and new and blank and I place it in her hand. I pat the grass next to me. "Sit, stay."

"Play fetch?" she asks wryly, but sits down anyway. I get to my feet and join Amber by the wall, wanting to give her some space. It can't help to have me looking over her shoulder.

She smiles at me shyly, appreciatively, then turns her head out to the view. The wind rushes up off the cliffs and tousles her hair. Her face, when it's not hidden by her dark strands, becomes pensive. Then she's slowly sketching. She's beautiful.

I munch on my sandwich and Amber and I talk about sharks since shark diving was the other option for the day (in a cage and all, but no thanks) but my eyes rarely leave Gemma. She seems to be caught up in a battle, staring at the ocean, that thin line of the horizon, then back at her book, like it's not matching up for her.

Frustrated, she throws my book and pencil to the side and puts her head in her hands. I exchange a quick look with Amber then go over to Gemma's side. I crouch down and place a hand on her shoulder.

"Hey, baby," I say softly and she whips her head to me in surprise. I'm surprised, too. I can't believe I just called her baby.

I try and play it off. "Take it easy on yourself, okay?" I pick up the sketchbook and see a very rough sketch of the view. You can tell that she tried to be as detailed as possible but then got frustrated and started pressing the pencil harder until the end broke off.

"I can't do it," she says.

I close up the book with a snap and smile at her. "But you just did. Now it's forever in this book. It's immortal. The day has been captured and when I look at it, I'll remember this. Isn't that what the point of all of this is? To rewind life a bit?"

She looks unsure. I help her to her feet but I don't let go of her hand once she's up. Amber turns to look at us as she shoves the remainder of her sandwich in her fringe purse.

"Is this a new development?" she asks cautiously, pointing at our hand-holding.

Gemma tries to take her hand away but I only grip it harder and raise it in the air.

"I think I've finally worn her down," I say to Amber with a cocksure smile.

Amber grins. "Took you long enough."

But Gemma still manages to wriggle out of my grasp and walk beside Amber.

I know I still have my work cut out for me.

The next day is a long, arduous journey through torrential rain from Kaikoura to the ferry terminal at Picton. Any hopes of a beautiful view are obscured by fogged windows and the endless gray outside of them. The inside of the bus feels damp with sweat and everyone is cranky and uncomfortable. Even though we'll soon be staying at Gemma's mother's place and it's bound to be a bit awkward, seeing as it's Christmastime for the family and all that, I'm actually looking forward to it. It will be nice to have a place to stay and unpack for more than a day. It will be good to get out of this bus and the constant Pink Floyd.

The clouds follow us across the choppy strait to the North Island, where we speed toward an unexciting-sounding town called Masterton. Once again we're staying in a hostel and once again I'm cursing Gemma for booking us in another dorm. I know she's doing this to save our broke asses money, but still.

This time there are only two bunks, but that still means there are two other people in the room when I need there to just be me and her. Aside from the hand-holding stint in Kaikoura, she's becoming standoffish again, at least physically, and I'm getting a permanent case of blue balls just by looking at her.

Especially today. She's wearing her denim short shorts again and a thin, low-cut white tank top with a lacy red bra underneath. The rain has her shirt looking a bit see-through and the delicate material of her bra has her nipples poking out like nobody's business.

I can barely contain myself.

When we settle down in the room—the other bunkmate is absentee except for their backpack—Amber and Gemma go to check out the rest of the hostel. I quickly shut the door behind them and lock it.

I go over to my bed, taking my cock out of my pants, and lie down. There's nothing around to make things smoother and I don't have time to go rummaging through the girls' bags for skin cream or anything. I spit on my hand and start stroking quickly. The need to come is so great that I know it won't take long. All I have to do is imagine Gemma's soft, wet lips around my head, a wicked look in her eyes. Maybe she could play with herself at the same time.

Oh god, I'm close.

A knock at the door pulls me back from the edge and the door handle jingles repeatedly.

"Josh?" Amber calls out from the other side.

"Goddamnit!" I yell slamming my fist down beside me. Frustrated, I shove my cock back in my briefs and zip up my jeans before I go over to the door and yank it open.

"What do you want?" I groan in exasperation, leaning against the door frame.

Amber and Gemma stare at me, puzzled.

"Why is the door locked?" Amber asks, coming inside the room and looking around warily. She sniffs the air like a hound.

"No reason," I say, pushing past Gemma into the hall.

"Where are you going?" Gemma asks as I start to walk away.

"To the shower so I can masturbate in peace," I answer. Then I pause and turn to her. "Care to join me?"

"Wow, TMI, Josh," Amber says from inside the room.

But Gemma is still staring at me and I can see the lust coloring her eyes.

"I'm serious," I tell her, lowering my voice. "You can just watch if you want."

She rolls her eyes, even though I know she'd gladly drop to her knees if no one was around. The sexual tension between us has been ridiculously high ever since our last fuck, and I've caught her looking at me hungrily more than once. She wants me as badly as I want her.

"Fine," I tell her and lean in closer so I'm whispering in her ear. "But just so you know, I'm going to explode inside you tomorrow. Taking the edge off now might make things easier, but it's your call. You're going to get it bad."

I slowly pull away, my eyes trained on hers until she feels their heat. Then I turn, a crooked smile on my lips, and head over to the shower stall to get rid of my raging hard-on once and for all.

Chapter Seventeen

GEMMA

I don't realize it's Christmas Eve the next day until we pass the town of Norsewood and I see a gaudy Santa display on someone's roof. I can't believe the month has flown by like this and that this holiday, of all holidays, has snuck up on us. If I were at home this whole time, I would have been subjected to Christmas songs on the radio and annoying jingles on TV. On the road, though, I've just seen unadulterated scenery and the pure spaces outside the cities, untouched by commerce.

"Guys," I say as I slow Mr. Orange down so a car from behind can overtake us. "It's Christmas in two days."

Amber laughs from the back. "Are you serious?"

I look at Josh and he looks mystified. "Wow," he says, "it does not feel like it *at all*. How can you deal with having Christmas in the summer?"

"Well, we have a thing called Christmas on the beach and it's awesome," I tell him. "It's also a song." I sing a few silly notes of it. "Which isn't so awesome."

Josh grins at me and places a large, warm hand on my bare thigh. "You could sing anything and it would sound good," he says earnestly and gives my leg a squeeze.

"Ugh," Amber calls from the back. "You guys make me sick."

I eye her sharply in the mirror. This makes her sick? Does she have any idea how hard it's been not to fuck Josh senseless in front of her? Yesterday when Josh invited me to take a shower with him, I was *this* close to going. The only thing that held me back was the fact that Amber was listening.

And yet him putting his hand on my thigh and paying me a compliment grosses her out? Yeesh.

"You think that's bad," Josh says to her over his shoulder, "just imagine all the things I'm going to do to her tonight."

I can't help but laugh. Leave it to Josh not to beat around the bush.

It doesn't take long before we're motoring past the vineyards of the Hawkes Bay area, heading toward the city of Napier, my home. Actually, the vineyard is a little north of the city and I find myself growing both relaxed and nervous with each kilometer we pass.

Relaxed because the bright, wide sky above us and the rolling green farms in the area will always be home to me, even though it holds a lot of difficult memories. Nervous because I'm not sure how Josh is going to react to my family or how they're going to react to him. The last they knew I was seeing Nick, I had a job lined up, and everything was in order.

My mother thrives on order. It's one of the reasons why she's been able to run the vineyard so successfully, especially after Dad died and our lives were thrown into turmoil. But where she thrives on order, it also means she doesn't allow for a lot of mistakes. She's hard on me but hard on herself, too. Even though she's closed off and reserved, we've made a lot of progress over the years. Believe me, I have the hours of therapy to prove it.

Still, I'm going to assume she won't be happy about leaving someone like Nick, who has it all, and being with someone like Josh, who . . . well, doesn't have it in quite the way she expects. I'm starting to think it would be best to keep our . . . whatever this is . . . under wraps, at least at first.

My auntie Jolinda, who runs the vineyard with my mom, will take to him like a fat kid to cake, though. I warn him about her.

"My aunt is a cheek-pincher," I tell him as we pass the airport and beaches, "and not the ones on your face."

He grins. "Those are my favorite kind of aunts. Is she hot?"

I give him a look. Not funny.

Soon the vineyards and orchards grow more vast and I'm pulling off the highway down a dirt road, past a sign my dad painted: HENARE WINES.

We bounce down the road for a bit among the rows and rows of pinot gris and sauvignon blanc grapes, then come to a stop outside the barn where the barrels are kept. I park Mr. Orange next to the beat-up old truck of Jez, our winemaker.

I turn to Josh and Amber and say, "Well, this is it."

It's like he notices I'm nervous because he briefly grabs my hand and gives it a squeeze. But he lets go and I think he knows not to act all PDA going forward. I breathe a sigh of relief and then step out.

The last time I was here was in the winter and everything had a look of cold death about it. Now the rows of grapes are young and bright green and the barn has a fresh stain on the gray-brown wood. Tibetan prayer flags hang between it and the house, remnants of my father; he was very earthy, very spiritual. My mother took them all down except for these ones.

The gravel of the driveway crunches under our feet as we walk to the front door, and before we can get close, it swings open and out comes my mom and my aunt.

My mother's smile is warm as she looks at us, although it falters for a moment at the sight of Josh. I keep forgetting he's this big, tall dude with tattoos and dangerous looks, nearly the opposite of what she expects from me.

"Gemma," she says, her voice light and airy. She gives me a hug, which generally consists of a light embrace and a pat on the back. Her eyes briefly flick to Josh and back to me but I don't say anything.

She moves on to Amber. "My, my, Amber," she says and embraces her the same way. That's just the way my mom hugs. "I haven't seen you since you were a little girl."

"Hi, Aunt Justine," she says brightly.

My mom smiles and then rests her eyes on Josh. "And is this your boyfriend, Amber?"

Josh steps forward, his hand out. "Uh, no. I'm just a friend. My name is Josh."

"Oh," my mother says, looking to me in surprise as she shakes his hand. "This is the Josh you were telling me about, the Canadian?"

I nod. "Yes, Mum, this is Josh. I still hope it's okay that he spends Christmas with us."

"Of course," she says without hesitating. She's nothing if not polite. "Your uncle Jeremy is coming over tonight with Keri and Kam. They'll leave on Boxing Day, so if you three don't mind sharing a room for a few nights . . ."

Inwardly, I groan. Loudly. But I smile at my mom. "That's fine, we're used to it." To get off the subject I look at my auntie Jolinda hovering behind my mother. "Hey, Auntie Jo!" I say, holding my arms out for the big hug I know is coming.

Auntie Jolinda isn't hot in the way that Josh was asking

about. She's from my father's side, as are most of my aunts and uncles, so she's got dark, sturdy looks, as we all do. But she's round-faced and has the prettiest greenstone-colored eyes and has a way of making you feel loved.

She pulls me into an embrace. "Gemma," she says happily. Like my mom, she's quiet and conserves her words but she doesn't have to say much to get a feeling across.

She strokes my cheek fondly and then lights up at the sight of Josh. I have to bite my lip from laughing as she goes for him. Thankfully she only hugs him hard and doesn't grab his butt, but I'll have to keep an eye on her after a few glasses of wine. Not that I can blame the woman. Josh has the best ass to pinch.

"I thought Nick was with you, Gemma," my mother says suddenly.

Amber, Josh, and I exchange the subtlest of glances before I put an appeasing smile on for her. "He went back to Sydney early," I say, which for all I know could be true.

To my surprise, she doesn't look disappointed. "No worries," she says, "that's one less person to eat Uncle Jeremy's famous kumara slices."

"Oh, kumara," Josh says excitedly. Of all the Kiwi things he's picked up on this trip, eating kumara—a type of sweet potato—and dipping it into sour cream and sweet chili sauce has become his favorite. That, and doing me, I guess.

We go back to Mr. Orange and haul our packs into the house and up the stairs to my old room. As usual, the house is immaculate but it still has this rustic, homey vibe. It's very much a Kiwi farmhouse, with wainscoting and rugged brown boards in all the right places and smooth finished wood in others.

"This is an awesome house," Amber says. "My parents' house is so boring and stucco. Total subdivision banality."

I lead them down to my room. It's quite large and has enough space for my queen bed and an air mattress or two on the floor. One wall is entirely devoted to sports medals and ribbons. Football, field hockey, women's rugby, netball, tennis—I've done them all.

Josh marvels at them, mouthing the names and dates of the competitions. "Wow, Gemma, you really like to whack balls around, don't you."

"I like them better in my mouth," I answer smartly. It brings out another annoyed groan from Amber.

"Seriously. You. Guys."

I stick my tongue out at her and place my backpack by the bed, opening my window. The view here is always beautiful. My room looks out onto the back vineyard and a dirt road that runs along the property all the way to the beach. I can see the holiday baches and Norfolk pines that line the bright blue ocean.

"Your view growing up was a lot better than mine," Josh says behind me, pushing my hair over my shoulder and kissing my neck. I close my eyes and melt into his touch.

"Hey, can we take a tour of the vineyards or something?" Amber asks.

I turn around and eye her. "Sure, but don't you have, like, Napa Valley by you?"

She ties her curly hair back into a braid. "It's not exactly nearby," she says. "Besides, I've been in the bus all day. I'd like some fresh air before I stuff myself with what smells like amazing cooking."

I nod and bring them outside. I lead them down a path lined with cabbage trees as it winds over to the vines. I can see Jez, his blue ball cap poking up way in the distance.

There isn't much for me to point out. We're a boutique winery and we're not open for tastings or anything touristy yet, so it's just the vines for acres and acres. We grow three types of grapes and would like to do more than pinot noir in the red department but the land doesn't quite get hot enough, except on the south end of the small rise near the edge of the property. But my parents started it back when my father was a struggling artist and, throughout the years, either the winery kept the art afloat or the art kept the winery afloat.

The money that my father left behind, thanks to what my mother calls carefully selected stocks, has kept this place going, and the winery even flourishes, depending on the year. It's a good life. There was a moment there after his death when I thought my mom was going to pack it up, but with Auntie Jolinda's help and Jez staying on as winemaker, it's still going strong.

I only wish I liked winemaking—or, really, wine in general—enough to want to be a part of it. Give me a brewery any day.

When we get to the crest of the low hill and can see over the vines to Hawkes Bay, Port of Napier, and the rolling hills on the other side of Highway 2, Amber decides she's had enough.

"Want us to come with you?" I ask and she shakes her head and says she wants to use the washroom. We watch her blond head pass along the vines as she goes back to the house. I have a sneaking suspicion that she's leaving on purpose. Seeing as we don't have a lot of privacy here, I could kiss her for it. Sometimes she really is the best cousin ever.

I start wondering what I should buy her for Christmas— hell, what I should buy Josh—when I feel his arms slip around my stomach, embracing me from behind. In the distance I can see plumes of dust rising from the long driveway, meaning Uncle Jeremy and his eight- and eleven-year-old kids will be here any moment. But out on this hill, surrounded by undulating green, it feels like we have eternity.

Josh kisses the rim of my earlobe, his lips pausing by my ear. "Can you remember the last time we were alone like this?"

I can't quell the excitement growing inside me. My hormones start to alight, starting off as flames and growing into Roman candles.

"I think the last time we were alone, you were fucking me against a tree," I say, almost whispering, as if my voice could scare him off.

"No trees here," he murmurs and presses his erection into my ass. "Only wood."

I grin at that but it melts away into hazy lust. I can't stand it. I turn around to face him and he grabs me, kissing me hard. I match his intensity, hot, hot, hot to the touch. His tongue, his lips, his mouth, they're all sparks to fuel the fire. He kisses me like he's addicted, needing his fix, and I can only respond in kind. The more he fucks my tongue with his, licks my neck, bites at my collarbone, the more I think I might spontaneously combust.

His fingers deftly undo my shorts and slide down into my underwear. He inhales sharply when he feels how wet I already am, but he must know by now what affect he has on me. He pushes a finger in deep, then two, then three.

I groan and my neck falls back, like my head is too heavy to hold up. I just want to submit and have him do terrible, dirty things to me here among the grapevines. I want him inside me, hard and fast or slow and deliberate—I don't care.

But then I find myself pulling away from his hand just when his other is slipping under my T-shirt. I drop to my knees, feeling the soft, cool earth beneath me, and reach up for his zipper. I glance up at him with mischievous eyes and he bites his lip before grabbing the hair at the back of my head in a tight fist.

It hurts but it's a good hurt. He's the master of hair-pulling. I slowly, teasingly unzip his fly, then pull his jeans down bit by bit. Once they drop to his ankles, I do the same to his boxer briefs, until his cock is free and jutting out in front of me. It really is a beautiful sight and I find myself marveling at it for a few moments. In the pool room at the house party, in his room, by the road in Le Bons Bay, I never really had the best look. His cock is as flawless as it feels between my hands, hot, silky steel.

I take a firm hold around his shaft, holding him taut as I lick a path up and down him, from base to shiny, swollen tip. His fist in my hair tightens and he moans. "Oh fuck."

I smile and continue. The sound of his pleasure only adds to mine. I go from slow to fast and back again, and before long he has both of his hands at the back of my head and he's fucking my mouth, his hips slamming into my lips in controlled movements. I try and let my lips and tongue be all he feels, but occasionally my tooth razes him; it only seems to turn him on more. Just when I think he's about to shoot his load down my throat, he pulls my head back and his wet cock bobs out of my mouth.

Somewhere in the distance I can hear voices, my family, but they're of no consequence. Josh tears his eyes away from mine and glances lazily at the horizon. When he looks back to me, a languid smile stretches across his face.

"They might start looking for us," he says, "if we give them something to look for."

Suddenly he crouches down behind me so that we're both hidden and pushes his hand between my shoulder blades so I'm on my hands as well as knees. He pulls me by the hips so my back arches and slides my shorts down over my ass and thighs.

"Jesus," he swears, and I can feel his eyes burning through me, as molten as his fingers. "I won't forget this."

He shuffles forward so his cock slides up between the crack of my ass. I'm about to move out of the way, thinking we have a lot more to do before we jump to backdoor action, when he pulls back slightly and begins to tease my ass with his cock before priming it at my wetness. One hand pushes my thighs further apart while the other grabs my waist, his fingers digging into me.

He guides himself inside, slowly, hissing sharply as he goes. He feels impossibly fat and thick from this angle and I inhale as he pushes in. My fingernails dig into the dirt.

He pulls back slowly and then thrusts in sharp with a low groan. Both hands grip my hips hard as his pace quickens. He pounds me so fast and hard I can feel my knees slipping in the earth and my breasts coming free of my bra. I reach below to help myself out and it doesn't take long before I'm coming. I try to keep my cries subdued in case the sound carries, and I can only eke out breathless little whimpers of his name over and over again as the world around me swirls in a beautiful dance.

He isn't done yet. He slams into me, his balls slapping against my ass, skin on skin, until finally he's moaning loudly and pushing in with three final thrusts, burying himself deep inside of me. He slowly wraps his arms around me from behind, then slips his cock out.

I hear rustling in the distance, so I straighten up and get to my shaky feet, pulling up my shorts. In my daze I can see people heading toward us along the rows. Uncle Jeremy's kids, Keri and Kam.

"Shit," I say, dropping back down before they see me. Josh stays low, pulling up his jeans, and I take his hand. We walk crouched down along the vines until we're heading down the rise on the side not facing the house. There, with the hill blocking us, we stand up, bathed in shadow.

I lean over and kiss him quickly on the lips, unable to keep myself from smiling or touching him.

He grins lazily at me. "Told you."

"What?"

"That I was going to explode inside of you."

"Well, you did just that." And once again I disappear behind a row of grapes to pee so I don't have the same problem as before. Either I have to stop wearing shorts or we have to stop having sex outside.

When I come back around the corner, I see Keri and Kam at the top of the rise, thankfully not where we had sex, and waving at us to follow them. I grab Josh's hand and we go.

———————•———————

No one seems very suspicious of me and Josh going missing for a while. When we get back to the house, only my mother is at the kitchen door, eyeing us warily, but when Keri and Kam, bless their innocent hearts, tell her that they found us talking, that probing look of hers goes away.

Ah, poor mum. If and when she finds out about me and Josh, she's going to have a conniption. I'm not sure if the fact that he's not staying in the country for long will be a good thing or a bad thing for her, in this case.

Keri and Kam are nice kids, and they seem to get significantly older each time I see them. I'm always surprised to see them taller and dressing differently, but they're easygoing and lighthearted. A bit like Amber in that respect, though they're from different sides of the family. Keri and Kam are also more closely connected to their Maori heritage than I am. It's nice to have those little reminders of where I came from.

My uncle Jeremy is a riot, though. He and my uncle Robbie, whom I borrowed Mr. Orange from—*and* now think a lot differently of, thanks to his porn collection—are brothers, born ten years apart. That said, they're pretty much the same, right down to their laugh. Robbie is more subdued because he's the older sibling and smokes more grass, while Jeremy is the loud one, but they're both nutters. We'll see my uncle Robbie when we go up to the Northland to spend New Year with my grandfather—he takes care of him, even though my grandfather is strong as an ox.

"Ever been to a *hāngi,* bro?" Uncle Jeremy asks Josh as we sit down to the wide kauri wood table my father made.

Josh shakes his head. "I don't think so."

Uncle Jeremy laughs and has a swig of his beer. "Then you haven't. When you go up north, you'll have one, aye? Robbie will make sure of that. So will Pops. How about the *hongi*?" Josh only stares so my uncle winks at me. "We'll let Pops deal with that one."

Josh looks utterly bewildered by all these Maori terms but he's taking it in stride. He starts talking about funny Canadian stuff, to which Jeremy cracks up. I look at Amber, who's drinking our own pinot noir and flushing at the cheeks, clearly enjoying herself. It's weird to think that in a few days she'll be flying to Australia on her own. I wonder if she can hunt down Nick and kick him in the nuts for me.

Though it's not quite the roast my mother has planned for Christmas Day, it's still a feast of roasted vegetables and homemade steak and onion pies. She's always been very good at stuffing us silly, which is probably why it's a blessing that my aspirations turned from art to physical fitness. I was already starting to go a bit doughy in the stomach, hips, and thighs when I was a teenager.

The thought that my physical fitness might no longer be as crucial to my daily life begins to eat away at me. I try to focus on whatever my family is talking about, especially what Josh is saying, but my thoughts keep going to the fact that when I eventually emerge from this vacation haze, I'm going to have to face cold, hard reality, and Josh's cock won't be there to distract me from it.

My mother loves to ask questions at the worst possible time, so it shouldn't surprise me when she says loudly and primly at the table, "Gemma, how is it going with you and Nick?"

"Is this the Aussie rugby player?" Uncle Jeremy asks, and I raise my brows, startled that even he knows about Nick.

I give my mother a steady look while the internal debate rages on. To tell the truth or not tell the truth, that is the question. I glance at Josh, and though his face is impassive, I know what he wants to hear.

I sigh and say, "Well if you must know, Nick and I aren't seeing each other anymore."

"Good," Uncle Jeremy says as he shoves pie into his face. "Aussies are no bloody good."

The Aussie and Kiwi rivalry is about as heated and constant as the Canadian and American one, but this has nothing to do with it. I eye my uncle. "It didn't end because he's Australian."

He shrugs as if to say it should have.

"What happened, dear?" my mother asks, and I can't read her tone. It's flat, like she could go either way. So I tell the truth.

"I'm not really sure what happened. It's a bit of a long story, but the gist of it is, he was an ass and became more of an ass on the trip. Possessive, paranoid, and just—"

"He was a shithead," Amber speaks up, her eyes wide and earnest. "Like, totally. Gemma kicked him to the curb."

That wasn't exactly true but I'm adding another round of Christmas presents for this girl.

"An ass?" my mom repeats, and there's a bit of a smile on her face. She smoothes her blond bob back behind her ears and hides her mouth with her hand. She's smiling.

"What's so funny?" I ask her.

Her eyes, light and playful, dart over to Auntie Jolinda before coming back to me. She composes herself and folds her hands daintily in front of her. "Oh, Gemma. I can't say I'm all that surprised. He struck me as an ass when I first met him."

That was the only time she met him, too. She was in Auckland visiting and came by the gym. Nick was a little brusque with her but he was that way with most people. Most people I brought into his life, anyway. Anyone who benefited him personally was always a different story.

Once again I berate myself for being so hung up on this loser that I had to fly all the way to North America to try to get over him and just ended up back where I started.

"Well," I say, clearing my throat and diverting my attention to the half-eaten pie. For a moment I want to focus on all the calories I've consumed and all the work I'll have to do to burn them off, but I'm not sure anymore if that's me talking. "The problem is that he said he'll trash my name all over town and I'll never get a job at another gym."

There's complete silence at the table. Not even a clattering of silverware. Finally, Keri says, "I don't think anyone will listen to someone who says that about you." She says it with such ease that I almost believe her, then I remember she's young and she doesn't realize yet how crap people can be.

"Awh, Gem," Uncle Jeremy says, "you'll be all right, aye? People will still want you at their gym because you're you. And if not, you'll find something else. You're only twenty-two, right? Plenty of time to figure things out."

Is that right? Because I've always felt that in your twenties you need to have everything figured out. Your job, your career, your body, your love life. Hell, the only thing I seem to have going for me at the moment is Josh, and he's fleeting.

At that thought, the ache in my chest rears its ugly head. I push it down with a large gulp of wine and finish the rest of my dinner while the conversation turns to other things.

When it's all over, I volunteer to help my mother and aunt clean up. As usual they wash the pots and pans and I dry so I don't have to deal with soggy old food stuck to dishes, something that always make me want to chunder.

After my aunt tutters on about this and that, my mother hands me the pie tin but holds on to it for a moment, looking me in the eye. "You're better off," she says, and her candor makes me jerk my head back.

"Really?"

She lets go of the pan and goes back to washing. "He didn't care about you. I could tell." Her eyes dart over to the living room where Josh is laughing with Uncle Jeremy about something. "But that boy, Josh, he cares."

I'm not sure how to approach this doozy so I go with the truth. "Josh is just a friend, Mum."

"Good," she says briskly, scrubbing the crap out of a pan. "You need friends. Sometimes I worry that . . ." She trails off and Auntie Jolinda leaves the room. My mother eyes me, ever so elegantly. "It's good to have fun, Gemma."

I slowly wipe the pan in my hand and then put it down. Somehow I still feel like a kid in this kitchen. "I have fun."

"I know," she says. "But I rarely see you smile. I saw you smile a lot tonight. You're having fun. And whoever that person is that makes you smile, I don't really care, as long as it's happening."

My brows raise. Who replaced my robot mother with *this* woman?

She notices and lets out a little laugh, her delicate earrings swinging back and forth. "I know I don't tell you this sort of thing often, my dear, but I've not seen it for quite a while. I know things have been tough—for the both of us. And I know you're trying your best to do what you think is right. But, as your mother, if you just do what makes you happy, I'll be happy." She gestures to the kitchen. "Cooking makes me happy. Running this place makes me happy. Tasting that perfect glass of wine that we created, that makes me happy. And yes, one day, I think another man may make me happy. There's a lot of happiness out there if you're not afraid to reach for it."

I don't know why but tears are springing to my eyes. She makes a tsking sound with her teeth and comes over, enveloping me in a hug. It's still a Justine Henare hug, the light, barely touching kind, but it counts. It's hers and right now it's for me.

"Take this opportunity," she whispers in my ear, "and find what makes you happy. You may never get that chance again. Time waits for no one."

I don't know why, but "Time" by Pink Floyd starts playing in my head, its lyrics finally sinking in with its potency.

No one told you when to run, you missed the starting gun.

But my mother is giving me the cue to run. I pull away and see the strange sincerity in her eyes. I nod and wipe away at the one tear that has dared to fall.

"Your father would want you to be happy, too," she adds, her smile soft. She nods in the direction of Josh, who at that moment is looking across the kitchen island and catching my eye. "Go. Sit down."

She hands me a glass of wine and ushers me away. I sit down next to Josh on the love seat and try to say more with my eyes than I can with my mouth.

I hope I'm brave enough to let go.

Chapter Eighteen

JOSH

Christmastime in the summer is a real fucking trip. That's the only reason I think the holiday has snuck up on me—it just doesn't feel real. In Vancouver, I would be working holiday hours, dealing with the constant rain and cold and the never-ending darkness and exhausted shoppers bumping into you in the streets armed with bags of Christmas gifts.

Here, on the other side of the world, the sun is high in that bright, blue sky all day, and it's warm—hot, even—and you feel like you don't have a care in the world.

Though, of course I'd be lying if I said I didn't have a care. It's officially Christmas Eve now and I haven't bought Gemma or Amber anything for tomorrow. I probably should get something for Gemma's mom and aunt, too, since I'm spending the holiday at their house.

When I wake up on a wobbly air mattress on the floor, I ask if there's some way Gemma can drop me off in Napier so I can do some shopping. Both she and Amber have this sheepish look in their eyes and tell me that they have to go shopping, too. We've all totally dropped the ball this holiday.

It's not long before we're up and dressed and clamoring downstairs, just in time to see her mother has laid out a spread of breakfast delights on the table—French toast, bacon, sausage, scrambled eggs, a pot of steaming coffee. Her uncle Jeremy and his kids are already digging in, so we sit down with them. I don't mind—Gemma's got a pretty awesome family.

I really like her uncle—he's easygoing and says the most inappropriate things. His kids are really cute, too—you know, for kids. Gemma's auntie Jolinda has yet to pinch my butt cheeks, but the week is young.

At first I wasn't too sure about her mother. She reminded me of my own mom in that cool, standoffish way. But she's actually not that bad. I can see how Gemma gets some of her traits from her, even if she didn't get the pale skin and blond hair. There's warmth inside of both of them; you just have to look for it from time to time.

With Gemma, I'm learning how to bring it out of her more and more. And the more I hear her laugh, the more I feel her, the more I want her. It's a bit addictive.

Sitting at the table, passing juice and coffee, laughing and talking, I start to get that ache that Gemma talks about. But I know exactly what it is. I like it here. I like being with her, feeling like I'm a part of something with people who care about me. I mean, they don't know me and I don't know them, but you can feel the love around the table and it doesn't seem to matter who it's directed toward. I'm treated just as well as Gemma and Amber and it's . . . nice.

At home, I don't have this. Even when I was little, I didn't have this. I had a mother and father who constantly argued—she was hard and impenetrable, he was having an affair with a woman who wasn't. My sister, Mercy, was the perfect one, and Vera was the screwup, lashing out at the world. I was the youngest, watching it all unfold and feeling slightly removed, sometimes too young to really understand what was going on.

I understood now, though. And now I could see what I was missing.

This.

I feel Gemma's hand on my knee, giving me a quick squeeze and bringing me back. Her eyes are asking me if I'm okay, and that ache is replaced with gratitude for her, for her concern, for her touch.

I only wish I could take her with me.

When breakfast is finished the three of us pile into Mr. Orange and head past vineyards and farms to the city. It's ridiculous how pretty this place is. I don't think I've seen an ugly part of New Zealand yet. I tell Gemma this.

She smiles at me. "Well, you haven't seen Invercargill. Mick Jagger called it the asshole of the earth."

I frown. "I bet New Zealand's asshole still looks better than his."

"Ugh," Amber says from behind us. "I do not need the mental imagery, thank you very much." She makes a disgusted sound and then suddenly adds, "Hey, guys. I'm going to miss this, you know."

I turn in my seat and look at her. "Talking about Mick Jagger's asshole?"

"No," she says. "This. Us. Mr. Orange. Going places."

As much as I've grown tired of being cooped up in this bus, I can't really imagine a life in which I'm not exploring a country in him, seeking out new places and adventures each day. That will be another thing I wish I could take with me.

"You're leaving on Boxing Day, right?" I ask.

She nods uncertainly. "Day after Christmas? Yeah. What's Boxing Day for, anyway?"

"I don't really know," I tell her, "but it's a holiday here and in Canada. Something about giving boxes instead of gifts?" I know that's totally wrong, though.

"I'm going to miss you, too," Gemma tells her sincerely, eyeing her in the mirror.

"Please play 'Wish You Were Here' ad nauseam after I leave and think of me," Amber says. "That can be your Christmas gift to me."

"Dude!" I exclaim. "I am never listening to Pink Floyd ever again after this."

"But every time you hear it," Gemma points out, "you'll think of us."

"True." But the truth is, everything is going to make me think of her.

We drive through the city streets and have a tough time finding parking. I guess Christmas shopping on Christmas Eve is sort of asking for trouble. After stalking shoppers back to their cars and trying to steal their spots to no avail, Gemma says she's going to drop us off and take Mr. Orange to an auto-glass shop to see if his window can get a quick replacement.

I offer to pay for it—I was serious when I first brought that up at the Routeburn shelter—but once again she waves me off. She tells us she'll be back in a couple of hours and then she's gone, puttering down the road.

Amber had asked me earlier if I wanted to go halfsies on a gift for Gemma's family and said she'd take care of picking it out, which totally saves my ass. All I have to do is buy something for her and Gemma.

It's not going to be easy. Amber and I split up and I stroll around Napier aimlessly. By noon it's hot as fuck out. The town is actually pretty neat, with all these Art Deco buildings re-created from the thirties when an earthquake wiped them out, and it's fringed with palm trees and blue surf. I want to ask Gemma about growing up here and wonder what she was like in high school, if she went to the beach to party with the other teens I spy there. Then I remember all her trophies and her comment about putting balls in her mouth and I laugh.

I've never been very good at picking out presents. I usually get people the same damn thing. For my mom, something for the kitchen, even though she doesn't cook; for Mercy, a gift certificate. For Vera I try to get her some rare music memorabilia, like a Faith No More single on seven-inch vinyl, or something astronomy-themed. For the ex-girlfriends who happened to be in my life during the holidays in the past, they'd get a nice date and maybe one of those tacky coupons for a free back rub or mindless fuck.

But Gemma needs something special. I just don't have the slightest idea what that is. I decide to get Amber's gift first. I wander into the least gaudy souvenir shop I can find, and after some searching I pick up a flask that has a Kiwi bird on it. It's classy and cute and also a bit badass, which suits her just fine. Amber has always struck me as a bit of a sheltered child with a hidden side to her. I think by the time she gets back to San Jose after her around-the-world trip, she's going to be a totally different person.

After I get that, I'm left to wander up and down palm-lined streets named after Dickens and Tennyson. It strikes me that this is the first time I've been alone in a very long time. I'm not sure if I like it. I've always been a bit of a loner but now I've grown accustomed to being around people all the time, people I like, people I love.

My thoughts jar me. People I *love*? Where the fuck did the L-word come from? I don't think I *love* Gemma, I just like her a lot. Like, an awful lot. Like, an absurd amount, to the point where I can't stop thinking about her, even when she's right beside me; even being away from her to buy her a damn Christmas present feels like ages.

I like her. So what? That's always been obvious.

I like being inside her. No, I *love* being inside her. And listening to her, talking to her, watching her smile, hearing her laugh. I love trying to bring her out of her shell, the real her, seeing those glimpses of sunshine inside of her that I know no one else can see. I love the way she smells, the feel of her skin, her muscles, her lips, her hair. I love that she's slowly trusting me and that she cares for me, and maybe one day it will be as much as I care for her. I love her battered little soul and artist's heart stuck in the body of a warrior. I love that's she more broken than me, because I think I can put her back together. I love that there is so much left in her to discover.

But I'm not in love with her.

Am I?

I blink and shake my head. It won't end well if I keep thinking like this. What do I know, anyway? I've never even *been* in love before.

And that's when it hits me. I know what I'll give her. The sketchbook I've been drawing, painting, and sketching in. I know I thought about giving it to her before, but now it's official. I'll give her that, when this is all over. It's the biggest piece of me that I can give—the world, the trip of a lifetime, her, all recorded through my eyes.

But since I'll be working in it until the day I leave, I'll have to get her something to tide her over, so she doesn't unwrap nothing on Christmas.

I go into an art supply store and buy a blank card and a dense pencil and head to a large, busy square at the end of the shopping center. I sit on the edge of a giant fountain, and while the palm trees wave above me, I sketch a different scene on the card, one of snow and ice. I draw Santa Claus *and* myself in a present-filled sleigh, flying up into the clouds.

Underneath I write: *Your present is coming.*

I almost write *and so am I*, but I figure that's probably not appropriate for Christmas morning.

"There you are." I hear Amber's sing-song voice. I quickly turn my head to see her coming toward me, shopping bag in tow, and make sure that her present is completely hidden.

She stops in front of me and spies the card. Her mouth drops open. "Shut the front door. Did you draw that?"

"Yeah," I say, sliding it inside the envelope but not sealing it. "I won't be able to give Gemma her gift until right before I leave, so it's just something to take its place for now."

"Please don't tell me it's your cock."

"Hey," I say, grinning at her. "If I recall correctly, you're quite fond of my cock."

She glares at me and puts a hand on her hip. "*Was*."

I get up. "Well, if you must know, I'm going to give Gemma my sketchbook when this is all over. All my drawings, paintings, every step of the trip that I've re-created. What do you think?"

I watch her closely for her reaction as to whether this is actually a pretty cheap and lame idea or not. As I said, I don't have the best gift-giving skills. But her eyes start to well up and her lower lip sticks out slightly. "Josh," she says softly. "That's beautiful."

"Really? You don't think it's a cop-out?"

She widens her eyes. "How could anyone think that? That sketchbook is art. It's your life, it's . . . *you*. Anyone would be honored to have that, but she's especially going to melt. Awh, I wish I could be there to see her face."

"I *don't*," I say, "because if she likes it that much, you know what's going to happen next."

She shakes her head, muttering something about me being a pervert. Then she gives me a reluctant, wry smile. "You did good, Josh."

Eventually Gemma comes to pick us up in Mr. Orange,

outfitted with a brand-new back window, and I'm feeling more confident about my decision. When we get back home, her house smells of fresh-baked cookies, or "biscuits" as they call them, and there are Christmas songs playing. I decide to start sketching more; I want to capture her family, her holidays.

That night, her mother has family friends over for dinner—the stiffly dressed Priscilla and Grant Richardson. It's apparently day two of amazing feasts. After we drink wine in the sun on the wide stone patio in their backyard, which is essentially composed of a dark blue lap pool and groomed grass, we head inside for barbecued prawns, crayfish, salmon, and grilled abalone with honey-roasted potatoes and carrots.

I make a remark about how different it is to be having prawns for Christmas Eve dinner when Grant Richardson fixes his eyes on me. He's a little drunk and he's got this smug look on his face that I didn't notice earlier. I feel like I'm not going to like what's coming next.

"So, how are you liking New Zealand?" he asks.

I smile before taking a bite of the salmon. "I love it."

"And when do you go back?"

"January tenth," I tell him, even though it pinches a bit to say it out loud.

"I see," he says. "And then what happens between you two?" He points to me and Gemma with his fork.

I raise my brow. "Excuse me?"

"Grant," Gemma's mom says, shooting him a look.

He ignores it and slips into a lazy smile. "Justine tells me you guys are," he coughs, "a couple. Just curious if you intend to stay in contact with her after you leave or if this is a shore-man-on-leave type of deal, if you know what I mean."

Who the fuck does this prick think he is? I look at Gemma with my blood boiling loudly in my ears. She's silent, shocked, maybe embarrassed. Everyone at the table is.

"Oye," Jeremy says to Grant, "let the lovebirds be, bro."

I give Jeremy a quick smile, raising my palm briefly. "No, it's okay. I guess it's a simple question," I say, but when I look at Grant, I know my eyes are hard. "Not that it's any of your business whatsoever, but I certainly hope to stay in contact with her."

He leans back in his chair. "I know young hormones, my lad. Just be honest with each other. You wouldn't want to lead her on." He gives Gemma a pointed look. "Or vice versa."

I look at Gemma curiously but she still seems frozen.

"Hormones?" I repeat. "What I feel for her is a hell of a lot more than hormones, *sir*."

"Grant," Justine says, getting to her feet. "I don't think their relationship is any of your concern, whether you mean well or not." She puts emphasis on the *or not* part.

Gemma suddenly seems to find her strength and gets up, leaving the table and going outside. I stare at the table, puzzled. Auntie Jolinda is giving me a sympathetic look while Grant looks smug. His wife Priscilla eats slowly, ignoring the whole, strange thing.

I get up and go after her. I find her walking down the road toward the ocean.

"Gemma!" I call out softly and jog after her. Once I catch up to her, I tug her arm to stop her in her tracks. "What the hell was that all about? Who the fuck is that obnoxious yuppie prick?"

She's upset, chewing on her lip angrily. "That's Grant Richardson."

"Yeah, I got that much. Who the fuck is he to you?"

She sighs and keeps walking, but slowly, so I walk beside her. "I used to go out with his son in high school. Remember I said I stayed at the hostel in Paekakariki with an ex? Well, that was him, Robin Richardson."

"Why is your mom friends with them still?"

"They were friends with my parents before my dad passed. Robin and I dated for a few years. It was inevitable. You know how high school is."

"So what happened? Does he hold a grudge or something?"

She exhales noisily through her nose. The back of her head is lit by the golden setting sun. I'm hanging on to her every word.

"Yes," she says, "though he shouldn't still. After high school, Robin went away to university in Australia and I found someone else. It was wrong, but I was young and stupid. Anyway, Grant saw us together and questioned Robin about it. Poor Robin had no idea. I felt terrible, I still do, though I know Robin is engaged in Melbourne somewhere and it all worked out in the end."

"I see," I say, understanding a little bit but not really liking this fact about her. "That was a long time ago, though, right?"

She nods. "It was before Nick. I think he wants me to get my comeuppance. Sounds like he wants you to do the same to me as I did to his son."

"That's a bit fucked up."

"Well, they were a pretty fucked-up family. Still are. He's a lush and his wife is a doormat."

"And Robin?"

"Actually, he was quite nice," she concedes thoughtfully. "I shouldn't have done that to him."

I purse my lips for a moment before saying, "Then why did you?"

She looks away and shrugs. "I don't do long-distance relationships well. I don't do relationships well, period. You saw me and Nick."

I did. But I can't help but notice that her mother was the one who mentioned the term *relationship*. Obviously that notion had to come from somewhere, whether it was accurate or not.

"You're a complicated little woman," I say, deciding not to bring it up.

She raises her brow. There's some relief in her face that the conversation is over. "Who are you calling 'little'?"

"Most women want to be called little."

"Not this one."

"And that's what I . . ."

She gives me a sharp look. "Why you what?"

What the hell was I just about to say?

"Want to fuck you senseless," I finish, wrapping my arm around her waist and holding her to me.

She laughs. "I can't believe I'm saying this, but no. The next time we fuck, we're going to be in my bloody bed. I'm tired of having your cum dripping down my leg."

"That's definitely something I have never heard before." I slide my hand down the back of her shorts.

"Well, it's a problem with us," she says.

"Not a bad problem to have," I say, "but fine. Next time we fuck, it will be in your bed. You know I'm happy fucking you anywhere. We could do it on the kitchen table right now, give your ex-boyfriend's father a little show."

She grabs my hand and starts to pull me toward the beach. "Come on, let's watch the sunset from there."

"You don't want to go back and finish that extremely awkward dinner?"

She grins at me. "We'll go back for dessert."

I wag my brows excitedly but she was being literal. After the sunset dipped behind the hills and valleys, tingeing the vivid ocean with gold and pink, we came back to find the Richardsons gone and a meringue dessert called pavlova on the table.

No one brought up the weirdness from earlier, and things continued on to the living room, where we sipped brandy and drank beer and slipped into an easy comfort. But in the back of my head, I couldn't help but worry. If she didn't do relationships, what were we, really?

What would I be to her when I left?

———•———

It's quite obvious to see whose presents are whose the next morning. Mine are wrapped in a plastic bag and Amber's are done up in a backpacker magazine about New Zealand, which includes a rather inappropriate ad for a campervan company: *Our prices are so Emo they cut themselves.*

I haven't had a fun family Christmas in a long time. Actually, I've *never* had a fun family Christmas, except for that time we were at the Big White Ski Resort and Vera and I climbed onto some condo's roof to use their rooftop hot tub. *That* was fun.

Here, though, it's nice to just relax as Keri and Kam hand out the presents, pretending to be Santa's elves, even though they're way past the age to believe in him.

Amber gives me a small sketchbook for writing on the go, which is pretty awesome of her. The art store was certainly the place to be yesterday. She loves her flask, too, and said she'd use it often. I believe her.

She then opens Gemma's present, which is a *pāua*, or abalone-shell, necklace, which fits right in with Amber's hippie-dippie style. The present she bought from us for everyone ends up being a giant box of very fancy Kiwi chocolates. Like, actual kiwifruit chunks covered in decadent dark chocolate. Keri and Kam go nuts over it and I give Amber the thumbs-up.

Somehow Gemma and I end up saving our presents for each other for last. She takes mine first, sitting down among a battleground of torn wrapping paper. She keeps wrapping and unwrapping the plastic bags I stuck together until she comes to the card at the middle.

She slips it out of the envelope and her features soften as she takes it in, reading it over. She looks at me with bright eyes and says, "Thank you."

I point at it. "But you know that the real gift is coming later, right?"

She smirks at that and I know her mind has gone the perverted route. "Yes," she says. She then shows the card to everyone else and they ooh and ahh over it, which makes my face grow momentarily hot.

Justine looks at the card and then at me. "I think you embellished your muscles a bit, Josh."

Everybody laughs and I shrug. "Artistic license," I say.

Suddenly Gemma grows serious, maybe even a bit nervous, and hands me a small, wrapped box. I take it from her, feeling the slight tremor of her left hand and the eyes of everyone on me.

I slowly unwrap it to find a black jewelry box. The first thing I think is, *I hope I like it,* because honestly, I've never been given a piece of jewelry that I've liked. I'm a picky guy and I hope to god I don't have to hurt Gemma's feelings. She can see right through me.

But when I flip open the box, I discover there's nothing to worry about. Lying there, attached to a black leather cord, is a brightly colored greenstone, or jade, pendant. It's not too big, not too small, in a simple twist design. I'd actually wear it proudly.

Jeremy gets up to get a better look. "Awh, that's choice, Gemma," he booms in his deep voice. "You know what that means, bro?"

I shake my head, taking it out of the box and holding it

up. The sunlight catches the edge of it, making it glow like a green sea.

"It's infinity," Jeremy says. He looks at Gemma and smiles softly, then sits down without saying another word.

"Infinity?" I ask.

She nods at it and a hint of color forms on her cheeks. "Put it on."

"This isn't some Maori curse or something, is it?" I joke.

"Nah, mate." Jeremy laughs. "The curse is if you stick around long enough, you have to put up with us."

Best curse ever, I think to myself. I put it around my neck and make sure it's lying flat. Again, everyone ooohs and ahhhs over it. Then they all separate, gathering their gifts and looking over the stash.

I remain on the couch with Gemma. She's tucks her feet under her, sitting like a mermaid.

"I'm glad you like it," she says. "Even if you didn't, greenstone is one of those gifts that's good luck to receive. It's not custom to actually buy one for yourself."

I cup her face in my hands and kiss her forehead, her nose, her chin, then her lips. I know this is the first public display of affection we've shown in front of her family, but I don't care.

They know. They would know from our gifts alone. We may not be in a *relationship* but whatever we have, it's something special. Something worth holding on to. I want nothing more than to take her upstairs and make love to her on the bed, like she asked.

But this is not the time or place. I just put my arm around her waist and haul her to me, grinning like an idiot. She laughs, burying her face into my neck. I'm lucky, so lucky, just to have this.

It's the best Christmas I've ever had.

Chapter Nineteen

GEMMA

It's Boxing Day and already hot as hell by nine a.m. We've—and by that I mean my mother, Auntie Jolinda, Uncle Jeremy, Keri, Kam, Josh, and I—have gathered in the driveway to say goodbye to Amber. Josh and I are still taking her to the airport but everyone else has to give her hugs and wish her well; Uncle Jeremy even tries to demonstrate the Maori tradition of the *hongi*, pressing his nose and forehead against hers and shaking her hand. She does it and manages to keep a straight face, too. Not that she feels much like laughing.

In fact, she's kind of a weepy mess all the way to the airport, which makes me feel like crying, too. I manage to hold it together, though, but just barely. I'm really going to miss that girl, and she's right—I'm going to think of her every time I hear Pink Floyd.

I park Mr. Orange in the temporary car park and it's hard to even get her out of the bus. When she does emerge, she runs her hands down his tangerine sides and pats him like you would a horse on the rump.

"Thanks for the memories," she says to Mr. Orange. She stares at him for a moment, like she's waiting for him to reciprocate, then joins me and Josh as we head toward the airport.

The Hawkes Bay Airport is small, so there's not much waiting around. She checks in for her flight, gets her tickets, and then we have to say goodbye.

I give her a big hug, bigger than I normally do. Josh does the same. She holds back the tears in her eyes and says she's going to miss us. She adds "heaps" at the end, proud of her Kiwi phrasing, then turns just as she's about to sob, hiding her tears and scurrying away to security, her kimono jacket flowing behind her.

She's going to be just fine in Australia. More than fine. I can't wait to see her updates on Facebook.

Instinctively, I grab Josh's hand, feeling the loss of her already. We were four, then we were three, and now we are two. It's just me and him, and I'm both excited and scared. There's pressure on us now that she's gone—on how we'll act around each other, what we'll say, how we'll get along. The dynamic has changed.

I loop my fingers through his and he pulls my hand up and kisses it, his mouth warm and real, his eyes looking deep into mine. His eye contact can be so unnerving at times, like he really is searching for my soul, but I'm growing used to it. He's starting to feel as close to me as a second skin.

There's a heaviness in the air when we get back to Mr. Orange, the result of Amber's absence. It feels weird, so I pop in Mr. Floyd to help balance the mood. "Fearless" starts playing, as it has *many* times before, but now it makes the short drive back from the airport a dreamy trip, green flying past us on one side, blue on the other, sunshine streaming down the middle. I curl up into the song, wishing I could be fearless.

I'm starting to think I'm losing it a bit. When I saw his Christmas present, I could have cried. It was just a drawing and a promise of more to come, but it was everything to me. When he put my greenstone around his neck, I nearly ran out the door from fear.

But it was a sweet kind of fear. The fear that hope hinges on.

I knew that Uncle Jeremy wanted to explain what the necklace really meant, but I'm glad he left that up to me. It's true it's a symbol of infinity, the twist going on and on, like a snake eating a snake eating a snake. But what it really means, for me anyway, is that he put his stamp on my heart, and no matter what happens in the future that won't go away. It'll go on and on, for infinity. This trip, this last month together, it can never be taken away from us. It means that, though we might take different paths, we will always be connected.

He's wearing it around his neck right now and the green shines subtly against his tanned skin. The design even matches the swirl of some of his tattoos. It's masculine and beautiful, just like him.

My Josh.

I blink a few times, trying not to think that way. But it's hard. He really does feel like *my* Josh. We're so undefined, so fleeting and fragile and new, but I don't think he could belong to anyone else, and I couldn't belong to anyone else but him.

So, for the next while, he's still mine.

Later that night, after we get back, we fuck in my bedroom. Uncle Jeremy and the kids have gone back to Aramoana, and my mother and aunt have gone to sleep. We finally have the place to ourselves and we waste no time. I'm barely through the door before Josh is trying to tear my clothes off and I'm doing the same to him.

The necklace stays on.

He goes down on me first, teasing me slowly until I'm

squeezing his head between my legs and I'm coming, hand over my mouth so my mother doesn't hear.

I'm totally sixteen again.

Then when I feel I'm too spent, too dazed, he thrusts inside me, bringing me back to life. I'm half off the bed and he's standing, my legs in his capable hands, and the necklace jostles slightly while he drives himself in and out. It's not long before I'm coming again, louder this time, caught up in the connection, in the sight of his long, hard body, of the gift I gave him, of the want and lust in his hooded eyes.

He collapses on top of me and then sinks into my bed, pulling me back into him, his legs and arms wrapping around me, much like they did on the top of Key Summit. I give in to his warmth, to the intimacy. I can't imagine anyone else ever holding me this way, and it's one more stab to the gut that I can't bear.

Every moment we're together now I'm so conscious that we're teetering toward the end. Tomorrow we leave for the East Cape, for that sunrise I always wanted to see, the first in the world. Then we skirt the Bay of Plenty, maybe popping down to Rotorua or Taupo, and then back up toward the Northland and New Year's Eve at my grandpa's. After that, we'll head back to Auckland, and then the real world begins. He'll go back home. I'll look for a job.

And try to forget him.

But the thought of him leaving me scares me more than anything, more than trying to figure out jobs and figure out my future. I don't know how I'll go back to living with Nyla and Chairman Meow again, just existing on fumes, succumbing to the emptiness inside, the sadness. I guess I'll have no choice but to harden myself once more and build my armor.

But my armor has chinks. If it didn't, Josh wouldn't be in

my bed right now, holding me like he'll never let go, and I wouldn't be loving every sweet second of it.

If I was smart, I would do it now. I wouldn't lie here with Josh, I wouldn't let him hold me and make me feel like I'm so fucking important to him. But I'm not smart. Not anymore, not now. Maybe I never was. I want to enjoy him while I can, even though I can see the Gemma of the future and she's lonely and cold.

I tried to tell Josh the other day, when Grant pulled that drunken bullshit at the dinner table. I tried to warn him, that I can't do what he thinks I can. I can't be that person he wants me to become. I can't hold on to myself and let go at the same time.

He kisses the rim of my ear, his favorite place, and murmurs a heavy good night.

He's burying the ache as well.

———————•———————

The next day we're up bright and early to keep our tight schedule. I know the drive up to the East Cape will take longer than it looks, thanks to Mr. Orange's composition and the Cape's remote and twisting roads.

After we have another hearty breakfast and I'm convinced I've gained another two pounds, Josh asks, a little too innocently, if I have any art supplies around.

I know we do. My father's studio, under Auntie Jolinda's room in the guest cottage, has been largely untouched since his death. I go in there from time to time when I'm back home, just to feel a piece of him, something tangible and real that he's left behind. But other than that, no one moves his stuff around. It's still his room and we like to pay respects.

But I know that my father would have loved Josh, would have loved his talent, and wherever he is, I know he wouldn't mind a little tour, even if it's to see if there are any leftover pencils or canvas or whatever Josh has his eye on.

Together we stroll down the gravel path, the morning sun high and strong. He grabs my hand and squeezes it hard just as I take out the keys. There are valuables in there, paintings that we could never bear to lose.

"Is this difficult for you?" he asks, eyes searching mine.

I manage a smile. "It's not easy but it's good. It's a good kind of pain."

He nods and waits as I unlock the door and push it open.

Dust rushes to meet our faces and floats in the air like mist, caught in the sun streaming through the back windows.

Most things in the studio, particularly easels with paintings my dad was still completing at the time of the accident, are covered with white linen, giving the room a ghostly look. I flick on the light but the bulb seems to have burned out. It doesn't matter; the natural light that floods in from the south-facing windows is more than enough.

Josh is silent as he takes it all in, and there's a wash of reverence in his expression. He's being respectful and I love him for it.

Finally, he looks at me. "This is a good space."

I nod. "He was in here all the time. Could hardly get him out. I used to sit right over there," I point to a stool in the corner, "and spin around and watch him paint."

"Where did you paint?" he asks.

He's getting closer to a question I don't want to answer. I clear my throat, feeling like the dust is getting lodged in there. I point at a spot in the corner, behind a shelving unit. "Over there."

He eyes it, frowning. "Where are your paintings?"

I feel the hot cloak of shame come over me. "I destroyed them all."

He stares at me blankly for a few long beats. "You what?" he whispers.

I look away, unable to handle this. I've never brought it up with anyone. After it happened and my mother found out, we had a horrible fight, but that was the end of it and it was never mentioned again. Now I can feel Josh's eyes on me, trying to understand.

He thinks I'm crazy. I think he's right.

I close my eyes and take in a deep breath. "I destroyed the paintings. All that were in my possession, anyway. I burned them in the fire pit outside. There's nothing left."

"Why would you do that?" His voice is shocked, saddened, heartbreaking to hear.

I put my head in my heads, blocking him out. He wraps his fingers around my forearm and pries my hands away. "What happened?" he asks.

My face crumples. Why doesn't he understand?

"What happened?" I repeat, shame and fear and anger competing in my heart. "He *died*. I was ruined. I lost the two things I loved most in the world, that's what happened!" I pull away from him and stumble to the middle of the room, gesturing wildly around me. "How could I look at what I used to be, what I used to have? I couldn't! The paintings would hang on the walls in here and they would mock me, they would make fun of me for not becoming what I could have been. Haven't you ever lost something, Josh?"

He stares at me, not saying a word.

"Well, I did," I go on, my heart racing, "I lost them in the worst way."

"So you shut down," he says, almost to himself.

I frown at him, my hackles rising. "It's called self-preservation."

He smiles sadly. "It's not a way to live, Gemma. Everyone

is going to lose something, someone, at some point in their lives."

"You don't understand," I snap, glaring. He thinks he has me all figured out. He doesn't know me, he wasn't there, he didn't have to go through it. "You have everything."

He raises his brows and gives his head a little shake. "I don't have everything," he says quietly. "I barely have you."

We stare at each other, the dust still hanging in the air. I try and compose myself, breathing in and out, but my breath keeps escaping me.

I need to escape.

I walk past him but he grabs me and hauls me to him. "Don't run," he says, holding me by the shoulders in place. "Not from this, not from me."

"Let me go," I say.

"You could make me," he says, his grip not loosening. "I know you can."

He's right. But the truth is, I think his arms are the only thing keeping me upright.

"It's done," I say, my chin dipped low, staring at the floor between us. "It happened. I can't get those paintings back. I was a different person before and I'm a different person now."

The child is grown, the dream is gone. "Comfortably Numb" plays in my head and I close my eyes.

"But would you do it again?" he asks. His voice sounds larger than life in here. "Or will you destroy something before you have a chance to lose it?"

He's in my head, he's in my heart. How did he get in here? There's an edge to his words, like he *knows*, like he knows *me*.

I'm numb, I'm numb, I'm numb.

"Gemma," he says in a hushed tone and plants a hard kiss on the top of my head. He wraps his arms around me. "I can't even begin to imagine what it must be like to lose your father. If I lost my sister, I don't know what I'd do. And if I lost the ability to create, the one thing that makes me happy, that would almost be worse. But . . . you have to understand . . . or maybe not . . . but your father won't stop being your father. And you won't stop being an artist. You just have to let it out. Don't think that because time has passed you're not allowed to grieve anymore." He pulls back and cups my face in his large hands, peering down at me. "And don't think that because you can't paint the way you used to, in the way you deemed as good—the *only* way—that you can't create. You're a different person now, as you say. Your art will be different. You don't have to stick to the only path you thought possible. There are others. Believe me."

I stare up at him, letting his words sink in. They're starting to stick.

Maybe I'm thawing.

I rub my lips together. "What did you want to get from here?"

His brows knit together but he nods, knowing I'm done talking about it. He doesn't have to know that he's gotten to me. He pulls away and looks around him. "Well, I was hoping to pick up something other than my watercolor pencils."

I tap my fingers to my chin, glad to have something else to think about. I walk over to the shelves and bring out a box full of supplies. My hand is shaking a bit but I decide that's okay. I'm still a bit shaken up over Josh's words, at the hope in them, at the way he managed to see inside me.

Will you destroy something before you have a chance to lose it?

I rummage through it and bring out black, green, and yellow oil paints. Their caps seem stuck on but they should be all right. I wave them at him. "How about oils? Only three colors, though."

"Nah," he says, coming over. "Too serious." He puts his hand in and pulls out a box of chunky pastels. "Bingo."

I eye him curiously. "Pastels? You don't strike me as a pastel kinda guy."

"I can't always be emo, can I?" he says with a wink and I laugh. "These are perfect."

I shrug. "Whatever floats your boat."

"You float my boat," he says seductively, and I know we have to get out of here before the air of respect totally disappears.

We go and pack up Mr. Orange. It's tougher than normal to say goodbye to my mother and Auntie Jolinda. Actually, it's never been tough before. I would just give them a wave and tell them I'd call them and maybe see them in a few months, and that would be that. I would leave without a second thought. I would feel no loss.

But something is different now. I feel this great link to the land here, to them, to their lives. I don't want to say goodbye. I've grown accustomed to having them around me, having them take care of me, and I've never liked or wanted that before.

Being home felt nice. Being home felt like . . . home.

It doesn't help that my mother has somewhat opened up to me. Or maybe, maybe, it's that I've opened up to her. Maybe we're meeting halfway now. Either way, I climb into the passenger seat with heavy shoulders. I roll down the window and wave to them as they stand in the driveway. They wave back and I think to myself, *I love them.*

Then I shake it off and slap the outside of the van door through the rolled-down window, signaling for Josh to drive on. We motor down the road, ready to resume our adventure, just the two of us.

The drive up the East Cape is easy for the first part. We

pass through farms and orchards and sunny fields, the highway skirting the endless blue ocean. Just outside of the Mahia Peninsula, we pull off the highway and have lunch sitting by a river. We devour a baguette sliced open and topped with brie and fresh tomatoes sprinkled with sea salt. It's the best thing I've ever eaten, the sun beating on our backs, cool water at our feet.

We laze about, lying in the grass at the river's edge, kissing sweetly and passionately. Sometimes we are full on making out and other times just staring at each other. His hands and eyes are always on me, touching me, roving over me, and I succumb each time, feeling prized and wanted in a way I haven't before.

This is so physical that it's beyond the physical.

Somewhere before the town of Gisborne, we fill up with petrol at a small, down-at-its-heels station, complete with rusted pumps. Josh goes inside to pay and when he comes back out, he's grinning, waving something in his hand.

"What?" I ask as he hops in the driver's seat.

He proudly displays it in his palm. It's a cassette tape of the best of Free.

"They had cassettes?" I ask.

"It was either this or Maori chants or Reba McEntire, so I picked this. Who doesn't love Paul Rodgers and Free? Now we can have new music for this part of the trip."

"The Josh and Gemma journey?"

"That has a very nice ring to it," he says. "In fact, it's all right now." He slides in the cassette and stares at it expectantly, figuring the song will start playing.

Of course "All Right Now" isn't the first song that plays, it's the Hendrix-like "I'm a Mover," but we're happy to have something new to listen to.

Later we stop to have dinner in Gisborne, which is a sort

of smaller, quainter version of Napier, then keep chugging on. I'm thinking that we'll find a holiday park soon but Josh scares the shit out of me by suddenly slamming on the brakes and taking Mr. Orange off the highway and onto a corridor of grass bordering the long but isolated Makorori Beach.

We bounce along over the uneven ground and just before he reaches the sand and I'm about to cry out, he turns to the right and takes the bus along the grass until we reach a long patch of trees and shrub. Once Mr. Orange is hidden from the road by all the brush, he puts it into park and switches off the engine.

He turns to look at me triumphantly. "Voilà, we have a whole beach to ourselves."

I give him a wry look and push back the swoop of hair that has fallen across his forehead from the bumpy voyage. "You know, you can't just camp wherever you like."

"Sure we can," he says with a grin and tries to fake-bite my hand. "No one is here, no one can see our car."

I sigh and point behind me. "Sure, no one coming down the hill over there can see this giant orange bus."

"Live a little," he says.

"Fine," I tell him, pointing a threatening finger at him. "But if we get busted by the Department of Conservation, you're getting us out of it."

We get out of the bus and I'm immediately glad he was so impulsive. Makorori Beach is a long sweeping expanse of off-white sand, bordered by sand and shrub along the highway and bookended by two green hills that jut out into the ocean. At this time of day there's no one around, there are barely any cars on the highway, and there are only a few baches in the area, hidden from sight. The air smells salty and sunbaked.

While Josh gets the camping stove and chairs set up for dinner, I decide to go for a barefoot run. I scurry down to the soft white sand and go slow but steady from one end of the beach to the other, just as the sun dips behind the low hills. When I get back, Free is blaring from the speakers and Josh has gone through a beer or two.

"There you are," he says, getting to his feet. "Daughter of Fire and Water."

"Huh?" I ask, wiping away the sweat from my brow. He comes over to me and puts his arms around me. "What are you doing? I'm all gross."

He grins and kisses my neck. "I like it. You're perfect." He starts to move back and forth, dancing with me, and it's only then that I realize the song playing is called "Fire and Water."

I try to pull away to towel off but he holds me in place, still swaying, rocking back and forth. The ocean breeze is stronger now, cooling the sweat on my skin, but inside I'm heating up.

"You've got what it takes to make a poor man's heart break," he sings in my ear, his voice low and melodic enough to send shivers down my spine. I take in a deep breath and rest my head on his shoulder and we just dance in the purple dusk.

After dinner is over—lamb kebabs—and the world grows dark, we retire inside to the bus. I've barely unfolded the bed before he's stripped naked and on me. Our soundtrack is the occasional passing car in the distance, the choir of crickets, the pounding surf and our hushed and ragged breathing as we thoroughly explore each other's bodies with hands, lips, and tongues.

He goes down on me and just before I'm about to come, he pulls up his head and slides his cock inside me with a low groan.

"I think I found a new calling in life," he says, his voice husky with desire. He places slow wet kisses along my jawline that shoot sparks down my body.

"What?" I whisper back, all my thoughts diverted to the languorous, steady way he's driving himself in and out of me.

"Fucking you," he says, his tongue snaking down my neck. "Fucking you in the morning, fucking you at night. Fucking you in a bed, fucking you in the ocean. Fucking you slow, like this," he withdraws his cock with deliberation before thrusting it back in, "fucking you raw. I would like to fuck you forever."

I close my eyes and groan at the way he's filling me up inside, the way his hands move over my hips and breasts like he's laying claim to different parts of me. "You like to say *fuck*."

"I like *to* fuck," he says, picking up speed. "And it takes on a whole new meaning when I'm with you." He licks a path to my nipples and sucks on them hard enough to make me gasp. "You," he whispers against them. "Everything has a new meaning with you."

I close my eyes and let the sensations take over. I can feel every inch of him. Inside me, around me, in the air I breathe, in the empty parts of my soul.

Even after we come and I'm snuggled into his chest, feeling his heart slowing beneath my fingers, I can still feel him.

He's buried in deep.

Chapter Twenty

JOSH

This woman is going to break my heart.

I knew it the moment she told me she destroyed all her paintings, all her memories. I knew she was going to destroy me, too.

I saw it in her eyes, in the dust of her father's studio: the fear that I had found her out.

I just wanted her to know, that's all. I wanted her to know that she didn't have to do this to us.

I can only hope she heard me. In some ways, I think she did. When we screw, I can feel her winding down while I'm winding in. The wall she has around her is coming down brick by brick. She's opening up. She's letting me in, even if she doesn't realize it.

I think she's starting to really like me.

I think I'm starting to fall in love with her.

I don't want to, of course. I don't want to fall because she's not someone I can trust with my heart. But if I could trust her to handle it with care, with understanding, with respect, then it might be worth everything. It might be the best thing on earth.

Or she might just toss it in a fire and watch it burn.

I may have to take my chances.

I get up in the morning before she does and take care not to disturb her. The inside of the van is a little damp, the way it normally is when you first wake and the sun hasn't had a chance to start kicking your ass.

Gemma moves a bit, pulling the sleeping bag up to her chin, her dark hair spilling around her like waves of black oil. She is so gorgeous, so perfect, that I can't help but stare at her. I love to do it when she's sleeping. Not because I'm trying to tip the creep scales here (I think I already did that when I followed her to New Zealand in the first place) but because she's finally at peace. Her face looks like a clean slate, with no anger or sadness or hollowness hidden in the corners.

I go outside to piss and contemplate going for a morning dip in the surf in lieu of a shower when I hear the crunch of tires going off road. I look over to see a policelike vehicle pulling onto the grass and head toward the beach. It doesn't seem like he's seen us yet but considering the bus looks like a giant orange Jolly Rancher, it's only a matter of time.

Shit.

I jump in the passenger seat, start the engine, and slam on the gas, peeling out of there.

"What the hell?" Gemma cries out, bouncing around in the back, her hair flying as I eye her in the rearview mirror.

"Stay down!" I yell at her. "I think the cops are onto us."

"What?" she says and looks behind her out the window.

Luckily the cop or the D.O.C. or whoever it was doesn't seem to have caught on that we were illegally camping there overnight, and soon we're speeding up the highway and on our way north.

Nothing like adrenaline to get your morning started on the right foot.

At our next stop, Tolaga Bay, some place with a really long wharf, we fill up with gas and try and make ourselves presentable for the rest of the journey. I've been driving in just my boxer briefs for about an hour, getting really weird looks from the truck drivers who overtake us.

The Maori presence on this part of the cape is really strong, and though at times I feel like I don't really belong here, being the tatted white guy and all, there's also something welcoming about it. It's mysterious. I want to explore the hidden coves and talk to elders with tattoos on their faces—*tā moko*, as Gemma explains—to understand their connection to the land. I find myself touching the greenstone pendant often, as if it will anchor me here somehow.

Gemma is behind the wheel now as we head toward our stop for the night, the East Cape Lighthouse, and I ask her about her heritage, if she feels more *pākehā* or Maori.

She seems to consider that for a moment. "I guess I'd consider myself more *pākehā* just because of my upbringing. But I don't really think about it. I can pass for either to everyone else, and no one really cares. I mean, I think one day everyone in New Zealand will have Maori blood in them, if they don't already. It's a good thing. I think it keeps people rooted, like they belong somewhere. The tribes, the *iwi*, around the country are all about family and your family beyond your family. I kind of like that."

I nod. I like that idea, too, it just doesn't apply to my own life whatsoever. My family may be tied through blood but the ties are weak and constantly unravelling. Suddenly, I think of Vera and can't blame her in the slightest for wanting to form her ties elsewhere.

I look over at Gemma, studying her. Her eyes are focused

on the road but are bright, clear, and sparkling. A few freckles have sprouted across her nose this last week. She looks healthy, content, happy. I wonder if I'm the reason. I wonder if she feels any ties to me. I wonder if she'll let me keep my ties to her.

It's a long, winding drive through tiny little settlements, overgrown forests, and encroaching bush, with clay cliffs rising up from the blue water. We take our time. I want to paint everything. I want to make a New Zealand superhero and call her Gemma, Daughter of Fire and Water. I'll give her a heart of ice and loins of fire and she'll sleep at the bottom of the ocean.

When we finally reach the turnoff for the lighthouse, it's growing dark. We drive along a narrow gravel road for what seems like for fucking ever, ocean on one side, a cliff on the other, and that terrible sense of loneliness hits me again. This is the easternmost point in the whole country. This is the edge of nothing. Out there, on the ocean, there's nothing.

There's nothing but me and Gemma. It feels like we're the only people left in the world. And it scares me, because she's all I have to hold on to. I can't be sure she won't let go.

There's no official camping at the lighthouse, so Gemma takes the bus off-roading, much like we did yesterday, and we come to a stop in a small valley in the middle of a field of cows. They all swivel their heads to stare at us with dark, inquisitive eyes. There's a small house up on the hill but we can barely see it. Horses graze on the hill's terraced grooves.

Beyond the hills, there's nothing but ocean. I breathe in deep, feeling strangely nervous and shaky. I don't think it's just about being on the edge of nothing, though.

I think it's that I'm on the edge of *something*.

We go to bed early, our alarms set for the early morning hour, predawn. Even though the ocean looks to be about a ten-minute walk, I pack a bag with my camera, my phone, my sketchbook, and the pastels.

I can't get enough of her. Our lovemaking is slow and lazy but necessary. Being inside her feels like being home, it feels like being in love, it feels like everything sweet and beautiful and nice in the world. Every time I come in her I hope I'm making a home for myself, a place where I belong.

The alarm on my phone goes off way too early. In my sleepy stupor I nearly turn it off but Gemma is patting my arm, then *punching* my arm, telling me to get up. The world around us vibrates with the sound of mooing cows and I wonder how the hell I slept through them.

Even though the days are hot, the mornings by the ocean are cold, and I can barely get on my jeans and hoodie in time. Armed with the pack and flashlights, we jump out of the van. The air snaps at us as if we're windblown flags.

Hundreds of cattle spread out in all directions, bound by the green hills to the south and the lighthouse to the north. I look east, to where the hills part and the sky is a paler shade of dawn. It seems to be growing lighter by the second, and our chances of catching the sunrise are dwindling.

We take off toward the light, cautiously creeping under barbed wire fences and avoiding the epic cow pies dotting the land. The cows, for the most part, seem to be ignoring us, but their piles of shit are like hidden land mines in the dim light. A meandering, narrow stream cuts across us and we have to head up into the terraced hills where wary horses eye us. I get the feeling that we've chosen the most difficult route to see the sunrise, and from our vantage point I can't even see the lighthouse anymore.

Just as the sky seems to grow frighteningly light, we reach the crest of the hill and I nearly collapse, out of breath from the quick, steep hike. A lone filly bolts at the sight of us.

Below us lies an empty beach, laid out like a sheet of velvet. Aside from the occasional hoofprint and driftwood, it looks totally undisturbed, like it has been waiting for us all this time. The South Pacific is spread out at the horizon's feet, a royal blue tinged with saffron edges. The sun is not up yet. We still have time.

We run down the hill and I nearly eat shit, several times, my shoes slipping on the dew-slicked grass, until sand sinks beneath my feet. I grab Gemma's hand and we run over to the water's edge just as the sun peeks its glowing crown over the wavering line.

I look at her and smile. We made it. We're standing on the easternmost point in the easternmost habitable country. We might even be the first people on this whole fucking earth to see this fiery sunrise. Only thousands of miles of rolling water lies between us and the southwest coast of Chile.

And yesterday.

Gemma lets go of my hand and lets out a whoop of joy and starts running up and down the beach like a horse that's been set free. I watch her, then take out my camera and start snapping pictures of her, of the beach, of the sunrise.

She raises her hands out, like she's about to fly, and tips her head back to the sky, eyes closed and smiling. I can feel the peace radiate from her, like she's being born anew. It's stunning.

I love you, I think as my heart seems to expand inside me.

And you'll hurt me.

You'll burn me.

You'll mark me.

But it's already worth it.

I sit down in the sand and bring out the sketchbook and pastels from the pack. Eventually she comes over to me, glowing even more brightly than the sun.

"Trying out the pastels?" she asks.

I shake my head. "No. You are."

She frowns and the glow seems to recede like the tide.

"Like before," I say to her, patting the sand next to me. "Like in Kaikoura. I want you to capture this, but with the pastels."

She frowns, but to her credit she crouches down beside me. She's not running away. "Why?"

"Because I think it will be good for you," I tell her.

She studies me carefully with those dark eyes of hers. "I'm not sure if you know what's good for me."

I grin at her. "I do. I'm good for you." I grab her shoulder and push her down so she falls back on her ass. She glares at me but again, she's not getting up, she's not leaving.

I place the box of pastels and the open page of the sketch-book beside her. "You won't see anything more inspiring than this," I say, gesturing to the sky, now gold. "Re-create it, capture it. Let it be wild, let it be messy. It's the first sunrise of many more to come. You can't screw it up. If you do, there's always tomorrow."

I know she's not the kind of person who looks kindly on the concept of tomorrow, but it seems to work. She chews on her lip for a moment, staring out at the ocean, before she rifles through the pastels and pulls out a goldenrod-colored one. She gingerly touches the pastel to the page and it leaves a waxy imprint. It's messy. It's abstract. You can't be precise. It's all about feeling and blurred edges and the loss of detail. It's the perfect medium for her.

She needs to let her soul out, on that page, like an artist. I feel like no one has seen it since her father died, since her art stopped. I understood what she meant by self-preservation. But it was more than that. It was like she had gotten rid of the only outlet she'd known.

I stand up and leave her in peace but she quickly mutters, "No, stay. I don't want to do this alone." She's never sounded so vulnerable.

So I stay. I sit beside her and watch with my own eyes as she re-creates a new version of the world; her version. It's imperfectly perfect and I'm lucky to be a part of it.

However much in love with her I was a few moments ago, I'm more in love with her now. And with each radiant smudge, each beautiful design, the feeling grows. And grows. And grows.

When she's done, she has tears rolling down her face. She has created art; gorgeous, heartfelt art. It's more than a sunrise. It's capturing a feeling, the right now. And she's just as proud of herself as I am of her.

I gently kiss her tears off of her face. I kiss her until she smiles.

I kiss her until we're naked on the sand and she's riding me and her bronzed body is lit by the morning sun, the pale blue sky behind her. We might be having the first sex of this day to follow that first sunrise. I hope we're setting an example for the rest of the earth. The sun climbs the sky and tomorrow creeps up in the distance, hiding behind the horizon.

Waiting.

"I should get a tattoo," Gemma says to me as she drives down the winding road toward Rotorua, dense forest and ferns blanketing either side of us and tossing long shadows across the bus.

I raise my brows and give her a look. "Really?"

It's been three days since that sunrise at the East Cape and we've managed to cram a whole lot of nothing into them. As we rounded the cape heading west along the soft curve of the Bay of Plenty, we stayed for a few nights on Ōhope Beach outside the town of Whakatane, renting a beach house for a few days. (Yes, pronouncing "F" instead of "Wh" still makes me laugh.)

We were right on the beach, and when we weren't relaxing on the balcony and enjoying the ocean view, we were eating, fucking, swimming—you know, all the good things. Though one of the days I managed to convince Gemma to stop being too cool for school and to come dolphin swimming with me.

That was definitely a highlight, getting into wet suits and going out on the open seas between the sandy shore and the steaming volcano of White Island, chasing down dolphin pods. The boat would get in front of the incoming pods and everyone would have to get in the water quickly. It was up to the dolphins to decide if they wanted to check us out or not.

One decided it liked Gemma a lot—it kept swimming around her and she kept humming a tune that sounded suspiciously like Pink Floyd to keep it interested. When we climbed back on the boat, she looked so elated I thought she was going to float away.

We're heading to Rotorua because it's apparently a really stinky place. Okay, well, there's supposed to be really cool volcanic remnants and hot springs and that kind of stuff, but from what I've learned it apparently smells. We're there for a night at a holiday park then over to Auckland, through the city and up into the Northland to other places I don't remember and on to her grandfather's place for New Year's Eve.

Time is flying and Gemma's statement about the tattoo has thrown me off a little.

"Where do you want to get it done?" I ask. "What were you thinking of getting?"

She purses her lips. "I'll know it when I see it." She turns her attention to me, staring at the tats on my forearms. "What are your tattoos supposed to be?"

I shrug. "A little bit of this and that. It's not so much what they are . . . most are just patterns I like. It's about what they represent."

"And what's that?"

"Moments in time. Tattoos are time stamps. That's why I don't believe in regrettable tattoos. I mean, shit, I've seen some pretty ugly ones and I'm glad I don't have any of those. But, really, as long as your tattoo looks nice and is aesthetically pleasing, then why regret it? It symbolizes a moment in your life in a world where everything passes us by in the blink of an eye. I think it's good to have these reminders to bring you back. Make you remember, reflect. Make sense?"

She nods. "Makes sense. That's kind of what I was thinking, too. I want something to represent this. Us."

I raise my brow and look at her in surprise. I can't help it. "Us?"

She swallows uneasily and looks back to the road. "The trip, everything."

But it's too late. She said "us." She wants a permanent reminder of *us*, something that I always assumed was temporary in her eyes.

Maybe I've been wrong about the whole thing.

Maybe I have something to work with here.

"So," I say, skirting over it in case she gets defensive. "Did you want to do it in Rotorua? Auckland? 'Cause I will totally get one, too. Not matching, of course."

She scrunches up her nose. "Hell no, not matching." But she's smiling. "How about Lake Taupo? They'll probably have better artists to choose from anyway."

"So we're going to Lake Taupo after this?"

"Guess so," she says with a smirk.

We decide to bypass Rotorua altogether (which, luckily, means I don't have to do something called "Zorbing"—being pushed down a hill in a giant hamster ball—and head straight to Lake Taupo, stopping at a few of the better volcanic hot spots like Craters of the Moon, complete with dangerous steam venting from the earth and bubbling, boiling mud.

It's late when we finally pull into the slick holiday park but the next day we're up bright and early and trying to hunt down the best tattoo shop that will take us on short notice. There's one in the center of town, among hostels and cafés and kiosks advertising skydiving and jet-boating and all those other ways to kill yourself. The lanky-looking dude in the shop is friendly and professional, and soon I'm being led to my chair. I take off my shirt and lie down. I've opted for a black-inked Canadian maple leaf but done in the Maori tribal style on an area of my shoulder blades that will fit in well with the existing tattoo there.

The needle buzzes and I feel the buzz in my veins. It's addictive, this high that I get from getting inked. I'm glad Gemma brought up the idea or I wouldn't have thought of it. She's been rather . . . distracting.

She stands across from me, flipping through the book of sample tattoos and I take the time to admire her ass. You can bounce quarters off that thing. One of my favorite things to do is slap it with my dick. It's like a cock trampoline.

I know she feels my eyes burning into her because she turns around gives me a wry glare. "I found my design," she says though.

"Don't tell me," I tell her, wanting it to be a surprise.

About forty minutes later, I'm done. I glance at the tattoo in the mirror and smile. It's pretty fucking awesome and couldn't be more perfect. A time stamp of a person and a place I don't ever want to forget.

It's what the Kiwis would call a *choice* tattoo.

I glance at her over my shoulder. "Do you like it?"

She can only nod but her eyes tell me more. She loves it, both of our cultures melding into one.

The artist covers it up as Gemma gets into the chair and pulls up her hair, piling the massive waves on top of her head.

"I want it on the back of my neck, here" she says to the artist, pointing at the base. "And I want it in an infinity twist. Just like his necklace."

The artist looks to me, briefly studying the greenstone. "Sure thing."

As he begins to sketch it out, I stand in front of her, my hand going to her neck, the very place I like to hold her sometimes. "I thought you said no matching tattoos," I say softly, massaging her there.

She cocks her head. "Your necklace isn't a tattoo. You didn't say it couldn't match something else."

Naturally, I'm flattered. More than flattered. I'm floored. I'm feeling a lot of things, and it's not just the adrenaline from the tattoo. I feel like I've hit the ground and I'm still smiling and there's another level below me that I'm about to fall through.

It gives me the craziest idea in the world.

When she's got her tattoo, her time stamp of infinity, and we're both buzzing from the needle and ink, I take her hand and lead her to one of the kiosks we passed by earlier. Two hours ago, it seemed like a death wish. Now I realize we're both falling. Might as well make it even more real.

Because if you're falling helplessly in love with someone, why not jump out of an airplane with them at the same time? I swear, I should write the advertisements for these companies.

I expect Gemma to scoff at my idea and call me a cliché tourist since Lake Taupo is the skydiving capital of the world, or at least question why someone with a fear of heights would want to do this crazy-ass thing.

But she doesn't. She smiles. She agrees. She's excited. She's gone as nuts as I have. I realize that both of us can't be trusted anymore with rational thinking. Everything seems to be coming from the heart, from some place that makes smart people do very stupid things, like get tattoos on a whim and then jump out of an airplane.

And so, the next thing we know, we're at a small airport being fitted into a jumpsuit, a bathing-suit-like cap, and goggles. Thankfully, we don't look as dorky as we did when we went black-water rafting at Waitomo. Holy fuck, does that seem like ages ago.

Of course we're doing this in tandem with a trained instructor. I get outfitted into a harness by mine, some guy who has the unfortunate name of Nick. I try not to feel like this is a bad omen. Maybe Nick doesn't always have to be followed by Dick.

I don't feel the slightest bit nervous though until we walk out of the hangar and I see the bright pink plane we're going to go up in. Once we're inside and the doors close and we're coasting up into the air, I want nothing more than to grab Gemma's hand. But she's chatting with her instructor like this is something she does every day.

It doesn't help that the instructor is a young, strapping Polynesian guy with just the kind of muscles she liked in Nick. Damn it. Maybe this is a bad omen after all.

It definitely at least feels like a bad idea when the doors open. I've been trying to distract myself with the view and the enormous blue expanse of Lake Taupo beneath us, but now that air is rushing in through the plane at twelve thousand feet, I'm not sure jumping out of a plane is necessary. Can't I just stay here and look at the scenery? Why would anyone jump out of a perfectly healthy plane?

But Gemma is up next and I barely have time to wave a fretful goodbye to her before she's out the door.

Pins and needles swarm my arms and legs, my chest grows hot, and I'm instantly regretting everything. *Shit, shit, shit.* And then I'm hit with the fear of actually shitting myself, or worse. Like, passing out and then waking up on the ground to a bruised ego and soiled underwear.

But there's no time for me to get lost on that panic-induced train of thought. The instructor makes me shimmy over to the door, and before I know what's going on, the air is blasting me in the face and the world is thousands of feet below me. I think he's counting down.

It doesn't matter.

My feet have gone over the edge.

I'm falling.

The only thing I can think about is how fast it feels, but my mind keeps telling me that I'm not falling at all, that I'm floating on a big cushion of air instead. Air is a lot more solid than you think. Up here, it's tangible, something you can hug or even fuck, I think to myself, almost smiling. I'm fucking the air, fucking the earth, and then the parachute is expanding above us, yanking us upward, and the weird little world I'm living in is gone and replaced with one my mind can better comprehend.

My instructor tells me something that sounds like we're at five thousand feet—I can't really recall from the safety videos where we're supposed to be when we pull the chute. Now the dizzying vertigo sets in as Lake Taupo and the white peaks of the surrounding volcanoes rush toward me. My brain feels blitzed out, short-circuited, and all thoughts shut down. I can only dangle in my harness as we slice through the air on the way to the ground.

I make it. And when I'm free from the harness, I run, stagger, to Gemma and scoop her up in my arms, embracing her, spinning her around like the sappiest little shit who ever fell in love. She giggles and laughs and her eyes are like a spear to my heart and her smile is the sweetest sword and I think to myself, *How can I possibly leave her, this place. How can I ever let her go?*

So, I decide on a new plan.

I won't let her go.

I'll stay.

Chapter Twenty-One

GEMMA

Dawn creeps up on us like flaming fingers reaching through the night. I stand outside of Mr. Orange, leaning against his solid mass, and watch the sky light up in the east. We freedom-camped along some unnamed river in the Northland, aka illegally parked overnight somewhere to sleep. When we stopped by the river so Josh could take a leak, we decided we didn't want to move. We'd be staying at my grandfather's soon, and it would be nice to be truly alone. No family, no other caravans, just us.

But the solitude is gnawing at me. I woke up early, feeling restless, anxious. Out here, in the chill of fading night, I can breathe.

Just barely, though.

It's New Year's Eve tonight, which means it's a whole new year tomorrow. Which means eleven days from now, Josh is leaving. I can't even comprehend the loss right now, and it's not because I'm numb. It's because I'm feeling too much. I don't know what to do with it. I don't know where to place these feelings, how to deal with them. I want there to be a cage where they can stay and not cause anyone any trouble.

But I'm struggling against my instincts. If I did that, locked my feelings away, then I wouldn't have anything for the here and now. I wouldn't feel like my soul is constantly in bloom. Every day it keeps getting prettier, feeling better, growing, and part of me is afraid it might never stop. It's infinite, like the tattoo on my neck, like the pendant on Josh's necklace.

When that first sun rose over that deserted beach on the East Cape and my fingers captured that moment, that *feeling*—hazy, grand, messy, warm—I felt like my heart rose as well.

I was shining on the inside.

It's all because of Josh. All because of this funny, sexy, handsome, generous, adorable man who knows my body better than I do, who sees the real me underneath the ice and isn't afraid of her. Who believes in who I am and what I can do, more than I can believe it myself.

That morning he showed me what he saw in me, and it was beautiful.

That morning I realized I love him. Deeply, desperately, dangerously.

I am in love with Joshua Miles, and it's bringing me to life.

It's killing me.

It's making me crazy.

I think I love that part, too.

It twists and loops around us, tying us to one another. It steals my thoughts and makes me think of him. It steals my hands and makes me touch his skin. It's brutal and kind and sharp and soft and warm and cold and freeing and imprisoning. It's an incognito imposter taking over my world, spreading itself like a disease.

It's a million and one things, and it's real to the bone.

It's *in* my bones.

It's love. And I have no idea what it's going to do next.

I can only hope that I'll have the strength to keep it in line.

I stand outside, lost in my thoughts until the black fades to blue and the sun spears my eyes. I hear Josh stirring inside the bus.

"Baby," he calls out, voice hoarse with sleep. I've started to love it when he calls me that. He doesn't say it often, but when he does it is *so* sincere I can't help but melt.

"Yeah," I answer, sliding open the door. He's sitting up with a mess of hair and my eyes dance over his bare chest, his tattoos, his wide, expansive shoulders. I drink him in, my hands itching to touch him.

I step inside Mr. Orange and climb back into bed with him. Now that he's awake, I don't have to be alone with my thoughts. Now I can breathe. Now he can distract me.

I run my finger over his forehead, down the bridge of his nose, stopping at his cushiony lips when he playfully bites me.

"Last morning of the year," he murmurs around my finger. "What are you doing up so early?"

I grin at him. "Trying to figure out how to make the last morning of the year . . . memorable."

His expression turns cocksure. He raises his brow and looks me up and down. My breasts are practically falling out of the flimsy camisole. "Sweetheart, just you here like this is already making a memory I'll fall back on again and again."

"Calling me sweetheart again, are you?" I tease.

"Only because it makes you wet," he answers with a knowing smirk.

He's right of course. But in this case, I love it when he's right.

I take his hand and guide it down the front of my underwear to prove his point. I don't mind feeding his ego. He deserves it.

Morning sex is the absolute best. We're both so sleepy and slow that it's like lazily discovering a new day. My hands find their way to his rigid cock and stroke it languorously. He sucks on my nipples while his fingers explore me in and out. We tumble into the bed, rolling, reaching, quietly yearning. It's a slow dance of tangled sheets and warm limbs and easy smiles. He guides himself into me, eyes half-closed, mouth wet and open. We kiss through our stupor. He fills me to the brim and I expand to let him in. Push and pull. Give and take.

In the mornings we take our time, relishing every lick, pinch, stroke, squeeze. When I come it's through shaky breaths and hushed groans, like it's a subtle surprise. He's louder but softer, and there's a moment where it's so easy to just fall asleep all over again, with him still inside me, and have another morning when we wake.

But we always have places to go. I tear myself away from him, clean up, and slip into shorts and a singlet, pulling my hair back in a ponytail. Lately I've been going makeup free and he seems to love it, always counting the freckles on my nose.

Soon we're hitting the road, stopping at a takeaway shop for coffees and sammies in the town of Whangarei and piloting toward my grandfather.

"Where are we going again?" Josh asks as he peruses a road map. "I mean, the name of the place."

I eye it briefly. "It's probably hard to find on the map. It's up in the Bay of Islands, a place called Bland Bay."

He snorts. "Bland Bay? How exciting."

"It's not so bland, you'll see."

Two hours later we're coasting down a hill toward a small peninsula. On one side of us is the bay, with its beautiful crescent moon of white sand. On the other side of the narrow neck is the protected Whangaruru Harbour. There's not much here except for a strip of road, a small store by the campground, and a scattering of holiday homes, all bordering the harbor.

My grandfather's place, where he lives with Uncle Robbie and Aunt Shelley, is past the narrow isthmus and up a gravel road that takes you across a crop of rolling farmland to his house at the very end. It's a large, isolated plot of land bordering the edge of the white-sand bay.

I put Mr. Orange in park beside my uncle's car, an old, shiny Datsun. The house, a white, sprawling one-level, sits behind a row of spiky flax and ornamental wind grass. Two giant pōhutukawa trees, their flowers still a brilliant pinkish red, flank the house on one end.

"This is it," I say. "End of the line."

"Boring Bay," he muses, taking in the wide green field rolling down to the beach.

"Bland Bay," I correct him and get out of the bus.

The screen door to the house swings open and my uncle Robbie comes out with his pit bull, Barker, at his side. My uncle looks as he always does—red baseball cap, hefty gut, barefoot. I have honestly never seen him in shoes.

"*Kia ora*, Gem!" he greets me, pulling me into a hearty embrace. He smells like lime and beer and aftershave, his usual combination. Barker sits at my feet and whines for me to pet him.

I do so, scratching the soft spots behind Barker's floppy ears, and say, "Hey Uncle Robbie. Look what I brought with me; Mr. Orange and Mr. Josh Miles."

My uncle fixes his twinkling eyes on Josh and goes over to him for a hug. "*Kia ora*, Josh Miles."

"*Kia ora*, Mr. Uncle Robbie," Josh says amiably as he's squeezed into a bear hug.

Uncle Robbie pulls back to assess him and then slaps him hard on the back. "Aye, you're a good mate." Then he goes to Mr. Orange and for a moment I think he's going to hug the bus but he just pounds his fist against a front tire. "Still in one piece."

I exchange a look with Josh. He won't be able to tell the window was replaced, and I really hope he doesn't notice the lack of porn because that conversation would be embarrassing.

"Gemma!"

I turn around to see Auntie Shelley coming out of the house, wearing one of her signature long sarongs, her curly black hair blowing in the wind. She's always had this ageless quality about her, and her cheeks have this rosy, freshly scrubbed look.

She hugs me and tells me she missed me, even though I just saw her in November to get Mr. Orange. She looks over my shoulder at Josh, who is talking to Uncle Robbie about Mr. Orange.

I quickly introduce them and Auntie Shelley gives him a warm if less boisterous greeting than Uncle Robbie did.

"How are you liking the winterless north?" she asks him.

"Winterless north?" Josh repeats.

"It's a right lie," Uncle Robbie says. "In the winter it will piss buckets for weeks on end."

Auntie Shelley narrows her eyes at his language. She's always been a bit of a prude, a bit churchy and proper, while her husband is the complete opposite. But somehow it works.

We're ushered inside and there's my grandpa sitting down on his recliner, watching the telly. I have a rush of trepidation as we stand in the TV room, wondering if he'll like Josh. My grandfather is lovely as all out, but he can be a bit hard to please, and for some reason I really want his approval. He's like the last test Josh has to pass before he's really welcomed into the Henare family.

And then what? I think to myself. I tell my inner voice to shut up.

"Pops," I say to him, and he slowly swivels around in his chair to face us. He's not quite Dr. Evil and he's not stroking a cat, but he's got to be an intimidating sight for Josh. For one, he's not smiling, and he's a tall, massive man. His long gray hair is pulled off his weathered face into a ponytail and his eyes shine with suspicion. Two, he's got the Maori *tā moko* tribal tattoos snaking up his neck and onto the sides of his face, making him look a bit primal.

Then again, Josh has ink everywhere.

"This is Josh," I tell him, and my grandfather stares at him for a beat that seems to go on and on.

Josh stands his ground. "Mr. Henare." He gives him a firm nod and then sticks out his hand.

My grandfather eyes his hand, eyes Josh, eyes his tattoos, and then looks at me. I can only smile.

"This your boy?" he asks me in a gruff voice.

Josh looks at me and I can tell he's on edge; his hand starts to shake a little. I'm not sure how fast the news of Josh and I being "together" spread through the family, but apparently it was fast enough.

So I smile and nod. "Yes, he's my boy."

Well, man. Very much a man. But I keep those thoughts to myself. I'm getting a bit flushed.

"And he treats you well?"

"He treats me far better than I deserve, Pops," I say honestly. If only he knew.

"All right then," he says and he rises powerfully out of the chair. He may have a bad knee, but his moments are so fluid you can barely tell he's limping.

He grabs hold of Josh's hand and pulls him toward him to do the *hongi*. They are both the exact same height and Josh holds his own as my grandfather presses his nose and forehead against his. They shake. My grandfather smiles. "We're not always so formal with each other like this but welcome to the *whānau*."

Josh smiles back. He's learned by now that *whānau* means family.

Pops breaks away and looks at me. "He seems like a good egg," he says. He appraises Josh. "So how have you been enjoying New Zealand? You showing her her own country and all that?"

"Well, actually," Josh muses with a cheeky grin, "she's been showing me."

"Aye, Gemma's calling the shots again, is she," my grandfather says and goes to sit back down. "Pushy little thing."

"Hey," I protest, throwing an arm out to Josh. "You try taking him and my cousin around the islands. Talk about indecisive. If it wasn't for me calling the shots, we would've been going around circles in Auckland this whole time."

Josh laughs. "It's true. I'm just along for the ride. And I've been loving it." He gives me a knowing look. "And I managed to get her to go dolphin swimming and jump out of an airplane."

"Skydiving?" Pops says. "You're crazy, mate."

"I can't argue with that," Josh says.

After we go and get our stuff from Mr. Orange and settle into the tiny twin bed guest room at the end of the house, Uncle Robbie invites Josh to sit outside with him while I'm talked into helping Aunt Shelley and my grandfather with the *hāngi* preparations.

Our *hāngi* are held on the beach at Bland Bay, even though traditionally they're held on a *marae*. I know a few of the neighbors probably started earlier today. Basically you dig a pit in the sand, start a fire, and then place hot stones on top. The stones heat up for hours and hours, then the food is added. Right now we're preparing wild boar, lamb, mussels, kumara, potatoes, zucchini, and pumpkin. Then you cover it all with sand (naturally the food has been wrapped in aluminum foil) and the food cooks for a long time. By the time the meal is ready, everyone has been on the beach for a while, having a few laughs and drinking the night away. That's why Auntie Shelley is preparing snacks; it's going to be a long night.

"So Gemma," Pops says while he cuts through the pork with a hefty knife.

"Mmmm?" I muse, pulling the disgusting hairy ends off the mussels. Blah.

"I had a talk with Jolinda the other day," he says.

My heart starts to speed up a bit. "Oh yeah?"

"She told me you lost your job."

I exhale sharply through my nose. "Yeah. That sucked."

"Do you know what you're going to do?"

I'm silent for a few moments, concentrating on the mussels, though I can feel Pops and Auntie Shelley's eyes on me. "No," I eventually say. "I guess try and start from scratch."

"Personal training and all that?" he asks.

I nod. "Yeah. I guess. I mean, what else can I do? That's all I know."

"That's not all you can do, Gem," he says. "You can do anything you put your mind to. You're only twenty-two years old. You've been out of high school for, what, four years? That's nothing. You're a baby."

"I am not a baby," I say, about to give him a look but remembering to rein in my feelings and show my respect at the last minute.

"Aye, I know that. What I'm saying is, you're young. No one has their stuff together at your age. Believe me, I didn't know anything at that age. It took years to know what I wanted, and years after that to know who I was. Take it from me, I've been around. Don't be so hard on yourself."

"I'm not."

"You are," he says pointedly. "I can tell. You've always been hard on yourself. Over time, it makes you hard. Get my drift? You'll be all right, though, if you believe you'll be all right."

"Has my whole family banded together to give me pep talks?" I ask, giving the two of them incredulous looks.

"We're your *whānau* and we're worried, that's all."

"You never seemed all that worried before."

He smiles calmly at me. "We've always been. Maybe now you're finally seeing it." He whacks his knife into the pork. "What was that saying again? When the student is ready the master will appear?"

"Sounds very *Karate Kid*."

He laughs. "Gemma, you aren't old enough to remember that movie. That's how young you are."

"Here," Auntie Shelley says, pushing me gently out of the way to take over the mussel duties. "Go wash your hands and take the food out to Robbie and Josh."

"Now who's the pushy one?" I point out but gladly oblige, eager to run away from the serious grandfather talk. I go into the sunshine where Uncle Robbie and Josh are sitting in wooden chairs and staring at the bay and smoking, Barker spread out on the grass.

"Gemma, what's wrong with you?" Uncle Robbie asks me as I bring over the tray of biscuits and fruit, setting it down on the driftwood table between the chairs.

"What?"

And then I see that he's not smoking a cigarette at all but a joint and passing it to Josh, who puffs back like an old pro.

"Josh here tells me this is the first New Zealand grass he's smoked this whole trip," he says. "You've been driving around our islands in a VW bus, listening to Pink Floyd, and you haven't even had a spliff? You're a disgrace to our culture." But he chuckles. Josh only grins at me happily.

I give Uncle Robbie a look. "Well, I guess he needs to work up an appetite if he's going to the *hāngi* tonight."

"You ain't wrong, girl," he says as I sit on the arm of Josh's chair. Josh wraps his arm around me, blowing smoke in the other direction.

I playfully pull at his hair and he momentarily closes his eyes in pleasure. "Is my uncle being nice?" I ask, shooting Uncle Robbie a wary look.

"Yup," Josh says. "I've been filling him in about the trip."

"Oye, Gemma," he says, adjusting his baseball cap, "Josh here tells me that you had to give away all my old *Penthouse* magazines. Is that true?"

I eye Josh and grimace. "Yes. And I don't regret it for a moment."

"All right, all right," Uncle Robbie says, relaxing back in his chair. "I thought maybe he was spinning a yarn and keeping them for himself."

This conversation has the ability to get all sorts of weird, so I get up.

"Where you going?" Josh asks.

"You'll find out later," I tell him with a smile. I walk to the back door of the house near our bedroom and find his sketchbook. I tear a piece of blank paper out of it, pick up the pastels and some old book about New Zealand trees to use as a hard surface, and go back outside.

I walk to the edge of the lawn and jump down into sand below, then make my way along the beach, fine white sand at my feet. Further down, by the holiday park, there are people gathered, the *hāngi* pit starting to smoke, the air filling with the smell of burning manuka wood. I go the opposite way, rounding the corner of low, red clay cliffs and find an isolated pocket of beach with stunning views of the neighboring rocks and islands.

I think about what my grandfather has said.

I think about what my mother has said.

I think about what Josh has said.

And I start to paint.

———— • ————

New Year's Eve has always been a big deal in my family. In fact, I think it's a big deal to every Kiwi, and not in the same way it is elsewhere in the world. Our New Year is about being with family and enjoying the summer. It's a weeklong event where people holiday at family baches and barbecue a lot of food, not just a one-night stand, as it seems to be elsewhere in the world.

At that, I look over at my one-night stand. He's sitting on a log with Auntie Shelley and one of our neighbors, Jono, the lanky fellow who runs the campground and likes to take tourists out for bushwalks. Josh is laughing hard at something Jono has said, and Aunt Shelley leans over to smack Jono on the shoulder.

It's dark, the stars are out, and the fire flickers and flames. We ate the *hāngi* a couple of hours ago, and as usual, it was delicious. It's not just the fact that we used high-quality meats and vegetables but the fact that it's such a process, such an event shared by many people, that makes it taste so good.

Josh seemed to love it. He ate everything he could before going back to drinking with my grandfather. It's almost midnight now, but if it's like any other year, we probably won't notice it's the new year until after the fact. No one here counts down. We just enjoy being with each other and slide into the next year that way.

Josh catches me staring at him. I was supposed to grab a beer from one of the chilly bins and come right back but I've been taking my time. I want to slow down. Time is going way too fast.

He excuses himself from between Auntie Shelley and Jono and strides over to me.

"Hey handsome," I say and can't stop myself from grinning. Even in the firelight, he steals my breath.

"Hi beautiful," he replies, grabbing my hand and a beer. "Care to join me on a walk? I heard you like long romantic walks on the beach."

He waggles his eyebrows in an overexaggerated manner and grabs my hand.

We walk away from the robust crowd until the firelight begins to dim and their voices fade. Occasionally you can still hear Uncle Robbie laugh. We go along the edge of the water, the waves gently lapping. Stars reflect on the bay. We don't talk but we don't need to.

I feel him in every part of me. I feel like we're saying enough with each breath we take in, with the way we squeeze each other's hand. We walk past our house and to the little cove I was at earlier in the day, when I sat down and made a pastel painting of the bay. It still hums with my creative energy, like it was waiting for me to return.

Someone in the far, unseen distance yells "Happy New Year!" and the sky behind us lights up with a few cheap fireworks.

"Happy New Year," he says, pulling me toward him and planting a long, lingering kiss on my lips. It's hot. The sand on our bare feet is cool. The sky is alive with light. The horizon is black.

I murmur it back to him, lost in his kiss, in the heat of his embrace.

"I was thinking," he says when he finally pulls away. From the way he cups my face and the earnestness of his words, my pulse kicks up a notch.

"Yes?" I ask with shaky breath.

"Maybe . . ." he trails off and looks away.

"What?" I ask, even though I think I'm afraid to hear the answer.

"I don't want to leave."

I exhale and smile. "I don't want you to leave either."

"So what if I don't?"

My smile falters. "I don't understand."

"What if I don't go. What if I stay here."

I nearly laugh. "Josh, you can't. You have school."

He pulls away briefly, and in the light of the moon I see him run his hand through his hair. "I know I do. I know. I just . . . Gemma. I can't leave you. If I can think of a way to stay, to make this work, I will."

I feel like there's a brick lodged in my throat. He can't stay here for me. I'm not worth it. He must know that, he must know the kind of person I am.

"Why would you do that?" I ask. "Why . . . I give you nothing. I'm just this girl . . . you deserve someone else, someone . . . better. Anyone."

"Gemma."

I manage to swallow. "What?"

"I'm in love with you."

Those words. *Those words* still my heart. They reach into my chest and make a fist. I can't breathe. I feel too much that it numbs me. The sharp stab of happiness sinks into me like a blade, but it's the blood, the aftermath, that makes me so incredibly scared.

"Did you hear me?" he asks quietly. He comes over and slips a hand to the base of my neck, holding me gently. I can see the moon reflected in his eyes as he peers down at me, trying to see the parts I'm trying to hide. "I love you." His voice is gruff and so heartfelt that it's almost like he's putting his heart in my hands. "I love you."

It hangs between us, heavy and weighted, like a hook.

I don't know what to do, how to handle it, absorb it.

I only know how to deflect.

I grab him and kiss him hard. Before he has a chance to react, I'm pulling his shirt over his head and tumbling into the soft sand with him. My shirt is nearly ripped off, the skirt I wore for the occasion is yanked down along with my underwear.

We're both naked in no time and I'm under him and he's in me and all I can think about is that this is what it's like to be devoured. To be consumed. To be loved. It all feels like the same thing.

There could be nothing left of me when he's through.

When we've both come, sated and breathing hard, we lie on the silky sand and watch the blackened waves roll in, their crests lit by moonlight.

It's a lonely sight, all that black on the horizon, all that nothing.

He loves me.

He loves me.

How?

"How can you love me?" I'm surprised that's what comes out of my mouth but it's the truth and it's out there, floating in the dark.

He's surprised, too. He balks at the question, his head jerking back.

After a long moment, the silence filled by the lapping water on the shore, he asks, "Do you want the truth?" Of course I want the truth. Of course I need to hear it. But I steel myself against it all the same. "It's not easy to love you, Gemma," he says, his fingers sliding up through my hair, gently, affectionately, in contrast to his words. "You are not an easy person to love because you don't seem to have any use for it. You don't want it. But the more you push, the more I pull. I fell in love with you because it was like staring at the frozen sea. I only saw the surface but I knew there was more underneath, miles of depth that no one has had a chance to discover."

"I thought it was because I'm a good lay," I say, attempting to make a joke.

His eyes harden. "It's a lot more than that. I fell in love with you because you made me crazy, and you were like this unattainable world that I'd never be able to get my hands on. And then I did get my hands on you. And you got your hands on me. And I saw into your depths and found what I was looking for."

"What?"

"You," he says, pushing the hair back from my face. "A funny, sweet, vulnerable little girl who hides from the world under a big sheet of ice. That's who I found. That's who I want. That's who I have. The artist, the poet, the dreamer, the risk-taker. The lover."

I feel like my lungs are being deprived of oxygen and my heart has too much blood to pump. I'm gaining and losing. I'm torn. I'm *loved*.

He plants a soft kiss on my forehead. "I know everything I've just said is scary. In fact, I think I've freaked myself out a bit. But it's true. And you don't have to do anything, you don't have to say anything. Just let me love you. That's all."

That's all, he says. But that's everything. How is it that *being loved* is even scarier than being *in* love?

I swallow hard and close my eyes as he wraps his arms around me. He's so good to me, too good to me. I don't belong with this man, not me with my heart of ice and he with his soul of fire.

The breeze off the bay is coming in colder now and I'm suddenly aware that we're both naked in the sand and not too far away from the house. I'd hate for Uncle Robbie to make a discovery with his flashlight.

"We should go," I tell Josh as I pull away.

He can't hide the disappointment in his voice. "All right."

Even though it's for the best, my heart sinks a bit and I feel bad that I can't say anything that he wants to hear. I lean over, grab his face and kiss him.

"Happy New Year," I whisper to him.

"Happy New Year," he whispers back.

Chapter Twenty-Two

JOSH

I have the mother of all hangovers. It's the kind that keeps you stuck to your bed, to the beach, to the grass, to whatever place you happen to wake up in, and you can't move because you know if you do, all the painful parts that make up your brain will become dislodged, bouncing around like razor-blade pinballs, and you'll soon wish for a swift and painless death.

I blink, staring at the ceiling. Gemma and I are in the small guest room at Pops Henare's house. She's squeezed in between me and the wall, sleeping soundly. I hate her for it. I know now that I'm up, I won't be able to fall back asleep, and I'll have to suffer.

My phone rings, the sound like bullets exploding in my head. Who is calling me? Why did I drink all that champagne and smoke all that weed?

Why did I tell Gemma I was in love with her?

She moans beside me, pulling the pillow over her face. I reach into my pockets because of course I'm still wearing my clothes from last night, all covered in sand, and pull out my phone.

It's Vera. And holy shit, it's already one in the afternoon.

"Hello?" I answer and try to get out of bed, lifting Gemma's leg off of mine.

"Josh?" she asks. "Happy New Year!"

I mumble something into the phone and then shuffle my way down the hall and out the back door. I can hear people in the kitchen and someone, probably Pops, watching TV, but I can't even begin to socialize. I walk outside into hot, blinding sunshine. It's like knives to my brain.

"Josh, are you okay?" she asks. "Don't ruin my buzz."

"What time is it there?" I mumble as I make my way to the chairs overlooking the beach. I'm squinting so much I'm almost legally blind.

"It's one in the morning. We're twelve hours apart, remember? I thought you'd be up by now."

"Well, as you can hear, I'm awake," I tell her. "Are you with Mateo?"

"Of course! Want to talk to him?"

Before I can tell her that I can't process his accent right now, I hear a muffled sound and then his voice on the other end.

"Happy New Year, Josh," Mateo says. His accent is always a lot milder than I remember. "How is New Zealand?"

"Great. I'm hungover."

"Well, I am sure Vera and I will be tomorrow. You are enjoying yourself, yes?"

"I think a little too much, actually."

"Then you're really living life now."

I can almost hear his grin. I nod and wince at the pain my head causes me. I'm living life for once, and it's a bit terrifying. "That I am," I tell him.

"Then keep it up, it's worth it. Believe me." There's a pause and I hear Vera in the background. "Okay, I shall let you go," he says and we say goodbye. Vera comes back on the line.

"How are you and Gemma?" she asks.

I would much rather talk about her and Mateo. "We're good."

"Anything happen since Christmas?"

"Been doing a lot of traveling," I tell her, which is true.

"Does she make you happy?"

I laugh. "She's driving me crazy."

"The good kind of crazy?"

I sigh and look at the sand where we made love last night. Where I told her that I love her. Where she didn't say it back.

"I'm not sure," I say. "All I know is I'm not ready to leave her."

A weighty pause rests in the air and then she says, quietly, "So don't."

"It's not so simple."

"Sure it is."

"Vera," I warn her. "This isn't like you and Mateo. You knew how you felt and you knew how he felt. That was easy."

"It wasn't *easy*—" she begins, but I cut her off.

"I know how I feel," I tell her. "And I've told her how I feel. But she doesn't seem to want it. She wants me but she doesn't want me to love her. Does that make sense?"

Another pause. "You love her?"

I groan. "Ugh, it's too hot to talk about this."

"If you love her, then you have two choices," she says. "You can either love her from afar, at home in Vancouver, or you can love her from there. Either way, the love part isn't going away. You just have to choose what scenario makes you the happiest."

I tug absently at my lip ring. "If she doesn't love me back, both scenarios will make me miserable."

She sighs. "When did you turn into such a pessimist?"

"I have art school to think about, Vera."

"I had school to think about but it worked out. You can work it out, too. They have art schools in New Zealand, right? You could apply to one, get a student visa. Problem solved."

"And the whole part about her not loving me back?"

"Love takes longer for some people than others," she says. "But if she gets there in the end, isn't that what'll make it worth it? The answer to that is *yes*, Josh. It does. I say go for it. That's what you once said to me."

"All right," I tell her. "I'll see how it goes. We still have another week here together."

"I bet it's nice and warm and beautiful. Enjoy it."

"I am."

I'm about to hang up when she stops me. "Oh, by the way, Mom actually called me the other day."

"Really?"

"Yeah, it was late in Vancouver and she sounded drunk. In fact, I know she was drunk. She started telling me that she missed me and you and wondered where she went wrong, why two of her children would want to go overseas, thousands of miles away from her. She thinks we hate her."

"I don't hate her," I say.

"Neither do I," she says. "But I don't think she really knows how she can be, you know? Anyway, she might call you soon. Talk to her. It was nice to hear her talk like that."

"All caring and shit?"

She laughs. "Exactly."

After we hang up, I lean back in the chair and stay that way until Gemma comes out and sits down beside me.

I slowly turn my head to look at her. "How are you, Peggy Sue?"

She raises a brow. "I feel like death."

"Well, you don't look like death," I tell her. "It's actually pretty annoying."

"I know what will cure you," she says, grabbing my hand and pulling me unsteadily to my feet. "It's about time you try marmite. In fact, a marmite chippie sammie."

"So many words I don't understand."

We go back into the house and straight to the kitchen. Her grandfather is watching TV, something Gemma says he does a lot of since he injured his knee a few years ago. The man moves slowly and painfully but refuses to take medication for it, so that's why her uncle and aunt live with him, to help out. He's a tough man, but a good man, and I like him. Once again, I find myself wishing I had the same family ties as she does.

"How are you two?" he asks.

"Been better," says Gemma.

He, like Gemma, looks great, even healthy, though I know I saw him throwing back shots of what can only be considered Satan's homebrew last night.

Within minutes, Gemma has thrown together a sandwich consisting of potato chips stuck between two pieces of bread smeared with brown stuff.

I start laughing and then laugh even more when she starts to eat it.

"That is the most white-trash thing I've ever seen," I tell her.

Her grandfather chuckles from the TV room, though Gemma only glares. "Hey," she says between mouthfuls, "the bread is to soak up the alcohol; the chips are for crunchy, greasy tastiness, and also for soaking up the alcohol; and the marmite is all B vitamins. It'll cure you right up."

I turn my head toward the TV room and yell, "Is this true, Pops?"

"It's worth a shot if you're that hard up, mate," he answers.

Gemma smiles sweetly and pushes the sandwich in my face. "Trust me."

I take it from her, not really sure if I do trust her or not. But I eat it anyway. It's actually pretty good, though the marmite has this strong, concentrated soy-saucey beer taste going on.

We take our plates and sit down on the couch across from her grandfather.

"So where you two off to next?" he asks, shutting off the TV and giving us his full attention.

Gemma opens her mouth but immediately shuts it. She takes a bite of her sandwich and then says, "I don't know. It's up to Josh."

They both look at me. I shrug. "I don't know."

"Well, start looking at the guidebooks, boy," he says. "How many days do you have left here?"

I swallow hard. "Ten."

"Then make them count, aye?" He leans back in his chair and taps his fingers on the arm. He's got tattoos on them, too. "If I were you, I'd go up to Cape Reinga."

"Is that the northernmost part?" I ask, recalling its place on our travel maps.

"Sure is. Where the Tasman Sea meets the Pacific Ocean. Our ancestors believed it was a very spiritual place, where the spirits jump off from this world to the next. No matter what you believe, it's very special, very important. *Tapu.*"

"*Tapu,*" I repeat.

"Sacred," he says, with a grave look in his eyes. "There is a very, very old pōhutukawa tree there at the end. The roots are where the souls slide down into the afterworld."

I nod, wanting to say "cool" but figuring that's too glib of a statement for something that sounds so serious. "Sounds like we have to go," I say, meaningfully.

He nods. I feel like his dark eyes are trying to tell me something else but then he abruptly turns back to the TV and clicks the remote to turn it back on.

In the end, we decide to stay only one more night at the Henares' place. The clock is ticking and Gemma and I don't have much time together. I'm trying to think of some way out of this, some way to lengthen my stay, to return, to take her with me, to do anything rather than let the two of us part ways. I know if we do, I'll lose her forever.

Our plan—well, actually, my plan, for once—is to take Mr. Orange to the Karikari Peninsula, a place that looks amazing for a few nights' stay, all white sand coves, clear blue tropical water, and lots of privacy, then we'll motor up to Cape Reinga, as far as you can possibly go in New Zealand, then on the way back stop by a ninety-mile beach to do some sandboarding on their massive sand dunes. We'll come back here on the way back, drop off Mr. Orange, and then get the next bus back down to Auckland.

It's a lot packed into a short amount of time, but like Pops Henare said, we have to make it count.

Even though we know we'll be seeing them all again in a week, it's almost an emotional farewell between us, Pops, Robbie, and Shelley. Once again I'm feeling that pang of losing family in the long run.

The ride up to Maitai Bay on the Karikari Peninsula is markedly different from our other ones. We're silent. Free blares on the stereo, but after a while Gemma slips in Pink Floyd. When "Comfortably Numb" comes on and she starts staring out the window, mouthing the lyrics, I wonder if she derives any comfort from the song at all, or if it's an anthem of sorts.

There's a heavy tension in the air between us. It's not necessarily bad, it's just that we both seem to be caught in our minds, our own little worlds. My fears are of losing this world, of losing her. There's much left to explore—here, in her. I feel like I'll be leaving when things are only getting started.

I wonder how badly I scared her last night by telling her I loved her. The look in her eyes wasn't of rejection; it was fear. And I don't have much time to help her overcome it.

I don't have much time.

When we pull down the unsealed road and into the campground, Gemma's spirits seem to lift. The spot is beautiful—but what hasn't been beautiful in this country? There are a few other campervans around but it's not too busy and we're able to secure a spot.

We park Mr. Orange and start getting ready for dinner. I want to stay here for at least two nights, just to really feel like I'm here, so we make ourselves at home, airing out clothes that we laundered at her grandpa's and setting up the table and camping chairs.

She's so beautiful here, her face turned to the sun. Sometimes I see her reach for the pastels. She usually just holds them, thinking about the scene, thinking about what she wants to do, but she rarely puts them to use. I think she's still afraid to create, to open herself up, to put her soul on paper for others—*for me*—to see. That's okay, though. That's a start.

I want to tell her again that I love her. I had no idea that once you realized you were in love, it was nearly fucking impossible to keep it to yourself. I always thought guys were such chumps for putting themselves out there like that, but now I'm doing the exact same thing. It probably makes me a chump, but the funny thing is, I don't care. Love whittles the world down into caring about just one thing.

It's not that I need her to say it back, though to be honest it's killing me that she hasn't, but I can't keep it inside. I'm thinking it all the time, over everything she does. I'm thinking it when I'm pissing in the outhouse, I'm thinking it when I'm talking to strangers. It's invaded me, and the longer I try to contain it the more it wants to escape, like an oil spill.

I try and fuck it into her instead. It always works. In bed she responds to me like she's an extension of myself, eager for more, eager for me. In bed I can trick myself into thinking she loves me, that she feels the same. It's so easy to do. So I do it, again and again. It's the only place that I've been able to find my peace.

Love is a fucking head trip. It's a bad idea. It's utterly distracting and, ironically, I think love is bad for your heart.

In the end, I think it's going to break mine.

———•———

Two days later we're doing the drive to Cape Reinga. It's a desolate, long journey through shack settlements and unchecked bush. There's a rampant, wild feeling here, a sensation that you're on the point of no return. We don't see any beaches, no ocean, just the same untamed forests and unsmiling faces. I think it's the first place I don't want to paint, mainly because it feels like I'm capturing something I shouldn't.

The weather changes. Gray clouds sit on the horizon like massive alien motherships, moving slowly across the wide expanse of blue sky.

"Goodbye, blue sky," I sing as I stare out the windscreen and the long, empty road.

When we finally reach the cape, there aren't that many cars in the car park, just a few tour buses. When we step outside, we aren't surprised why there's no one here. The wind is vicious, battering into us, turning us around, and rain sporadically whips us in the face.

We slip on light jackets, grateful that at least it's not too cold. Grabbing each other's hands, we make our way down a long path toward the famous lighthouse, which is periodically shrouded in passing mist. Unlike the East Cape Lighthouse, there are others here.

I'm immediately hit with the foreboding sense of isolation as the path becomes more narrow, sloping off on both sides to wave-beaten beaches. You can't even see the horizon.

This is *tapu*. This is sacred. This is a place where things end.

We reach the lighthouse and look below to where the land continues onward as a few humps of black rock. That's the point where Pops told us the spirits leave this world. You can barely see it through the cloud cover and the crashing waves. The water here, where one sea meets an ocean, is violent and rough and loud.

It seems like a terrifying bridge for the dead.

I want to leave.

I want to go back to the sunny, happy-as-fuck place we were in before, but then I'm thinking maybe it's too late now. Maybe there's no going back. The sand is almost at the bottom of the hourglass.

I'm at the end of the country, the end of my stay.

I have to do something.

I turn around and see the tall signpost in the middle of the bluff. There are signs pointing to Sydney, London, Tokyo, the Tropic of Capricorn, Los Angeles, and Vancouver.

Vancouver.

Eleven thousand two hundred and twenty-two kilometers away.

I can't do it.

I can't go back there, not without her.

I face Gemma, who is looking at the sign with apprehension. Her eyes flick to mine, the wind blowing her hair across her face.

She can feel this coming. She looks ready to run.

"I'm not going back," I say to her, my voice raised over the wind.

She rubs her lips together and shoves her hair behind her ears. "What do you mean?"

But she knows what I mean. Just because I didn't bring it up again, what I told her on the beach on New Years still stands. I still love her, and I still don't want to leave.

"I mean, I'm not going back to Vancouver."

"But you have school. You have to go to school." She sounds like a broken record.

I smile at her. "No, I don't. I don't have to do anything. I can take courses at a later time. Hell, I can go to school here. I know you have an art school in Auckland, I Googled it."

"Josh." She looks at me with wild, staring eyes. She looks like an animal caught in a trap, about to gnaw her leg off in order to be free.

I throw up my hands. I don't understand why this is so hard for her to comprehend. How does this affect *her*? "What? Why not? If I don't get in, I can get a working visa and get a job somewhere. I'm twenty-three. This is the time to do this stuff, to try and figure life out, see what works. See what's worth it."

She shakes her head and looks away.

My lips are moving, can't she hear what I'm saying?

"Gemma," I plead, grabbing her shoulder and making her face me. "What is it?"

"Why are you doing this?"

I frown at her. "Because of you, obviously."

She smiles but it's cold. "You can't do this for me. It has to be for you."

"It's for everything. I love this place, too; it's imprinted on me as much as you are. But in the end, it's still for you. I love you. I'm in love with you. I'm not going home. *You* are my home. I'm staying with you." I sound desperate, I know I do, but it's the truth and I can't stop it from falling from my fucking lips.

"And if I don't want you to stay with me?" she asks. It's quite loud with the wind but I hear her words. I hear them because I feel them stab me like ice picks to the gut.

"What?" I ask breathlessly. The chill spreads through me.

"What if I don't want you to stay here? What then? Will you still want to stay?"

Her eyes are like black holes in the sky.

"I don't understand, Gemma. Please. Just . . ." Something inside is starting to sink. It's growing. Dread. "You don't want me here?"

"This was only supposed to be a temporary thing."

My eyes nearly fall out as anger rushes through me. "What the fuck are you talking about?"

She steps back, away from me, and looks around her at the few people who have looked our way. "Let's go talk somewhere else."

"Fuck that," I sneer, grabbing her. "We're talking here. Temporary?"

She yanks out of my grasp, her eyes pained. "Yes! You came to visit and now you're leaving. That's the way it's supposed to be. It's what we agreed on."

"I didn't agree to anything!" I yell. "I just wanted to be with you."

"You don't belong here!" she yells back.

My jaw drops. "I don't belong here?" I feel like everything she's saying is a lie. It makes no sense. It can't be real, can't be happening.

She exhales and covers her face in her hands. I'm breathing hard, my chest squeezed so impossibly tight I'm afraid I might collapse. "This isn't your home, Josh," she mutters into her hands. "And you'll see that. You'll realize it when you stay."

I don't fucking understand her. I never will. "Home isn't a country or a place," I say. "It's where you belong. I thought I belonged with you." I suck back the pain. "I guess I don't."

She takes her hand away and looks me dead in the eye. "No, you don't." Her face is impassive, a stony mask. It gives me nothing.

She never gave me anything but my shattering heart in my chest.

"You know what your problem is," I tell her, having a hard time keeping my voice calm. "You don't know when to stop being such a stone cold *bitch*."

Gemma flinches like she's been slapped. That got a reaction.

She blinks a few times and says, "You're right. I don't know when. I don't know how."

"It's called fucking trying to be a nice, caring person," I tell her. "You should try it one day when you pull your head out of your fucking ass."

I whip around and march through the violent wind, back to Mr. Orange. But I'm not going back with her.

I can hear her running after me. But I'm done caring. I'm done bleeding.

She grabs my hand and yanks at me to stop.

"Josh," she cries out, and for once I see some emotion in her eyes—the fear, the panic, and maybe pain. But it's too late. The damage is already done. "Josh please," she begs, "I'm not trying to hurt you. I'm trying to prevent you from being hurt. You know how I am, you just said so yourself. If you stay here for me, I'll fuck up. I'll ruin things because that's all I know how to do. I'll only end up breaking your heart."

I lean in close to her, close enough to kiss her. But that's the last thing on my mind.

"You've already broken my heart," I tell her, my voice rough with anger and pain.

Then I walk away, fast, up the hill back to the car park. I'm going to run like hell.

I take out the car keys and open Mr. Orange's back door. I grab everything I can see that's mine, everything of importance. Most of my stuff is already in my backpack, including my passport. Everything else I can buy at home.

I swing it on my back and take out my wallet from my jeans. I have about five hundred dollars in cash that I took out the other day and I place it in the cutlery drawer. I won't owe her anything after that.

I look up and see the sketchbook on the counter. I have no use for it now.

I pick it up, feeling its weight in my hands just as Gemma comes running up to the door.

"What are you doing?" she cries out in horror.

"Everything I owe you is in the drawer." I shove the sketchbook in her hands. "This was supposed to be your Christmas present," I tell her. "Feel free to toss it in the fire."

Then I'm brushing past her and heading over to one of the buses loading wet and weary sightseers. I climb on board, and with a wad of cash and pained eyes, convince the driver to drive me as far as he can.

I take my seat at the back and avoid looking out the window, at the faint outline of Mr. Orange as the rain against the window blurs the image.

It's over.

It's not until the bus gets farther south and the sky turns blue again that I start to cry. It's beautiful again.

And it's all over.

I'm going home.

Chapter Twenty-Three

GEMMA

"Excuse me miss? Are you all right?"

I barely hear the voice. I only clue in when someone touches my shoulder. I slowly raise my head and see a Department of Conservation officer staring at me quizzically. He appraises me and then folds his arms. "Do you need help?"

I do need help. I need all the help in the world.

The gray, stormy sea beckons me. I wish to be a dead soul, to have a soul, to slip through the roots and shed this world behind me.

I've broken Josh's heart.

I've smashed my own.

The pieces are jagged and lodged deep in my chest. My heart needs a tourniquet. Every breath I take hurts. The pain is so physical, so real. It's like when my father died and I was just this lost, wounded creature for days, weeks . . . years.

At the time, I only had my friend Robin, who later became my boyfriend. He was there before the accident and he was there after, but he never changed. I changed. I let the pain define who I was. I let pain ruin me, hold me down to the earth with an iron fist. I let pain scare me.

I thought burning my paintings would help. And it did. For a time. I wouldn't let myself grieve for them, though, for the art. What was the point? Why should I let myself feel over and over again when I have the choice to not feel anything at all?

I never understood why anyone would choose to go out into the world without armor on, to feel all the stabs, punches, and stings of life. That's not how I wanted to live. I wanted to be free from pain, from loss, from broken dreams.

Art was a dream—but it's fine, I don't want it anymore.

My father was everything to me—but it's fine, I don't grieve him anymore.

Life isn't what I want it to be—but that's fine, I don't deserve a better one.

That's everything I tell myself, just to keep going on each day. I'm good at stressing, testing, building my body, so I do that instead. Being a personal trainer is a good job. It's fine. It's okay. It's good enough for me. With this armor, I can't do much more than the things I'm already doing, things I don't care that deeply about. I can't involve myself with people other than the ones I don't care deeply about.

It's not living—I know that. But that's the point. It's not living.

It's a wall.

And now I'm standing at Cape Reinga, long after the crowds have gone home, frozen to the bone, staring at the sea. My wall has come down. And I threw the bricks at Josh. To maim, to kill.

It worked. He's gone.

He's gone.

I burst into tears.

The D.O.C. officer doesn't know what to do. "Miss?" he

says, softer now, and that bit of pity, of empathy for someone like me, does me in.

I start bawling.

He awkwardly puts his hand on my shoulder. He's probably frightened to death. But I don't care. I don't deserve comfort, but any amount will do. I lean into him and sob on his department-regulated uniform.

I never deserved him and he never deserved to be treated the way I treated him. But it was all the truth because he doesn't belong here. He doesn't belong with *me*. He called me a stone cold bitch and it hurt because it's true. He needs to be with someone less selfish, more open, warmer, nicer, better.

He needs someone else.

But I need him. I need him to keep pushing me. To keep believing in me. I need him to make me better.

I need him.

I lift my head off the officer's soaked chest and look around. It's nearly dark. This is a wild, heavy place. The mist is thicker, faster, swallowing things whole. The wind is stabbing. It matches my mood, my bleeding heart. But I can't stay up here. I can't do this all over again.

"Sorry," I mumble to the man, wiping my nose on the sleeve of my jacket.

He stares at me with kind eyes. "Are you going to be all right? It's getting late, I'm about to close the car park."

I shake my head, too tired to feel embarrassed. "I don't know if I'll be all right. But I'll be on my way."

I take the windblown path back to Mr. Orange, and as I sit in the driver's seat I'm demolished by the emptiness inside. His stuff is gone. His sketchbook remains on the backseat where I put it.

I want to curl up inside my body to find warmth. I'm so cold.

Mr. Orange starts with a rough purr. The sound echoes across the empty bus, emphasizing how alone I am. I turn on the heaters full blast, and with a deep breath pull the bus out of the car park, the D.O.C. officer waving at me as I go.

I drive south, through desolate villages and past darkening trees. The night is coming and I want to escape. But there's nowhere to go.

It's late when I end up at my grandfather's place. I wanted to make it to Auckland, but I knew I couldn't bear to be alone in the house with my roommate out, probably working. My *whānau* is what I need. I pull Mr. Orange to a stop and sit for a few moments, the engine ticking down, sounding hollow.

Eventually the front door opens and I see Auntie Shelley coming out, a shawl wrapped around her and billowing in the breeze. It seems the clouds and wind have chased me down here.

She comes to the window, peering in at me. "What are you doing here?" She looks in the back. "Where's Josh?"

I close my eyes and the tears start again. I'm afraid I'm compromised now, the wall destroyed, the damage too deep.

I feel everything. Every little horrible thing.

Auntie Shelley opens the door and I practically fall into her arms. She leads me into the warm house and sits me down on the couch. I can't stop shivering so she wraps me in blankets and bustles off to the kitchen to make tea.

My grandfather is staring at me but I avoid his eyes. I could tell he liked Josh. He's going to be mad at me for ruining things.

But he doesn't say anything. No one has asked anything because everyone knows. I'm crying. Josh is gone. That's the whole story.

When I start to warm up a bit, the hot tea coursing through my veins, Pops switches off the telly.

"Do you want to talk about it?" he asks. He's neither inquisitive nor curious, just courteous.

My instincts tell me they wouldn't understand, to keep it bottled up inside, rebuild the wall. This would be the first step, the first brick. But my instincts aren't my own. They are of the person I told myself to be. They are conditioned reflexes. They don't come from my heart.

I take in a long, shaky breath. I tell them everything, from our start in Vancouver (leaving out the sordid details, of course) to him appearing in Auckland, to traveling with him and Nick and Amber, to the way he got under my skin, to Christmastime, to finally painting at East Cape, to getting tattoos and jumping out of airplanes, to New Year's Eve when he told me he loved me, and to the Cape Reinga, where he told me he would stay and I told him he should go.

It's been a crazy seven weeks, and when I'm done speaking I'm utterly exhausted and feeling brittle to the bone. We had gone through *so* much and I had just thrown it on the fire.

The whole time Pops just listened. Only now he nods slowly, studying me, thinking. I fear what he's going to say; I respect him so much that if he tells me I'm a terrible, irredeemable person, I will believe it.

"I think you were right in telling him to leave," he says finally, and the sentence drops between us like a bomb.

My jaw comes unhinged. "*What?* I thought you liked him."

"From what I saw of him, yes. I liked him very much. I think he's very good for you. And I think you have been good for him. You have pushed his boundaries and made him brave. He would have never come here, seen all that he saw, if he hadn't met you."

"Then why do you think it's good he left?"

A wisp of a smile traces his lips. "You were right in thinking you would hurt him. You would have. Not because you mean to. You're a good girl, Gemma. You have a good heart. But it's all you know how to do: push people away."

I stare at the ground, knowing how right he is.

He continues, "He would have stayed here for you, just for you, and there would've been a lot of pressure from that. New relationships shouldn't have that kind of weight on their shoulders. If you weren't stable enough, open enough, selfless enough to shoulder that weight with him, you would crumble."

"So we were doomed from the start," I say wearily.

"No," he says quickly. "You aren't doomed. This is a blessing, for both of you. If he hadn't left, you wouldn't be here, opening up like you never have before. At least not to me. Sometimes you have to bulldoze something to the ground before you can rebuild. Do you know what I mean?"

I swallow. "I thought I did that back when . . . when . . ."

I don't have to finish. He knows when he lost his son. "You didn't, Gemma. That was not building. There was no rebirth from those ashes. You just stood in them for a very, very long time. You have to make a conscious choice to become better, do better. It's scary, opening yourself up to be hurt, I know. But even if you don't, you'll hurt anyway. You're hurting right now, aren't you?" I meet his gaze. He only needs to look at me to see. "So you are," he says gravely. "Then you know. You can't escape everything in the end, so you might as well open yourself up to the good stuff along the way. You know, after your father passed away, I turned to the drink. I know you were busy dealing with your own stuff, as was your mother, and we didn't see each other much. That was for the best. I was a mess. I did everything to numb the pain, and it worked. For a while. But then I missed things like Kam's birth, your aunt and uncle renewing their vows, and I missed you. With Robbie's help, he pulled me out of it, even though my boy was hurting, too. I vowed not to hide anymore. And sure, it hurts.

Losing your son hurts. Losing your father hurts. But don't let that pain color your whole life." He sighs, thinking I'm not getting it. But I am.

I get up out of the pile of blankets and go to give him a hug. A big hug. I bury my head in his neck and let out a few tears. "I miss Dad," I whisper before I break down again. He holds me tight and cries, too.

I break many times over the next few days. But each time, my *whānau* lifts me back up.

It's January eighth when I bring myself out of my stupor. I feel worn down, naked, raw. But the sun is shining. The air is fresh. The world hurts but it's beautiful, even with the pain.

I pick up Josh's sketchbook and the pastels he left in the bus and start roaming over the peninsula around my grandfather's place. I sit in three different places and draw, paint, smudge the landscapes. It's so messy and imperfect, but life is messy and imperfect.

I put myself on the paper, bare for the world to see.

I paint and paint and paint.

———— • ————

"What are you going to do now?" my grandfather asks. He, Auntie Shelley, Uncle Robbie, Barker, and I are taking Mr. Orange to Paihia to catch the bus back to Auckland.

"I have ideas," I say. I'm going back to my apartment, taking stock of my life, and then figuring out the next scary step. I'll probably have to move back to my mother's for a while to save money, to make money, but that doesn't bother me. I need her at a time like this.

We say goodbye at the bus depot and I promise to call them, e-mail them, visit them more. I promise to reach out and reach in. I'm going to miss them to pieces.

But after I get on the coach bus for the journey back home,

I notice that the ache I thought would multiply in their absence feels like it's getting smaller. It's healing.

There is of course, the pain I feel for Josh. The pain I caused myself. That hasn't gone away. It hasn't left me. It's weird going back to a city that I know he's still in. I wonder if I'll run into him somewhere. I wonder what I'd say.

I know what I'd say. I'd tell him I'm sorry. I'd tell him I didn't mean to hurt him. I'd tell him what he means to me in the big, bad world, how his arms are the ones that kept me safe, that his eyes are what still coax me out of my shell. He gave me the courage to try again, to create, to lay myself bare, and that won't stop, even after he's gone.

I want to tell him that I love him. So deeply that I'm afraid I'll never be able to remove it, that I'll have to carry it with me forever, like a badge. And I want to tell him that's not a bad thing. It's an honor to love him.

When I get back to my apartment, it's just after dinner. Of course it's empty except for the cat. I busy myself, cleaning even though Nyla is a neat freak. It's weird to be back home after all this time. It doesn't feel like home anymore. It feels cold and impersonal. Then I think, maybe it's always been this way.

Maybe now I'm finally realizing that I need more than that.

I pour myself a glass of wine, sit down at the kitchen table, and watch Pink Floyd YouTube videos on my phone. The music stirs my sensitive heart, making me feel unbelievably restless inside.

I don't know how long I sit there for, with Chairman Meow snaking around my legs, but I'm almost done with the whole bottle of wine when Nyla comes home.

"Gemma?" she asks in surprise as she places her messenger bag on the kitchen counter. I barely look at her. She smells like the hospital, her pale, freckled face looking tired from her shift, her red bun a mess. "I didn't know you were coming home today."

I nod. "Plans changed."

She chews on her lip and says, "Okay. Well, I'm glad you're home."

She turns around, ready to head to her room, but I speak up.

"Hey, um, do you want to have a glass of wine with me?"

I rarely drink wine and never ask her to drink with me so she looks a bit stunned. But maybe she reads something on my face because she says, "That sounds great. Let me just change out of my scrubs and freshen up."

Moments later, she's back and I pour her a glass, and with it my soul. I tell her everything that happened, from beginning to end, with painful emphasis on everything that went wrong with Josh. She's speechless the whole entire time.

Eventually she says, "Well, I suppose I should tell you that Nick came by yesterday."

I raise my brows. "What?"

"Yeah." She gets up and grabs another bottle off the rack. Naturally, they're mostly all Henare wines. She pours us both another glass and sits back down. "He told me about the breakup. He dropped off a box of your stuff. It's in the closet."

"Oh."

"He said don't worry about the stuff he left behind, you can keep it. And he said if you still want a job at the gym, you've got it."

Now I'm really surprised. "Seriously?"

She shrugs. "It's what he said. Now that I've heard your side, maybe he realized he had been an overreacting asshole."

"Did he say he was sorry?"

She smiles. "No. But he looked sorry. Like a mutt looking for scraps. I was tempted to slam the door in his face since you know how I feel about him, but I was very cordial. You would have been proud." She sips her wine while I absently twirl a piece of my hair. "So, are you going to take the job?"

Now I shrug. "I don't know." I had come to peace with the idea that the world had better things for me. If I didn't take the job, it would mean I'd have to move back in with my mother. If I did take the job, it meant I'd stay here. And my life would stay the same.

But I don't want it to stay the same.

I know what I want.

Realization slams into me like a heated fist. I nearly knock over my glass of wine before I quickly fish out my phone and Google the number of the hostel that I knew Josh was staying at before. Sky Tower Backpackers.

"What are you doing?" Nyla asks, but I ignore her.

I get a woman on the third ring. "Good evening, Sky Tower Backpackers."

"Hi," I say, feeling flustered. "I have a friend staying with you. Josh Miles. He's Canadian. Can you tell me if he's there right now or . . ."

"Oh, Josh," the woman says brightly. "He was here. He left this morning."

The words get caught in my throat but I choke them out. "To go to another backpackers?"

"No, he went to the airport. I called the shuttle for him."

I shake my head violently. "No, no, no. His flight to Vancouver is on the tenth. It's the eighth."

"I'm sorry," she says. "I guess he caught an earlier flight. He had to work in the kitchen the last night just to pay for his room. Maybe he ran out of money."

Maybe he ran away.

"Is there anything else I can help you with?"

"No, thank you," I whisper and hang up the phone.

Now he's really gone.

"He left?" Nyla asks.

"Yes," I manage to say. I can hear the emptiness in my voice, like an echo in a dark room.

She reaches across the table and puts her hand on mine. "I'm sorry. Really, Gemma. That sucks."

It does suck. I literally feel like my heart has been sucked from my body and there's nothing but a gaping hole in my chest.

I nod, swallowing hard. "Thanks." I exhale loudly, like I've been holding in air all day. "I think I'm going to go to bed."

"Why don't you and I go out for lunch tomorrow?" she asks, something else we've never really done together. I'm starting to realize we were living together without knowing each other. But how could she know me when I didn't even know myself?

It's not too late to change both of those things.

"I'd like that," I say gratefully and manage to give her a small smile before I shuffle away to my room.

I walk over to my bed and collapse on it. Chairman Meow, as if knowing I need quiet comfort, lies by my head, curled up. I tell myself it's okay to cry, it's okay to break down, that I can rebuild. Maybe not a wall, but a window.

The tears don't come, though. I'm all cried out.

The ache returns, and for days it stays. Empty, throbbing cold. Nyla and I start hanging out together more, which helps soothe the pain, and soon I start driving out to Piha Beach in the late afternoons. It's the only thing I want to do, the only thing I think will help me. I sit at sunset and paint the horizon, where sea meets sky. I paint the infinity, the melding of the two elements. I paint the messy beauty that changes from day to day, from dark and dramatic to bright and colorful.

It's beautiful.

Chapter Twenty-Four

VANCOUVER, CANADA

JOSH

"Tell me more about New Zealand," Katy says from across the table. She's staring at me with those big blue eyes of hers, twirling her dark blond hair around her finger.

"I've told you everything there is to tell," I tell her, leaning back in my chair and sipping a beer. "Nice people, beautiful scenery."

"But there's more to it, isn't there?"

I shake my head and pick up the dessert menu. "Nope."

We're at a Cactus Club restaurant in downtown Vancouver. It's our third date. I'm putting on the charm but it's half-hearted. She slept with me on the first date already. It was the first time I'd had sex since New Zealand. It wasn't bad. Good enough to warrant another date. And a third.

But I'm not sure about a fourth. Katy is pretty and funny and she makes me laugh. But she bores me to tears. There's no depth to her, no substance. She is who she says she is. And

I guess that's refreshing, the lack of mystery, but I just don't find myself intrigued by the real her.

I want more. I always want more.

I had a lot more at one point. But that's neither here nor there.

It's been three months since I left. They've been the hardest three months of my life. After Gemma told me to leave, I went straight back to Auckland and switched my plane to the next flight out. I couldn't stand being in that city anymore, knowing she was out there. I couldn't stand being in the country.

Thankfully, Air New Zealand was able to find me a flight two days early, but of course there was a hefty fee for the switch. It was worth all my money. It was worth having to work at the hostel to pay for my stay.

When I got home, I was more angry than hurt. The weather here was dark and gray and inhospitable. It rained every day. It made me a miserable person to be around, even though I was just starting school. I had to throw myself into my studies to try and bring myself out of it.

Gemma tried to contact me once, on Facebook, not long after I left. I never read the message; I just saw it there. I blocked her account. I didn't need any reminders of her. If I heard Pink Floyd playing anywhere, *anywhere*, I had to get up and leave. Once I left a Foo Fighters concert because the band started covering "Have a Cigar."

After some time, though, the anger started to fade. Sadness filled in those cracks. I'd never been in love and never had my heart broken. Now I'd experienced both in a very short amount of time. And when I let myself breathe a bit, I realized just how badly Gemma had affected me.

Vera had said I went after Gemma because she reminded

me of my mother. It was a disturbing thought, that's for sure. But maybe Gemma was more of a challenge to me because of that, a lock that needed a key.

I thought I'd found the key. I thought if I kept pushing at Gemma, again and again, she would let me in. But maybe she needed the time to do that on her own, without me breathing down her neck, needing her to love me. Or maybe she was welded shut, and no matter what I did, no matter what happened to her, she would never change.

I wish things ended differently. I wish I hadn't called her names. I wish I hadn't run off. I could have stayed and talked to her and tried to make the best of those last days. I wish I hadn't pushed and pushed, put that pressure on us, and especially, her.

But I can't do anything about it. It happened. It's over. And three months later, it still hurts. It's not so bad—the comic book I'm illustrating is helping me funnel those feelings and fears into something worthwhile. I'm trying to date. I'm at least trying to get laid.

I've moved out, too. In February, Toby, the guy who threw the Halloween party where I met Gemma, needed a new roommate. Though my new job at the art supply store on Granville Island is only part-time in order to fit with my school schedule, I jumped at the chance. I'm barely scraping by but the rent is cheap and it's a share house. I figured why not dive into the cliché and become a starving artist?

At that thought, I close the dessert menu. I'm only buying lemon meringue pie for someone special.

When dinner is over, I drop Katy off at her apartment in North Vancouver. She asks me in. I let her down gently.

"Who is she?" she asks. Her features sharpen. She can tell. Still, I play dumb. "Huh?"

She sighs. "The girl you're hung up on. Gemma, is it?"

I frown, bewildered. How could she know her name?

Katy smiles stiffly. "You called me her name the other night. In bed."

Oh shit. I had no idea. I give her a pleading look. "I did? I'm sorry."

She shakes her head. "Don't worry about it. God knows I've been there. Take care, Josh. It was fun." She gets out of the car and gives me a little wave. No hard feelings, thank god.

I watch her walk inside and then lay my head against the steering wheel. Jesus. Now I can't even date without having Gemma invade me somehow. What did Amber call love when we were talking on the shores of Lake Wanaka? A fungus?

It was fitting. Love is a fungus. It's hard to kill. Apparently this strain is lingering on, living in my pores and cracks and crevices.

I can't tell if I'm grossing myself out or making myself sad.

I sigh and drive back into Vancouver. The city looks cold and lonely in the dark. Spring is on its way but feels so far off that it's no more real than a ghost ship in the night. I go home and straight up to my room. Someone is in the kitchen, eating late, but I don't stop to say hi.

It's weird, ironic maybe, that my room is the very same room where Gemma and I had sat on the couch and watched people play Rock Band. I had wanted so badly to devour her.

She had bewitched me back then, and she still bewitched me now.

Only then, I welcomed it. Now, I wish it away.

But the feeling stays.

———————•———————

It's April and I'm about to take a giant leap.

I have to call my dad to ask to borrow money. We're not so close but it's necessary; there are a few classes I want to take that start outside of the range of my student loan. I'd ask my mom but I always feel like a burden to her, even though she's been texting me often, inviting me over for dinner. I just can't. Art has taken over, and I'm glad.

"Dad," I say when I hear him answer the phone. I'm sitting on the roof deck on the shoddy furniture, watching the city in the background and the budding maple trees that line the streets.

"Hey Josh," he says, sounding warm and surprised. I hate that I'm not really calling to talk.

"Hi, listen, Dad, I have a big favor to ask you," I say, just launching into it.

He sighs. "What is it?"

"Well, there are a few extra classes I would like to take at school but my loan doesn't cover them and I'm just not making enough at the supply store to cover it. I was wondering . . ."

"How much is it?" He also gets straight to the point.

"In total, six seventy-five," I tell him, wincing. "That is, six hundred and seventy-five dollars."

The line goes silent. I can almost hear him thinking, stroking his mustache. Finally he says, "Fine. But if I do this for you, you have to do me a favor."

I frown. What could he want from me? "Okay."

"Why not come to Alberta when school is up and stay a week with me and your stepmom? We'd love to have you."

This is a first for me. "Really?"

"Yeah. We miss you. We're not getting any younger, and neither are you. I think it would be good for you to get away for a bit, out of the city."

He's right about that. I love Vancouver but it's starting to make me feel both boxed in and lonely. "Okay, sure. That would be great. If I take these courses I won't be free till the summer but I can come then. Oh, maybe we can go to the Stampede!"

He chuckles. "Anything you like. All right, I'll get the money into your account. How is your mother?"

He rarely asks about her, and I can tell he doesn't really want to know. "She's fine. I don't talk to her much, though. School keeps me busy."

He coughs. "Right. Well, she's still your mother. You should spend some time with her."

I sigh. "Yes, fine, I will. Hey, thanks, Dad."

"You're welcome."

When we hang up, I look at all the texts my mom has sent to me over the last month. She's asked me over for dinner. Asked me to pick up my mail. Asked to come to my apartment to say hello. Asked me to come out with her and Mercy. She's been asking and asking, and I keep answering her with *I'm busy* or *Later* or *Sorry, can't*. Or I just don't answer her at all.

I don't know why I've been pushing her away. It's like I'm punishing her for something she didn't do. It's like I'm punishing her for just being my mom.

Feeling guilty, I decide to answer her last text, sent a week ago: *Come stop by and say hi. And pick up your mail.*

I text back, *Okay, I'll stop by today, I don't have school until the evening.*

I head on over, thinking she won't be home but at least she'll know I made somewhat of an effort. When I get there I see she's home and the door is open. On the kitchen counter is a pile of mail, probably all junk, for me.

The shower is running but I still yell, "I'm here!" so she doesn't come out and think I'm a robber and attack me with her pointy nails. I know those things hurt.

I grab a can of Diet Coke from the fridge and crack it open

as I stare at the mail on the kitchen counter, expecting to see a mound of letters.

It's not a mound of letters at all. There are two envelopes and a postcard from Amber in Bali, but the rest are packages. Some are a square foot, others half that size, and they're all wrapped in plain brown paper.

I pick up the one on the top. It has my address but the return address is Henare Wines in Bay View, New Zealand. I feel the blood drain out of me.

My heart is waterlogged.

With shaking hands, I pull back the paper and reveal a pastel-painted canvas. A seascape at sunset. Blues and corals and tangerine. It's so gorgeous I want to cry. I blink a few times, turning it over. It doesn't have Gemma's name on it or a note but it's from her. It's her soul.

And she's showing it to me.

I put it down and open another. And another. There are about fifteen of them, all gorgeous horizon lines, sunsets, sunrises—dark and stormy, happy and light. I'm surrounded by her.

"Josh?" I hear my mother say, and I whirl around to see her tucking her wet hair up into a towel, her face bare, her glasses off.

I point to the paintings. "What the hell is this?"

Her brows furrow as she comes closer. "Oh, they're paintings. Quite nice. What do they mean?"

I'm incredulous. "I don't know what they mean," though I do. "How long have you been getting these?"

She shrugs, picking up one of a red sunset on a black sand beach. "For weeks now. A new one comes almost every day."

"Why the hell didn't you tell me?!"

She gives me a sharp look. "I did tell you. I kept telling you to pick up your mail. It's not my fault you don't have a second to spare for me."

Oh, I see. She's using the mail as leverage.

I sigh, rubbing my hand vigorously across my face, trying to force some sense into my fried brain. "Okay, I'm sorry that I haven't been around."

"It hurts, Joshua," she says. "Everyone is gone. Everyone has someone except for me."

I wince, my heart sinking even more. It's hard to hear my mom be vulnerable. I don't know how to deal with it. I don't know if she'll just go back to being the cold stone that she usually is.

"I don't have anyone, Mom," I tell her, though now, looking at the paintings—Gemma's soul, her love, her passion spread out on the table—I think she might have me. "I'm sorry I haven't been around. Things are . . . tough sometimes. You know how it is."

She sighs and nods. "I do. Just say you'll try."

"I will, Mom," and I mean it. "I just can't believe these are all here. How did she even know where to send them?"

"Who is sending you these? Seems like promotion from a winery."

"It's a girl, Mom. One I . . . she's in New Zealand."

She studies the art. "Did she make these?"

"Yes," I say proudly, as if I had something to do with it. "She's very talented."

"Very," she says. Her eyes flash. "Oh, I forgot, someone came this morning with something for you. But there's no return address on it."

She disappears around the corner and comes out with a thick package in her hands. She places it on the counter, and just from the shape and the weight I know what it is.

"When you say someone . . ." I say, my eyes glued to it.

"I don't know. A girl dropped it off. Not the regular post-man. Must be a courier."

I feel my face growing cold. I can barely speak. "What did she look like?"

"Like a girl," she says. "Pretty. Long hair, tanned. Healthy looking. She looked a bit mixed."

That would be my mother's way of saying "not totally white."

"Didn't you ask her questions, like where this came from?"

She taps her long nails on the package and nods. "I did. But the girl just turned and ran down the steps. For a second, I thought maybe it was a bomb."

"It's no bomb," I say.

I start unwrapping, slowly at first, then fast.

Mom pats my shoulder. "Well, I'll leave you to it."

When I rip all the paper off, my sketchbook is in my hands. I marvel at it, turning it over, and I start flipping through it. I see the inscription, *If you lose this, please return to Josh Miles*, and my address on the inside cover. I flip through, hoping to see something new, but all it does is bombard me with a million memories.

Each page is a trip back to New Zealand—every beautiful day, every moment captured. The clear, pale water and golden sand of Abel Tasman. The cold, dramatic ice of Franz Josef Glacier. Dawn at Key Summit. Foxgloves and milk-blue Lake Tekapo. Dolphins. Gemma's attempt to paint in Kaikoura. Christmastime. The sunrise at East Cape.

This is where I pause. Her painting is glowing brilliantly off the page, like I'm seeing that sunrise all over again in her satu-rated, waxy lines. I feel just how messy life was at that moment.

But the painting is a bit different now.

Across the horizon she has written, in orange, *This where I first loved you*.

My throat closes up, my nose growing hot. I blink my eyes fast, trying to move through the love and pain competing for space in my heart.

She loved me.

I don't even want to look at the rest. But I do. It's more of my work, reflections of a journey and love that were slowly winding down.

I get to the last page. It's the picture of a cold, cold sea.

She has written, *I'm sorry*.

I close my eyes and hold the book to my chest.

I'm sorry, too.

I stand there for a few minutes, in my mother's kitchen, trying to absorb it all. The courier has to have been Gemma. It just has to be.

I whip out my phone and start Googling Vancouver backpackers. She has to be here; I can feel it. I know it. She delivered it this morning in person, she just had to. She wants me to see this, to have this. She wants me to know she's here.

Yeah, I'm probably thinking like a lunatic, but at least when you're nuts you take chances. I remember her saying she stayed at the Hostelling International on Thurlow Street when she was last here, so I call them up.

They don't have anyone called Gemma there.

I call another backpackers nearby. They can't give out info.

I call another and another and another. No leads, no answers.

No Gemma.

I log on to Facebook and search for her, hoping I can unblock her. She's there and her picture is of one of her paintings, which thrills me in a weird way, but her privacy settings are high and I can only send her a friend request.

After all the paintings have been carefully stacked, I put

them in my car and drive them back to my place. I'm not sure what I'm going to do with all of them, but while I wait to get her to accept my friend request, I end up placing them all over my room.

Toby steps in and tells me it's like living in an art gallery. He knows all about Gemma and doesn't bug me about her. Apparently the same thing happened to him and some girl he met at his parents' place in Shanghai. We've become quite good at commiserating.

My evening class on illustration starts soon and I have no choice but to go. I'm tempted to leave my cell at home, just so I'm not checking Facebook every five minutes in class, though let's face it, that's what everyone does anyway.

Class drags on. My palms itch to take out my phone. I can't concentrate and I need to. My computer is slow and Adobe keeps fucking up.

A war wages inside me. I'm all kinds of messed up.

But I feel alive for the first time in a while.

I feel a sense of hope I didn't even know was missing.

When class is over, I stay a bit later, just to finish up what I should have. I take my time, giving the drawing the concentration it deserves. I have nowhere to be, no one to see. A beer sounds good, though.

I grab my stuff and make my way down the hall toward the back doors, where I parked.

There's a familiar melody filling the air the closer I get to the end.

Pink Floyd's "Wish You Were Here."

It unravels me.

It's coming from a classroom at the end of the hall, and I slow as I pass by the open door. I peer inside. It's empty and filled with canvases of all shapes and sizes. I can hear a tap running in the background.

I wouldn't normally stay and linger but there's a painting in the middle of the room, staring me in the eye.

Actually, it's *me* staring me in the eye.

It's a black and white pastel drawing of me with a wild teal background, painted with blue watercolor.

My mouth gapes. Thoughts dislodge. My heart shrinks and swells.

What the actual fuck?

What kind of dimension did I just wander into?

I walk into the room, quietly, as if I'm going to scare the painting, scare the *me* staring back at me, with its lip ring and asshole smile.

Suddenly the water turns off and I hear the *tap tap tap* of a paintbrush against a sink. There's movement behind one of the canvases.

I hold my breath.

Gemma emerges into the open.

She's wearing a white tank top, black jeans, tall boots. Her hair is piled onto her head. She has teal paint everywhere, on her chest, her arms, her face, her hands.

She doesn't seem surprised to see me, not like I am to see her. She just smiles and stands still and gestures to the painting.

"Do you like it?"

I can't even look at it. I can only look at her. And that's when I see the line of fear across her brow, the uncertainty in her eyes. She wants me to like it, she needs me to like it.

But I don't care about the painting.

My mouth feels full of sawdust. I'm surprised I'm still standing on my own two feet. "Gemma," I manage to say. I can't say any more.

She swallows and nods, perhaps expecting a different reaction. "Surprise, right?" She sighs and walks over to the painting, standing in front of it. I can't believe her ass is within touching distance again, her hair, her skin.

"I moved into the vineyard, worked there part-time, saved up money. Then I took a leap of faith and enrolled in school, here," she says as the questions linger on my lips, her back turned toward me. She touches up something on the painting. "I followed my passion. And my passion led me here. To you. I've only been here for a few days. I've been wanting to find you, say hello but . . . I've been shy."

She shoots me a look over her shoulder, slightly embarrassed, her cheeks flushed beautifully. "I don't expect anything from you, just so you know. I'm here to find out what I want from life." She licks her lips before turning her face away. "I just wanted to give you my art. I owed you at least that much."

I reach out for her and touch her gently on the shoulder, just to make sure she's real.

She is. Her skin feels soft enough to sink into, though she's still got her muscle. She's still got everything I love about her.

And now she has art.

And now she has me.

I grin to myself and spin her around so I'm staring down at her beautiful face, those deep dark eyes that look up at me with a need I've never seen before.

"Welcome home," I tell her before I grab her and kiss her. She tastes as sweet and spicy as I remembered and melts into my arms, into my touch. We kiss with deep heat and fired intensity, which only makes me hungrier for her, for everything about her.

I can't believe she's here.

Gemma is here.

She pulls away, breathing hard, her hands gripping me tight.

"Josh," she nearly whimpers in my ear, her voice soft and on the edge of breaking, "I love you."

My heart does a warm somersault in my chest—the best kind of ache.

"I love you," she says again, placing her hands on either side of my face and staring at me with those deep eyes of hers, now wet with waiting tears. "I couldn't stop loving you. You're so easy to love." She kisses me again, soft and slow, and murmurs against my lips, "I'm so sorry I didn't realize it before, that it took me so long. I never meant to break your heart."

"Gemma," I say through a groan, my body and heart igniting. "Don't be sorry. I couldn't want for more. You're here. And I love you." I place her hand on top of my chest. "See, it's not broken at all."

"You still love me?" She sounds so shocked, so vulnerable. I can't help but smile.

"Always," I tell her and pull her tank top over her head, unable to keep my hands off of her, my skin from her skin. I need to be closer than this, I need to feel her in every way that I can. I need her to be real, to stay real in this room full of art.

She shoots a nervous look to the door, and as she swiftly removes her bra I head over and lock it, ensuring us privacy. When I'm back at her side, my lips graze her nipples before sucking them, and she moans in response. Such a gorgeous sound, one I never thought I'd hear again.

She's here.

She loves me.

I pick her up in my arms and stride across to the counter in the corner of the room, placing her ass up on the edge beside the sink before pulling down her jeans and underwear.

"I'm having déjà vu," she says, her smile wanton, her voice throaty. "Though I think the pool table was more comfortable."

"You won't be complaining in a moment, sweetheart," I tell her with a grin as I pull her legs to the edge of the counter and unzip my jeans.

"I like when you call me that," she says as she wraps her strong legs around my waist.

With one hand I position myself against her and brush a strand of paint-coated hair behind her ears with the other. "Good. Because you're going to be hearing it for a long time."

I want nothing more than to take this reunion slowly but I'm fueled by the almost delirious desire to be inside of her again. She holds me close as I push myself in, my eyes squeezing shut as she envelops me, tight and warm, the most decadent feeling.

She gasps then moans, and I do the same.

She's here. She's home.

"Please tell me you're here to stay," I say to her, my lips finding hers again as I slowly thrust in and out.

"I'm here to learn," she says softly, her hands gripping my shoulders, my hair. "Not just at school . . ." She breaks off and gasps as my fingers slide around her. "I'm here to learn from you. About art, about love, about everything. I'm not going anywhere." She looks me in the eye. "You've got me."

She then punctuates those beautiful words by moaning softly, her head thrown back as we sink into the feel of our love for each other. It is so, so impossibly good.

As we move as one, slow then fast and frantic, she gets paint on me, staining my skin, my clothes. We make love in the art room like lovers reunited after war. It gets messy.

But life is messy.

And life is good.

Acknowledgments

It's funny how you can make plans that you know aren't even slightly adjustable and yet somehow the universe ends up rearranging things for you. Case in point: back in 2002, after a few years of working mindless jobs; of going to film school for things like make-up, production, and screenwriting but not following up on it; after backpacking around Australia and New Zealand; I decided to get real and continue on with education. I decided on a local college, in their journalism program, and everything was all set for my "real" life to begin. I would go to school and then get a job in my field and that would be the end of that. No more finding myself, no more searching.

Well, when it came time to enroll in my classes for the semester, I had a rather rude awakening. There were no classes. None in the journalism program, none in any program, none at all. There was just *nothing*. I couldn't even take Advanced Pyrotechnics 300 if I wanted to. The entire school was booked up.

But that couldn't really be, could it? I mean, I *paid* for the school already. I was accepted. I was ready to go.

It turned out that I wasn't the only student this had happened to. On that day, hundreds of potential students couldn't sign up for any courses and were consequently turned away from the Vancouver college (which shall go unnamed, but there is a news clip of me being interviewed because of this and saying, and I quote, "It's like when they oversell an airplane, but I don't want to be on standby for my education." How's that for a sound bite?).

Anyway, apparently this happened because they had "accidently" accepted too many students, and as it turned out, most of them were international (this was right after 9/11 so there was influx of foreign students opting to study in Canada instead of the US). And international students pay more.

So there went my whole damn plan. If I had known there would be no classes for me, I would have applied for another college. Now it was too late in the year to do so and I was screwed.

And so, I decided to apply to a foreign school. Sure, I'd be paying those higher fees, but at least I'd have somewhere to go and I could make an adventure out of it.

Long story short (too late!), I decided on New Zealand. Not only had I spent a few weeks there in 2000 backpacking the country and totally falling in love, my sister Linda and her family lived outside of Wellington. Within a few months I had applied, been accepted, and had selected my course load for my bachelors of communication. It was kind of a bullshit degree, but it would do.

In March of 2013, I moved to New Zealand by myself. I shared a flat off campus on the north shore of Auckland and commuted to the city every day where I attended the university downtown. I made some amazing friends—and met my best friend—and spent my days falling in love with the country's people, culture, scenery, and outlook, all while lamenting the traffic, the overpriced groceries, and the fact that no one heats their house in the winter.

It was one of the best years of my life and because of that, this book was so easy to write. Though I ended up finishing my degree back at home (journalism, again) I've been back since then for my friend's wedding in 2009, and I was able to add more amazing experiences to my memory bank, some of which have found their way into this book.

Where Sea Meets Sky is, in some ways, my love letter to New Zealand. It's also a love letter to those who are just finding their way in life, who are too afraid to take risks and chances. You have to learn to go with the flow, and if I hadn't taken that chance on New Zealand, I'm not sure where I would be right now.

So, my biggest thank-you goes to New Zealand. Then, of course, to everyone I met there, especially Kelly St-Laurent and the Robson family, whom I won't call out because it will be quite obvious when you discover their names in the book (Hi Tony!).

Thank-you as well to: my gentle, welcoming, and all-around lovely sister Linda, Hamish, and the boys Tor and Bjorn. Kass Healy. Titus Rempell. Gemma Rushbrook. Graeme Marshall. Everyone at Akoranga housing and AUT. My parents for making it all possible. Then of course my lovely beta readers, Laura Helseth, Shawna Vitale, Lucia Valovcikova, Nina Decker, BJ Harvey, Barbie "Ovaltine" Messner, Sandra Cortez. Danielle Sanchez and her buzz skills. Hang Le for her awesome map. The cottage for being such a great writing space. Pink Floyd (OMG I listened to so much Pink Floyd) and Free. Bruce, for being the best dog in the world, even if you are such a pain in the ass. And of course, my husband Scott MacKenzie (who is not a pain in the ass). You WILL come with me to New Zealand one day.

Last but not least, I have to thank my "team" for making this happen: Taylor Haggerty for being such a wonderful agent and the Waxman group. My editor, Jhanteigh Kupihea, for her belief in the story and for being so enthusiastic about Josh and Gemma. Ariele Fredman, Lee Anna Woodcock, Judith Curr, and everyone else at the Atria team for everything from the amazing cover to the tireless support.

Thank you and *kia ora!*

Read on for a sneak peek at the next novel
by Karina Halle

Racing the Sun

Available as an Atria Paperback and eBook in July 2015

I think we've all thought about how we're going to die. My friend Angela Kemp, whom I've known since we were playing in saggy diapers together, is convinced she's going to choke to death on something. Every time we go out to eat, she searches the restaurant for the person most likely to know the Heimlich maneuver and tries to sit by them. It doesn't seem to matter that *I* know the Heimlich maneuver; she just wants to know that she'll be safe if it happens.

Personally, I've always thought I'd fall to my death. I think it all started when I was seven or eight years old and had dreams of my house turning over and me falling from the floor to the ceiling, dodging couches and tables. After that, my dreams turned into me falling off of balconies, getting stuck in plummeting elevators, and finally, being in horrific plane crashes. Actually, it was never the crash that killed me, nor was it the scariest part of the dream; it was that I was always sucked out of the airplane first and fell to my death in a horrible rush of cold air and mortality.

It shouldn't surprise me then that I currently think I'm about to die, and by falling, no less.

In fact, I'm sure there's no way I can possibly survive this. It's not that I'm in a taxi that seems to be coughing black fumes out of its tailpipe every two seconds, or the fact that the driver—with a mustache so big he looks like a land walrus—is looking more at me and the two other backpackers in the backseat instead of at the road, but that as we round the corners of the "highway" toward the famously postcard-worthy town of Positano, we're going full speed and there's nothing but a sheer cliff face on my side of the vehicle.

"Shit," I swear, trying to hold on to something—*anything*—that will keep me in the car and not falling to my death, as my sordid dreams have foretold. I look over at Ana and Hendrik, my Danish traveling compadres for this leg of southern Italy, and they don't seem all that concerned. I'm especially not going to grab onto big, blond Hendrik since Ana has a problem with random girls touching him.

Not that I'm random at this point. I met up with the couple in Rome and spent a few days with them there before we took the train down south. I know they have plans to keep going all the way to Sicily and hunker down on some beach hut with a bunch of goats (I don't know, but whenever Hendrik talks about their plans, goats are involved somehow) but I'm starting to believe that Positano is the end of the line for me.

And it's not just because I'm certain I'm going to die on the way there. It's because I am flat fucking broke. We all knew this day would come (and by we, I mean my parents and I). After all, I've been traveling for six months around the world, and even though I've been trying to spend as little as possible, the world isn't as cheap as you'd think.

It probably doesn't help that I went a little overboard in Europe and went on a mini shopping spree in every city I was in. But I like to think of my new shawls and sandals and jewelry as souvenirs, not just clothes. I mean, do you get to wear your post-cards or ceramic doodads or tiny calendars with pictures of the Eiffel tower on them? No. But you can wear a scarf you picked up from a market in Berlin.

But of course, in hindsight, maybe I should have managed my money a bit better. I just thought that my savings were enough. And then when my parents started bailing me out, I thought I could coast by on that. Just for a little while. Until I found out they sold my shitty 1982 Mustang convertible to help pay for this trip. And then after that, they just stopped putting money in my account.

I've now eaten into the money that's supposed to pay for my return ticket home, a ticket I didn't think I'd have to buy until I got down to Morocco, or even Turkey.

So, Positano, Italy, on the Amalfi Coast, might just be the end for me.

Or this cab ride. As we round another bend, I can see crazy people parked on the road and selling flowers—not the side of the road, but parked on the actual road. So now people are swerving and going around them, but when Italians swerve they don't slow down—they actually speed up.

I decide to close my eyes for the rest of the journey and hope I end up in one piece.

Even though the journey from Sorrento to Positano doesn't translate into many miles, it still feels like it takes forever for us to finally get there.

The walrus-mustached cab driver pulls to a sudden stop, abruptly enough that I fling forward, my curly blond hair flying all over the place as my seatbelt barely restrains me.

"Amber," Ana says in her deep accent. "We're here."

"I gathered that," I say, and do the very awkward act of pretending to search through my messenger bag for euros. I don't really have any euros to spare. Thankfully Ana thrusts some bills into the driver's hand as we clamber out of the cab.

And so here is Positano. I'd been so busy closing my eyes and praying, I hadn't really gotten a good look at the town on the way over.

It's fucking charming. I mean, it's beautiful and stunning and nother. But I do love him, and

e right thing to do. So why not

esn't work out, at least I'll have

f a story." I'll admit that even

antic, the jaded and cynical side

that she's doing all of this for a

ove that fast. But that's probably

men a few times already on my

r phone and showing me a pic-

for him, wouldn't you?"

onso *is* hot. Dark-skinned with

e's tall, too. Not that it's too out

ed me that Italian men are short

e case at all.

wish you both the best and hope

he way it wants to."

mber the real reason why I came

some financial difficulties at the

bit in London and all that. Any-

w if there was any work available

ell, there's no work here."

ur job.

e. I just meant in town. Or in the

nks. "Well, there would be jobs

t to work there. Have you tried

t? Sometimes they need English

otice board they put up for for-

l are one-offs for guys, like a day

photogenic as all hell, but its charm is the first thing that comes to mind. The cab dropped us off at the top of the hill and you can see just how packed the town is. Building after colorful building crammed below cliffs, staggered down the hillsides, tucked into every nook and cranny. It makes you wonder what crazy person decided to put a town here, of all places.

The one-way road leading down to the beach is narrow, with cars and pedestrians and patio seating vying for space, and lined with stores that beckon you to come inside. Actually, knowing Italy, the minute you walk past, some shopkeeper will come out and literally beckon you to come inside because, like, you can't say no (maybe that's how I've ended up with so much stuff). In the distance, the Mediterranean Sea sparkles from the sunlight, glittering on the water, and hydrofoil ferries glide through the waves with ease.

"Wow," I say softly, trying to take it all in. "This is like the movies."

"Yes, it's very nice," Hendrik says blankly. He's never really impressed with anything. When we saw the Coliseum, he said he thought it would be bigger. Well, I thought it would be bigger, too, but that didn't stop me from being overwhelmed by the structure and history of it all. "Luckily the hostel is at the top of the hill."

That *is* lucky, considering that if it was at the bottom of the hill on this one-way road I'd have to lug my overflowing backpack and duffel bag up to catch a cab or bus when it's time to leave. Then again . . . I have a feeling I'm going to be here a while. I have enough money to stay at this hostel for a week and then I'm officially fucked.

I try not to dwell on that as I follow the Danes down the road for a few minutes as cars and motorcycles—ubiquitous here— zoom past, narrowly missing me by an inch. Even being on foot and at your own pace, there is still something so dizzying about this place. All these houses, burnt orange and pastel yellow and faded rose, looking down on each other. When I turn around and look behind me, the steep, rocky hills rise up into the sky.

It feels like the whole entire town could topple over at any minute.

This could be a metaphor for my life at the moment.

After we've settled into a rather pleasant looking dorm room (pleasant compared to the fleabag we stayed at in Rome), Ana and Hendrik invite me to go with them down to the beach. I really do want to go and explore, but I have a feeling they'll want to eat at some restaurant, and that would be more euros than I can afford. As much as I hate it, I have to stick to my weird Italian granola bars and fruit for as long as I can. Besides, I'm sure the lovebirds would rather stroll on the Positano beach with each other and not have some broke, frazzle-haired American girl tagging along.

So they leave and I take my time exploring the hostel. It's small but even though it's the only one in town, it's not as packed as I thought it would be. It's the beginning of June so I thought all college kids and post-college kids (like myself) would be flocking to this area but I guess not.

That's fine with me. After living out of a backpack for months on end and never really getting any time for myself, strolling around a quaint but quiet hostel is a pleasure.

I end up back at the reception desk where a girl with shiny, poker-straight, chocolate brown hair is sipping some lemon drink. I get major hair envy over anyone with straight strands.

"*Buongiorno,*" the girl says with a smile—and an American accent—once she notices I'm there. Then she recognizes me from check-in earlier. "I mean, hello. Amber, right? From San Francisco?"

"San Jose," I correct her, finding her easy to talk to already. I've always been a fairly quiet girl but that changed real quick once I started traveling by myself. "Listen, I was just wondering . . . well, I mean, I know you work here, right?"

tionship seriously, not even his n
he loves me, and I know this is th
take the chance, you know? If it d
a hell of a story."

"You already do have a hell o
though I think it's sweet and rom
of me thinks it's a bit ridiculous
man, that you could even fall in l
because I've been screwed over by
travels.

"See," she says, pulling out he
ture. "This is Alfonso. You'd stay

I let out a low whistle. Alfo
piercing light-colored eyes. And
of the ordinary—everyone warn
and hairy, but so far that's not th

"Nice," I say to her. "Well, I
it all works out."

She shrugs. "Life works out t

"Uh-huh." And then I remen
to talk to her. "Listen, I'm having
moment. You know, overdid it a
way, I was wondering if you kne
for someone like me."

Her eyes narrow slightly. "W
Relax, I think. *I'm not after y*

"Oh, I don't mean here, per s
area. Even Sorrento or Salerno."

She purses her lips and thi
in Salerno, but you don't wan
the English cafe down the stre
speakers. There's also a work-n
eigners. Usually the jobs poste

spent painting a house or something like that. But sometimes you can get lucky."

This sounds promising. "And it's just down the street? It's a long street . . ."

Amanda smiles and pulls out the hostel map and proceeds to draw on it. "Follow the road all the way to here and then take these stairs here. You'll come to Bar Darkhouse. Beside it, kind of tucked in the back, is Panna Café. That's the one."

"Thank you," I tell her, folding the map before shoving it into my bag.

I walk down the streets with an extra spring in my step. The air is fresh (when you're not inhaling diesel fumes) and the sun is warm, baking my bare arms. I'm feeling a bit optimistic about the whole money problem now. If Amanda can find work here, I can too.

That should also mean that if Amanda can find love here, I can too. But thankfully, that is the last thing I'm looking for. I've had enough fun and heartbreak during this trip, falling for boys who either have their hearts set on someone else (like Josh in New Zealand) or who love you and have to leave you (like the Icelandic boy, Kel, whom I spent a sex-filled week with in Prague). No, the next guy I was going to fall for would be a Nor Cal boy when I returned home to San Jose. No drama, no heartache, no tragic goodbyes.

No fun either, I think to myself, but I quickly push that thought away.

The café is easy enough to find but it takes me a while to get there. The town is just so pretty and tightly packed that I want to linger in every single store. Eventually I find it and order an espresso at the bar. Unlike most cafes in Italy, this one actually has tables and chairs where you can sit down and sip your drink, obviously catering to tourists. But at this point I've gotten used to doing quick shots of coffee while standing up. It's at least more efficient.

After I ask the British barista whether they are hiring and find out it's a big fat no, she points me to the corner of the cafe where the notice board is. Though most of the postings are actually fly-ers for parties or advertisements for ceramic sales, there are a few work notices.

One of them looks fresh—none of the phone number/email strips on the notice have been taken.

It reads:

Need help. Want English speaking woman. Two children. Must be good to young children and help with language. Fluency needed. Italian is helpful to have. Please email Felisa. Locate to Capri.

I quickly take the notice off of the board before anyone else notices. Like hell I'm going to compete for this job. Even though I'm not really sure what it entails, other than possibly teaching English to two kids, or what it pays or if it includes room and board, I'm not going to give the opportunity up. If it doesn't work out, then I'll just put the ad back.

I immediately connect to the cafe's Wi-Fi on my cell phone and shoot an email off to Felisa. I make myself sound as good as possible: graduated from college with an English degree. Worked as a receptionist for a prestigious company (before I was fired). Great with children (I think I baby sat once when I was fifteen). Willing to work in Capri, provided help with housing is included. Have spent a great deal of time building up life skills while travers-ing Southeast Asia. Knows how to bake a mean tiramisu.

That last part is a lie but I thought they might find it endearing.

I press send and then wait.

And wait.

And when I realize I'm not going to get a response right away, I head to the bar next door, taking the work notice with me.